A Rose in Winter

Catherine Miller

ISBN: 1494862905
ISBN-13: 978-1494862909

DEDICATION

For Beth, who not so silently encourages, and for Mum, whose discerning eye has saved me from many an error, and whose tales of motherhood and wifedom have been a source of limitless inspiration...

ACKNOWLEDGMENTS

Once again I must acknowledge the work of Gaston Leroux, for it was his characters within *The Phantom of the Opera* that have served as the foundation for my little work of fiction. And my humble thanks to Ann Maggard, for without her prodding I never would have put my pen to paper.

I

He did not know what possessed him to do it.

He could begrudgingly acknowledge that he did indeed have a certain connection to broken and damaged things, and it was not as though he was unfamiliar with the prostitutes who found their employment in the forgotten corners of Paris. Not that he had been the one to employ any of them—even though at times he felt nearly desperate for the connection only a woman could offer. However, he could never actually bring himself to pay for such attentions, no matter the temptation. And while he had seen the haggard and weary appearance of many of them as he slithered through the darkened city streets, he had never felt any urge to help them. He knew full well that his corpse-like visage would make any such offer unwelcome, even in the direst of circumstances.

In the past his sympathy had only been stirred by the occasional animal, all too obviously abused by the world, much as he had been.

But never a girl.

He had been walking back to his home and had heard the quiet whimpers and the low grunts and knew exactly what was transpiring. It was not his business, and so he kept to the darkened stone walls of the alley, though night had already long since fallen and little of the world could be seen beyond what the occasional street lamp illuminated. His fingers began to itch for the instruments buried away in his underground home, but the sound of a pained cry and filthy words hissed into a feminine ear made him pause and turn and truly *look*...

The girl was staring at him. He did not know how she could see him as he was always certain to walk in only the darkest portions of the alleys in order to avoid such interactions. From the sight of her it was quite clear that even if this particular assignation had begun as a willing exchange, the girl pressed harshly into the wall was no longer amiable to the man's ministrations. And though surely he imagined it, her eyes—her clearly terrified eyes—were pleading with *him* for help.

Curious.

The man's hands tightened on her throat as he continued to thrust into her cruelly, knocking her head against the brick behind her with a sickening thud. Her eyes rolled, and she had evidently lost consciousness, slumping against the beast that had apparently finished with her. He allowed her to fall unceremoniously into the dirty snow at his feet as he began to tuck himself back inside the placket of his worn trousers.

There was blood plainly visible on his softening member.

The lasso was taut around his neck before he had time to finish, and soon he was also slumped in the sludge next to the girl. But while she still breathed, she now lay crumpled next to a corpse.

He considered leaving her. Perhaps it was a kindness for her to pass from this world that had quite evidently shown her little benevolence. If she did manage to awaken, the immediate danger was gone, leaving her free to...

What? Continue as a prostitute, allowing any manner of unsavoury man to find his fulfilment within her for yet another coin?

He watched her crimson blood mingle with the dirty snow surrounding her, and felt yet another stirring of pity.

Very curious.

Perhaps he should not have shuddered when he lifted her into his arms. He firmly reminded himself that if she was awake she would not willingly allow herself to be carried by him, and would surely have rescinded her unspoken plea for his aid had she been granted a closer look. He had no idea of her age, and it was apparent from the state of dress as well as the filth that clung to her that she lacked any semblance of a home. He adjusted her slightly in his grasp, taking note that she weighed very little.

Not that he knew what girls of any age should feel like as he held them.

And now she was lying on his settee, getting all manner of dirt on the spare bedclothes he had placed beneath her.

For it would not do to pollute his furniture.

He wanted to draw her a bath. Though he could take little pride in any aspect of his appearance, he always ensured that his person was neat, tidy, and most of all *clean.*

This girl was anything but clean. She wore what he supposed was once a sturdy cloak, but was now a faded brown rag tied loosely around her shoulders. It would do little against the harsh winter winds, and he wondered that she had survived so long while living in such conditions. Her dress was torn over her right shoulder, leaving bared skin and the tattered remains of dingy undergarments visible to his view.

What he noticed most were the bruises. Her shoulder bore evidence to the putrid yellow of some close to healing, while others stood out prominently—black and harsh and angry. Her tangled and matted hair covered much of her face, and he eased most of it away, grateful for his gloves so he would be sure not to touch her with his own pallid skin.

Too many monsters had touched her this night.

Her lips were chapped and her skin was drawn and slightly sallow, obviously suffering from severe malnourishment. He suppressed a dark chuckle that she was beginning to resemble *him.*

He allowed one hand to pull slightly at her lip, revealing surprisingly intact teeth given the abrasions that confirmed someone had struck her quite soundly on the mouth.

She stirred suddenly, moaning in her sleep as she tried to pull her shabby cloak more tightly around her and he yanked his hand free from her person.

Well. There would be no more examinations.

He left her to continue sleeping as he went to the kitchen to prepare a light broth. He was not particularly hungry—never truly was—but it was apparent that she would be starving when she awoke. Perhaps if he had food readily available she would be less frightened at waking to the masked countenance of a complete stranger.

Though he should hope that she would remember little of her attack, he almost wished she would at least remember him—that she wanted him to help her. He was not in the habit of kidnapping young girls for sheer amusement, no matter what his reputation implied.

Realistically however he knew that she would awaken to a slightly chilly sitting room—though he *had* lit the fire and it was gradually warming the small space—and find herself trapped within a house of stone. She would fear for her life, plead and cry with him for her release, and the broth he had set to warming would go uneaten as he doubted he could stomach it after seeing her imagined display.

He heard a sharp cry from the sitting room followed by the rustling of fabric, and knew she must have woken. Stirring the broth one woefully final time, he sighed and vacated the solitude of his kitchen in order to face his new guest.

She was indeed awake, and her clear blue eyes were wide as she stared at him. As he had predicted, her fear was nearly cloying in its intensity.

He would not be angry. She had the right to be afraid after what had transpired, and though he could feel his blood begin to pound as she continued to watch him with such panic, he tried valiantly to keep from snapping at her to mind her staring.

"Who..." Her voice was soft and noticeably unused. It rasped slightly and she coughed, while he openly scorned that she managed to keep her eyes trained on him even as she struggled for breath.

"Where am I?"

He swept his arms wide and gave a low bow, his irritation making him slightly sarcastic in his movements. "You are in my home. I was under the impression you required assistance."

She blanched, her eyes *finally* moving from him and fell to her lap. He almost wished she had continued to stare at him for as soon as she saw the state of her dress, and most likely registered the pain in her womanly places, her eyes welled with tears. "I… he…"

He coughed uncomfortably. "Yes, it would appear that your *caller* was more than you could handle."

He would not have thought her capable of such ferocity, and mingled with the tears still glistening on her cheeks she look slightly crazed. "I am *not* a whore!"

She stood suddenly, limping towards the door. He made no move to stop her as he knew with certainty she would be impeded by the lack of handle.

"My apologies then." Guilt was not a feeling he often experienced. He had few interactions with others, and usually when doing so he cared little for social niceties. If the girl had not agreed to lie with the man for money nor of desire, then he has maligned her dignity—what little she could afford living in such squalor.

She lifted a trembling hand to the door, pushing at the heavy obstruction feebly. "Please, I should like to leave now." Her voice was rapidly returning, though it still quavered and hitched with disuse and her continued tears.

He sighed. "Mademoiselle…" he looked at her expectantly.

"Christine," she mumbled and he nodded.

"Christine, sit down before you harm yourself further."

She pushed futilely against the door once more before acquiescing with another sob as she returned to her makeshift bed.

"Now, if you would remain seated I shall bring you some broth. I assume you are hungry?"

Christine eyed him warily. "What do you expect for it?"

He blinked. "I expect you to eat it."

Her tears had finally slowed but he found her look of complete resignation to be equally discomfiting. "Men always want something. I told you I am no whore so I will not... do... *that* for a bit of broth." She raised her chin defiantly, and he could not stop the chuckle that escaped him, though it stopped short when he heard the loud grumble of protest her stomach gave.

Whether or not she would accept the food freely given, her body obviously was imploring her to do so.

He sighed and approached her slowly. Comfort and assurance was not something that came to him naturally. "I expect you to eat what I give you, and then I expect you to take a bath after you have eaten. You insult me by suggesting I am as monstrous as that previous fellow." No, they were not the same. He was far, *far* worse.

Her lip trembled again and he sighed. "Do not cry. Remain here and I will bring you something."

He tried to prolong his time in the kitchen as much as possible, but eventually he ran out of tasks. A lone spoon and bowl were placed upon a silver tea tray, along with two slice of passably fresh bread and a cup of water, all which he eyed ruefully.

It looked to him more akin to prison rations than a proper meal.

But it was the best he could do under such circumstances, and the girl should probably not eat anything too decadent on such an empty stomach in any case.

He passed his dining room table and considered calling her to sit with him at the overly large structure that could easily seat four. It would feel *so* good to have someone to eat with. To set the table for two and dine over a fine meal that he had prepared.

Would *learn* to prepare.

He had little interest in food for himself, but the prospect of having someone to cook for was an appealing one. Having someone to do *anything* for was an appealing thought—one he had not allowed himself to contemplate since the days of his foolish youth.

Perhaps he should begrudge the girl's presence for reminding him of these long forgotten fantasies, though he supposed he knew it was no fault of her own. Her only error had been to make the dreadful mistake of appealing to him for help—and *his* being to provide it.

As soon as the thought entered his mind, he felt the prickling sensation of guilt. He had not been wrong to save her...

Though by no means well versed in what constituted proper knowledge and behaviour, it was readily apparent that he should have no knowledge about the intimate atrocities that had befallen the young girl. Yet the fact remained that he *did* possess such knowledge, and as such he decided against seating her in the dining room. The settee would be far more comfortable for her more delicate places and wounds, and it was not as though he would be joining her in the partaking of the meal. To do so would mean removing his mask— if only slightly—and that was something he would never do in company.

He scoffed.

Company.

He had company.

Christine had tucked her legs within her skirt and wrapped her cloak entirely about her person, so she more resembled a brown lump than a girl. She grew visibly uncomfortable when he came close enough to place the tray upon the side table nearest her.

"Eat."

Her gaze flickered from him to the proffered tray, but finally the scents of steaming broth and soft bread proved too much for her. She must have burned her mouth the way she was devouring the soup, but he was disinclined to scold her.

He knew what it was to be starving.

He watched her eat with interest. Christine's wrists were terribly frail. While he knew he had been born with shockingly long fingers, he was certain even a normal man's hand could encircle her wrist completely with quite a bit of room to spare.

"How old are you?"

She froze, obviously not expecting him to carry on conversation. Christine cleared her throat awkwardly, clutching the soup bowl possessively near her chest along with the bread. "Fifteen," she said quietly. "I think."

He could not say if he was surprised, either by the number or by her uncertainty. Part of her seemed impossibly young, evidenced by her delicate wrists and hands as well as her small stature. Her eyes however bespoke of someone much older—someone who had lived and seen far too much for their short years.

She swallowed thickly. "How old are you?"

He laughed, and it was startling to both of them. "Not fifteen."

The girl nodded and returned to the last of her meal, using the remainder of the bread to ensure she had sopped up every drop of soup.

"Christine, I must ask you something." The look of fear was back, and he sighed impatiently. He could well understand why she was so nervous, but that did not mean he appreciated her ready assumption that he was intent on harming her.

"Yes?"

"Are you in need of a physician?" What colour had entered her cheeks by the warm food quickly dissipated.

"I… I do not think so."

He was not entirely sure he trusted her opinion on the matter so he enquired further, articulating the question that had been pressing quite insistently on his mind. "Was tonight the first time that has happened?"

Her eyes welled once more and she shook her head slowly. "No. It is…" She sniffled loudly, putting aside her bowl and wrapping her arms around herself tightly. "There are cruel men who like to…" She seemingly could not give voice to what perversions the men of Paris were inclined to inflict on her.

"I am well aware of just how cruel men can be."

Her eyes rose to meet his, and for a brief moment he felt she could truly *see* him. Her eyes roamed over his mask, and for the first time he did not begrudge her for it.

"What is your name?"

He gave a slight smile though he knew she could not see it.

"My name is Erik."

II

The girl was quiet after he had given his name. While used to silence himself, he did feel rather uncomfortable with hers.

The itching of his fingers was returning, made worse with the knowledge that his instruments were so close by and were yet unused. Though never one to play strictly for the enjoyment of another—he played for *his* pleasure, not for foolish mortals and their pedantic musicality—he found himself almost willing to offer Christine a small performance if only to alleviate the unease he experienced at her stillness.

That was until he saw her smudge the grime on her face with a dirty sleeve, the tear tracts clearly the only thing that had washed her features in quite some time.

Erik shuddered.

"I believe it is time for your bath."

Whatever moment of understanding they had shared was obviously ended as the girl started violently, her eyes filling once more with suspicion.

"I won't share a bath with you."

Erik rolled his eyes. "Yes, you have made it quite clear that you do not make it a habit of sharing your body with all and sundry. You are, however, filthy and are sitting on my furniture."

A blush stained her cheeks and she had the decency to look rather ashamed. "I just do not want there to be any misunderstandings."

He looked at her incredulously. "You think the men who have abused you cared for your protestations? That simply informing them that whoredom was not in fact your profession would have gotten you anywhere?"

Her eyes flashed dangerously. Or he supposed they were *supposed* to be dangerous in their viciousness had they been directed at anyone but him. "I am well aware of what those men have done; I do not need you to constantly remind me!"

Erik sincerely doubted they had been in each other's company long enough for him to have *constantly* done anything, but he did not press the matter. He wanted her to get into a bath, and apparently continuing to discuss her current appearance was getting him no closer to his aim.

"Christine, I can assure you there is a lock upon the door and you will be granted privacy, but you *will* bathe." Though he did not relish having to notice such things, now that the room was warm he could readily detect not only by her appearance but also by the odour that she was unwashed. He also felt no need to mention that a lock would do little to bar him entry should he feel so inclined.

She must have finally realised that had he any untoward predilections toward her person she was incapable of stopping him from enacting them. He resolutely ignored the silent tears, and instead led her slowly to the bath, mindful to keep his pace slow due to her delicate injuries.

Erik was actually quite proud of his bath. He had it made especially to accommodate his long frame, so he imagined that the girl could potentially drown if it was filled to its maximum capacity. Though he indulged in few physical pleasures, a long, hot soak was amongst his most treasured indulgences.

The girl was mesmerised by the running water, and she squeaked when she held out a trembling hand and found the water to be pleasantly warm.

He sniffed.

Of course it would be warm.

Did she think him so primitive as to have to heat the water on the range?

She seemed content to sit at the edge of the bath and run her hands under the spout, so he quietly left and retrieved a towel before he returned unnoticed. "You will wash, and then you shall tell me if you have any wounds that require tending. Then we will discuss what to do with you."

Christine had the good sense not to protest but he noticed that she watched him carefully to ensure he made good on his promise to leave her alone during her bath. He heard the distinct click of the lock behind him.

Not that it mattered in the least. There were two doors into the bath, one visible and one not. Should the need arise and she do anything foolish, he would easily be able to intervene.

Again.

Erik sighed. Troublesome girl.

He had taken her through to the bath attached to the second bed chamber in his underground home. He looked about the covered furniture with an appraising eye. The dust clothes would have to be removed and the bed made. He had furnished the room with his mother's things on a fleeting whim, but had promptly covered it all with a tremendous amount of self-reproach. At the time he was certain no one would ever have need of it, as he would never exchange his coffin beneath the red brocade canopy with the mahogany bedstead, deeming a casket more fitting for his person than a featherbed.

After all, one had to get used to everything in life, including the sterile comforts of an eternal resting place.

Though the idea of company was still of such a novelty as to keep him from becoming entirely resentful, he still felt a twinge of annoyance that he was currently playing housemaid when his music beckoned to him so enticingly. Perhaps he should have made the girl make her own bed once she surfaced.

Erik froze.

The entire purpose of her bath was to keep her from continuing to dirty his furniture, as well as to make her slightly less wretched to his eye.

He did so have a love for pretty things.

She had been soaking and presumably scrubbing for nearly a quarter of an hour, and while he assumed she would want to relish in the healing affects of the bath for a while longer, it occurred to him that all his efforts to see her cleansed would be negated once she placed her tattered rags back on her body.

With a final crisp tuck the bed was made to his precise standards, and he hurried to his own elaborate wardrobe. If he had more time he would venture above and spirit away a costume from one of the forgotten nooks of the Opera House, but as it was he plucked out a black nightshirt that he rarely wore. While he favoured the Persian style for his own use, he had tested out the more traditional nightclothes so as to determine preference based on optimum comfort.

The nightshirt would puddle, but given the girl's own emaciated frame that was similar to his own, he doubted it would be uncomfortably large.

As an afterthought he also procured his heavy dressing gown, assuming from the way she held her cloak about her that she would also appreciate the preservation of her modesty.

He almost *did* believe she had drowned when it was not until a half an hour later that he heard the steady churn of the bathwater as it escaped through the drain, though the sound did not linger long enough for the tub to have been fully emptied before the sound ceased.

Erik knocked on the door firmly. "I assume you will accuse me of salacious intent when I tell you this," he clearly heard a gasp from beyond the door, "but I have gathered some clean clothing that I insist you don instead of your own miserable garb."

The girl gave a startled cry of protest, but did not obey and open the door. "My clothes are now soaking and I am sure they will soon..."

Erik scoffed openly. "Your clothes will disintegrate before they even consider coming clean. You will put these on and then you shall tell me if you have found any abrasions that require further attention."

He was mildly surprised to hear the lock click and the door open a mere sliver—the small, pale hand emerging only long enough to grasp the clothes before disappearing once more.

Though he had been abundantly clear that his aim was to see her properly cleansed, Erik was not prepared for the sight of the girl when she re-entered the bedchamber. Her hair was still a mess of tangles, but was now tinged with gold instead of matted together with gray filth. She was as skinny as ever, and he had grossly overestimated her size, as the dressing gown wrapped around her nearly twice, trailing behind with all the regalia befitting an empress.

But to his utmost surprise, she was *pretty.*

He stopped such thoughts with a scowl. She was not *pretty.* She merely no longer resembled a common street urchin. Perhaps now he would no longer fear she would steal his silver if he left her unattended.

His heart tugged suddenly, and he knew that was a lie.

The girl was comely, and dressed entirely in his clothes, and she was *here...*

Erik's thoughts were diverted when she whimpered slightly, evidently uncomfortable with his steady gaze.

His scowl deepened. Pretty or not, she would be like every other young girl and turn from him in horror, whether he had provided food and shelter or not. "Well? Are you very much injured?"

She nodded hesitantly, gesturing to her upper left thigh. "One of the... when he was... he had a knife and it did not look this bad before, but now it is red and oozes a little..."

Erik clenched a fist tightly before expressing a calming breath. It would not do to be angry. This girl faced the same horrific underbelly of mankind that he did—though admittedly in a very different manner. While he was shunned, ridiculed, and ostracized, she was used most viciously.

And now he would heal her.

It had been quite some time since he had to call upon his knowledge of doctoring. In his youth, learning such methods was out of sheer necessity as no one would help him should a cruel soul see fit to maim him. Though now he was a man grown well adept at defending himself, he still kept all the necessary materials on hand for just such unexpected occasions.

Perhaps it was a touch self-congratulatory, but when he had completed a rather extensive and arduous series of medical texts he had commissioned a leather bag like he had seen many doctors use as they rushed between house calls. He would never have been able to attend a university had that even been his inclination, nor would any doctor carrying such a case call upon him in the lowly depths beneath the Opera. But he now had cause to pull out the still crisp leather bag, feeling quite professional as he did so.

Given the location of the wound he felt it would be more prudent to return with the girl to the sitting room. Asking her to lie upon the bed and raise her nightgown would surely be asking for yet another one of her speeches of denial and rebuff, and while there was a small sofa within the bed chamber, he felt it better to vacate the room entirely.

Though he tried to remind himself that her assumption was based on previous experience, it still insulted him that she should so readily assume that he had a predilection for lust and violence.

He quickly stripped the soiled linens from the settee and piled them neatly with the rest of the dust clothes from the Louis-Philippe room, telling Christine to sit as he did so.

Erik was perhaps too relieved when he turned to find she had situated herself so that the wound was already within view. It would be mortifying in the extreme to have to ask her to lift her—*his*—nightshirt, only to be met with the tearful and quivering bout of tears that was sure to follow.

Christine was resolutely looking away from him, shoulders tense and not a stitch of skin uncovered that was not strictly required to be visible.

He pulled a chair close enough to be seated comfortably during his work, ignoring that she shivered at his approach. His leather gloves were removed and his spindle-like fingers doused in a small vile of alcohol before Erik turned his attention to the girl's thigh.

He had seen worse. The wound itself was long and angry, and the depth was cause for some concern. Though he tried to keep his attention solely on the wound she had apparently given him permission to treat, he could not help but also notice the large, hand-shaped bruises that littered her pallid flesh.

Erik knew he was a monster. Of that one fact he had been absolutely certain nearly since birth. But though he had lied, cheated, stolen, and murdered, he had never forced a woman to lie with him.

He quickly focused once more on the gash, lest his anger at the injustice of both their situations distract him from his task.

"I am afraid this has begun to fester. It will require disinfecting and I shall need to sew the wound closed to allow it to heal properly." Christine was staring at him with wide eyes, and he attempted to soften his tone so as to keep her from being overly frightened of the relatively simple procedure. "It will be very painful, so I would suggest you be unconscious while I work."

"No!" Christine hurriedly pulled the nightshirt down over her leg before also bundling the dressing gown around it protectively.

Erik sighed. He had no wish to cause her undue pain, but he was willing to allow the decision to be hers. "Very well then." He waited a moment, expecting her to once more reveal her leg to his view, but she only continued to stare at him. "Shall I proceed?"

She nodded, but again made no move to assist him.

He found that this time it was *his* fingers that trembled as he eased her leg down to lay flat upon the cushions, and he slowly moved the black fabric up—past the point of any semblance of propriety.

His mouth suddenly felt terribly dry.

The girl was eying him warily, but did not stop him either, so he patted her leg softly in what he hoped was reassurance, before pulling out another vial and pouring it directly on the wound.

Christine howled.

There was no other word that could quite describe it, though Erik in his shock supposed a shriek could more aptly describe the pitch and intensity.

He did not know why seeing the girl in such pain made his own body tense. "Erik offered you unconsciousness! You should have listened!"

She shook her head forcefully, and he found the more she began to calm as the sting began to abate, the more he did also. "I am sorry! I just... was not expecting it to be that bad."

He gave her a withering glare. "Why do you think I offered you anaesthesia?"

Christine shrugged and nibbled her lower lip. "Do you... do you really have to sew it?"

He fixed her with another glare. "I can assure you, I am not putting you through this for my own amusement."

She took a bracing breath before motioning for him to continue.

Suddenly he felt as though his fingers lacked the ability to function. Though he had taken the lives of men with little trouble, it seemed as though the very concept of causing this little waif of a girl any additional distress was nearly impossible now that her cries of pain were still ringing in his ears.

"Please..." He swallowed thickly. "I ask that you trust me, if only a little. I do not wish to cause you pain, and if you will not allow me to give you complete respite, at least allow me to offer you something for the discomfort."

She need not know that the dose of laudanum he had in mind would severely impede her mental faculties. But she would at least see what he was doing, and would hopefully not feel the piercing and tugging that would soon follow.

He did not think she would acquiesce, but she must have seen something—some evidence of his sincerity for she gave the tiniest of nods.

His relief was tangible.

Erik placed a few drops of the bitter liquid within a small glass of wine, hoping to mask the taste. The coughing and gagging that followed her swallow revealed that his hope was for naught.

When her eyes became glassy and a small smile graced her lips as she snuggled into his overlarge dressing gown, he felt sure enough of the drug's effects to begin working. In total the gash only required ten stitches, and though he was pleased with his work, he did not like the look of the black thread holding her fragile skin together. It looked harsh and dark, and he was all too glad to wrap it in ointment and gauze, hiding it from his view.

"You have terribly long eyelashes." Christine's eyes widened and she clapped a small hand over her mouth, almost as if she could stem the flow of embarrassing comments through physical impediment. Erik tensed, as she had been quiet while he worked aside from the occasional whimper, and he was completely unprepared for her to make any comment regarding his physical appearance.

"Why would you say such a thing?" He knew it was the effects of the laudanum calming her fears and loosening her tongue, and he hoped she would soon begin to feel the unavoidable urge to sleep—if only to save her the indignity in the morning when she remembered what she had said to him.

She shrugged, and as he hoped her eyes were beginning to droop. "Because it is true."

It most certainly was *not* true. Was it? It was not as though he regularly studied his appearance. In fact, he did not even own a looking glass...

Christine's eyes closed for a moment, but she opened them again obstinately. "Are you quite angry?"

He chuckled, a dark humourless laugh. "Yes, I am angry, but not with you."

Christine nodded, though he doubted she truly understood that he was angry at the entire world for making them both such unhappy creatures. "That's good then." With that, she ceased her attempts at fighting the drug's affects and fell asleep.

Not wanting to waste all the effort he exerted in making up the Louis-Philippe room for her stay, he carefully picked up the dozing girl and carried her to bed.

Erik had never allowed himself to imagine how it would feel to carry a woman to bed, but he found that when he gently laid Christine down in his mother's bedstead, he felt the smallest stirrings of something he supposed could be considered genuine affection.

Very curious, indeed.

III

Though his intention was simply to see that Christine suffered as little as possible, he could not deny that he also appreciated that the small dose of laudanum also allowed for him to continue his compositions while she slept.

He welcomed the distraction.

Erik could not explain why, but though he had only spent a few hours in the girl's company, he was already beginning to grow fond of her—something for which he berated himself thoroughly.

Was he truly so desperate that he would accept any feminine attention, regardless of the fact that this particular girl was young, hurt, and entirely at his mercy?

His fingers pounded a melody with a punishing intensity, hoping to clear his mind of any such thoughts. She had to leave. Perhaps he could give her a few *francs* that would ensure her immediate comfort and then take her aboveground. He would not use a lantern, but would simply walk her above stairs and allow her to wander away as she pleased.

He cursed that such a thought was not as equally pleasing to him.

She was not a stray kitten to be taken in; she was a living, breathing young lady that would inevitably grow to despise him—if she did not do so already.

Erik sighed and ceased playing, the organ notes still ringing faintly in the air before eventually dissipating into silence.

Except... it was not all silent. Perhaps it was not even actual sound, but instead a pure *awareness* of her presence, making his underground home feel not quite so lonesome.

She needed to leave at once.

To grow attached to her would only lead him to despair all the more when she turned from him. It was far better to focus on her flaws, feed her a simple meal, give her a small purse that should allow her to find shelter in an inn, and then never see her again.

It was obvious that it was not specifically *her* he wanted, merely the vague concept of a companion. A kind woman with soft eyes that would be happy to see him whenever he returned home...

A pet. He would take the girl above and immediately seek out a familiar who would satisfy his growing fondness for company *without* any ridiculously romantic notions of domesticity.

Almost without conscious effort his fingers resumed their playing, only this time with the soft cadence of a lullaby long since forgotten.

His attention however was diverted by the sound of a quiet thump from the Louis-Philippe room.

Erik hesitated before rising from the instrument and going to knock on her door. "Christine?"

The sounds of yet more sobs was her only reply, and he found himself growing frustrated. There seemed to be no end to her tears! Though he had also faced the cruelties of humanity—for much, *much* longer than her—he had coped quite well. Christine seemed only capable of crying whenever humanly possible.

Though he turned to stalk back to his organ and continue his composition regardless of his guest's emotional outbursts, he found himself unable to do so. She was just a girl and there might be something seriously wrong with one of her injuries that would require his intervention.

"Christine, speak now or I am entering your chamber!" He chastised his own reference to the room being *hers*. She was not staying and a mere one night's sleep most certainly did not count toward a transfer of ownership.

Receiving no reply, Erik walked into the room.

She was a huddled mass in the corner, the sheets he had so carefully arranged on the bed the night before wrapped tightly around her as she sobbed her seeming despair into her knees.

She had never looked so much like a child.

"Christine?" Erik ensured that his voice was a soothing lilt, as he was certain anything more would merely force the girl into further hysterics. "What has happened?"

She hiccupped quite unbecomingly and raised a red and tear-stained face toward him. "I do not know where I am and my leg hurts and you..." Her voice took on an ethereal quality that startled even him. "*I will send you the Angel of Music..."* The look of devastation on her face was paralyzing. "Why did you not come sooner?"

Erik blinked rather stupidly. "Of what are you talking?"

"Papa said that when he died, I would be visited by the Angel of Music—that you would look after me. But then Mamma Valérius died and I had nowhere to go, and you must not have been able to find me!"

Erik was by no means a simpleton, but he found himself quite unable to understand what the girl was saying. Her father was dead, as was her mother? Guardian? And apparently he had now been promoted from monster to angel—at least according to the girl.

Christine continued to sniffle even as she choked out the rest of her thoughts. "I know now why you wear a mask." He stiffened. "I am no longer pure enough to look upon your face!"

Now he was truly dumbfounded. "Christine..." Where to begin? Selfishly he had absolutely no desire to disillusion her as to his identity. That someone would choose to believe that he hid his face for some other reason than to mask his hideousness would be refreshing in the extreme. But could he allow this girl to take such a burden upon herself as to believe it was due to her own failings that he hid from her?

He cleared his throat and rose to his full height. "Christine. You *must* not question me about my mask. But I can assure you, your own past dealings and sufferings have nothing to do with it."

She did not look at all convinced. "But, Angel..."

Erik shook his head determinedly. "I have told you, my name is Erik. You will make use of it."

He should have disabused her of any childish stories of angels and her father's ability to command them. She was hardly a woman grown, and he knew how much he would have liked to hold on to his own childhood for as long as possible. But it seemed as if circumstances were determined to strip such fantasies away from them both—though Christine obviously held hers with far more tenacity than he.

Christine nodded, but it was readily apparent from her expression that she still considered him an angel, and therefore her acquiescence was based solely on his perceived command.

He did not know how this development would affect his plan of sending her on her way. To do so now would mean she was being rejected by her father *and* the keeper he had supposedly sent to see to her care.

"I shall make you some tea. Do you have any preferences?"

Her mouth opened, but she closed it quickly. "Whatever you see fit to provide."

Erik scoffed. "That was not the question."

Christine apparently felt she had displeased him, for she quickly amended her statement. "Sugar please. And cream if you have it." Her request was so soft he barely heard it, but as soon as she had spoken he quickly vacated the room, grateful for the respite of the kitchen and its uncomplicated activities.

He would see to the girl's breakfast, and then reconsider his options. The goal must remain the same—he simply could not allow her to continue on as his permanent guest. The concept was far too appealing. Besides, there was evidently something wrong with the girl's mental faculties if she should think *him* a heavenly being.

She *had* recently suffered a trauma to the head...

Erik had no idea what to offer her, but remembered vividly that the after effects of the drug he had administered used to cause unpleasant nausea in his youth. With that in mind, he prepared simple toast, opting to provide butter and preserves for her to apply should she feel so inclined.

It still felt bizarre to be making breakfast for *anyone,* let alone a clearly disturbed girl.

He placed everything once more on a tray, this time laden with its intended teapot and cups. He had no penchant for cream and sugar himself—it inhibited the vocal range terribly, no matter how seemingly pleasant the texture. But he would not begrudge the girl her own tastes.

She had apparently had enough of the floor for she was now sitting on the small sofa in her—*his*—spare room, and was rubbing at her leg absently.

"I trust you have not damaged your stitches. I would be rather cross if you had after that dramatic display." He placed the tray on the side table, pouring himself a cup of tea before taking the seat farthest away from her.

Christine immediately pulled her hand away from her leg. "No. At least, I don't think I did." She blushed, and he noticed that her complexion was improving from the red mass it had turned after her morning histrionics. "Would I be able to tell?"

Evidently she had never had stitches before if she did not immediately know when a stitch had pulled. "Yes, you would know. It would be very painful and would bleed quite a lot."

"Oh."

She was staring at him again, though her gaze was very different from the day before.

It made him no less uncomfortable.

"Drink your tea."

He was pleased when she complied and that she also added large helpings of preserves and butter to her toast, humming happily as she began eating her small morning spread.

Erik did not have the least idea how to begin the discussion of her relocation. He still was not convinced she would not do herself harm if he should make it perfectly plain that he was not in fact the angel she supposed. But if he played along with the charade, would that not make him the same kind of monster that preyed upon an impressionable girl's innocence?

Just as she had with her previous meal, Christine tried to hold all of her food and drink as close to her body as possible. The teacup rested precariously on the arm of the sofa while the toast was kept in hand—getting crumbs over his fine Persian rug, he noticed with a grimace.

His own black tea was sipped placidly.

"Have you given much thought to where you will go once you leave here?" Perhaps she would make this easy for him and offer a brilliant plan that would negate him from any feelings of responsibility—and also desist thinking him some sort of benevolent creature sent from above.

But apparently the girl was determined to make him feel as wretched as possible as she clutched her tea and toast tightly and turned to him with over-large, shattered eyes. "You do not mean to keep me?"

Oh, what a question! He chastised himself thoroughly for the hope that swelled within him at the possibility that living, breathing person should actually *choose* to stay with him. There could be no mistaking her reaction, as just as her eyes had spurred him into disposing of her attacker, they now clearly communicated her desire to remain.

To be *cared* for.

As if he knew how to care for anyone, let alone a damaged girl. She needed nutrients and quite a lot of them if she would ever lose the gaunt and slightly sallow appearance that turned her youth into fragility. He barely remembered to eat one meal a day.

And surely, she would know nothing of music, and that was his one true joy in life. He would not cease his composing, and surely she required sleep like *normal* people. Some of his best work was produced at night.

He would have to be *considerate.*

No, it would be far better to point out to her the inadequacies in her deluded plan. If he did so successfully, she would want to leave of her own accord. And though it would sting at first, he would huff and say 'good riddance' and think of her no more.

But looking at how upset she was at the prospect of returning to the streets, he decided a few more small enquiries could not possibly cause further complications. "Child, why do you call me the Angel of Music?"

Her eyes brightened considerably. "I heard you playing my lullaby! And you made my leg feel so much better." She picked at a crumb of toast with her finger, even as Erik was convinced she had confused his medicinal prowess with the pain relieving properties of the laudanum. "And if you were a man you would have wanted to do *that,* and you did not. So you must be an Angel."

Erik stared at her incredulously. Because he had not *violated* her, that meant he was not a man? How many scoundrels had used her after her father had passed that *that* should be her conclusion? As for the lullaby, it was not one of his own compositions, but was fairly well known throughout the continent. What troubled him most was how accepting she was of her erroneous assumptions.

How could he allow her to wander off alone to be further abused? Whether or not he particularly liked her, or whether or not this was pure selfishness on his part, he had begun to steadily feel a responsibility for her. And if that meant that she should stay with him—grow to love him? Would that be so very terrible?

He firmly pushed away such thoughts. "Is there nowhere else you might stay? An acquaintance perhaps?"

She looked away thoughtfully. "There was a boy..."

Erik stiffened. "Yes?"

Christine shrugged. "I have not seen him since before Papa died. He... he kissed me once and said he would remember me..." She sighed, looking forlorn once more. "I tried to find him when Mamma Valérius died, but..." she shrugged again and took a large mouthful of toast.

"What was his name?" He could not justify keeping her if there was a home available to her—one that did not include the likes of him.

"Why does it matter? He could not have been with me when I was just the poor daughter of a violinist, why would he care for me now?" She made a vague gesture over her person, clearly referring to her recent injustices.

Erik grimaced as he saw yet more crumbs falling onto the rug below.

"Your father played the violin? Did he teach you also?" Maybe she would not be entirely opposed to his compositions flowing throughout the house at all hours of the day if she had been subjected to such musicality since birth.

The girl actually *laughed.* It was short and breathy, but the brief twinkle in her eyes affected him more than he could say. "Oh no! Papa would play, and I would sing!"

Erik remembered the strained and hoarse voice she had used yesterday and tried to imagine anything of quality being produced from her vocals. This morning her timbre was more pleasing, but still held a twinge of disuse.

"And if my Angel has finally come, then I can sing once more!" He nearly groaned when he saw her eyes turn misty. "I tried to sing in the parks for spare *centimes,* but when Papa died... my voice died with him."

"Did you sing with him often?"

She *smiled,* and again, it caused an uncomfortable feeling in his chest. "Every day! We used to play and sing for Professor Valérius. He always called me his little soprano songbird. But then he died too..."

Erik was tempted. If her father had been a musician of such quality as to have any sort of patron, she would have been trained from birth. Tragedy often had unexpected effects on the vocals, but with proper coaxing—and if anyone was able to coax potential from a soprano it would be him—he would have a companion not only for meals, but also for his *music.*

Assuming she *had* potential of course.

But he had to admit, he was intrigued. The idea of sending away someone with talent—someone who had expressed a sincere desire to stay with him—seemed like an absurd handling of the situation. And if in the meantime while her voice healed she came to understand that he was simply a man, and that not all men were quite as dreadful as the ones she had encountered, so much the better.

"Can I not stay with you? I promise not to be any trouble." Her voice was so small when she asked it of him, and his thoughts briefly drifted to his previous determination to find a pet familiar in order to fill the void this girl would leave once she abandoned him. How quickly he had adjusted to the thought of her intruding upon his solitude...

"If you stay with me, Christine, it will not necessarily be easy. To live in this realm of darkness means to devote oneself entirely to music. You say you were promised the Angel of Music, but you have yet to prove to me that you are worthy of his attention."

She nodded emphatically. "I could try to sing for you now! And I know I will not be as good as I used to sing with Papa, but I will improve now that you are with me."

Erik moved quickly and took the teacup away from the arm of the sofa, as he feared in her enthusiasm she would manage to topple the remaining liquid onto his rug. "You will do no such thing. You will heal and you will eat. When I feel it is time to test your voice, I shall tell you." Of what seemed to be their own accord, his fingers twitched as if to grasp her chin, and he was grateful when she looked at him without his unwelcome prompting.

"And if I find you are worthy of my tutelage, Christine, you shall never want for a home again."

Christine wept, and Erik sighed.

IV

Erik had not the least idea of how to comfort her. Surely his attempts at physical reassurance such as a consoling pat would not be welcome. His mind froze at the idea of giving useless platitudes, never one to appreciate lies.

In truth, the problem stemmed from never being comforted himself. When the despair became too great he would find his own little corner and weep, aching for someone—*anyone*—to be willing to offer him respite.

But no one ever came.

This girl deserved far better than he. She was victim of horrific circumstance, with too many deceased relatives that should have been the ones to comfort her through life's trials and tribulations.

And he was so *very* tired of her tears.

Tentatively, bracing himself for the pain of her recoil, he wound his long fingers around her small hand, and tugged slightly. To his great surprise, she in turn grasped his hand tightly with both of hers, following him trustingly as he led her back to the sitting room—the room which housed his organ.

He supposed it was reasonable that she had made no comment regarding the magnificent instrument that rose imposingly on one wall. Too consumed by her immediate concerns such as food and safety, she would have had little time to question him regarding his decor.

Extricating his hand from the unyielding pressure of her own proved quite a task, and it was only with a quiet word that she relented. "I shall play for you, Christine. Would you like that?"

The girl hiccupped unbecomingly as she nodded her assent, and he stole quickly to his favourite instrument. If her father was truly am accomplished violinist, he reasoned that playing the same could potentially create a pleasant nostalgia for her. But there was also the possibility that hearing the musical whine would only further her grief and Erik refused to take such a risk.

So instead he sat down upon the bench of the organ, and began to coax the tune she had already stated was so familiar.

It was simple to the extreme, just a soft lullaby obviously meant to quiet fussy children and soothe them back into slumber. Erik had not had the pleasure of such a caregiver offering him comfort after awakening from a nightmare. He could not remember precisely when he had first heard it, but it had most certainly been in boyhood, and he vividly recalled the many nights he would hum it to himself after particularly harsh terrors—anything to balm the loneliness.

Upon the third repeat of the melody, Erik turned slightly in order to assess Christine's mood. To his great relief, he found that she had once more resumed her position cocooned within the folds of his dressing gown, and was sleeping quite soundly.

Excellent.

If she would be staying with him for a time—at least until he had gauged the quality of her voice for himself—she would be in need of clothes. He had no issue with her continuing to roam his home in nothing but a nightshirt and overly large dressing gown, but he presumed that she would prefer to have some modicum of propriety through actual female accoutrement.

And heaven forbid she attempt to wear those rags again.

He had actually been slightly surprised that she had risen so early given the amount of drugs that should still have lingered in her system. He guessed she would sleep for some time now that she would be promised the silence of his home. He would not attempt to move her, as his errand depended on her slumber. But he did re-enter her bed chamber in order to fetch a coverlet so she would not be cold while he was away.

But most assuredly he did so because she could possibly awaken from an errant draft, not because he cared so much for her comfort—of this he was sure, even as he smoothed the blanket around her, ensuring she was tucked in properly.

Satisfied that the girl would not be disturbed, he fetched his outerwear and crept silently out of his home—quite grateful that the heavy door was greased so thoroughly as to make only the slightest *click* when he closed it.

He was going above.

If he were not pressed for time he would place an order at a dressmaker.

Of course, he would not actually enter the shop, and instead he would pay one of the street urchins a few *centimes* to carry in a list of items that he would require. But the girl needed garments that were already created, and shops were often limited in their wares.

And truly, anything at all that he would require could be found in the floors above.

He carried no lantern, and even in the darkest places where even he could not see clearly, he was surefooted and navigated the numerous traps and divots with expertise.

It was after all, *his* domain.

He did not often *borrow* from the costume department. On occasion one of his more fanciful escapades throughout the Opera would demand something more eccentric than what was currently housed in his wardrobe.

Erik was quite proficient at sewing his own clothes, but he often delegated such responsibilities to hired hands. He did not like how the needle and pins would occasionally prick his fingertips. The twinge of his sore fingers would interfere with playing, and that was not something to be tolerated.

So while not one of his normal routes that he took as he surveyed his theatre, the way to the many rooms filled with costumes was by no means unfamiliar.

He entered one of the empty rooms, moderately disgusted by the lack of organisation. Ruffled skirts, heavily ordained tunics, and the occasional plumed hat were all strewn about the room in absolute chaos.

The managers would be receiving a strongly worded letter regarding a change in the costuming department...

But for now, he would sift through the mess, looking for anything that would remotely suit the needs of the girl housed within the cellars.

Chemises were the first to be located, and the most versatile, doubling as both undergarment and nightgown. He ignored all of the various corsets and stays for he despised the contraptions. They impeded lung capacity and made the critical stomach muscles lazy that were so necessary for proper vocal control.

He was pleased to find a trunk that contained perfectly normal looking dresses, as well as a few skirts and blouses, though he could not immediately place what production they could possibly have been for...

Unless these were *not* in fact costumes. He grumbled again realising that one of the dressers was obviously utilising these rooms to store personal items.

Well. They would be properly punished by losing the privilege of owning such items.

Deciding to simply take the entire trunk with him, Erik stole from the room with his plunder.

He would need to question Christine about what kinds of foods she liked to eat, and though stocked with what he considered essentials—mostly wine, bread, and the occasional cup of tea—he would defer to her tastes when next he procured food.

But for now they would make do, and he wasted no time in traversing the many stairs and passageways to his home below.

When he opened the front door, he was filled with trepidation. Christine was awake, and while she was *blessedly* not crying, something about her seemed quite odd. She almost seemed... frozen.

"Christine?"

She blinked mildly. "You were gone. You were gone and I could not open the door." Her eyes rose slightly to meet his, though he could not place the emotion within them. "You do not have any windows."

Erik placed the trunk down on the floor before closing the door firmly, giving it his full attention as he did so. He supposed he should have expected these questions at some point, but still found himself quite unprepared with answers that could be given safely.

He turned back to her carefully, quite uncomfortable with her cool composure. "Do you wish to ask me something?"

Christine took a bracing breath. "Am I dead?"

Erik gaped at her. "You think you are dead because you are in a house with no windows? Christine, you have reached some of the most ludicrous conclusions I have ever heard, but that might be the most ridiculous."

He could clearly see the beginnings of anger flicker through her features. "I do not *know* what to think! You were not here to make me think otherwise!"

Perhaps the fact that she mentioned his absence twice was worth noting, but he quickly dismissed it as he felt the stirrings of irritation at having to explain his comings and goings.

He had taken time and energy out of his schedule in order to see to *her* needs. And yet she stared at him so accusingly, as if he had done something hurtful by leaving her!

"I was not aware that I had to account for my actions to *you,* you foolish girl. I am sorry you were so distressed at finding you still dwell within my home." His voice had taken on a cutting edge, and by the way she began to cringe it was apparent they found their target acutely. "You were not so upset by remaining here this morning! I believe you *asked* to be allowed to stay!"

Any anger seemed to leave her in one swift breath, and to his absolute *horror* she slid from the cushions of the settee to the floor, her hands clasped at her breast. "I am sorry for questioning you, Angel. *Please* do not make me leave." Her head bowed, and she looked a perfect picture of winsome piety.

Seeing her blatant supplication and feeling deeply disturbed by her display upon his carpet, he quickly bade her rise. "Get off the floor, Christine. I have something for you."

That seemed to grab her attention. "For me? What is it?" Her eyes seemed to finally take in the small trunk at his feet, and he could practically feel the excitement pouring from her—though to his displeasure she remained perfectly still, disobeying his command to rise.

"What kind of a surprise would it be if I opened it for you? Get *off* the floor and open it for yourself." She was not a dog, or any other sort of animal. Living on the streets meant that she had slept undoubtedly on alleyway cobblestones or perhaps the occasional bench should no one shoo her away. But in his home she was a guest, and though he had chastised her for mussing his furnishings, he felt distinctly uncomfortable seeing her on the floor.

She smile at him timidly and *finally* did as he directed and came over to the trunk, and he realised stupidly that in order to sift through the contents she would have to once more kneel. Only this time he assured himself that she was doing so in order to receive essentials for being a proper guest, so it was not at all the same thing.

The girl actually *squealed* when she lifted the lid. "Clothes!"

So despite being forced into urchinhood, she still possessed such feminine qualities as to show such excitement by simple pieces of sewn cloth.

Erik sniffed.

Christine looked up to the looming presence above her, eyes shining. "Thank you. No one has done as much as you have in..."

He cleared his throat. "Yes, well. If I did not want you to steal the entirety of my wardrobe, it was necessary to procure some of your own." And in order to stop her from looking at him like he was the angel he knew he was not, he added, "I do not know how they will fit you."

She shook her head fiercely. "It does not matter! I can sew well enough if you have any needles and thread, or I shall simply wear them a little loosely."

To his relief her attention finally turned from him in order to begin inspecting and sorting through the contents of the trunk, and he could not quite explain how he felt when happy little cries would escape her when something particularly pretty or soft was pulled from its confines.

Ladies. Such distractible creatures.

Though loath to distract her when she was so engaged, he did need to enquire as to her tastes and appetites. "I am afraid that my food stores are rather low and I shall need to acquire more. Is there anything in particular you want or need?"

Christine was currently holding up a light blue dress to her frame, but looked to him cheerfully at his question. "I would never presume to tell you what to purchase! Whatever you wish to provide will be more than enough."

Erik groaned. "Christine, let me be clear. I realise you suddenly hold me in very high regard, but when I ask a question of you, it is because I would like an *answer.*"

Patience. If there was one thing he would learn from this girl it would most assuredly be patience.

He nearly felt like stalking away from the room when the light that had graced her eyes dimmed and it was apparent she knew she had displeased him. "I am sorry, Angel."

This girl would be the death of him, of that he was absolutely certain.

Erik wanted to berate her for the use of her preferred title when he had so explicitly stated she was to make use of his name. But to do so would merely distress her more, and he had experienced quite enough of her tears.

"I shall fetch some paper and you will write down at least three items you would like for me to acquire." He rose and moved to his large stacks of compositions but suddenly paused. "You are literate?"

The girl had the audacity to look slightly affronted. "Of course! Papa and Professor Valérius made sure of it." Then, in such a quiet tone he would have missed it had he not spent years in complete silence, she added, "I am not stupid..."

"My apologies, I was not questioning your intelligence, merely the extent of your education."Christine blushed and opened her mouth to apologise but Erik silenced her with a wave of his hand. "No, do not apologise. I have had quite enough of your contrition today."

Locating a clean sheet of paper proved difficult, as most had compositions or illustrations either covering the entirety of the page, or at least a portion of it. Eventually he grew tired of sifting through his works and simply tore off a strip from an incomplete concerto, and with a bit more scrounging, located his favourite fountain pen.

Christine ceased her organising and returned to the settee with her paper and pen, and stared at it thoughtfully for some time before making careful scribbles. Leaving her to her task, Erik began transporting her numerous piles into the Louis-Philippe room, not relishing the idea of an entire trunk's worth of ladies' garments scattering across his sitting room floor.

In any case, was it not the gentlemanly thing to do?

He did not consider the making of a list to be any great task, but Christine evidently did not agree. She would often cross out items and then make new additions, her browed furrowed and lip tormented with nibbling until she was seemingly satisfied.

"You do not have to buy all of these just because I wanted them..."

Erik silenced her with an exasperated huff. "Yes, you have made it perfectly plain that I do not have to provide you anything at all unless it is my express wish to do so. I shall add that to the ever growing list of things you have made *abundantly* clear."

He cursed his tongue when he saw how deflated the girl became at his sarcasm. "Perhaps... you would care to join me as I obtain these items?"

Christine brightened considerably. "I would like that very much!" She glanced down at her clothes. "But perhaps I should change first."

And so it began.

Just like any other man, Erik would have to constantly wait while the female in his life took an inordinate amount of time preparing for whatever simple outing required her presence.

He felt that strange stirring in his chest once more, and rubbed at it absently.

Nothing could have prepared him for when she finally did emerge.

He noted ruefully that he had forgotten a hairbrush and comb, but she had managed rather well to maintain her tangle of curls with a hair ribbon and a low *chignon*.

And while he had not taken any of the corsetry, it was obvious that the dress would have required one for any woman of normal weight and size. Christine was so slight however that it fit her remarkably well without any such additional confinement.

The pale blue of the dress drew out what small amount of pink still remained after her malnourishment had robbed of her natural complexion, and he truly glimpsed what under his guidance and care she could become—a beauty.

His mouth felt suddenly dry.

"Am I presentable?"

Erik could only nod.

It was too light outside for them him to safely traverse the markets, so for the second time that day he would need to make use of the Opera House's stores.

He shuddered when Christine pulled out her tattered brown cloak and began tying it about her shoulders. "What are you doing?"

She froze, looking unsure. "You said I could go with you. The trunk did not have a cloak, so I shall use my own."

No guest of his would wear a rag masquerading as a proper winter cloak.

Grunting his displeasure, he moved once more to his wardrobe and pulled out one of his many spares. He knew the hem would be ruined, as while on him it skimmed his ankles, on the girl it would trail through all manners of filth as they ascended the cellars.

But no matter. He had plenty of others, though he did give it a comforting pat goodbye as it faced its own demise as he handed it over to the girl.

Erik could tell she was about to protest, but she quailed when seeing his challenging glare. It did not escape him that she burrowed quite thoroughly into it as a sigh of pleasure escaped her lips.

He also noticed her delighted gasp when with a quick flick of his fingers, the front door with no handle opened silently, revealing the location of his home for the first time.

The girl looked both frightened and curious as she peered out into the darkness beyond. "Where are we? And where are we going?"

He chuckled softly as he pulled her hand into the crook of his elbow, knowing full well she would be unable to see the path before them. "My dear, we are going above."

And when the door behind them shut with a quiet *click,* he relished the tightened grip on his arm.

For this time, the Opera Ghost would have an accomplice.

V

What Erik had not considered was how anxious she would be in the total blackness. What had started with a simple hand clutching at his arm became an entire body pressed against his, her frightened breaths coming out in pants. "You will not leave me down here, will you?"

For a brief moment he cursed his decision not to bring a lantern. He never liked travelling with a light as he felt too exposed—for if any person had stupidly wandered into his cellars, they would immediately be able to see him coming. It was far better that they only be aware of his presence when they felt the rough sting of the Punjab lasso as it coaxed them into death's waiting embrace.

But this trembling girl had obviously had quite enough of the dark, and he felt strangely moved that she looked to him for reassurance—that at a simple promise she could believe he would never leave her down here to be lost and alone, confident that he was utterly incapable of such a cruel notion.

He had not at all expected how *good* her body would feel against him. Though little more than a child, nearly all skin and bones like he was, she still radiated a warmth that his own body lacked.

But his blood ran cold when he realised she apparently feared this darkness more than she feared the possibility of rape, as she was clinging to him quite completely.

He snorted. No, she simply thought him an ethereal being who could not possibly want her in such a visceral manner.

If only that were true...

His attention returned to the girl when he felt the small pricks of her fingernails pressing insistently into his arm.

"No, Christine, you have my word that I shall not leave you here. And Erik always keeps his word."

Never mind that he generally twisted his word to suit whatever purpose he so desired. The girl did not need to know such things, as he saw little issue with keeping his promise to her.

The only reason he could tell she even remotely accepted his assurance was because she had her head nestled into his arm, and he could feel her slight nod.

Erik shuddered.

He had believed it to be true before, but he was even more positive now—this girl would be the death of him.

He quickened his pace so that his torment would end all the sooner, though he eventually was forced to slow when the girl tripped yet again. When she did so she would release a startled cry and his fingers would be forced to grasp whatever part of her was most near—usually a thin arm, or even once her nipped waist. Each time he revelled in the way his hands fit so completely around her, and he was even more determined that he would ply her with all sorts of nourishment so that she should eventually feel less like a corpse, and more like the woman she should become.

The trip to the kitchens of the Opera House in theory should have taken far less time than his previous excursion to the costume department, as the kitchens resided in the lowest levels of the upper floors, as did the pantry that was his ultimate aim. But he was trying to be mindful of the girl, so what should have been a relatively short jaunt turned into a carefully manoeuvred maze wherein he had to struggle with the nearly uncontainable urge to flee from here whenever he felt her press all the more firmly against his side.

He let out an audible sound of relief when at last he reached the short tunnel that led directly to the back wall of the pantry. The door itself on the other side was lined with all manner of foodstuffs, so he always had to be particularly careful to ensure that nothing fell when swinging open the panel.

There had also been that unfortunate incident when someone had actually been *in* the pantry when he had opened it.

The terrified kitchen maid had quite the tale to tell of her near death experience with the illustrious Opera Ghost—who apparently had a taste for preserves!

Never wanting such a mistake to again be possible, he had quickly installed a small sliding peephole, so he could always ensure that whatever ghostly mischief he intended to inflict was always of *his* explicit purpose and design.

Erik never did care for surprises.

He made swift use his hidden panel, and surmised that their little raid would go unnoticed.

Christine gasped when the wall in front of them suddenly opened, and he could not help but be rather amused by her enraptured expressions whenever he did something unexpected, yet so uncomplicated. Well, uncomplicated to *him.*

It was always nice to be appreciated.

The girl blinked rapidly as she adjusted to the dim light of the pantry. The exterior door was closed, but he imagined she could see well enough by the light that poured in through the sizeable crack beneath the door.

He pulled out the slightly crumpled list and his heart, generally untouched by much of anything beyond his own substantial wounds inflicted by his past, gave a sharp pull when he finally looked to see what had been written.

Sweet Biscuits.

Scones.

Apples.

Such simple things, yet utterly unattainable when living on the streets. Whatever fruits or vegetables she could have found would most likely have been rotten, and her first request revealed more of her childishness than he would care to admit.

He turned to her. "Why scones?"

She blushed, and found the scuffed leather of her shoes peeking out from beneath her long skirt to be suddenly very fascinating. "I liked to stop at this little tearoom and watch all the fancy ladies take their tea. The scones they would eat looked *so* very good, and I was very hungry and..." she trailed off with a shrug.

This poor little urchin girl, coveting a scone.

He knew what such hunger was like, and while desperate for any nourishment at all, one would especially desire something that was warm and soft—though he used to fantasise about freshly baked bread, not English fare and *fancy ladies.*

Christine looked suddenly horrified. "Is that wrong? Am I asking too much?"

Erik wanted to rage. He wanted to find everyone who had ever hurt her and show them exactly what it *meant* to be hurt. And though he would *never* voice this desire to the girl, he wanted to hurt her father for not providing her guardians who could remain alive long enough to see her through to womanhood.

"No, Christine, you are not asking too much."

And though he would not admit to himself that he had done so, he prayed that her voice was worthy of his attention so that maybe—just maybe—he could keep her.

Though he began to strongly suspect he would offer to keep her even if her voice more resembled a frog than an angel.

Erik already had many of the things necessary for making baked indulgences. His underground home was excellent for storing goods as the cool temperatures allowed for a natural form of refrigeration. But still, he could readily tell that if Christine stayed with him for any length of time he would require much more sugar than he normally kept on hand. He was therefore gratified at the abundance available within the pantry. In addition, he was pleased to find apples—though most were already dried and preserved. The only fresh ones were very small, obviously the last remnants of the late harvest.

But as he handed them to Christine to hold, she positively beamed as if he had presented her the most wondrous of gifts. He also took a few jars filled with applesauce, just in case her tastes were not limited to fresh fruit. Fruit was difficult at best to find in winter, and she would require more nutrients than simple carbohydrates that appeared to be her preference.

If he wished to raid the larder in order to procure proteins for her, he would have to return at night. As it was, the kitchen would be too full and he had not built any tunnels backing into the enclosed structure. So for now, he would have to be content with his current spoils, though he did take a few more titbits that would hopefully prove useful for future meals.

He really did need to begin investigating his cookbooks.

When the door of the pantry opened suddenly and a piercing screech was heard, Erik knew they had long overstayed their welcome. He pulled from one of his pockets a small ball and threw it down upon the ground with a cackle—smoke and sparks emitting instantly and filling the pantry.

And that time the shriek of terror was from his own little accomplice.

Though mindful of the girl's delicateness, he shoved her through the back panel and slammed the door shut.

This is why he usually purchased—or stole—from the market.

Christine was trembling again, and with her arms filled with apples and other necessities, she was having a difficult time latching on to him as she had before. "Angel, I am frightened!"

Erik groaned, keenly aware that her ever growing use of that title meant that her delusions were only growing more potent. But here, in the total darkness where he could *feel* her fear as it sent her quivering into his side, he could not begrudge her whatever comfort she gleaned from such fantasies. "There, there, Christine. I am here."

His own arms were burdened with far heavier items, so it took quite a bit of shifting and manipulation of goods in order for him to manage to fit one of his arms through hers. When this was accomplished, however, and she practically burrowed into his cloak with him, he yet again felt the need to flee from her.

This was wrong.

She was a poor, broken, damaged girl who thought him a heavenly being—free from lusts and sin, when he knew acutely that he felt the encumbrance of both every day of his miserable existence.

Her warmth suddenly felt like a cloying presence, slowly suffocating him with thoughts and feelings he had long since buried—hidden within his own mind even as he had concealed himself physically within the bowels of the Opera.

He extricated himself from her with a sharp cry, *needing* to be free and alone once more in the darkness he knew so well. She drew comfort and solace from people. He drew it from his one constant companion.

Erik began to move away from her, intent on finding some remote corner where he could simply *think*—reformulate the plan that she had dashed with her tears and strange philosophies about his person. He was meant to be alone. He had finally reached a small level of *contentment* being alone, and here this girl, with her clinging grasps and frightened yet oh so hopeful eyes had all but...

He turned back when he heard the thuds. When she could no longer touch him she had dropped all her apples so that her arms were free to grope blindly through the darkness looking for him. "Angel, please do not go! I am sorry for whatever I did!"

But he remained frozen, knowing that it would be far less painful if he allowed her to come to him than if he were to once more willingly seek out her touch. Christine had grown so disorientated without her guide that she walked sharply into the wall beside her, her nose bearing the brunt of the injury. She had started crying and her hands were now clasping a bleeding nose and not the apples she had treasured only moments before.

"Erik!!"

It was the last cry that broke him. He determinedly bit back his own sympathetic sobs, knowing that she was now hurt simply because he was too afraid to become attached to her—because of his weakness. "Calm yourself, Christine, I am here." And because he could not quite help himself, he added, "You dropped your apples, you foolish girl."

She sobbed pathetically, and he pulled out his handkerchief and placed it into her hand, drawing it to her nose and stopping her natural instinct to lean her head back with a gentle press of his fingers. "Shall I save them for you?"

Christine whimpered, grasping at his cloak and refusing to let go, even as he picked up her apples and slipped them into hidden pockets. He would have stored them there to begin with had she not seemed so enraptured by them.

She made no move to touch him further and seemed resigned to merely gripping his cloak as they travelled down below once more.

Erik could not remember a time when he felt more wretched.

Yes, the girl possessed her eccentricities, but it was her tremulous trust in him that he had besmirched with his own selfish needs.

Christine was still sniffling when he gently pulled the fabric of his cloak from her clenched fists, and before she had time to let out a wail of despair, carefully slipped his one free hand between hers.

So ingrained was the fear of rejection that he almost expected her to fling his hand away in disgust. Instead, he felt her pull it closer, clutching it to her warm body as she followed him blindly back to his home.

Not a word was passed between them, not until Erik poured the small bag of sugar he had filched into its proper canister, and the other items put to rights. Christine stood in the doorway, her pallor ghostly—the stark contrast of his black cloak overwhelming her small frame doing nothing to improve her complexion. "Why did you leave me?"

Erik sighed, expecting she would not allow the matter to simply fade away from his thoughts and memories so he would no longer have to remember her cries and know he was responsible.

"Christine, I am not certain you will be able to fully grasp how... I am unaccustomed to..." He growled, setting down a jar of applesauce with slightly more force than strictly necessary.

Gathering his thoughts so he would not bumble like a foolish schoolboy untrained in the art of speech, he tried again. "I am a solitary creature. Your touch overwhelmed me, and I am afraid I moved without thinking. I apologise that you were frightened."

There. That was the best he could do.

How could he hope to explain that his responses were conditioned from years of abuse from the entirety of mankind? Though Christine would certainly understand better than most, it still made him no more willing to discuss such atrocities.

She had suffered enough of her own.

Erik could not quite put into words how her dour expression unnerved him. So moving slowly and deliberately toward her as not to startle her overly much, with a quick flash and a twist of his wrist he produced one of her apples from seemingly thin air.

Perhaps timid and a little watery still, her answering smile was genuine as she took it from his gloved fingers. "Thank you," she whispered, cradling the fruit.

"You are most welcome."

Erik was never one to relish awkward interactions. Running and hiding, or cloaking his anxiety under a heavy layer of sarcasm or vitriol was his usual method of dealing with individuals—whenever such a thing was absolutely necessary of course.

But the girl would surely not appreciate such techniques.

So he simply nodded and would have been quite satisfied had she remained silent.

Apparently this particular girl was sent to him merely to test his self-control.

"You did not... it was not because I am undeserving of your touch?"

That urge to flee from her came upon him once more. *Surely* this was beyond his capabilities. Someone else—someone kind, and gentle, and who knew how to *love* should have intervened for this girl so that she might learn to heal from someone who knew what it was to be whole.

But no. She was saddled with him, and it could not possibly be his responsibility to make such assurances.

Erik turned to face her, waiting until she stopped looking down at her toes and glanced at him. "*No.* There is nothing unworthy about you, Christine. You are goodness and light and I..."

He would not tell her of his many sins. He would not explain to her precisely why he was so unfit for the title she bestowed upon him as that would only make her all the more uncomfortable to be in his presence and in his home. Until he had found a suitable living arrangement for her, she would have to remain with him. While he still drew breath he would not allow her to return to the streets.

She looked so lost. It was obvious she wanted to believe him, but from the way she pulled her cloak—*his* cloak—more tightly around her, he could tell she was not ready to begin reshaping whatever distorted ideas she had concocted regarding herself.

Perhaps she required a distraction.

"Are you hungry?"

Christine looked hesitant, and Erik knew she was grappling with her first instinct to inform him she would eat only if he felt the need to provide her with something. It pleased him greatly when instead she answered him directly. "Yes."

"Very well. You may find a seat of your liking and I will make you something."

He had meant for her to return to the sitting room or the guest bedchamber, and was quite unprepared for her to glance around the kitchen before hopping onto his counter with a slight grimace.

Foolish girl. She was still healing and the hard surface would be quite unforgiving and painful.

Stalking from the room he took one of his dining chairs and brought it into the kitchen, pointing at it a glare. Though he had dismissed it yesterday as it was not as soft as his settee, it was certainly better than the counter. "You will never heal properly if you do not take proper care of yourself."

Christine slid down and settled herself, looking not entirely chastened. "But you take care of me, so I am sure I will heal just fine."

Erik had no response to that.

So instead of feeding her impudent delusions—he was a *genius,* not a childminder—he pulled out one of his cookery books and proceeded to make the first item on her list, handing her an apple to munch as he worked.

"Do you have a preference for a specific type of biscuit?"

The girl practically beamed at him.

And Erik could not help his returning smile, however slight it might have been.

VI

Whatever concerns Erik might have had about the girl's weight were rapidly being assuaged.

She had so far consumed *five* biscuits, and showed little outward signs of stopping.

Earlier he had considered it a victory when he managed to ply her with some slices of cheese and more water for her meal, and a few slices of bread rounded out her little supper feast. He had intended for her sweet biscuits to be an accompaniment to her meal as he felt it more important that she eat promptly and regularly, without waiting for his questionable baking skills to produce something edible. Cheese was perhaps a poor excuse for protein, but Christine ate it all happily, and the way she *thanked* him made him very much aware that with one of her smiles and a pleading look, he would do nearly anything for her.

And it frightened him more than he could say.

So instead he now distracted her with more biscuits, until she released a contented sigh and her eyelids began to droop.

It did not surprise him that she was so tired. When the body was long denied proper nutrition the act of digestion would most certainly cause sleepiness, simply so that other functions would not have to also be sustained.

And it gave him more time for thinking and planning.

He moved to take the rest of her biscuits away, meaning to store them in one of his few tins so they would last longer. To his relative surprise, she followed him, obviously intent on knowing precisely where her morsels were going to be kept.

Erik dreaded to think this action was because she feared he would seek to hide them from her, and she wished to circumvent such intended unkindness.

She eyed him warily as he made a very great show of placing her remaining titbits into their proper container and leaving them well within her reach. When he designed the kitchen it was for himself alone, and though he supposed in a vague recess of his mind he knew the shelves and cupboards were higher than for a normal kitchen, seeing Christine's stature made it abundantly clear that she would need assistance to reach *any* of the upper storage.

"Thank you for supper, it was perfect." Her eyes were soft as she said this, and he was glad to see that her demeanour no longer resembled one focused solely on survival, but one that lent itself toward appreciation, not simply desperation.

"Perhaps you should sleep now that you are *satisfied*." Satisfied was a proper word—engorged was not, even if that was the first his mind had supplied. Just because her appetite had stunned him did not mean she should be censured for eating—surely that would lead to disastrous future meals.

Erik did not think he would be met with any resistance, but the girl was apparently full of surprises. Or perhaps he was simply dreadful at understanding her.

Both could easily be true.

Christine seemed to hesitate, and he braced himself for whatever strange and unpractised thing she would ask of him.

"Could you... could you perhaps..."

Erik groaned, the anticipation causing all kinds of untold horrors to supplement themselves for whatever request she would make. A bedtime story perhaps? No one had ever read *him* a bedtime story, and he most certainly would not do so for the girl.

"What is it you want?"

He had not meant to sound so curt, but his nervousness was influencing his tone more than he had supposed.

She flinched, "Nothing. Thank you again." She made a hasty retreat with only a timid glance in his direction, before practically fleeing to her bedroom.

Erik sighed. He did not want to think about her anymore. For a few blissful moments he wanted to lose himself in what he knew best—music. She was complicated and frightening, and cried entirely too much for comfort, and she made him feel like the unsure boy he had been in his youth.

But he could not play because that would keep her awake, and he just wanted her to *sleep.* Sleep and become restored so that maybe her mind would miraculously heal and he would not feel compelled to keep her with him, caring for her and ensuring that nothing ever harmed her again in this life.

He had not slept the night before, or the night before that. Erik never required much sleep, but even he was beginning to feel fatigued—though he rightfully supposed that had more to do with emotional strain than any physical exertions.

Perhaps sleep would do his own mind some good.

What he had not told Christine was that his home only had one bathroom, and that the hidden, secondary door connected to his own bedchamber. To inform her of such a thing would surely only cause her distress and it was not as if he would ever dream of invading her privacy.

He scoffed. And to inform her that he indeed *did* bathe would imply he was not an angel. Heaven forbid he disillusion her in that respect.

So he waited an appropriate amount of time, hearing the pipes work while she seemingly drew water to fill her basin, then when all was quiet, he slipped through his own door and performed his own ablutions—making *quite* sure that the connecting door to her room was locked.

That accomplished, he returned to his bedchamber and donned his own comfortable nightly attire, suddenly remembering that the girl was still in possession of his dressing gown when he could not find it hanging on its usual hook within the wardrobe.

Erik debated on whether or not to sleep in his mask. He did not generally, as while hideous and accustomed to being covered, the skin of his face did require some time in which to breathe after being confined in its leather tomb for the majority of the day. But now he had Christine to think about, and while he was certain he would awaken before she could possibly see him, he still felt another pang of unease as he slowly peeled it from his face. He listened intently for a long moment, waiting for any sound that would indicate his *guest* had somehow managed to enter his locked bedroom and had seen his deformity.

But all was quiet, and with careful steps he blew out his lone candle and climbed into his tight coffin. And for the first time he found his sleeping arrangements slightly morbid. He blamed the girl for that, as now he knew there was another human being separated by a few layers of stone that slept in a featherbed enclosed in brocade, while he tried to find respite in a casket befitting his corpse-like features.

Christine denied it, but he *was* a man... was he not?

It took quite some time before he could eventually will his body into relaxation—and with it his mind—until ultimately sleep took him.

Only to be startled awake by a piercing scream.

He cursed his decision to sleep without his mask as his usually precise movements were hurried and fumbling as he tried to don it as quickly as possible, even as he hastened over the walls of the coffin. With his dressing gown still held hostage by Christine he was forced to stalk from the room in nothing but his sleep clothes.

And though he could clearly hear whimpers and cries from beyond the next door, his hand froze on the handle.

She had scampered off to bed so quickly she had no time to extract a promise that he would not enter her bedchamber while she slept. But he had unconsciously known that while she resided with him that room was going to be *hers*—to cross such lines would be dangerous to his already fragile emotionality.

But when he heard a gasping, *"Angel!"* from beyond the door, any thoughts of privacy fled his mind.

He thought her cry had been a conscious one, but instead he walked in to see her thrashing in the bedclothes, obviously still in the throes of a nightmare.

How many had he suffered throughout the years? And no one had been there to wake him from the terror—the *pain.*

But this poor slip of a girl had *him.*

So while cautious and wary of furthering her fear, knowing she would inevitably waken to a mask looming above her, he placed a hand on her shoulder and shook it gently. "Christine, you are all right. You may wake up now!"

She lurched away from his hand, and he chastised himself for having touched her at all.

Of course she would not find it a comfort.

Would anyone?

He tried to stifle the hurt she had caused by her unconscious refusal of his person, but the wounds were imbedded too deeply and he felt the overwhelming urge to storm back to his own coffin and leave her there to suffer through her own night terrors—just as he had been forced to do for the entirety of his miserable existence.

Before he could even move she startled awake with a gasp, eyes darting around the room furiously before her hands groped in the total darkness, nearly hitting him in the process.

Belatedly he realised she was reaching for the match in order to light the small kerosene lamp on the bedside table. Of course she would be frightened of the dark—how quickly he forgot that *normal* people did not have his ability to see in such blackness. It was unnatural.

He took the matches from her trembling fingers, resolutely ignoring the shriek she gave when his own icy digits came into contact with her own, before allowing a small amount of illumination into the bedroom.

Erik added yet another issue that needed to be ignored. Christine had made use of the chemises he had supplied, and unlike his own black nightshirt he had loaned her before, these items were made of a thin, white cotton that was bordering on transparent.

He felt every bit the monster he knew himself to be that he should notice such a thing.

Here she was shuddering back sobs and he was admiring the way her nightgown caressed the pale flesh that it not so completely covered.

Erik stood hesitantly by her bedstead, waiting for some instruction. "Is there something you require?"

Christine burrowed under the covers more thoroughly, peeping at him through swollen eyes. "No."

He nodded, but made no move to vacate the room. "Would you like to tell me what you dreamt?"

She opened her mouth slightly, but shut it again firmly. "No."

Perhaps he should fetch her another glass of laudanum. It would at the very least allow her to sleep...

But that was the coward's way of dealing with this damaged girl, and Erik was most assuredly no coward. Though unversed in the art of comfort he would not allow Christine to sleep unaided, nor would he make her dependent on medicinal intervention.

"Would you..." He felt stupid offering, but if one thing was certain to distract her from whatever plagued her mind, it would be this. "Would you like me to play for you?"

Her relief was palpable.

Christine made to rise from the bed but he stopped her with a wave of his hand. He wanted for her to sleep. And the fact that he almost wished she would fall into slumber on his settee so he might have an excuse to carry her to bed once more made it abundantly clear to him that such was the wrong thing to do.

So instead he fetched his violin, ever aware of the potential that hearing what her father played might distress her, but finally he decided it was worth the possibility.

The girl was sitting up in bed, and he noticed gratefully that she had pulled the bedclothes up around her so she was now covered modestly. Her eyes were wide and he was pleased that she was not crying.

His hands ran over the carefully polished wood before raising it to his throat and beginning to play.

Christine did not cry for which he was very glad, but the look of awe and wonder that was clearly displayed on her features unnerved him. He was acutely aware that every note he coaxed with his bow was only furthering her confidence that he was her Angel of Music.

But that did not stop him from playing. At first he played something slightly more dramatic so as to distract her from whatever remnants of her nightmare lingered. But then Erik shifted to the simple lullaby she had claimed as her own so that she might be persuaded to sleep longer.

Her sleepy and drooping lids were a testament to his skills, and his eyes shone triumphantly thinking she would drift off at any moment. But instead she pinched her arm rather harshly, apparently determined to continue listening to the personal concert he offered her.

Finally he could tell that no matter how long or how softly he played, she was not going to allow herself to sleep.

Erik gently lowered his violin and placed it back into its velvet lined case before turning back to Christine. "Why will you not sleep?"

She hummed softly, "I do not wish to dream."

Erik never talked about his dreams, but on many occasions he thought perhaps if he gave voice to his fears—the nighttime terrors that plagued his mind with increasing intensity—they might in fact be purged.

"Child," he used his most persuasive and enticing tone, noticing her shudder with a tinge of satisfaction. "Tell Erik what you dreamt."

Her eyes were wide and glassy and he thought at first she would simply shake her head in refusal. But after a few moments, in a quiet voice he could barely hear, she spoke.

"It was the first time a man... he... he was the worst. I tried to tell him that I was not what he thought I was—that I wasn't a *whore,* but he just laughed at me." Christine sniffled, and though looking at him, it was clear she could not *see* him. Erik moved slightly closer, waiting for her to continue.

"I had not been on the streets for very long, and was still thinking I could find Raoul to help me." Though Erik did not actually know who this Raoul person was, he felt the intense stirrings of hatred that he had been yet another person to abandon this poor girl when she needed assistance most.

"Anyway, he dragged me into an alley and threw me down. I had not learned yet that it is better not to struggle... they beat you more when you fight them." A few tears escaped, but she wiped them away angrily. "I dreamt that he was doing it again, but this time *you* were there and I was calling for help but you could not hear me..."

Erik's stomach roiled as he remembered how he had considered leaving her. He would have been just as guilty as any of those other cads, turning away from this poor child in such desperate need of help.

He swallowed thickly, taking a step closer to the foot of her bed. "Christine... I must apologise."

Her brow furrowed in confusion. "Why? You saved me."

Erik found that he could not speak the words. He could not shatter her innocent assumption that he was *good,* and that his intervention towards her plight was inevitable—not something nearly dismissed by his own prejudice and experience.

So instead, he merely shrugged and looked away from her. "I am sorry you had to endure so much."

Christine sniffled once more and he expected she would finally concede that she was ready for sleep. Instead, her eyes turned imploring and she reached out to touch him. He had the good sense to pull away before she could do so, though at her crestfallen expression he supposed she might not have agreed that keeping a physical distance was an imperative.

"Why did you snap at me before bed?"

Erik groaned. "Christine, I have explained to you that I am a solitary creature. You are... an enigma, and I am afraid that sometimes my thoughts and assumptions run away from me." He forced his voice to sound as contrite as he could manage. He did not think he had ever in his life apologised as much as he had to this girl.

Foolish thing.

Christine did not acknowledge his explanation, but again had the faraway look in her eyes that made him so uneasy. He cleared his throat awkwardly. "What were you going to ask of me?"

She blushed, looking down at her coverlet as she registered his enquiry. "I was..." The small hand attached to the impossibly delicate wrist went to her mess of tangles, pulling at it slightly. "Papa used to always brush my hair, and I was wondering if..." Her eyes turned beseeching, "If you would."

Erik felt as though he had lost all ability to move. This little slip of a girl wanted *him* to brush her hair—as if he was a lady's maid!

He should rage and bellow his insult, reminding her of his genius and that he had far better things to do than tend to her girlish vanity. So what if her curls looked more akin to a haystack than actual hair?

But then his mind flashed to his youth when he would stare through the crack of his mother's bedchamber, watching her rhythmically pull her comb through the long, shining tresses. And how he had so desperately wanted to go behind her and offer to do it for her.

And now Christine was offering him the same opportunity.

He had obviously waited too long to reply for Christine was already recanting her request, but he stopped her with a choked reply. "I will... fetch a comb. Perhaps you should move to the sofa."

The idea of settling behind her on the bed was too much to contemplate.

Christine obliged happily, and he went through the Louis-Philippe dresser until he found his mother's pewter comb and brush, then proceeded to the bath-room to fill the pitcher with water. It would be far less painful if her hair was wet and pliant.

And he was completely unprepared for when his trembling fingers first made contact with her curls.

Erik had never experienced such bliss.

While her hair obviously had suffered through her time without a home, the tactile sensation of running his hands through her golden locks—with her permission!—was entrancing. He loved watching the curls straighten as he passed through the knots, only to bounce back determinedly when he had reached their ends.

And each time the comb would graze Christine's scalp, she would release the tiniest of whimpers.

When he realised this was due to pleasure and not because he was hurting her, Erik felt nearly overwhelmed.

Someone could find pleasure in the touch *he* provided.

He was grateful Christine could not see the few tears that escaped him.

VII

Erik could not sleep after what he had experienced the night before. He had enjoyed playing for her as she obviously appreciated his skill and musicality, but ultimately it was the lingering feel of her hair upon his fingers that kept his mind from resting.

She had said that her father had been the one to brush her curls, but he was most assuredly *not* one of her progenitors. He felt not familial attachment to her and so when he had done it, it had not even felt as he imagined it would to touch his mother's hair.

No, though the gesture was innocent enough, when he had touched her it was with the full and cognisant understanding that he was a *man* and she a beautiful girl.

Who could never love him.

And that was the crux of the matter. The longer he spent with Christine the more apparent it became that it was only a matter of time before he was fully enchanted by her smiles and beauty. Even though the world had been cruel to her as well, that did not inherently mean she would be any more ready to accept him than the rest of the human populous had been.

Instead, she would most likely despise him more. If a *normal* man was capable of the abuses she had suffered, what would a monster like him have to offer?

Certainly not the love he so desperately wished to bestow on another human being—but only if there was the possibility it could be reciprocated.

So instead of sleeping Erik went to his organ, scribbling notations and measures onto his many stacks of compositions, playing softly only when essential to the production of a melody or harmony. Not that it was ever *truly* necessary, as he knew each note and sound by heart. But still, sometimes his fingers would ache to play the notes that filled his mind, and he had to oblige—even if the girl could possibly awake by his playing.

It was midmorning before she emerged from her room. Erik had eventually abandoned his music in favour of making the second article on her short little list of desired culinary items. Scones were not as complicated as he would have imagined, and he was very pleased with how symmetrical the small circles were when he cut them out of the round of dough. He had no idea if she cared for dried fruit, but he thought that any additional nutrients he could provide would do her good so he added a small sprinkling to the mix before placing them in the oven.

Erik felt practically domestic. The only thing lacking was an apron and cap and he could take over as Head Cook for the Opera above, not simply the Opera Ghost.

He snorted at the thought.

Christine startled him when she entered the kitchen and it took every ounce of self-control to keep from snapping at her for sneaking.

That did not stop his scowl however, which she apparently noticed with a frown of her own. "Did I do something wrong?"

Erik's scowl deepened. "No, you did nothing wrong." She did not seem to believe him and he could see her visibly inching back through the doorway. "You simply surprised me."

"Oh," she murmured, looking chastened.

He sighed, not at all liking how this morning had begun. "Let us start again. You walked into the kitchen and I would turn," he gave a low bow, "and say, 'Good morning, Christine! Did you have a pleasant night?'"

She smiled faintly before mimicking his formality with a fumbling curtsey of her own. "Good morning, Erik, my night was pleasant enough."

Knowledge of her nightmare hung heavy between them, but both refused to speak of it. Seeing that he was not intent on mentioning it, Christine began to relax.

"We have a little time before your breakfast is ready. Would you perhaps like to finally show me your vocal talents while we wait?"

Christine looked torn between excitement and severe trepidation. "What if... what if you do not like it? Will you make me leave?"

It still baffled Erik that leaving him would seem such a *bad* thing. And while he had implied that she could only stay if her voice proved worthy of his tutelage, he highly doubted that even his cold heart could bear to shove her back onto the streets—even if her voice proved disastrous.

"Do not fret about such things now. Come."

She followed him from the kitchen, standing by the organ without coming too close as he sat upon the bench. "Normally I would have you sing scales in order to prepare your vocals, but I admit my own impatience. Sing whatever you would like."

Christine nodded, and he was pleased to note her change in posture. Instead of slightly hunching as she was prone to do, she squared her shoulders and prepared her breathing. Perhaps her father was an apt instructor after all.

It was a simple song, and he was surprised when he identified the language as Swedish. Christine's French *did* possess a hint of an accent—noticeable only to a highly trained ear—but he had not questioned her origins. But hearing her sing in her native tongue was unexpectedly pleasing, as each word trilled and flowed from practiced lips.

What he was not at all prepared for was her *tone.* The potential was obvious, as her voice was clear and precise, not corrupted by haughty airs or abundant conceit. Whatever she might have thought of her person, her *voice* clearly showed just how pure a soul she possessed.

And he in turn would possess it.

There were imperfections to be sure. Her singing voice clearly had not been used in some time, and there were a few improper habits that would have to be dealt with swiftly. But the potential was tremendous, and Erik found himself assessing her in an entirely new light.

No longer was she simply an abused girl he was sheltering—now she would be his muse.

Her little song ended, and she looked to him expectantly. While he could tell plainly that she was nervous, singing had evidently lifted her spirits and she bore an unmistakably hopeful expression.

Erik found that he was quite incapable of putting into words the plans and dreams that rapidly were filling his mind. So instead he rose and stood before her. Her eyes still held more life than he had seen before and he was once more struck by just how lovely she was—especially now that her hair was full and buoyant and returning to the healthy tresses she should have always possessed.

"Christine, I would be honoured to become your Maestro."

If possible, her eyes shone all the brighter. "Truly? I know that I am terribly out of practice."

He would not lie to her. "Yes, you are. And while I commend your semblance of posture, you will need to work on that also." His own mind reeled with all the small techniques she would need to learn, but he stopped himself before giving them voice. Surely an overwhelmed Christine would not prove an amiable student.

"And... that means that I might stay with you? Forever?"

Erik stopped short. Just because he offered her a home with a promise that its doors and comforts would be available for the entirety of her days did *not* in turn mean that she would desire to remain with him for always. He would be an overbearing maestro, and he was positive there would be times when she regretted her decision to be tutored.

But he could hear his heart cry out to make her such a promise, even when he was so acutely aware that to make such an offer would mean all the more pain and agony when she chose to leave him.

Unless...

Could he really extract a similar promise from such a damaged soul? She would cling to anything—*that* much was readily apparent—and it would be an abuse of her trust to ask her to stay with *him* for all eternity.

But Erik found himself horribly tempted.

His silence was not ignored as Christine began to look disappointed.

"I promised you that should I become your tutor, you would never be in want of a home. Whether that be here with me or some other location of your choosing, I swear that you will always have a roof over your head."

"Oh, *thank you!*"

Nothing could have prepared Erik for her attack on his person.

Frail arms entwined around his waist as she buried her head in his chest, her shoulders trembling all the while with what he assumed were barely contained sobs of relief. "Papa *said* you would come, but I confess, I had started to doubt it after... all that happened." All of this was said into the crisp buttons of his waistcoat, but then she raised her head to stare up with such gratitude it made his knees nearly buckle. "I promise you will not regret this."

In truth, Erik already regretted it.

For feeling her pressed up against him this manner made it all too obvious that there were certain attributes to Christine's body that most assuredly did *not* resemble his own bony frame.

And it woke things that had long since been quieted.

Before he could extricate himself from her person she froze, pulling away from him with a start. "Forgive me, I should not... touch."

She was blushing again, and he was temporarily distracted by how pretty she looked—her pink cheeks overtaking the slightly yellow appearance of her skin that bespoke to her past starvation.

The scones!

Erik had never been more grateful for a distraction as when he choked out that the scones would be burning, and he nearly ran from the sitting room in order to rescue Christine's breakfast—and by extension, his own sanity.

Though he had feared that in his preoccupation with Christine he would have burned them beyond recognition, he found them to be a pleasant golden brown and settled a few on a plate and busied himself with preparing the tea things.

Now that she was to be his pupil he would have to wean her off her preference for sweetened tea, but he would allow it for now. In time however he would see to it that she began eating a diet more befitting a singer of her capability—at least, the capability she would acquire once he was finished with her.

He found her sitting at the dining room table and he almost felt distressed that she had not followed him into the kitchen as had become her wont.

Erik dismissed such foolish notions quite resolutely.

He poured their tea and handed the girl her cup and a plate of scones. Once again she slathered her breakfast in incredible amounts of preserves, and though Erik knew it was traditional for scones to be served with clotted cream, Christine would have to be satisfied with butter.

The delighted moan she gave at the first bite would indicate she was *very* contented.

Feeling the need to divert himself from this ever distracting girl, he attempted conversation—although he realised with a touch of chagrin that with her mouth so full of scone she might not be very able to reply to any questions. But regardless, he felt it worth the attempt.

"You are Swedish?"

She nodded, taking a sip of tea as she swallowed her first bite. "Papa brought me here after Mamma died. He wanted to play at the Opera House, but they would not have him." This was said with a bitterness that gave him pause. "But Professor Valérius liked him very much!"

If he had in fact been employed at the Opera, he would have been able to enrol Christine as one of the little ballet rats—where she might have later joined the choir and learned nothing of man's harsh brutalities. But the world was full of *what-ifs* and dwelling upon them would cause nothing but longing and discontent for what might have been.

Erik knew that all too well.

So instead he listened while the girl prattled about her fondest childhood memories—her father telling her stories, how he would play the violin in the park and she would sing and how *very* exciting it was when one of the fancy ladies while on the arm of a dashing gentleman would drop a coin for their efforts.

Christine rose up indignantly, her scone temporarily forgotten. "But we did not do it for the money of course. We just wanted them to experience the music."

Erik disagreed with her, as if a man's only profession was as a violinist without a proper patron and he had a young daughter to feed, money would most certainly have been on the man's mind. But he could appreciate that Christine's father had filled her head with the importance of music for music's sake alone, not for monetary gain or notoriety.

He reached over and tapped her plate, drawing her attention once more to her breakfast. She looked down at her crumbling scone and took a large bite—and thankfully did not try to talk while she chewed.

"Your father did not think to ensure you had a guardian before his passing?"

The girl's mouth dropped open and Erik looked away. No matter how pretty she was, seeing masticated scone was not something he relished. She swallowed thickly before giving him the deepest glare he had yet seen from her. "Most certainly he did! He was sick for quite a long time before he..." She took a bracing breath, and he almost felt bad for having seemingly maligned his aptitude as a father. Almost. For the girl had still been forced to live on the streets, and had been horribly abused because he had not picked a proper minder.

"I *told* you, I was supposed to live with Mamma Valérius. But then she got sick as well, and even though she *promised* she was fine she... was not." Her eyes turned glassy, and Erik did not know what to do to turn their conversation back to her excited retellings of tender years, so he poured her more tea and slid it surreptitiously toward her.

She barely glanced at the peace offering, turning her ferocious glare upon him once more. "My papa loved me more than anything, and everything that has happened since his passing was *not* his fault." Christine reached for the proffered tea and nearly mumbled into its depths, "If you had come sooner..."

Now it was Erik's mouth that fell open, though he at least had not been attempting to swallow half of a scone at the time. While Christine's glare had been formidable, Erik knew his could strike fear into the hearts of men fully grown.

"You will *not* blame Erik any more than you blame your father!" Christine quailed, and he purposefully made his voice a lilting rapier. "You would question the timing of an angel?" That was as close as he had come to acknowledging her ridiculous notions, and he comforted himself that he had not actually lied to her. If he did in fact believe in supernatural beings such as angels, why would they respond to the demand and plight of mere mortals?

"No," she all but whispered.

Erik groaned, his anger leaving him as he took in his charge. Whenever he raised his voice to her—no matter how seemingly justified—he did not like the timidity that overcame her. He realised that while his interactions with the world had taught him to lash out as strongly and efficiently as possible, Christine had learned instead to withdraw, wholly and completely, and agree with whatever opinion was thrown at her.

And was not it natural that she would wish to blame something for her situation? She obviously loved her father too much to do so, and if some mystical angel was to be her guardian upon his death, Erik supposed he could understand why he would be the next victim of her ire.

"Christine, listen to me carefully." He waited for her to look at him before he continued. "I understand why you wish to blame someone for all that has happened. Someone *should* have helped you, much sooner than I was able." Erik suddenly realised that comforting her was not as difficult as he had thought. All he had to do was speak the words he had so longed to hear when he was a child. "The men who abused you are the ones to blame. Not you, not your father, and most certainly not *me.* You would do well to remember that."

Her eyes had filled with tears, and he could tell she was struggling to keep from crying outright. Would she never run out of tears? "Do you think God was punishing me for something?"

Erik froze. All too often he had thought the same because of his own sad fate. What could he have possibly done that warranted this curse? To be scorned by every person he had ever come into contact with—including his own mother—seemed like the cruellest form of punishment.

Only in the deepest recesses of his mind had he acknowledged the burning anger for whatever deity had created him— that one who possessed the ability to create the entire world with such beauty must have hated Erik so much that he cursed his appearance so completely.

But as Erik also grudgingly recognised, to be angry at God was to believe that he existed. And no matter how he tried to deny it, that resentment and begrudging belief could not be expunged.

Looking at Christine however, with her pretty features and beautiful voice that housed such great potential, he knew that God could not have been the one to send those foul beasts to do her harm.

"There are monsters in the world, Christine. Dark beings that seek to purge the world of all the goodness and light, simply because they covet what they can never be. That is what those men saw in you."

Though he would *never* tell her, Erik knew that was also what he wanted from her. But while men had taken it from her body, he sought her goodness through her voice and her very soul.

And perhaps, as he sought to give *her* healing through song and music, he might also purge whatever darkness inhabited his own.

VIII

And so began their lessons. In the early mornings Erik would make his own breakfast and glumly notice that his pupil felt able to sleep nearly the entire morning away as she lazed about in her overly large bed—though he never once considered waking her himself. It gave him time to tend to his own projects, and to also be able to replenish his pantry in a more usual manner. There were always poor children wandering about that were quite willing to bring him whatever foodstuffs he required, as long as they either were provided a cut of the bounty or a few coins to fill their pockets.

He never allowed them to take his coins without first regaling them with tales of just what disasters would befall them should they run away without first bringing back his items. Eventually, however, he became rather well known around the market street corners in the early morning hours, and while he never felt particularly attached to any of the little scamps, he did suppose he was glad that they were slightly better off for having come into contact with him.

When Christine would emerge from her bedchamber—and it was with grudging acceptance that the Louis-Philippe room was now *hers*—she was always freshly washed and looked quite handsome with her braided hair and her new dresses. Well, new to her at least. Erik *had* made sure to write a rather scathing letter to the managers relating his displeasure at the sorry state of the costume department, and on one of his morning jaunts had ensured that all was once more in order and to his specifications.

Erik was always rather awkward while Christine ate, especially once his careful attention to her diet began to show such positive effects on her appearance. Her skin was pale but had lost the yellowed appearance and the bruises and cuts that had once littered her flesh had finally begun to fade. All of this meant that her body was healing and becoming all the more lovely, while his remained in its permanent state of near decomposition.

But where Christine truly flourished was in her music. Every day her eyes seemed brighter, her smiles more genuine, and often times it would be *he* who insisted that it was necessary for her to stop for a midday meal, even if it was for something as simple as a few slices of baguette and a small wedge of cheese.

"It makes me forget," she told him one evening, as she lay curled up on the settee reading one of his many books. "When Papa died it was like my music died with him. But then with you..." She blushed then, hotly and prettily, and his fingers twitched with desire to *feel* that warmth for himself. "You made it come alive again."

Erik was never one to feel bashful, but at that moment he felt it nearly enough to be called so.

The only true interruption to their lesson was the day he was determined her stitches required removal. Christine had looked terribly nervous when he mentioned the need to check them, but she acquiesced quietly enough. He also noted that she did not tremble nearly so much this time as she arranged her skirts about her as she lay upon the settee. The wound was still rather red but it no longer oozed, and overall it had closed as well as could be expected given the length of time before it had been treated properly.

She would most likely bear quite a scar but he did not tell her that. He merely fussed and gave her leg little awkward pats as he carefully removed the black threads, and quite inexplicably he found that he missed her befuddled ramblings as he worked.

Their evenings were perhaps his favourite, which he found quite remarkable as he originally felt that *nothing* could compare to the joy and triumph he felt when coaxing new and beautiful things from his protégée's vocals. And in turn, she inspired him in ways he had never thought possible. While he was always composing, the sheer ferocity in which he scribbled page after page left him nearly exhausted.

Exhausted, yet exuberant.

But even so, their evenings were still his favourite. He knew that many cafés served hot chocolate at breakfast time, but he preferred the occasional cup as an indulgence when his rare sweet tooth became too insistent. This urge generally came at night, and one evening after he had first made them the warm liquid treat, Christine had nearly begged him to make the concoction part of their nightly ritual. So after their supper they would retire to the sitting room with their individual books, sipping hot chocolate and making conversation only when strictly necessary. And in Erik's case, perhaps stealing a few more glances at the girl beside him than at the book held within his grasp.

And then when Christine would begin to yawn and her eyes to droop, they would retire to their respective bedrooms, only to repeat the process the next day.

On this particular day however, a mere two weeks since she had joined him in his little home, she was not so enthralled. Every correction, no matter how gently given—though he would admit, not all of his instructions could be considered *gentle*—made her cry or stick out her chin in rebellion.

"I have always sung it this way!"

Erik was nearing the end of his patience. "Then you have always sung it *incorrectly.* I would hardly deem a habit correct merely because it is your custom."

He knew he was not asking for too much. The squabble was over a simple matter of technique, and it was her responsibility as his pupil to merely *obey,* not fight him at every turn.

He grew even more upset when pushed to such frustration by her refusal to accept *piano* instead of her instance on *mezzo piano,* he threw down his hands upon the organ with a thundering crash.

If there was one thing Erik was meticulous of, it was the care of his instruments. "I am your maestro, Christine, and you shall listen to my instruction!"

That earned him tears *and* the pushed out chin of rebellion.

He rewarded her with a magnificent eye roll of his own.

To which she responded by sulking on the settee she normally inhabited with such pleasure.

Erik did not know what he had done wrong. He had been no stricter than usual, and had ensured she had all manners of tasty items to eat and plenty of tea to drink—even if he had not yet managed to get her to cease taking sugar in her tea. One morning he had simply refused to place it on the tray but she had meekly—and he supposed rather sneakily—fetched it from the kitchen herself.

What Christine did not know was that Erik was equally if not *masterfully* disposed to sulking, and he found himself perfectly prepared to ignore her for days if it meant she would apologise. And *obey.*

In her mind and from the confession of her own lips she thought him the Angel of Music. Why then did she fight him?

He was therefore entirely unprepared when she burst into tears and began to sob out her troubles. "I was ill this morning."

Erik did not want to know such things and he wondered why she felt the need to inform him. He was certain that the roast chicken he had prepared for supper the night before was far from spoiled, so there could be little cause for concern that she suffered from some sort of food poisoning.

He remembered that she had sounded restless in her room, and he had thought she had another of her nightmares, but had quieted before he had time to offer comfort. He had thought it odd when he heard the rushing of the pipes to the bath soon after, but even *he* knew not to enquire about a lady's bathing habits.

"You vomited. So your response to this event is to abuse your poor instructor through disobedience and tears?"

That impudent glare of hers returned, and he wondered if he should react to it in some way. There were not many that gave him such looks and lived very long after to gloat.

Not that he would ever do such a thing to Christine.

"I was ill and I am worried and upset and you should help me feel better!"

Erik always thought of Christine as a girl, except for those rare occasions when she had so thrust herself on his person that he was nearly *forced* to recognise which attributes of her were most decidedly womanly. But seeing her sheer irrationality at how he could *possibly* know and be responsible for assuaging her distress when she had so annoyed him with her impertinence and tears...

She had never seemed so much like a woman.

He quickly determined that sulking either in his bedroom or even in plain sight at the organ was a far better method than trying to converse with her, so he turned his back and hoped that she would take up her book and allow him silence for awhile.

Of course, he had forgotten that Christine was highly uncooperative and would therefore never do precisely what he needed.

"Erik, what if it means..."

Her tone was so desolate it broke through the great stone wall of his frustration, and he turned to *truly* look at her. She had resumed her ball-like posture on the settee—one that she had forsook the more comfortable she became while living with him. He could see that she was trembling, and her eyes bespoke of a fear he could not name.

Erik sighed, coming to sit beside her in his own leather reading chair. "What is it you are afraid of? Erik may be many things, but a mind reader is not one of them."

She blushed and looked to her lap, her fingers touching her middle absently.

Erik felt as though he could not breathe.

Although she had only been with him for so short a time, he had not thought to provide her any means for dealing with such *feminine* issues, and the fact that she was not asking for them now...

There was one startling consequence to her abuse that he had not previously considered—had banished so thoroughly from his mind that it nearly hurt to think of it now—and he could quite easily see why Christine had been so obstinate today.

She had vomited.

She was irritable and weepy.

His voice quavered, even as he told himself that this hardly mattered. "You are... with child?"

Her expression was one of absolute horror and for one brief and sickening moment he thought somehow his mask had slipped from his face, so he found his hand moving nearly of its own accord to ensure his features were still carefully hidden.

His mask still firmly in place, he realised it was his query that had caused such a visceral reaction. "I do not know! That is why I need you to help me!"

Erik could think rationally. It would do no good to panic, as Christine could hardly be expected to deal with her own fears in addition to his.

He was the man in the room after all, whether he felt well equipped to be or not.

His throat felt tight and restricted, so he took a moment to tug slightly at his collar as well as to collect his thoughts. He was well familiar with the reproductive processes having studied what possibly could have accounted for his own misshapen birth, and he felt he had sufficient knowledge to ascertain if the girl *was* in fact pregnant.

He shuddered at the word.

"Very well, Christine. I must ask you some questions and you must answer them as truthfully as you can." He waited for her tearful nod before beginning his interrogation. How he wished this *was* an interrogation—only of some poor miscreant that had stupidly fallen into his torture chamber. But no, it was his own pupil asking him to allay her fears that she now bore the child of some unnamed scoundrel.

"When was your last menses?"

Never did he think he would have this conversation.

Christine's brow furrowed, obviously deep in thought. If she could not even remember if she was fifteen for *certain,* Erik sincerely doubted she could provide an exact date. "An estimate would be fine."

"It was at the beginning of autumn. It was just beginning to turn cold, and I had to..." If possible, her blush deepened and for a brief moment he wondered if she could do herself damage from her crimson colour. She shrugged again, but by his expectant look seemed to find the will to continue. "I had to use my petticoat for... protection."

Well, that was far too much information for his liking, but he sent such thoughts away. The more he knew the more informed he could be about her condition.

"Had you been on the streets for very long?"

"No. Only a week, maybe two. I had trouble keeping track of the days. I still could not believe that everyone had... died." She looked haunted for a moment, and Erik could well imagine the girl who had once known a childhood of love and happiness would have been in quite a stupor at the deaths of every person she had once known. Then to learn she had no friends or family who were able to take her and that she no longer had even a bed to lay her head...

But she had one now, and she always would for as long as she chose to stay.

He refused to think of what he would do when eventually she chose to leave him—and if she was with child he would not pretend that day was not looming within the *very* near future—and he was once more all alone.

He would consider such things later. For now, there was a terrified girl before him and Erik felt quite wretched for having to ply her for such intimate details of her pain and degradation. "How far after that were you first... assaulted?"

Christine whimpered and somehow managed to pull herself into an even tighter ball. If there was in fact a living being in her womb, he wondered that it could survive such cramped conditions.

"Not very long."

Erik nodded, staring at her thoughtfully. In theory, for her to have last had her menses over four months previously would indicate that she was in fact quite far along. While his reading had made plain that women often did not show until even their fifth month, Christine was so slight, so *frail* looking even now as she finally had begun to fill out once more, Erik sincerely doubted that she could be hiding a baby of such an age.

"And you are certain that you never... bled... again at any other time?"

"Of course I *bled!* They *always* made me bleed! Those horrible men who took and took and did not care that I would cry and beg for them to stop!"

There was a distinct flicker of *hatred* in her eyes that surprised him and he was glad when it died away, though he did not care much for the sheer sadness and resignation that replaced it. "And now they might still be *in* me, just as they haunt my dreams." She shook herself, seeming to finally remember his original question. "But no, my monthly never came back."

Erik did not know what to address first. While his father had lain with his mother by her willingness, he felt an uncomfortable pity for the potential babe that might be born of Christine's suffering. It had no part in her affliction, but surely she would see it as the product of a monster and would never love it.

And if she could never love the product of her own womb, how could she ever love *him?*

He grew cold at the thought. It should not matter if she could never love him—that was not why she was here. She was here for his music, and if that meant he was forced to listen to her concerns about pregnancy and hypothetical motherhood, that was the price he had to pay.

"Christine, I understand your concerns. But the fact remains that besides your one instance of nausea and your *considerable* rudeness to your poor instructor this morning, I see little evidence of pregnancy." She flinched at the word, and Erik found that it disturbed him greatly to watch her do so. "Have you experienced anything else? Headache? Fatigue? Have your..." Oh God, to have to say it aloud, "have your breasts been tender?"

She looked positively mortified, and the arms that had been holding her legs to her chest now moved to curl protectively around the bosom in question. "You know how much I sleep, and I would have told you if my head hurt." And then, so quietly he would not have heard had he not been seated so closely, she added, "They are a little tender."

Erik sighed. This enquiry was getting them nowhere. Each symptom could easily be explained by the fact that she was now once more in a safe environment—he inwardly scoffed that *his* home would ever be considered safe—and was now being fed regular meals. Either she was experiencing the return of her menses that had understandably been delayed by the stress and malnourishment she had suffered during her urchinhood, or a pregnancy was finally beginning to make itself known.

The only way to know for certain would be through a manual examination, and although Erik prided himself for his medical knowledge and he possessed a basic understanding of what to look for, there was no possible way he would *ever* offer to perform such an assessment.

"I am sorry, Christine, but I am afraid you are correct. You might indeed be with child." His heart broke at the terrible sob that tore from her throat, and he chastised himself for thinking of the potential damage and strain she rout upon her newly tuned vocals.

"I will see about finding a midwife who would be able to tell for certain."

IX

Christine had retired early for the night claiming that the book she had been pretending to read had made her sleepy. Erik knew that all her tears had simply exhausted her, but he kept such observations to himself.

He had not the faintest idea of where to find a midwife. Any doctoring of his person was performed *by* his person, so he did not even know of a medical physician who could be contacted. The Opera House had their own medicinal staff, but they were trained for the sprained ankles and occasional broken bones that accompanied rehearsals, not for determining pregnancy.

Much to his dismay he realised that he was so distraught that he could not even find distraction through music. Instead he found himself pacing in his bedroom, glaring at the coffin when at the fifth circuit of the room he rammed his knee quite thoroughly on the corner.

Erik was so preoccupied with the duties he would have to perform on the morrow that he was quite unprepared for the timid knock on his door. He jumped slightly which annoyed him greatly, but he pushed down such emotions while stalking to the doorway. It would not do to frighten his overwrought charge with his own foolishness.

He thrust open the door with perhaps more force than necessary, only to find a teary Christine beyond the threshold. She had a very odd expression on her face which puzzled him. Embarrassment was clear, and he noticed that she was clutching his dressing gown tightly around her body. But what was most peculiar was that there was an apparent note of *relief* about her.

"May I assist you in some way? Or did you simply want me to be awake also since you found yourself unable to sleep?" Perhaps that was uncalled for as he was obviously still in his day clothes. He had forgone his nightly rituals as he wanted to be ready to complete his errand immediately should an answer have presented itself during his pacing.

She blushed, her cheeks flooding that pretty shade of pink, and he was momentarily absorbed watching just how deep it would grow. "No, I just wanted you to know that a midwife will not be necessary."

Erik blinked rather stupidly.

If possible, her blush deepened. "My monthly has arrived."

He winced, trying viciously not to picture exactly what her *monthly* entailed, and specifically what body parts were affected. "You are certain? Is it..." How glad he would be when they could never discuss such things again! "Is it more than just spotting? It is possible for a small amount of blood even when pregnant."

Christine shifted in front of him, clearly uncomfortable by his question. "No, I am quite sure. I... it might have gotten on the bedclothes." She hung her head ashamedly, and for the first time Erik noticed a bundle of linens on the floor. And amongst the bedclothes a slightly visible chemise could be seen with a distinct imprint of red blazing in one of the corners. Christine must have caught his look and hurriedly stooped to ensure that all evidence of blood was completely hidden from view.

"I see. Well, I shall congratulate you for the return of your cursed state."

She positively *beamed* at him. "It is quite horrid and terribly embarrassing to have to talk to you about it. But regardless, I am ever so glad it came."

"Yes, I am certain you are." Never mind that *he* felt as though a vice which had clamped itself around his lungs at her suspicion had finally released and that the pleasant normalcy they had found for the past few weeks could be reinstated. As soon as Christine stopped being weepy and uncooperative of course.

She nudged the linens with one bare toe, and Erik marvelled at the strangeness of it. She had a very fine toe, pale and delicate just like the rest of her. But he realised that ever since his time in Persia he had never once seen a woman's feet. He most assuredly never watched any of the ballet girl's dress, and though some of the costumes of the Opera demanded bare shoulders and exposed legs that in polite society would equate to sheer indecency, never once were there uncovered feet.

It felt horribly intimate seeing Christine's toes and he found himself inexplicably embarrassed and endeared to her by the sight of them.

"Why do you think I was sick? I have never done so before when my courses came."

Erik coughed, wishing they could stop speaking of such womanly matters. "I do not know if you are aware, but you had a nightmare last night. It is possible you had a physical reaction to whatever you were experiencing."

Christine was nibbling her lip again and Erik felt that tingle in his fingers as they desired to *touch*—just to know what the plump, pink flesh felt like against his own ghastly digit.

He settled for balling his hands into fists and stuffing them into the pockets of his trousers.

"What should I do with the linens? I would hate for them to be ruined just because I... was silly and unprepared."

Erik snorted, giving Christine an incredulous look. "You were most certainly not *silly.* It was a perfectly logical explanation for what you had experienced, as well as your seeming ability to begin crying at every juncture." He could not help the imperious sniff that followed. "It also would have explained your deplorable manners when speaking to *me.*" And just because he was certain she would agree with him as she still held the remnants of her blush and had a pile of bloody sheets and a soiled shift at her feet, he added, "That piece requires *piano* at that section. You will do well to remember it."

The girl had lost her mind, of that Erik was certain.

He had never expected to cause her to *laugh,* but perhaps that was too small a word. The loud, boisterous sound that escaped her was closer to histrionics, and he had to examine her face closely to ensure that her expression was one of merriment and not those dreadful tears that she seemed to shed so very often.

But to his great relief her amusement was genuine, and though she did indeed wipe tears from her eyes they were ones born of amusement and relief, not sorrow. "Yes, Maestro, I will remember that." She had the good sense to look sheepish. "I am very sorry for arguing with you about it. I was just so worried and all I could think about was if..." She eyed him warily, and with that hint of resignation that he hated with an ever growing passion. "I was worried that if I had a child, you would make me leave."

Of course she was. Because even though she believed him an angel sent to guard her, her subconscious obviously knew he was a monster—a monster that would hear that she was pregnant with another man's child and demand she return to the streets from whence she came. Even after he had promised her a home—that even if she chose to no longer live in *his* home, she would be given a place to call her own.

And while his first thought was to snap at her until she rescinded the hurtful insinuation, he forced himself to remember that Christine was just an insecure little slip of a girl. She might have once known the security of a home but had since been forced to forget and adjust to more cruelties than she should have ever had to endure in her short years.

Erik also noticed that Christine had to tilt her head quite a distance in order to look at him, and he felt this was too important to allow her discomfort. Or worse, that she should continue to study the linens and toes she found so fascinating while he tried to communicate his sincerity.

So Erik knelt.

He even surprised himself at the gesture, as he was never one to show any form of supplication. But as he considered the girl before him, he felt no shame in the action. She needed to know, to *understand,* that he would care for her in all things. Even things that were too painful to truly contemplate.

His knees would have been pressed into the harsh floor had it not been for her bedclothes providing a modicum of cushioning, as he had no rugs within his doorway.

Christine looked positively startled, and already he could see that her hands were moving to tug at him until he rose. But he stilled her with a glance and a wave of his hand, and she looked down at him with a wariness that made her look much older than she truly was. "Christine, I thought you understood. I promised you that I would provide you a home for *always.* Perhaps you do not appreciate the magnitude of the word, but allow me to assure you, *I* do. Of course I would not wish for you to bear a child conceived in fear, but that does not mean I would shun you should that have happened."

No, he would certainly not turn from her. But that would not keep him from demanding a description of every man that had harmed her so that he might massacre them all. None deserved to live after causing this poor girl such pain.

He might still do so, simply for the worry it had caused her.

"Do you understand? Erik has made you a promise. And this one I mean to keep."

It hung heavy upon them both that he had nearly broken the promise he had given her before—that she would not be left alone in the darkness of his tunnels. Though he had never intended to truly abandon her, the fear she had shown was genuine and forceful and he knew she felt the sting of betrayal whether it was intentional or not.

This time her hands did tug, but he would not relent to her insistent prodding until she gave voice to her acceptance. Finally she stopped her urging, and simply leaned forward—and it was with mild surprise that Erik noticed she did not have to learn very far as she was so much shorter than he—and put her arms around his neck in an embrace.

Erik wanted to cry.

This girl, this poor damaged and nearly broken girl had shown him more affection than any other person in his entire miserable existence. Here he was, kneeling before her in the oddest form of proposal and her response was to hug him until he could scarcely draw breath.

He wanted to lose himself in her, to merely enjoy the warmth she provided. But with her hands behind him and so near the ties of his mask, he found that the sheer terror that she might accidently—or worse, *intentionally*—remove his safeguard kept him from truly enjoying her closeness.

Yet when he felt the whisper tickle his ear, his eyes closed even as a terrible shudder ripped through his entire body. "Thank you, Angel. I think that God sent you to me, and I am so very grateful."

How desperately he wanted to believe her—that in some strange and unbelievable way he had been used as a tool for some goodness of which he had not even thought himself capable. He had wanted to help her, and in turn help himself in some great form of selfishness. But to even consider that his motives could be deemed wholly pure and good, that was something else entirely.

Without his conscious thought or permission one of his hands found the back of her head, and he patted it rather awkwardly. "You are welcome, Christine. But I think you have it quite reversed. *You* are the angel and I the recipient of your kindness."

She pulled away from him suddenly, and he rather thought she was going to argue and scold. But her smile was soft and warm, and for a moment he was lost in her beauty. "Then perhaps we were meant to save each other."

Indeed.

That was as close as she had come to even mildly suggesting he was not in fact one the heavenly hosts, but he did not press the matter. If he was allowed to consider her to be his own personal angel, he supposed she was allowed to hold her own fancies about him—however wrong or misguided they might prove to be in future.

The moment was shattered however when Christine shifted away from him entirely. And for a moment he knew despair until very quietly she said, "Erik, might you have something for my... protection? There was nothing in the trunk and I..." Her cheeks were once more scarlet, and he found himself cataloguing each individual shade. Perhaps eventually he could tell her level of mortification based solely on the exact hue. "I need something for the... blood."

Erik rose rather stiffly, though he hoped it retained a semblance of fluidity. "Of course."

"And how will I wash the linens? That chemise was my favourite, and I would hate for it to be ruined."

He eyed the now squished pile thoughtfully. Erik had his own methods of laundering but that would not help with the immediacy of blood. On the few occasions when he had gotten blood on his clothing—most certainly not from any natural source of his own—he would generally just discard the item, giving it up for lost.

But it was obviously important to Christine that she not have permanently spoiled these items. So with a shrug he scooped them up in his arms, noting with a slight chuckle her intense mortification that he should have touched them. At first he moved to go through his own bedroom and cross to the bath from there, but quickly remembered that Christine would most assuredly *not* be pleased to learn of his secret doorway and rapidly changed his direction.

He dumped his burden in the large tub, eyeing it thoughtfully. He knew hot water was best for cleaning properly. At least, that was how he washed his dishes. But blood was a unique substance and perhaps it would be best to staunch the stain with a shock of cold. With that in mind, he turned on the flow for cold, watching the white bedclothes begin to swirl in the rapidly rising water and eventually shift enough so that the stains in question was readily visible.

Christine had knelt beside him and was poking at the laundry, and he noted with amusement that she was ever so subtly trying to hide the stain from his view under the pretext of ensuring that the linens were all submerged to her approval.

"Have you hidden it to your satisfaction, or shall I leave you to continue while I search for some soap?"

She had the audacity to appear indignant. "You know far too much about these matters, Erik. I was simply trying to maintain a little feminine mystery."

Erik scoffed. He knew now more about this girl's *feminine mystery* than he had ever cared to, and the least of which had to do with seeing actual evidence of its presence.

"Perhaps... before we look for soap, might you find me something before I have to add another shift to the bath?"

Erik had not the least idea what women generally used for such matters and he was torn about what to propose. He could offer her some strips of kitchen towel as those proved sufficient for drying his dishes and surely they would be able to absorb a bit of blood. Or he could use the medical gauze within his doctoring bag that was available for compresses and actual wounds.

He rather liked his kitchen towels and thought he might offend her with the offering, so he went to his medical bag and pulled out one of the numerous rolls of gauze and handed it to her. "I will leave you to..." He made a vague gesture over her person. "I will be in the kitchen if you should need anything else."

She smiled at him softly and a little bashfully, and he felt his chest warm. "Where you will be looking for soap?"

"Yes."

Erik could not escape her company quickly enough.

He did not have any soap specifically for laundering, as he most generally employed one of the Opera's washer women to take care of any such needs. She never actually saw him of course. She merely received a weekly bundle of clothes and black bedding—for even he needed to use sheets and blankets while resting within the coffin—in addition to a pouch full of coins that would ensure her silence. When he had originally made use of her services, he had also deposited a letter stating the importance of her silence and discretion, as well as the potential consequences should she ever feel the need to discuss her unnamed employer.

Erik cut off a chunk of dish soap, deciding that even if this only slightly lightened the stain, it would show Christine that all possible efforts have been utilised. He could always send their failure along with his other weekly washings for Hélène to see to. Or he could simply burn them in the fire while Christine was sleeping, or attempt to drown them in the lake. He would have to study the chemise first so that he could provide her an identical one, as she had said it was her favourite...

He waited for Christine to emerge and then they both made their way to the bath, kneeling beside the high sides as they stared at the stain which had once more situated itself at the top of the water.

Erik rolled up his shirt sleeves, intent on beginning the tedious process of scrubbing when he noticed Christine staring at his naked forearms. There were scars there to be sure, just as there were scars most everywhere on his body, and he plunged both arms into the water with great haste in his attempt to cover them. As he did so, the water splashed Christine slightly. "Oh! It is *cold!*"

He decided her shocked expression was quite amusing, but he would have forced himself to apologise in any case had he not already seen the smile tugging at her lips—though she feigned righteous indignation. "That was dreadful of you, Erik! And if you were not currently scrubbing my sheets in the middle of the night, I would ask you to say sorry." She sniffed rather imperiously, and Erik could not help the laugh that escaped him.

He found himself nearly resentful when the stain began to give way with his makeshift laundering soap, for it meant his time with Christine would soon come to an end. To his great surprise it was most enjoyable to do the wash with Christine as she giggled and occasionally splashed him, to which he would covertly do the same, blinking innocently at her all the while.

Erik was rapidly discovering that the domestic life suited him quite wonderfully.

And that terrified him more than anything.

X

"Erik, I know you said I am in your home, but where exactly is that?"

They had finished their evening meal—well, Christine had, while Erik sipped wine and made occasional conversation—and they were now in their preferred seats, passing a pleasant evening before the fire as they read.

But of course Christine would not be content to allow them their simple joys of silent companionship. Erik sighed.

"Where do you think we are? You have not pressed the matter before now."

Christine stared at her lap thoughtfully. "I did not think it mattered, and I suppose it still does not. I miss the sunshine sometimes, but I am quite... happy to no longer be living in the city."

Erik chuckled softly at that. "I am certain you are, and I hate to disillusion you, my dear, but we are still in the city."

She looked rather startled. "We are? But it is so quiet!"

He nodded. "Living underground is one of the surest ways to be guaranteed privacy."

"Underground? Are you trapped here?"

Now Erik truly *did* laugh at that, and he noticed that Christine's cheeks turned a lovely shade of rose. "You were with me when I ventured above—I took you right off the streets! How would you think me trapped?"

She shrugged, and Erik felt a twinge of discomfort that she was so embarrassed by her enquiry, or perhaps because of his reaction *to* her enquiry. He sobered, and repeated his question, making sure to keep any trace of amusement from his tone.

"It seems an odd thing, to *choose* to live belowground."

Erik gave her a look of mild surprise. "Really? I would think you of all people should understand the impulse. Think for a moment, and tell me what you conclude."

That little crease between her brows returned, and Erik occupied himself while she thought with studying it and wondering what it would feel like to smooth it away with a lone finger tip.

"I suppose," she said haltingly. "You would want to escape. You could live in the country and have no neighbours for miles around, but you could still be found. If you live underground..." Her eyes found his and he could see the clarity within. "No one can find you. You are safe." Her hands abandoned their fiddling with the book in her lap and instead she held them around herself, obviously intent on finding whatever comfort she could from her own embrace. "I think I like that idea."

Erik had expected to feel contended that another living soul could *understand,* that instead of thinking him some sort of strange mole that would seek to burrow within the earth instead of face the world above, they should know that he had done so for protection. But instead he found that while there was a tinge of happiness that Christine should be capable of comprehending his motives, there was an inexplicable sadness that overwhelmed him. She should not be *able* to infer such things. She should feel safe in the streets above, absorbing sunshine and basking in the perfectly normal interactions of merchants and shopkeepers as she deemed to patron their businesses.

But instead he had to watch her grapple with the knowledge that she might prefer the solitude and darkness of a subterranean home, if that so meant she could be safe.

"Erik, I hope you do not think me a horrible nag, but you still have not told me *where* we are."

It was a fair question, and he did not quite know why he hesitated to answer. She was free to leave at any time—though he begrudgingly admitted to himself that he would gladly haunt her for the rest of his days, teaching her from afar and ensuring her safety even as he did so.

Or perhaps it was simply indulgence on his part, that he liked the air of mystery, knowing that she trusted him enough to live with him regardless of not knowing precisely where that dwelling was located. But with startling clarity he realised that it was not *he* that she trusted, but the figment of her angel, bound by the laws of a heavenly being that could not possibly harm her. The thought chilled him.

"You said that your father auditioned at the theatre. While he did not know the satisfaction of living and working within those hallowed halls, his daughter now knows the pleasure."

Christine gasped. "We are below the Opera House?"

"Indeed."

Her eyes flitted about his sitting room, and he idly wondered if she would give herself a headache as she took in his home with freshly awakened admiration. "How did all of this get here then?"

If there was one thing that truly filled Erik with pride, it was his work. For the next hour he regaled her with tales of the construction and architecture of both his home and the building above—how although a silent contributor, many of the unique details were carefully crafted and expedited on Erik's insistence.

"So that is how we entered the pantry, you fashioned the tunnel and the secret panel!" His chest began to tighten as she looked at him with such awe and esteem, and he felt strangely humbled to be the recipient of such value. "It seems so obvious now that the Angel of Music should want to be involved in the building of the musical heart of Paris."

Erik's mood instantly plummeted. He knew exactly why Christine held so dearly to this notion, regardless of his protestations and gentle nudges that he was not in fact the apparition she suggested. He truly did not think her delusional—after all, he preyed upon the superstitious nature of the people above, and knew them to simply be reacting to concepts instilled in childhood. But he had not sought to manipulate Christine in such a way. While he knew that his fondness for her was growing daily, her trust and affection for him was based on the lie she told herself—the only method at her disposal to allow her to cope with the horrors she had suffered, and to make the act of living with a man more tolerable in her delicate mental state.

She must have noticed the change in him, even as he tried to stifle his irritation and dismay at the confirmation of his belief that she could not care for him for simply *himself*. "Are you upset that we did not sing today?"

After their late night interlude with the laundering, Christine had slept even later than was her usual time, and he had been glad of it. It gave him time to set his home to rights while also providing him some much needed time to compose and distance himself from the easy enjoyment he had found caring for domestic tasks with her.

When she had finally risen and after he had given her breakfast, he had moved to the organ in order to begin their customary lesson. But she had held back, looking at him with pleading eyes that he was helpless to refuse. "I am sorry, Erik, but I do not think I feel well enough to sing today." Her hand strayed to her womb, and desperate to keep her from telling him even more of *that* subject, he hurriedly acquiesced. He found that when he periodically gave her tea and things to nibble, her moodiness greatly diminished, and she happily had spent the day reading on the settee while he either composed or read as well.

"No, I am not angry." Inwardly he scoffed, knowing that when he was truly *angry* there would be little doubt in her mind as to his feelings.

She nodded, but did not seem wholly convinced, eyeing him suspiciously every few minutes while she pretended to have turned back to her book. Eventually she tired of her little game and closed her novel, settling it once more in her lap. "Papa once said that there is a lake beneath the Opera House. Is that true?"

Erik looked at her for a long moment as he wondered at just how terrified she must have been the last time they have ventured above because she surely must have noticed it. But perhaps she was too preoccupied in the darkness by ensuring that she had stayed practically soldered to his side to pay much attention to any of her surroundings.

"Yes, it is true. Would you care to see?"

"Yes, please!" Her enthusiasm loosened the pain of his earlier musings, and he fetched their cloaks. She still did not have one of her own and so he once again provided her the borrowed garment he had leant her previously. As he had predicted, the hem was in a sorry state indeed, but it would serve its purpose well enough and they would not be out long. He did not really require a cloak, used to the temperatures of the cellars, but he knew Christine would be far more comfortable with a covering. And if he was honest with himself, he rather liked the way his cloak *whooshed* as he walked. Not that he would ever inform Christine of that—better she think him cold.

She was waiting for him in the sitting room, practically quivering with excitement. He had failed to realise she had not left his home since their raid on the pantry, and she never said she had any inclination to do so. He carefully placed his cloak upon her shoulders and walked to his front door, but Christine's voice gave him pause.

"Can we... perhaps take a light?"

He had intended to simply keep the front door open, but when he turned and saw the look of severe trepidation that had crossed her once enthusiastic features, he realised that his temporary abandonment of her in the darkness had done more damage than he had first thought.

"Of course."

He located his solitary lantern, lighting it deftly and turning the small knob until it produced as much light possible. This was a jaunt for Christine, and her comfort was paramount. They would remain on his side of the lake, and none of his traps had warned of intruders, so a light would be of little danger to them.

Erik was startled when he felt Christine grasp his cloak with two of her fingers—not enough to touch him at all, but enough for them to be connected as he walked through the door out to the lake beyond. Though the winter above was harsh, there was a consistent temperature here that while chilly, was not nearly as unpleasant as above. He held the lantern high so as to distribute the light more evenly throughout the cavern, and he felt Christine move away from him with a gasp.

"It is beautiful!"

That was hardly the word he would use for it.

If looking objectively, the lantern light did twinkle on the occasional ripple in the lake, and the stone walls around them glistened with moisture in a manner that was almost friendly. There were no plants except for small patches of moss that grew on some of the stones.

His boat was moored close by, and for a brief moment he imagined a candlelight picnic between lovers on the lake, feeding each other bits of cheese and olives, tittering of nonsense and foolish words of fondness and admiration.

And he wanted it.

So lost in his imaginings of things that could never be, he did not notice Christine moving from his side as she sat down upon the shore. He had thought she merely meant to sit and watch the water, so he was slightly startled when she lifted the hem of her skirt and removed her slippers. He noted with some amusement that she wore no stockings, and he was glad as he was certain that the garter would irritate her still healing cut.

When she had made her feet properly bare, she lifted her hem a little more and dipped her toes into the icy water of the lake.

Her shriek of delight echoed upon the walls, as did the giggles that followed, and Erik was too stunned to offer proper chastisement for her apparent determination to give herself hypothermia.

"What on earth are you doing?"

She wriggled her toes and patted the hard ground beside her. "Enjoying the lake. You should join me."

He did not know exactly what possessed him to comply, but he supposed it might have had something to do with the way her eyes were shimmering in the glow of the lantern, and how she looked so peaceful and contented in that moment that he knew he would grant her any request, no matter how ridiculous.

Or undignified.

Erik placed the lantern down at his side and sat down next to Christine. He kept his own feet carefully free from the water's edge, but this apparently was dissatisfactory to his pupil.

"Oh no, you cannot properly enjoy if your toes are not wet." She poked at his shoes teasingly. "You have seen *my* toes."

Yes, but her toes were pink and perfect and surprisingly small for a girl her age. The shoes she had been wearing when he found her had nearly worn through, but evidently not to the point where her feet had been damaged.

But with a sigh of resignation as well as the acute knowledge that there was no one else in the entirety of the world that he would willingly do this for, Erik removed his black leather shoes as well as his socks, and rolled up the hem of his trousers so that his own pale ankles were visible.

Then, begrudging the girl for her preposterous notions, he placed his feet beside hers.

The water was indeed cold, though not quite as much as he expected given Christine's reaction. He marvelled at how large his feet were compared to hers—his toes long and his skin yellow. While the water had not made him yelp, when she nudged his foot with her own a noise escaped him that was certainly similar.

"What are you doing?"

She laughed again, and although his toes were slightly numb, his chest felt warm at the sound. "You already asked me that. I am enjoying the lake."

Christine left his person alone after that, seemingly satisfied to pull her—*his*—cloak more tightly around herself while she watched the water ripple and took pleasure in the gentle lapping of the water on her feet. "The Seine is so dirty compared to this; I had trouble finding clean water to drink."

Erik shuddered as he considered how desperate Christine must have been if she had resorted to considering the filthy river as potential drinking water.

"Do you ever sit here? And just... think?"

"No." It had never occurred to him to do so. Thinking was not a good thing for him. Sometimes his thoughts would become muddled, and he felt the tinges of madness as all the years of loneliness compounded into terrible thoughts and despair. So it was much better that he be indoors, where his organ and his violin were welcoming, and he could distance himself from any such *thinking.*

"I think it is very peaceful here. Quiet. Safe."

Erik stiffened. "Christine, you must promise to never try and swim in this water. If you should ever want to leave, I will... take you across and let you go, but you must not try to leave by yourself. Understand?"

How it hurt him to say the words! He had known from the beginning that she would leave, but the thought that she might someday be so frantic to escape him that she should try to swim in the icy waters—*hear* the siren's song—it was not something he cared to contemplate.

Christine cocked her head. "Why? What would happen? And why would I ever want to leave you?"

Where to begin? "Firstly, the water is too cold for swimming, and I would not want you to catch your death. I would have to drag you back in and you would get water all over my carpets." He said this with a sniff, and he noticed that his caution was merely met with a soft smile. "Secondly, there are many traps that protect us from prying eyes and invading peoples. What is the point of living belowground if just anyone could stumble in?"

She nodded. "That seems reasonable."

He highly doubted she would say so if he mentioned just how many people had died over the years as they foolishly entered the Opera Ghost's domain.

"And lastly, you will want to leave poor Erik once you allow yourself to understand. But now I think you are still too desperate and sad to believe me."

He was of course referring to her insistence of his supposedly angelic nature, and while he wanted to deny it, he *knew* she would turn from him once she had healed enough to realise that he was simply a man.

A man who would *never* hurt her, but there was no way of knowing if she would allow herself time to recognise that before the fear and distrust took hold.

This was why he did not care for *thinking.* Pondering was good—solving puzzles and agonising over every detail of a project until it was perfect. *Thinking* depressed him.

Christine sighed, and moved her foot so that it sent a small wave in his direction, thankfully not soaking him in the process. "I do not know what that means, but I do not like that you have so little faith in me." Her eyes were wide and he so wanted to believe their assurances.

"Christine, this has nothing to do with my faith in you. This has everything to do with the fact that you are not yet ready to face the *truth.* And until you can do so, any promises you give me are not sufficiently informed."

Her hand twitched slightly and Erik watched it warily as it came closer to his arm, wrapping around it as she laid her head against his shoulder. "When do you think I will be ready to make those promises? That you will accept that I want this to be my home? With you?"

Erik's eyes stung with tears—the amber eyes that glowed only in the darkness—and looked down at the little waif at his side. *Never.* She would *never* accept it. But when he opened his mouth, he heard the foolish dreams and hopes slip through even as he was desperate for them to return.

"With time."

She pressed more firmly against him, and he heard her soft sigh. "I like time."

And as they sat upon his shore, staring at the lake that had once only seemed a protective and dramatic measure against the world, Erik found that he liked time very much as well.

XI

After their evening beside the lake, Erik locked himself in his room for three days. He emerged but rarely, and even that was merely to sneak a bottle of wine and a slightly stale baguette from the pantry and then steal back to his bedchamber—and only when he was completely sure that Christine was asleep.

She had cried at first and unlike the previous irritation he had experienced at her obvious signs of distress, he now felt quite dreadful for being the source of her pain. She would knock upon the door and call out his name, sometimes slipping to her moniker of *Angel,* but mostly remembering to use his true form of address.

He knew that there was sufficient food to keep Christine well fed, so he tried not to worry overly much that she would starve during his withdrawal.

And true to what he had told Christine previously, he was not *thinking.*

Instead he sat in the corner of the room, trying not to think, and more importantly, not to *feel.* But every time he closed his eyes he could remember every detail of her pretty blonde head pressed against his covered arm, how his toes had not felt so very cold once she had moved her own small feet to settle against his, and just how wonderful it had felt to be connected to another person in such a manner.

Eventually he had noticed the blue tinge to her once pink toes, and had insisted she must return indoors. She had indulged him and sat before the fire as she warmed, but in his concern he had still felt it necessary to select one of his own pairs of cashmere socks to ensure her feet would not suffer any permanent damage.

Seeing her once more in some of his clothing did little for his already tenuous control. So he had escaped to the kitchen and made her a cup of hot chocolate, and upon delivering it to her bright smile and breathy thanks, had locked himself away.

It was better to be alone. It was better to dream of these things as far away figments that while torturous, were not excruciating. This girl was a tangible example of the affection and goodness that he would never be able to truly experience—not when she was once more well and strong and could see the fallacy of her belief in his character.

Erik was not a good man, and the longer she stayed with him, the more he wanted to forget—to pretend that he was who she believed. But that would be to deceive her in the worst possible manner, and hurt her in a way he could not bear. Not when she had already lost so much.

It was the worst when he heard evidence of her nightmares. While she had them nightly, they had gradually lessened in intensity and duration, if substantiated by the sounds coming from her room. Erik had taken to playing his violin as she slept simply so she could be granted a few hours of rest, and it seemed quite effective at quieting her overactive mind.

In his self imposed solitude, however, he had found the idea of playing an abomination. So he had listened to her whimpers and cries, knowing that the longer this charade continued the harder it would be for her to understand that he had never meant to truly deceive her. And above all, that he wished with all his heart that she could come to trust him for *himself,* not because of some childhood belief instilled by her father.

And he felt that this was slowly killing him. Perhaps not physically as he thought it impossible for his corpse-like countenance to actually succumb to the afflictions of normal men, but emotionally. The longer he remained in her company the more his attachment to her grew—and his chances of surviving once she knew of his true nature and rejected him grew slimmer.

But brooding away in his room was doing little to improve matters, and instead was only causing him to miss her all the more—miss the music they created, and even the simple pleasure of her company as they prepared meals, washed dishes, and read together in the evenings. And he realised with startling clarity that he was sacrificing what precious moments he was granted with her due to his fear.

She was curled up on the settee when he emerged, staring at a dismal looking fire. It had not occurred to him that while she was capable of making small meals, she would not have the skills necessary to produce any flame of substance.

The guilt that she had been cold while he squirreled himself away in his bedchamber was nearly stifling.

He had expected her to ignore him when he entered, and was therefore entirely unprepared for when she flung herself into his unresponsive arms.

"I thought you had left me!"

Of course she had. Because Erik was a Ghost, and though he had made use of the bath-room when necessary, it had only been when she was fast asleep and she could not have known he had never vacated the premises.

That also explained why she had eventually given up calling out against his door.

Erik wrenched himself away from her, finding her warm body against his to be the ultimate of torture when he knew full well that it was her *Angel* she cared for, not him.

"Christine, this must end. I told you that time would prove you ready to hear this, but I simply cannot continue how we have been. It is too *painful."* The last word was naught more than a choked release of air, and he felt the sting of tears that he fought valiantly to contain.

She looked hurt by his rejection of her touch, but that had given way to a peculiar panic. "What do you mean? What have I done?"

Erik growled. "You have not *listened.* Over and over I have tried to explain that Erik is not an angel, that he is only a man. But you in all of your sweetness..." He trailed off, pulling roughly at his sparse hair and trying to calm his rising temper.

"Angel, I do not understand..."

"I am *not* an angel! That is what I have been trying to explain, but you seem incapable of grasping that simple concept!" He knew he was shouting at her—that he was frightening her in his anger—but he was too far gone. The stress and emotions this little waif had stirred in him were too close to the surface, and no matter how he had tried to stifle them over the past few days, they had only returned tenfold.

And as he took in her quivering form, the tears pooling in her eyes and the thin arms that were practically the only thing holding her together, he realised with startling clarity the issue.

He was ashamed.

She thought she could give her affections freely and without recourse because in her eyes, he was not a man. No matter how she pressed her loveliness against his own thin frame, there would never be any consequences, as he would never dream of taking advantage. She could hold his hand, rest her head against his shoulder, and he would simply offer her silent comfort with no other urge for *more* that would plague an actual man.

But Erik knew these urges. And while he had tried to maintain his distance, he found himself craving those small attentions, and holding them jealously in his heart when they were so willingly bestowed.

And she did not *understand* how this was hurting him—to maintain his distance and always remember how damaged and hurt she was, and that she would *never* want anything more, even from the most normal and beautiful of men.

So how could she want anything with *him*?

"Erik, please, I know I have angered you somehow and I am truly sorry. If you will just explain..."

She was crying.

He had made her cry.

His compositions had faced the brunt of his anger before, and they did so now with as little complaint as they always had. He cleared his work table with a swift swipe of his arm, scattering the many papers and pens across the sitting room floor, even as he tried to contain the desperate sob of frustration. How he wished that he would never have to listen to one of her apologies again! She was everything that was pure and innocent, regardless of her past experiences. They had not tainted her. They had simply made her more aware of the evils of the world, and how separate she was from their influence was readily apparent.

"Let me be perfectly forthright then, since hints and insinuations seem entirely lost on you." She cried harder at that, and he knew that he had once more managed to insult her intelligence. "I am not an angel. I was a man walking home from an errand, and saw that you need help. And Christine? I almost did not intervene. I thought you a prostitute with a client, and very nearly continued on my way."

"Why are you telling me these things?!"

"Because they are true! Because I want you to know *me,* not a figment of your imagination!"

She collapsed. She had not fainted, but apparently the sting of his words was too heavy for her frail shoulders, and so she fell to the floor and tried mightily to muffle her cries into her hands. But despite her best efforts, he could still make out quiet mutterings interspersed with harsh sobs. "Papa promised to send the Angel of Music... He *promised!"*

Erik growled, and acutely aware that he was looming over her and that action was doing nothing to quell her oncoming hysteria, knelt before her. "I am just a man, Christine. Just a man, who feels as other men do. Your father told you that so you would have reason to hope after he died, not so that you would try to find a saviour where there was none!"

Her face was read and streaked with her tears, and for a terrible moment he wished he could take it all back. So what if this charade was slowly furthering his madness? The girl had needed the security and comfort it had given—things that he could not have provided otherwise.

But there was no going back.

She stuck out her chin in that petulant way of hers, and her eyes flashed. "I think this is a test of my faithfulness. It is a horribly mean one and I admit I am angry about it, but I will not fail it!"

Erik's mouth opened in shock.

A test?

A damnable *test* of her fortitude—that above all odds she would cling to her belief that was so decidedly based in her own mind?

And with surprising calm and resolve, though admittedly his fingers shook even as the knowledge burned his heart that she would never forgive him—*never*—he removed his mask.

To her credit, she did not scream. She was already crying and they grew no more pronounced as she stared at him. It was her eyes that revealed her thoughts, and what they told him hurt most of all.

Monster. Her angel had been revealed as a demon, and she was scrambling within her own mind to reconcile her foolishness with what knelt before her.

And that broke him.

He grasped her hands tightly in his own and brought them to his face, and it would have cut him had her nails not been so short—still recovering from the abuse they suffered when she had not the luxury of proper hygiene. "Oh yes, Christine, this is the face of your *angel.* You thought I wore a mask because *you* were the tainted one, when really it is your poor Erik that has the corrupted soul! Perhaps you now think him a demon sent from the fiery depths to further your torment!"

She was shaking her head furiously even as she tried to pry her hands from his, but he would not relent—her warm, small hands that had once touched him of their own volition. And it was with great horror that he realised she would leave him after this, and she would never choose to touch him again.

His grip softened then, not enough to release her hands, but he no longer forced her fingers to claw at his face. Instead, he gently turned her hand and placed one, solitary kiss in the middle of her palm.

Erik did not know who cried loudest. His anger and frustration was rapidly cooling and he was left feeling bereft and horrified at his treatment of her, but found himself too frightened to release her completely. She would scuttle away, would raise her hands above her head as she feared whatever blows that he knew would never fall.

Christine was openly weeping, but through gasping breaths managed to ask one of the fundamental questions that he knew would be paramount in her mind. "If you are a man... why did you not hurt me?" She tugged against his hold on her wrist once more and her unspoken addition of *yet* hung thick and heavy between them.

He pulled away from her suddenly and moved to the other side of the room. "Because though I look a monster I do not make it a habit of ravaging young girls! Have I ever given you the impression that I somehow wished you harm? That I wanted you for anything more than to sing, and to read, and to cook for?" Her question had stung him more than he realised, and he practically snarled his response. "But you see this face and think me worse than those cads that abused you—that I lured your here with promises of music and safety only to then bed you when you least expected it, is that it?"

The air in the sitting room was stifling, and all he wanted was to sleep—to forget any of this had ever happened and he could go back to being alone. Loneliness was uncomplicated, and while not exactly pleasant, he had grown quite used to it. He was able to do what he wanted, *when* he wanted. He had no reason to dirty his kitchen more than strictly necessary, and had never needed to learn such useless confections as sweet biscuits and scones, and whatever recipe had caught her interest.

He realised then that his mask was still on the floor before her and he moved hurriedly to get it, suddenly feeling quite naked and exposed. She flinched from his speed and his outstretched arm. While in his more calm and understanding moods he had quieted the hurt feelings that generally accompanied that particular action with a firm reminder that such was simply an ingrained response and was *not* in fact a personal insult, this time he felt the pain all too acutely.

"Do you see now, Christine, why I had so little *faith* in you? Because I knew that once you truly comprehended the truth, you would *beg* to be free of me. I promised you a home, and I am certain that now all you can think of is how to ask ever so nicely to be guided above!"

He took her silence as confirmation, and the knowledge that she would rather be at the mercy of anyone else than remain with him nearly kept any air from entering his lungs.

This was a disaster. The whole miserable situation was a disaster, and he had known it from the beginning.

Perhaps it was not too late to exchange her for a pet—something warm and soft that would feel good as he held it, just like she did. Something that would never want to leave him, not after he had cared for it so nicely...

But even he knew that was a lie. No one could take Christine's place now. Even if he managed to capture the prettiest songbird, it would only sing its own song, never the one he taught it. And though a cat would most likely come to him for cuddles and other such affections, it would never be the same as when Christine looked to him for protection and comfort.

And now she would want to leave him.

He had told her that he would lead her from his home whenever she decided to abandon him, but now when faced with the prospect he found that he could not bear to do so. He would then have to watch her walk away, knowing full well that she would take his heart with her.

He gasped.

He sobbed.

He *loved* her.

Erik fell once more before her, raising the hem of skirts to his lips and brushing it lightly with a kiss, even as she tugged at it insistently for him to release it. "No, do not do that!"

He moaned, and knew that he could not bear whatever was to come next. To hear the bitter words of betrayal would surely break him more completely than any other she might have spoken. So instead he rose and with as much composure as he could muster, addressed her.

"I will leave you now. Feel free to gather what you will. The boat and lantern will be available for when you are ready to depart, simply follow the moss to the aboveground." He hesitated, knowing well that to soften his tone would also lead to a softening of his resolve. "Please, try to keep yourself safe, as I was obviously unable to do so."

She looked at him with such horror, and kept repeating *no* in such a pained voice that he could quite easily feel his heart shatter, even as he looked at her for what he knew was the last time. "I love you, Christine."

And with the sound of her sobs still echoing in his ears, and the sight of her crumpled form weeping upon his floor etched into his memory, he fled the room, stopping only long enough to grab his cloak and hat before vacating his home.

And for the first time in his memory, he left the front door unlatched.

XII

Of course it had to end.

Living with Erik had been too good to be true, and he had proven that with his venomous words and actions. Her wrists and hands still ached slightly from where he had gripped them, and she was suddenly terribly grateful that her fingernails were still down to the quick. If she had torn his flesh—had added blood to the gruesome sight of his already deformed features, she surely would have fainted.

But even without any blood he had frightened her, though not enough so that she would have chosen to leave. If indeed he was a man, which she now begrudgingly was forced to acknowledge, he had ample time to do... *that*... if it had been his desire.

What upset her most was how she had practically flung herself at him! All those times when she had clung to him, had touched him, and he had probably felt... *things*... when she had done so.

His first assessment had been correct. She was a whore.

And now he wanted her to leave.

She picked herself up from the floor, remembering vividly how upset he usually was when she spent any length of time on his carpet. Christine liked his rugs. They were soft and plush and were finer than anything she had ever experienced, even when visiting Professor and Mamma Valérius. But it would upset him and she had wanted him to be pleased with her, so she had contented herself with his comfortable settee—even if she would have liked sometimes just to lie before the fire, sipping the delightful hot chocolate he would make for her in the evenings.

Christine shook herself. If she continued to dwell on such things she would never stop crying. He wanted her to leave, and that was that. She had overstayed her welcome and while she trembled with fear at having to once more face the world above, she knew she had no desire to trespass on his generosity.

But in the far recesses of her mind, she could feel the twinges of hurt and anger that he had promised her a home for *always,* even if it was not with him.

How foolish she was. No one kept their promises. Not her papa when he told her of an angel that would come and inspire her music, nor Mamma Valérius who had pledged to take care of her when her father died.

She moved slowly to her bed chamber, and she could not stem the tears when she realised that her lovely room was not hers any longer. She went to the trunk that still housed all the clothing he had provided, as she had not felt it prudent to move them to the wardrobe. Perhaps some part of her recognised that all of this would eventually come to the end, and it would be far better for Erik that he be able to easily remove any trace of her once he grew tired of her presence.

Christine carefully removed her dress and tucked it gently back into the trunk, pulling out her old tattered garments as she did so. How she wanted to take one of her new dresses! But they were not truly *hers* but his, and it would be better not to draw undue attention to herself on the streets. To be pretty was to be noticed, and she nearly sobbed when the vivid nightmares of that kind of *notice* filled her mind.

The only things she allowed herself to take were the last of the sweet biscuits that he had made for her before his self-imposed absence. He had always taken such care to ensure that her little tin was always full, and she had thought him so wonderful for his dedication. So she hid them away in the pocket of her ragged cloak, which now looked so much worse after having experienced the warmth and richness of Erik's.

But she would never steal from him, no matter how he broke her heart by telling her to leave.

As Erik had said, the lantern and the boat were waiting for her. She had never steered or rowed before in her life, and she found that for quite some time she merely managed to make the small boat creep around the edges of the lake without coming close to the other side. She wiped angrily at her eyes, hoping that would stem the ever increasing flow of tears.

She was so tired of crying!

And more importantly, she was tired of having a *reason* to cry. She had always been happy and cheerful with her papa! And for a blissful few weeks, that had mostly returned while with her Angel.

With *Erik.*

Did it matter if he was a man? He had not hurt her. Not until today in any case, and she would hardly consider his tight grip to truly count as a hurt, not when she knew the pain of actual abuse. His face was dreadful, there was no denying it. All withered skin and skeletal features, she had to admit that it had frightened her. Especially when he had made her touch it as he had.

But when he had kissed her palm so sweetly...

There was also no denying that he could be tender and gentle. And perhaps if she had not been flinging herself at him like a common trollop...

No matter. She was leaving.

With new determination, she managed to find the rhythm necessary for proper rowing, and made it to the other side of the lake where she tried her best to moor it to what she presumed was the correct post. Not a moment after she had carefully placed the lantern on the shore did she make a slight hop as she tried to vacate the boat, only managing to capsize the entire craft in the endeavour.

The water was shallow so she was in no danger of drowning, but she managed to slip further on a mossy rock and tumble fully under the water, soaking herself completely in the process.

Grateful that the lantern had not overturned in the upset, she put the boat to rights and sniffled in the cold of the underground as well as from tears, and cautiously began her journey. Erik was correct, as there seemed to be a line of green moss that was only visible in one direction. So though fearful of every rat, spider, and other fearsome creature she come across, she believed that she was going in the right direction.

She tripped numerous times on the way as her feet were soaked and terribly cold as the cool temperatures would not allow for them to dry at all. They were chaffing in her worn stockings, and she fully anticipated that painful blisters would appear relatively quickly.

Christine was miserable, and no matter how firmly she told herself that she would survive, just had she had survived before, she now remembered what it was like to have a warm bed and a good meal and sweet water, and she did not *want* to go back to doing without.

Eventually she came to a door and while she expected it would require much more effort on her part, she found that it opened quite easily at her touch.

The afternoon sun was blinding after the dim light of the tunnels, and though Christine wanted to keep it for the dark nights of Paris when she was frightened and so desperately wanted a bit of light to scare away the shadows, she mournfully placed the lantern on the inner side of the door and closed it behind her.

From the outside the door looked simply like a stone wall, and unless one knew to look for the subtle seam that belied its location, Christine imagined that no one would ever be the wiser. And since it had no handle, she would never be able to enter Erik's tunnels again.

Her eyes burned with yet more tears, but she choked them down stubbornly. There was no more use in crying. It had only served to irritate Erik, or at the very least cause him alarm judging by the wide and frantic look he would give her whenever she had started.

She was hungry. With frantic hands she remembered her sweet biscuits and sought them in the pocket of her cloak. They were soggy, but not inedible, and she knew from experience that she would have to ration them carefully. It would do no good to assuage her stomach now, not when she still had her faculties and could go about hunting down her own food.

Or perhaps it was better to be honest with herself. More often than not she would *steal* food, as asking or begging only got her shoved and kicked—or in the case of the fancy ladies, they would merely pretend they had not seen her and carry on their way to the beautiful tea shops that housed the delicious scones and steaming cups of tea...

Her stomach grumbled, and she remembered how foolish she had been not to have had luncheon earlier. She had been so upset that Erik was ignoring her that she had forgotten many meals, more consumed with considering what she could have done wrong that he should wish to shun their lessons *and* her company.

But dwelling on her failings or how perfect her life had been for a while would not do any good—it would only prolong her pain.

So looking forlornly at the door that led back to what she had begun to consider a home, she shuffled further down the street.

The Opera House itself was a large and imposing figure. Christine had nearly forgotten how cold a Parisian winter could be, so cocooned had she been in Erik's world of tunnels and passages that while cool, had not the biting wind that did nothing to help her already chilled state. She tugged feebly at her brown cloak, trying to eke out a small bit of warmth from the wet fabric. The snow was still frozen on the ground, and mixed with the dirt and grime of the streets made for a truly grotesque gray colour that well matched Christine's mood.

It took all of her attention to put one foot in front of the other so as to keep herself from returning to the hidden door. She wanted to simply wait there where she could eventually beg Erik to allow her to stay—reminding him of his promise as well as provide assurance that she did not mind so very much if he was a man. Things would be different of course—she would have to reassert that while she would do practically *anything* to be allowed to stay, she would not willingly submit to anything untoward.

Her father had raised her better than that, and no matter how cold or hungry, she would not be anything he would find disappointing.

But even there she had failed. He would never have approved of her pilfering scraps of bread or bruised apples when vendors were not looking. She had cried after she had done so, as her belly was once more slightly filled and the regret and frustration would well up as she shivered in alley corners and she tried to seek forgiveness.

Only to repeat the process the next day.

Jobs were scarce, especially when one did not have proper clothes or admirable skills. Her voice was only now properly tuned after its years of disuse. For a while she had tried to sing in the park as she had once done with Papa, but she found that whenever she opened her mouth to do so, her throat would constrict and all that would come out was a trembling croak.

But maybe now that she had experienced Erik's lessons, she would be able to make at least a little bit of money—hopefully enough to keep from starving. And then she would not have to steal, and perhaps someday she could buy a new dress and audition at the Opera House, and she could at least remember fondly the weeks she had spent in such comfort...

So consumed was she in her own revelry that she failed to notice that she had crossed to the front of the Opera. More importantly, she had managed to crash headlong into one of the well-dressed gentleman that actually *belonged* at the foot of such a grand structure, and she stumbled back forcefully.

"I'm so sorry!"

She made to walk on, thinking her apology sufficient to diffuse the situation when she felt a hand clamp onto her wrist. Startled, she turned to look at the gentleman, fully prepared to demand he release her.

Raoul!

Christine thought he had stopped her because he recognised her, but there was a scowl on his face, and though his grip was not wholly unkind, it did nothing to help her already sore wrist from Erik's earlier treatment.

"I know your tricks! You bump into me and steal my purse while I am unawares. I shall take it back now." His voice was firm but not cruel, and she supposed for a man in his position it was common to be a target for thieves and pickpockets.

But that did not mean she was prepared to be thought as such!

She knew she looked a fright after her quarrel with the lake, and even before that, she had not given her appearance much attention when Erik had been ignoring her. Her hair must be a mess, and in her old clothes she found she could not blame him for thinking her a bandit.

But that made it hurt no less that he did not recognise her.

She lurched from his grasp, jutting out her chin as she glared at him. "It was an honest mistake, *Monsieur;* I was not watching where I was going. I am sorry for any disturbance but I am sure you will find that your purse is where it should be."

And she prayed it had not been filched by someone else, because the last thing she wanted was to involve the law.

Raoul gave his pocket a quick tap, and his cheeks flushed with colour when he felt the slight protrusion of his money still properly housed within its purse. He released her arm quickly. "My apologies, *Mademoiselle,* I spoke too hastily." Now that his features were not contorted in accusation, she could see how handsome he still was, even after all their time apart. But if she was unworthy of him before, she was most certainly beyond his notice now. It had been foolish to think him capable of giving her any assistance. She realised that now.

She only nodded to him, afraid that if she opened her mouth to speak she would begin to cry. Christine had treasured the memories of their friendship, and though she deeply regretted and would later weep for the loss of her last friend, for now she would allow him to go on his way unencumbered.

A fine looking man of middle age approached her, and she eyed him warily. "You must forgive my brother. He is a little excited today as we are now financing this establishment." Christine blinked at him, realising that this must be Philippe. She had never met the Comte, and she felt awkward and silly that he was speaking to her.

She nodded again, simply wanting to go away and nurse her wounds in privacy. Philippe pulled out a *franc* and handed it to her with a soft smile, and at that moment he looked so much like Raoul it pained her. "To make up for my brother's deplorable manners."

Christine mumbled her thanks and gave a quick curtsey and scurried away.

She just wanted to go *home.* Somehow in the weeks she had been with Erik his dark little home that was so cosy with the aid of his fires and kitchen range had become her home. She had a *franc* now that would at least buy her a few things, so she allowed herself a moment to find an alley and sink down onto the cobblestones.

Erik had *said* he loved her. She had not given it much thought before as she was consumed with the fact that he was telling her to leave. But now as her heart broke still further at the realisation that she was so unrecognisable to her childhood sweetheart, she realised that all she wanted was for someone to love her—to know of her scars and her nightmares and continue to think her good and pure and worthwhile as a person, even if that naught but a lie.

She pulled out one of her soggy biscuits and nibbled on it, suddenly needing the small reminder that someone, though for only a moment, had cared enough about her to make them for her—just because she had asked.

Christine did not care that Erik was a man. As long as he had continued to be kind to her—to feed her and give her a home, and help her to forget her troubles through their music—she might not even have struggled too much even if he did want *that.*

She *was* a whore.

But as she cried into her knees and the biscuit was still sweet on her tongue, she knew that it was true. She so desperately wanted to stay, even if he did have fits of temper that he used to frighten her, and even if he would not let her believe in the Angel of Music. Whether man or not, he *was* her Angel. He had saved her, and reminded her that beauty still existed in the world. And truly, what more could she ask from her father's promise?

Her heart clenched when she realised that someone was standing at the mouth of the alley, and she sobbed all the more. This was to be her life for always it seemed—weeping and mourning until some scoundrel took note of her weakness and had his way with her.

But when the figure drew closer and she saw the dark smooth leather and the fine black fabric swishing around the man's ankles, she looked up, hope nearly choking her with its intensity.

Erik said not a word to her, but when he reached out a gloved hand in invitation she forgot all thoughts of fear or anger, and gripped it with all the strength she possessed. "Are you taking me home?"

Erik sighed, and she could easily tell it was not one born of irritation, as the pain was clear. "Yes, Christine, I am taking you home."

And though she would chastise herself for her forwardness later—perhaps when properly bathed and fed and curled up in her warm bed—she hugged his arm to her and rested her head against the softness of the black cashmere that enshrouded it.

And with a sigh of contentment, allowed him to lead her back into the darkness.

XIII

Erik was furious.

He had gone to the Opera simply because it was a rarity that he would walk the streets during daylight hours, and it was impossible for him to remain within his home. He had left the boat for Christine's use which meant he had to use one of his own lesser used tunnels. It was cramped and uncomfortable to navigate, but it bypassed the lake and allowed for him to still travel above.

He felt as though his brain had ceased functioning the longer he walked, and was therefore surprised to find that he had walked all the way to the managers' offices—and to even greater anger, discovered that his faithful puppets Debienne and Poligny were retiring. Not only retiring, but were at this moment turning over all keys and legal documentation to two new individuals—men that Erik knew nothing about.

They looked like idiots, though it could possibly have been Erik's ire that made him think so.

Had he truly been so blind? Christine had apparently preoccupied him to such an extent in the past few weeks that he had missed something so terribly obvious during his few visits above. Debienne and Poligny might have been trying to retire in secret, but that would generally be of little concern to Erik. Their office was his playground and he had spent many afternoons agreeably engaged with amusing himself at their expense. He had probably done them a tremendous favour by being so disengaged from their activities, otherwise he would have been able to discourage their leaving through a little persuasion of his own.

It was always so troublesome to train new staff to his exacting standards.

Moncharmin and Richard were their names, and Erik filed away the knowledge for later use. He would need to send them a greeting worthy of their new position. They were currently regaling the old managers with news of their recently acquired patron, extolling their triumph at being able to obtain the good will and attention of the Comte de Chagny.

The name meant nothing to Erik, and while he was always appreciative of people's investment in the arts, he sincerely doubted that any individual that these two men could have dealings with were the type he would want involved in his theatre.

Erik grew tired of their chortling and watching them toast their celebratory beverages. When he heard that the new patron would be arriving shortly to take a tour of his new investment, Erik knew he would much prefer to first view the man as he entered. One could always tell the pomp and arrogance of a personage from their method of arrival.

But before he left, he made sure to allow a lone chortle of his own filter through the walls—and he relished the looks of bewilderment of the new managers, while the old paled as white as the sheets of paper still in their hands.

Satisfied with his brief introduction, he hurried along his passages, trying not to think of the previous time he had made use of his tunnels. He had company then, and while he tried to tell himself that it was much easier and far less cumbersome to haunt on his own, he knew he was being absurd. Genius was only satisfying when it was acknowledged and appreciated—and every time Christine had bitten into an apple or dipped one of her sweet biscuits into her tea and smiled at him in that welcoming way...

Erik growled and hurried down below, pushing all the painful thoughts away with a vicious resolve.

He had seen this Opera House grow from its infancy, and he would not allow it to become tainted just because he was distracted by things that would never be.

This particular tunnel ended in the foyer—or more specifically, in the exterior wall of the front entrance. There was a peephole that would allow him to look out at the incoming guests, assessing who it was that was coming to appreciate the music.

How he wished he could say *his* music, but that would remain forever entombed down below.

There was a carriage waiting near the front steps—a grandiose and obnoxious structure if there ever was one. He begrudgingly noted that the horses were magnificent creatures, with glossy brown coats that bespoke of proper care and attention.

Perhaps when he had seen enough of these new *intruders* he might just see about hunting down the pet he had promised himself. It would not be Christine, but it would at least be *something*—which was more than he would have when he returned to the barren, desolate rooms that had only recently begun to feel so very homey.

A young man exited first, and Erik was surprised that someone his age would be a count. But he supposed Christine's own sad tale was evidence enough that parents could die at any age, leaving their children behind with burdens too large for their inexperienced shoulders.

What he did not expect was to see Christine shuffling across the front steps. She was back to wearing her rags, and he berated himself for not ensuring that they met their ultimate demise in his fireplace. He could not fathom what had possessed her to wear those, not when he had made it clear she could take anything she wished. Though he knew he was perhaps a little too selfish with his possessions, he truly had meant what he had said. Anything he owned he would have gladly sacrificed it if meant she would be comfortable—regardless of where that meant she would lay her head.

He wanted to chastise her when he saw her lack of attention. While she had only knocked into the young man, she could have just as easily wandered into the streets and been struck by a carriage.

He had *told* her to be safe!

To make the situation far worse, Christine was being *manhandled* by the boy. He steadfastly refused to remember that a mere hour before *he* had been the one to grip her too harshly. And by the slight flinch that crossed her features, he could tell that she was discomfited by his hold.

He was very grateful when an older gentleman intervened, but his relief ended when he saw the small coin being pressed into her palm.

Erik was more an idiot than those bloody men upstairs who fancied themselves the managers of his theatre.

He had promised her a home, and although he knew she would eventually want to leave him, he had not provided the means necessary for her to take care of herself properly. She had shunned the clothes he had given, and so of course she would not have also seen to search out his purse that contained enough *francs* to see to her comfort for years to come.

His own feelings did not matter. If she ran away at his approach then so be it, but he would not allow her to suffer for his own misjudgements.

Aside from the peephole, this part of the tunnel had no door to the exterior, so it took some roaming and creativity in order to find an exit hidden in as much shadow as possible. It took him some moments to decide on which direction she could have gone, but when he started walking, somehow he just *knew.*

Erik was never one to readily believe in the metaphysical, but when he turned down an alley and barely made out the huddled form swathed completely in the dirty bedraggled brown of a cloak that would most *decidedly* be meeting the inside of his fireplace, he had to acknowledge that something was responsible beyond his own senses.

He had planned to offer her money—for her to come with him just long enough to fetch some coins and then tell her she was free to be on her way. But when he approached and she looked at him with such *rapture,* he knew that he had misjudged her.

She might still fear him, think him a monster unworthy of her affections and company, but it was plain even to him that she was happy to see his approach.

And when she asked if he would take her home, her voice tight with tears but yet so *hopeful,* he knew there was nothing he could do but acquiesce.

Christine had once again pressed herself against his arm as they walked, and though a part of him wanted to slow his pace so as to relish the contact for as long as possible, he knew it was important that they be seen by as few people as possible. He led her back to the hidden door she must have so recently passed through, knowing it was the only exit that the moss could have guided her to. It took only a few touches of his fingers upon specific stones and the inner mechanisms recognised their master and opened for his use. The lantern had been placed carefully inside, and mindful that she had already been traumatized enough on this day, he lit it with yet another flick of his fingers.

With Christine so close to him he realised just how soaked she truly was. Had she met with a sudden rain? He had not been paying particular attention, but he did not remember any heavy clouds that would have indicated a downpour.

"Are you cold?"

He felt more than saw her response as her head was burrowed into his arm and whatever vocal response she gave was muffled, but he did feel the subtle nod of her head.

Erik always felt exposed travelling without a cloak. The voluminous fabric was what allowed him the pleasure of disappearing into shadows, and also kept the air of mystery should anyone ever have the misfortune of stumbling upon his person. But for Christine he would forego such comforts. After swiftly placing the lantern on the ground, he disentangled her from his arm, easing her quiet protests with a gentle hush. And with a swirl that even he found quite remarkable, he placed his cloak upon her shoulders.

"Better?"

She looked at him thoughtfully for a moment, and he realised just how becoming she appeared in the lantern light. "But will you be cold now? I do not want you to be uncomfortable."

Erik's throat tightened that she should be concerned for him, and for a moment he could form no reply. So instead he held out his arm once more. And although he wished he could have withdrawn the words as soon as they were thoughtlessly spoken, he answered, "Then you shall have to keep me warm."

Christine blanched and looked at him warily, and he cursed his foolish tongue to the darkest depths—which he realised was a ridiculous thing to do since it did not *get* much darker than the depths he called his home.

"I... I did not mean to give you any ideas..."

Erik groaned, hating this aspect most of all. When he was her angel she never doubted his motives, and while he knew it important that she recognise that her modesty must be maintained, he loathed that she would now reconsider every action in case it could be construed as innuendo. "That is not what I meant. It is perfectly acceptable for a lady to hold a gentleman's arm so as to keep her from any danger. Would you not agree?"

She smiled, but it could hardly be called thus as it looked wane and slightly watery, but he was relieved that she still reached for his arm. She did not quite clutch it as she had done before and her head did not settle against it, but he hoped it might do so the longer they walked.

Erik stooped to pick up the lantern and upon doing so noticed that the hem of his cloak was pooling on the ground. He looked at Christine sheepishly before reaching out and bundling it up slightly and putting it in her hands. "I already lost one cloak due to your short stature; I should hate to have to bury another."

Christine blushed and nodded, and he was happy to note that this time when he held out his arm her face indeed made its way to his sleeve. And even knowing it was simply to hide her embarrassment, he was still glad of the contact.

He had made sure their pace was quick while on the streets, but Erik could admit to himself that he walked more slowly than strictly necessary once in the tunnels. He knew they would have to converse when they were once more locked away in his home, and he dreaded the conversation.

Would she ask him to rescind his foolish admission of love, asking him to never speak of it again? Would she cry and remember that he was a *man* and they were to be feared above all else?

No, it was much better to simply appreciate this walk—where they were quiet and he could just enjoy the feel of her before *talking* ruined things.

But eventually they reached the lake and Erik could not help but notice that when he carefully lowered her into the boat, her blush was voracious in its intensity. He eyed her shrewdly, remembering the wet state of her clothes. "Christine, did you and the boat have a disagreement?"

He began rowing softly, and he watched with amusement as her hands fiddled with the folds of his cloak, her cheeks never quieting. "I did not realise how careful you had to be when getting out. Someone had always helped me before."

Any amusement died as Erik remembered that *he* should have been the someone helping her. Regardless of his feelings, he had left her to a dark and dangerous tunnel, with a lake that could have drowned her if she had taken too much of a tumble, all because he did not want to have to watch her walk away from him.

He was the epitome of a coward.

Erik ceased rowing for a moment and stilled her hands with one of his own and bade her look at him. "I am sorry, Christine. You should not have had to manage by yourself."

Christine transformed before his eyes. Her slightly huddled posture rose and she now sat primly before him. He had expected her to cry and ask him why he had left, and in so doing abused her trust—in every way since they had met—but instead he saw a tinge of anger in her eyes. "Perhaps we should discuss this further once we are inside." And though what they had to *discuss* terrified him, he found that he appreciated her vehemence. He found that he was quite disappointed when her shoulders hunched yet again and she began nibbling at a fingernail. "That is, if you do not mind..." She looked at him so hesitantly, and dare he say, *fearfully* that he wished with all his heart that she had remained angry.

He resumed his rowing, taking out his frustration upon the water with relish. "You are allowed to be upset with me. I will not pretend to like it, but you are allowed to feel how you wish." No matter how much he disliked it and wished he could simply will her into caring for him.

Christine brought her knees up to her chest and tucked his cloak around them. "But how do I know you will not make me leave again, just for saying the wrong thing?"

His limbs suddenly felt as though they had lost the ability to function.

"Make you leave? Foolish girl! Why would I *make* you leave?"

She tugged at her hair and her agitation was obvious. "I do not know! I know you were angry that I was being... stubborn... but before I could apologise you had told me to leave!" Christine buried her head in her knees, and she seemed startled when the boat suddenly landed on the opposite shore. She tried to scramble from the craft, and from her jerky movements and the way she tried to leap over the side, Erik could easily see how she had managed to fall into the water.

Ever mindful that she was upset and probably did not want his touch, he still warily extended his hand and held her elbow so as to ensure she made it safely onto the shore before following, mooring the boat to its post as he did so.

He allowed Christine to carry the lantern, despite his brief moment of worry that the flame could somehow manage to set his cloak aflame, near as it was to the bunch of fabric still clutched in her opposite hand. But there was no incident as he opened the front door and gestured Christine inside.

She hesitated, looking back at the lake. "Maybe we should talk out here. I liked when we talked out here before, even if you did lock yourself away afterward."

Christine could not possibly know how he would forever treasure the time spent enjoying the lake together, but she was still wet and his cloak would do little to keep her warm for any significant duration. "No, I am afraid not. You should come inside and warm yourself. We can be perfectly amiable and discuss our... misunderstanding like civilised people." He secretly considered that locking himself away in his bedroom while she bathed and thereby avoiding any such discussion was not a wholly unappealing idea.

She would be with him—safe, warm, and theoretically contented—and while he would not be able to enjoy her smiles or her company, his home would not feel desolate. He would be able to hear her movements through his door, and perhaps she would sing sometimes in the evenings instead of reading one of her novels.

But that was ridiculous. She deserved to express her disappointment in him, and he could stand to listen—even if it hurt him dreadfully to do so.

Christine finally sighed and entered his home, handing him the lantern as she passed.

He knew he was stalling, but he made doubly sure that the boat had been tied properly and that the lantern was sufficiently full of kerosene in case there was a later emergency that would require it.

Erik had expected Christine to be in the bath when he finally did enter his sitting room, but found her instead staring at the fire, seemingly lost in thought. She looked almost tall in his cloak, and with her golden curls a tangled mass around her features, she had an air of mystery that impressed even he.

"Christine, you should probably take a bath. You have been in those wet things for far too long."

She nodded absently and finally turned to him, her expression unreadable. "I did not think I would ever be able to come back here—to come back *home.* If you had not changed your mind..."

She cried then, and though he knew she would be angry with him later when they did finally have their *discussion,* he could not deny the absolute thrill he received when she flew into his arms and cried into his chest. "Please, no matter what happens, I want to stay with you."

He allowed one hand to come around her in an embrace, fearing for his self-control if he should allow the pleasure of both to feel her softness. "That is excellent to hear, Christine, as I do not think I could let you go a second time."

And when she gave a hiccupping laugh, he wondered if she understood how perfectly serious he had been.

XIV

Christine had eventually calmed herself enough to return his cloak and whisper a quiet, "Thank you," before retiring to her bath. To Erik's dismay she also removed her own tattered rag—as it was unworthy of being called a cloak—and placed it before the fire to dry.

As if he would ever allow her to wear that monstrosity again.

And while Erik was of course satisfied that she would finally be clean and warm—how she should *always* be—he found himself quite unsure about what to do with himself in her absence.

Tea.

They needed tea.

It had been days since he had made her anything, and it was with renewed determination that he went about fixing their afternoon repast. He would need to go to the market soon, as to his alarm, he realised that most of the food had begun to spoil instead of simply disappearing as it should have if Christine had been fixing proper meals during his self-imposed absence.

Erik did not think he could possibly feel any worse than he did at that moment.

While in his mind his intentions had been good by allowing her to leave unimpeded, he had not seen to her care in the least. She had not taken any clothing, money, or food, and he knew it was because he had failed to tell her she could do so.

He did not like feeling this way. He liked to be the one in control, carefully orchestrating either music or the people in the Opera House above to his every whim. And this girl...

She confused him. He, who could master the most complicated mathematical equations, learn languages with ease, and design the most grand and impressive of structures. But when it came to a young fifteen year old girl, he was floundering.

It did not take overly long to make fresh biscuits, and he was grateful for the distraction, although he did not particularly enjoy the way the flour clung to his black attire.

With a dry chuckle he supposed it contributed to his ghostly air.

But to Christine, he was no ghost, nor an angel, and while he knew she would never look at him as something desirable, he still wanted to look presentable.

He had not yet heard the release of her bath water by the time the biscuits were complete and the tea water was boiling. But he set them all on the tray in any case and took them into the sitting room. The tea cosy would ensure the pot remained properly heated by the time she emerged, and for a moment he could not remember how he had acquired such a thing.

Ah yes.

It was one of his most frivolous purchases when he had first moved into his subterranean home. He had discovered that when he was in the throes of composition he often forgot about the tea he had brewed, and often the fire itself. And there was nothing quite as vile as tepid tea.

So he had gone on an expedition and tried to find one that was not *too* feminine, but the more he looked—both in stores after hours and in the above kitchens—he realised that there was nothing masculine about a tea cosy. But finally he had grown tired of the search and had simply taken one, leaving a few coins in its place for the merchant to find the next day.

No need to admit to stealing something so hideous as this chintz atrocity, even if he begrudgingly found it to be tremendously useful in his everyday life. There had been little need for it since Christine arrived as she was devoted to her meals whenever she had them, and there was little worry of the pot growing cold by the time she had finished with it.

Erik placed the tray on the side table before sitting in his reading chair, his eyes lingering on the sodden bit of cloth before his fireplace. Remembering his earlier resolve to burn it so she would never be tempted to wear it again, and he hurried to it, suddenly aware that she might try to stop him should she walk in on him doing so.

As he picked it up however, he felt something lumpy in a hidden pocket, and remembered the *franc* that man had given her. He reached in to remove it—only to find a crumbled mass of what appeared to have once been biscuits.

Erik felt as though air was suddenly being blocked from his lungs, and he stumbled back to his chair and sank into it with a croak.

She had refused all of the things he had sought to provide her, except for the most menial and least important. He made them for her just so she would have something to eat and nibble in case he would be so consumed in his work that any of their meals were delayed. And, a small part of him recognised, he made them because he loved to see the rapture on her face while she ate them. She always had a special smile when he would place a plate of them before her, and she always watched *so* vigilantly when the remainder were carefully placed in the tin—always within easy reach of her greedy fingers, should the need for further nibbling overtake her.

And that was what she had chosen to take. There was other food in the kitchen—much more nutritious and long lasting—but she had chosen what *he* had made for her.

Perhaps he should not read quite so much into it, but Erik felt as though this was evidence that she *cared*—that it was important she take something of his with her.

But obviously her slight tumble into the lake had deprived her of even this last remnant of his affection.

So lost was he as he stared at the ruined biscuits and the tattered garment in his hand, he did not notice that Christine had appeared. She was once more in his dressing gown, never having given it back even after receiving a shawl of her own, and she was looking at him strangely.

"I had forgotten those were in there. I am sorry if they left crumbs on the rug. I know how you hate your lovely things to be soiled."

Erik could not help it.

Before he had even realised he had moved, he found himself before her feet, crying into her hem as he held the evidence of her caring. "Oh, Christine..."

He chanced a look at her face, and instead of the look of disgust he had partially expected, she appeared nearly alarmed. "Erik, I do not like it when you are down there!" She was tugging at him again, and although he wanted nothing more than to pour his love at her feet—that she might see it and judge him worthy—he allowed her to raise him up and followed obediently as she held his hand and led him over to the settee where she invited him to sit beside her. And he did try valiantly to stem the tears that overwhelmed him.

He felt rather detached when she removed the biscuit remnants from his hands and bundled them up in her old cloak, putting it down at her feet as she did so.

While he was upset and overcome, she was calm and collected, pouring their tea and dressing it to their respective satisfactions. And he found that the longer he watched her, the more in control he began to feel.

They would talk.

They would both understand.

And maybe, just maybe, she could learn to love him even a little.

He sipped his tea, more because Christine was looking at him so expectantly than for any true thirst or desire. As he had expected, the tea was hot and soothing, and the chintz had once more done its job—even if it looked so odd placed in the middle of his sitting room.

Christine was smiling at it as she squished the plush cushioning between her fingers. "I would have thought you would have picked something dark. It seems like everything you choose is black." She eyed him carefully after that, obviously interested to see if she had offended him with her comment. "All you *wear* is black..."

Erik shrugged, trying to force his body to relax by easing toward the back of the settee and settling his teacup on his knee. "Everything goes with black."

She laughed then, and he wondered if it would ever cease to send a thrill through him when she did so. "Yes, I suppose it does. Though I am glad my bedclothes are not black. I would feel as though I was being swallowed up!" He did not tell her that *his* bedding was black, nor did he mention that the only reason he had any white for her bed was because that pair had been hidden away in one of the dresser drawers. He also did not point out that she would be glad of his black sheets should her *monthly* make such a disastrous appearance the next time.

Perhaps it was better if he did not speak at all.

Christine popped a warm biscuit in her mouth and sighed in contentment. She pulled her legs up onto the settee as was her usual way of sitting on his furniture, but he found that he did not begrudge the action. It was an endearing thing, something he was privileged to know about her—that contrary to what he thought proper manners, she liked to put her feet up on furnishings.

She took a small sip of tea and turned to him, her expression one of resolve. "I would almost rather we pretend this day never happened. We would read our books and then I would get sleepy and go to bed," this was sounding like a fine idea, "but I do not think that would accomplish much of anything."

Erik sighed, and took a bracing sip of tea. "No, I suppose you are correct. You may ask your questions if you have them."

She nodded, and with slight amusement he watched her pop yet another biscuit into her mouth before continuing. "Am I allowed to ask about... your face?"

He froze. He should have expected this of course as he had given her little explanation at the time, and it was only reasonable that she would have questions.

Erik would keep his temper.

Erik would not lash out at her simply for remembering what he had shown her.

Why had he shown her?

He nodded, though even that felt forced. It was not all right that she asked questions, but he would pretend for her sake. "You may. But please... it is a delicate subject."

Christine put a consoling hand on his arm, and while normally he would marvel at the gesture, he now felt it confining and uncomfortable. He wanted to shove it away, but he thought that would perhaps insult her. And causing offense would likely accomplish nothing but to inspire more tears between both parties.

"I understand." Erik sincerely doubted it. "Were you... born like that?"

Erik felt the bubbling of his sardonic laughter, as did the long winded speech he had perfected for when people had the misfortune of witnessing his visage. The Daroga had been the last one to receive it, and it had ended with harsh words on both sides. He would mind his tongue. Christine was all innocence and natural curiosity, and he would not scoff at her simply for being banal.

"Indeed. A face even a mother could not love."

Christine looked at him with *sympathy,* and though he wanted nothing more than to lock himself in his bedchamber until she would look at him with *anything* else, he allowed her to pat his arm and say she was sorry. "You should not have made me touch it like that. All you did was frighten me, and I could have hurt you terribly if I had not filed my nails down with the things you gave me."

He had not been aware that the trunk held any such items. And in the heat of the moment he had wished she *would* hurt him, if only so that the physical pain would dull the emotional one that had threatened to drown him.

"I was... very wrong to have made you touch me. I hope you are not still frightened."

She looked at him for a moment, and Erik knew she was not really seeing what was truly there. His mask was firmly in place, but he knew she was seeing past it—was remembering each vivid detail of what lay beneath, and he had to fight the impulse to cover his face with his hands. "No, not of that. But I will admit, I did not like that you were... forcing me. It reminded me of other times."

She did not expound on those *other times* for which Erik was very grateful. While his purpose had been well meaning as he simply wanted to be honest with her about the state of his person, his methods had been all wrong. They had caused her pain, and it was with sudden memory that Erik remembered just how tightly he had gripped her poor hands.

"Do your wrists require attention? I am well aware that I was not gentle with you and I am..." His throat felt tight and his mouth dry, and it took nearly all of his self-control to swallow the sob that wished to burst forth. "I am so very sorry for having caused you pain."

Christine smiled softly, yet he could easily see that there was little joy in the expression. She pulled up the sleeve of his dressing gown slowly, and while by no means were the marks dark, he still felt as if a knife was being pushed into his chest at the sight of them. "Christine," he choked.

He grasped her hand *so* carefully, holding it loosely so that if it should be her wish, she could pull away with only the slightest of effort. He kept her hand within his and he could feel it trembling—as was his. He kept his gaze steady with hers, wanting to ensure that she was fully accepting of his action before he pulled her wrist to his mouth and placed a lone, dry kiss upon the mark. "You must forgive your poor Erik. He did not mean to be so careless."

She whimpered then and pulled away, and he could see that while physically present, her mind was far from him. "You cannot... I want to trust you, but how..." Her other hand covered the marks on her wrist, twisting in agitation, and it was all Erik could do not to moan and crawl away.

He would never be worthy of her.

It had *never* been his intention to hurt her, but with his horrid temper he had forgotten himself and inexcusably, had forgotten just how delicate his Christine truly was.

Erik looked at her miserably. "What can I do? You may ask anything of me, Christine. Anything at all."

She blinked, and it was apparent that whatever dark corner of her mind had overtaken her had been driven away, if only for the moment, and she relaxed slightly. "You are not very good at keeping your promises, Erik. It makes it difficult to put my faith in you."

He grimaced. While he had always meant to keep his word, he understood how she could doubt his sincerity.

"Of what matter in particular would you like reassurance?"

Her mouth dropped open and he scrambled to find what had been so very stupid about his question. Before he had come up with a satisfactory answer, Christine had drawn herself up as she tried to look down at him from what he supposed was to be her righteous indignation.

"I would like to know that when you promise me a *home,* the next day you will not rescind on your offer. I would like to know that when you reveal yourself a man—whether or not I had been foolish to think you anything else—that you have no improper intentions." She nibbled her lip then, and she seemed to lose whatever spark had lit her ire. "Because if you do... I have thought about it and even though it would be my preference to not... allow you to... *know* me in that way, I find that I would rather be forced to do so with you than to be on the streets once more." Christine was whispering, and Erik dearly wished that he could not hear the vile situation she was presenting for them, but he found himself entirely unable to stem her ridiculous flow of words. "I would not fight you too much..."

With a shaking hand Erik moved his teacup to the tray before he rose, and if his compositions were not still scattered all over the sitting room he was quite sure that they soon would have been once again. "After all this time, how can you even suggest such a thing to me? I *love* you." His voice cracked at the words and he stumbled, but he knew with certainty that she needed to hear them. "I was not aware that people generally showed their fondness by *forcing* themselves on the object of their affection. I may be a monster, Christine, but *never* in that way."

And he hoped to God she would believe him. Even if their music could offer her some semblance of healing, if she could not trust him in this fundamental way there was little hope that their relationship could survive—in whatever form she would allow.

"I want to believe you, truly I do. But I do not know how to be loved by a man other than my papa, and it frightens me. I do not know what you will want or what you expect. I thought maybe for a time that Raoul loved me but today..."

Erik froze. "That boy was Raoul? *He* is the new patron? He hurt you!"

Christine cocked her head and regarded him with a strange expression. "How do you know about that?"

He shifted awkwardly, and finally decided that resituating himself with his tea was far better than looming over her as he sought answers. "It is my job to know all the details of the Opera House. I am paid handsomely to do so." Never mind that his payment was akin to extortion.

She shook her head, but this time there was a slight smile on her lips and he was satisfied that she was not too upset for him having watched her without her knowledge. "Raoul hardly hurt me beyond the fact that he did not recognise me. I did not realise I had changed so very much."

Erik wondered then what she had looked like in her prime. She was still pale, and no matter how he plied her with sweets and regular meals he knew that his home would never provide her an infusion of colour beyond her many blushes.

He took her hand in his, this time a little more firmly, and she did not protest in the least. "I did not want you to go, Christine. I thought *you* had wished it, and I know now that you felt you were being evicted for some perceived misdeed. The last thing in the world that I wish is for you to be anywhere but here."

His expression was beseeching and she looked at him for what felt like a very long time. Eventually she gave his hand a small squeeze and moved a little so she could lay her head on his bony shoulder. "If I choose to trust you, will you make me regret it?"

Erik kept very still, thinking that if he moved even the slightest bit she would somehow disappear. "I can say with utmost sincerity that there will be days you wish you had never met me." And with only a shift of his tone he knew she could hear him whispering in her ear, so he added, "But if you could love me, I would be as gentle as a lamb, and you would want for nothing."

Christine made no reply, but since she did not leave and only settled more firmly at his side, Erik found that he did not mind at all.

XV

Christine was sleeping. Knowing how upset she was prone to being when he was not at home when she awoke, Erik silently entered her bedchamber and placed a small note on her bedside explaining that he had an errand to attend to and would return shortly.

He felt rather strange entering her room when she was unawares, but reasoned that she would be more upset finding him gone without a word than she would at realising he had seen her in a vulnerable position.

Erik's first stop was to procure a few groceries, seeing as their supplies had begun to dwindle. It was very early in the morning, and to most civilised people it would still be considered night. But the bakers were already slaving over their craft and willing to part with some to even masked individuals who asked for a loaf freshly emerged from the hot ovens. Even Erik could not help pulling off a piece of crust and munching on it in the darkness, too delectable was the smell.

His true errand however took him farther into the city.

Yesterday's conversation with Christine had not at all been what he expected, but he could not say he was wholly unsatisfied with the exchange. He had apologised for his misdeeds, and he felt that she had offered enough of her trust in him that their relationship was not strained. The rest of the evening had been a quiet one, and Erik had realised it primarily had been so because Christine had fallen asleep against his shoulder. He allowed himself to enjoy the sensation for quite some time before he begrudgingly acknowledged that she would wake with a painful neck should she sleep the entire night away in that position.

So he had carried her to bed and tucked her in, and while he would never admit it, had allowed himself to touch a lone curl that had fallen across her forehead.

He had to do so otherwise the misbehaving coil could have tickled her eyelid and disturbed her rest.

Erik was merely being helpful.

And although he rather wished for sleep himself, he was too plagued by lingering guilt to allow himself the respite. He had paced for a while, knowing that he was too distraught to produce any music that would not wake Christine with a start. The longer he did so, the more it became clear that he needed to provide her a gesture—something tangible that visibly showed her that she would forever be within his care.

And that whenever she looked upon it, she would remember that he would hold himself to the promise he gave her. A promise of *home.*

In addition, it would also be there for *him* to see should he ever require a similar reminder.

He was not perfect and he would not pretend to be, but he could at least offer her the assurance that he would *try.* He would be better for her, and she would teach him to be who she needed, just as he proved to her that not everyone wanted to see her harmed and abused.

Erik rather liked the idea of learning together—learning with *her.*

Only with her.

So Erik walked the streets of Paris, this time not clinging to alleyways, but instead perusing shop windows in the darkness before dawn, enjoying the crisp air and the wayward snowflake that dared drop from the lingering night sky.

It was not long before he found what he was looking for.

There were many baubles in the window, which rather surprised Erik. He would have assumed that many jewellers would lock away their stock at night in case any thieves were drawn by temptation—though he supposed that the bars on the windows were meant to be a discouraging factor.

But Erik was no ordinary thief.

It took only a moment and a few careful clicks with his lock pick and the front door swung open. The shop was entirely dark inside aside from the few streams of light from the streetlamps that the windows allowed in.

He sincerely doubted anyone would notice his entry but he still made sure to close and relock the door in case any patrolmen happened to pass by.

Satisfied that his errand would not be interrupted, he bypassed all of the glittering gemstones that would certainly seem gaudy and out of place against Christine's effortless beauty.

In the far corner he found the perfect item. It was a plain gold band, simple and elegant, and immediately he could see it upon her dainty finger.

He wasted no time and snatched up his gift, placing a small pile of coins in its stead. Christine would not be tainted by stolen goods, as it would most likely offend her sensibilities if she were ever to ask how he had acquired it.

And he would not lie to her.

He reminded himself firmly that the trunk of clothes and other feminine goods he had spirited away from the costume department could hardly be considered stolen, as it never should have been placed there in any case. His theatre was to be run with the utmost of efficiency and professionalism, and superiors were allowed to dock their employees' privileges when they misbehaved.

He slipped the ring onto his littlest finger, emerged from the shop, and returned to the Opera House, an unusual excitement flowing through him as he did so.

This was a boon purchased from guilt, not for any other reason. It did not matter that he would also enjoy the sight of *his* ring upon the third finger of her left hand...

Erik stopped himself short. He had not considered which finger the ring would rest upon, but any other digit seemed wrong. Perhaps she would not mind when that was the one he slipped it onto. Surely she would tell him if it offended her.

He was slightly nervous when he entered his home, and he busied himself in the kitchen while she slept. She would most likely be overly tired as the day before had been especially arduous. He would not resent her sleeping in, even as he felt quite agitated as he set about fixing her breakfast.

He would conquer muffins, he decided. She had never given any indication that she had a particular fondness for them, but given her palate he sincerely doubted she would voice any true objection.

What he did not anticipate was just how anxious he would feel once he sat staring at the oven, waiting for the muffins to plump, and listening intently for any sound of Christine awakening.

Taking the opportunity, he tried to rehearse what he would say when he gave her his gift. He was not one for show—at least, not where Christine was concerned—so he did not think wrapping it in paper would be necessary. Besides, how would one wrap a ring? No, he would simply slip it onto her finger, and tell her that this was a tangible offering of his protection and his care, and as long as she wore it she would not have to fear anything. Least of all him.

He knew it was slightly unreasonable for him to give her a wedding ring, taking the rightful place of the band her husband would someday give to his bride. But as his lip curled and he felt his temper rising at the thought of her married to another, he knew that he would much rather pretend that she had willingly accepted his own gift of play-marriage than allow her to appear unwed.

And when he was alone, he could imagine that she bore his ring after they had taken their vows, and that he had a living wife—someone who was happy to see him in the evenings after he had shooed her away so he could compose, and who loved her husband very much.

But he would not ask that of Christine. She feared too many things already, and it would be wrong to thrust such fantasies upon her.

No matter how much he might wish to.

He should let her sleep. She needed to recover from the day before and there was a very distinct possibility that she had in fact caught some sort of sickness from her prolonged exposure to the cold while dressed in her wet garments.

The guilt of yesterday's disaster was growing steadily worse, and as he piled his muffins and their tea onto the tray and snuck into her bedchamber, he knew it was an absolute necessity that he gift his ring to her immediately.

He comforted himself with that thought that she could not be *too* angry when he brought her breakfast in bed. Only married ladies of considerable status were afforded such luxuries, and surely she would enjoy the indulgence.

Erik placed her breakfast feast on the side of the bed not currently occupied, as he feared that if he placed it *on* Christine, she would awake in a fright and disrupt his labours. He was not experienced in how to awaken sleeping beauties, and while the tale would indicate a kiss or even more lurid methods, Erik was not so brave as to try anything so drastic.

So with a lone fingertip, he prodded her side.

Nothing.

"Christine."

She slept on.

He looked at her thoughtfully for a moment knowing that the muffins would be cooling soon and they would most certainly be at their most scrumptious when warm. With that in mind, he bent over her sleeping form, very much aware that he could have used his ventriloquism in order to achieve the same result but chose instead to whisper in her ear directly. "Christine, you must wake up now. Your angel has brought your breakfast."

Erik did not know what possessed him to refer to himself in such a manner, except that he *did* feel rather angelic for having made such a lovely tray of food—which she was currently neglecting because she felt the need to sleep until all hours of the day.

This time she shivered, stirred, and with fluttering eyelids, woke, and Erik was quick to straighten before she startled by his presence looming over her.

"Erik?" He felt a moment of regret at hearing her sleep befuddled voice and seeing her furrowed brow, but as she took in his position and her eyes flickered over to the bedside breakfast, she smiled.

"You are going to spoil me."

His smile was waning, but genuine. "That is my sincere intention."

Christine suddenly blushed and looked at him sheepishly. "Would you mind if I made use of the bath-room before we enjoy our tea?"

Erik blinked, wishing that he had just placed the ring on her sleeping hand and departed just as quickly. He made a vague gesture of acquiescence and he was very glad that he had put her into bed with his dressing gown still wrapped around her so that he would not have to further his torment with the sight of her in naught but her chemise.

To her credit, she was quick, and from a brief whiff as she passed he knew she had made use of her toothpowder. Silly girl. As if he would be concerned with something like the state of her breath upon first awakening.

But somehow it seemed a very great compliment that she would want to be sweet smelling, even if he was the only one near.

She did not return to the bed, but instead curled up on the sofa and looked at him expectantly. "Will you not join me?"

Oh, Christine.

If only she knew that he would join her anywhere she wished.

He moved the tray to the side table and sat beside her. She reached to pour their tea and he could see her greedy eyes roaming over the muffins with abandon. But before she could grasp either, Erik softly took her hand in his.

Perhaps he should have made his speech first, he later mused, but suddenly it felt absolutely imperative that he see the ring upon her finger.

She was silent as she watched him slip it onto the third finger of her left hand, and as his fingertip stroked the plain gold band in reverence, he felt a peace he had never known before.

She wore his ring.

Christine wore his ring.

And although he wished with all his heart that it was a true wedding band, he would settle for this.

"Christine, with this ring I offer," he began, only to stop short when he took in her expression.

Her eyes were wet and glistening, her breath coming in short gasps, and for a moment he thought he had done the worst possible thing. He must have frightened her horribly and now she was regretting ever having returned with him.

But the longer he studied her and forced his thoughts to focus on the present and not his own suppositions of her intent—that had not worked to either of their benefit before—he knew without a doubt that should he say or do the wrong thing, he would completely shatter her.

She looked so expectant, so *hopeful* that it left him reeling.

Did she think this was an actual proposal?

Did she *want* it to be?

He was silent too long, and her eyes flickered to the ring before returning to look at him. "Are you proposing?" She was nibbling on her lip, and while he told himself he was imagining it, he thought he saw that she was doing so in order to quell a burgeoning smile.

"Yes?" Erik did not mean to be hesitant. He had meant to be reassuring and that could only be done with conviction. But she obviously expected something in particular with the giving of the band, and the last thing he wished was to disappoint her.

And apparently his answer had been the correct one, even though her eyes were streaming with tears and her lower lip quivered. "You... you want me to be your wife? Even... after everything?"

Stupid girl.

As though something like her tragic past would somehow make her *less* desirable. His own sordid dealings were another matter entirely, and the fact that she seemed excited at the prospect of being a wife—*his* wife— was not something he ever truly considered.

Erik forced himself to calm, to say things properly even as his mind reeled and his breath became short. "Christine, my treatment of you yesterday was deplorable, and I will forever beg your forgiveness." He allowed the feel of his ring upon her finger to give him confidence, and he carried on. "I would be the happiest of men to take you as my wife, though I do not know if I could ever please you as a husband." He grasped her hand a little more firmly, mindful to remain gentle even as he did so. "But I would *try,* Christine. Your Erik would be a faithful husband who would love you and care for you for all of your days."

His heart was in his throat, and although this step was a far greater one than he had anticipated, he was rapidly falling into the dream—the dream of a wife who could maybe, someday, *love* him. But not just any wife. Christine.

She was sniffling, and if she was not also smiling in that soft, tender way, he would have believed that he had frightened her. However, her expression shifted and she was once more worrying her lip and looking at him imploringly. "You truly love me? You will not marry me and then dismiss me later once you see everything that has been done?"

Foolish girl.

As if he would ever be the one to judge the appearance of another human being. Certainly, he could judge the hygiene or quality of an individual—and *had* on many occasions—but he was no stranger to scars.

Slowly and deliberately so she could stop him if she so chose, he shrugged out of his black coat, removed his glove, and rolled up the sleeve of his shirt. It would have been simpler to have removed his mask and reminded her of what *she* would be marrying. But the part of him that wanted to do nothing that could truly discourage her from considering the union made that a less than desirable prospect.

So instead he settled for exposing a yellowy forearm, complete with many raised scars that had twisted into crisscross sections that resembled slightly crinkled parchment. "I know you saw them before, my dear, so perhaps you would like to do so now with my permission."

She was looking at his arm with wide eyes, and he could clearly see her fingers nearly twitching with a desire to touch them. He did not know how he felt about allowing such a thing, wondering if it would be far too much pleasure than he could ever deserve. But he found himself nodding at her silent question, and he nearly gasped when her own delicate fingers began to examine his flesh for the first time. "Who...?"

Erik shook his head. "That is a story for a very different day. I believe you had asked me a question. You are getting the far worse end of the bargain, Christine, and I would be a monster indeed if I did not tell you so. Your husband would be ugly at best, grotesque at worst. *You* are the beauty, and nothing that any of those villains did have tainted you in any way." He allowed one finger to trace a lone curl, and he whispered, "You must believe your Erik..."

She continued to trace his scars, seemingly lost in thought. Though he began to feel the stirrings of unease and impatience, he would allow her this. It was more than he had dared hope, and if time was what she required then he would provide it—especially when it also included her touch upon his person.

"Will you want to be married... properly?"

Erik froze, his thoughts flooded with images of *making love* to Christine. She would not be quivering with fear and repulsion, but instead enraptured by the bliss he could provide in the darkness.

But that was never something he would demand.

"We would have whatever marriage you would allow."

She was chewing on her lip again, and this time he allowed his hand to move from her curl and tug gently at it until she released it with a smile. "I think I would like to be married to you. And..." Her cheeks were crimson and while she could not meet his eyes, Erik found that he did not mind so very much—not when she was speaking the words he had never dreamed would be uttered in regards to the likes of him. "Doing... *that*... with you would be different. I know it would."

Something vice-like within his mind and heart suddenly loosened, and he nearly gasped at the sheer relief that she believed that to be true.

"I *swear* it, Christine. Should you ever wish to fully be my wife, it would be so *very* different."

He kissed her ring and she nestled into his side, finally reaching over and popping a bit of muffin into her mouth. Erik noticed with a half-hearted grimace that she was getting crumbs on his shirtsleeves. But when she swallowed and looked up at him with smiling eyes, any complaint died as easily as it had been born.

"Then I will marry you, Erik. And we will be a proper married couple."

She returned to her breakfast, using Erik as her personal armrest, and he was quite glad that she did not seem to notice that some tears escaped the seam of his mask and settled in her curls.

Erik would have a living wife after all.

XVI

Erik was not used to hurrying and whisking about attending to wedding preparations, and it was not an activity he had ever considered before today.

A part of him had been content to simply proclaim that Christine was his wife and be done with it, but he knew such things were not traditional. And if his fiancée hesitated in believing that she was worthy of being a wife, then denying her a wedding would certainly be unacceptable.

The issue of course was that no priest would ever consider marrying him to any woman, let alone a young girl that was barely regarded as of marriageable age.

He had left her to primp and dress in whatever she saw fit. Perhaps if he allowed himself more time he would have desired to see her in the fashionable white arraignment that brides had begun to wear in order to showcase their purity. And while he would never impugn Christine's character, the sentiment did not seem truly fitting. They were not stylish creatures, and it seemed almost wrong to base anything upon the whims of a society that shunned them so completely.

And while Erik would not readily admit to *not* knowing something, he realised he knew very little about Scandinavian marriage customs. Just because a British queen decided to wear white on her wedding day, did that negate whatever Swedish traditions that Christine would been raised to observe?

But no matter. She would wear her best dress like all the brides of old, and he would provide the ring—had *already* provided the ring—as well as his promises of love and cherishment.

And perhaps she would not be too upset that while he could not provide a priest, he could grant a church.

He had wanted to depart that moment in order to see to the beginning of their marriage, but Christine had laughed at his enthusiasm and forced him to sit with her and read and sing at her leisure. The only reason Erik allowed her to utilise her feminine charms to keep him from planning was because he begrudgingly acknowledged that his schemes would best be contrived in the dark.

The fact that it felt so very nice to sit with her on the settee or listen to her voice after days of abstinence might also have been a factor, although Erik quickly dismissed it.

Christine had started a rather peculiar habit since he had given her permission to touch his withered flesh. Whenever he was seated closely enough, even when he had returned his shirtsleeves and jacket to rights, her little fingers would delve under the fabric on his wrist to stroke the tight cord of scars that encircled it. She had not asked why he had such a thing, and he had not offered to speak of their cause.

But as she continued to stroke and massage, he found that the pain of their memory began to be replaced with a tentative gratefulness for their existence—if their presence meant that Christine would willingly touch him in such a manner.

That afternoon she had been perfecting this small and admittedly distracting habit, and while he was entirely focused on the movement of her fingers, her thoughts seemed to be quite far from the action. "Erik, what month is it?"

Wary of its potential importance, he cautiously responded, "January."

"Oh." She was quiet for a minute and he wondered if she was upset by his answer. "Then I must amend my statement. I am sixteen."

Erik was not one for birthdays. He did not know his own and knew there was little to celebrate by the turning of yet another miserable year. But as he regarded the girl still stroking his wrist, he felt inextricably sad that she should have missed such a day. "I am very sorry you were not aware of your birthday, my dear. You shall have to tell your Erik of it next year so we might celebrate."

She smiled at him then and nestled further into his side. He would have thought that the end of her sudden melancholy, but then she whispered and his heart nearly broke. "If I cannot have my papa to celebrate my birthday with, then I would rather have you than any other person in the world."

Perhaps he should have been offended that her heart belonged more to a dead man than to the man she had agreed to marry, but in that moment he only knew that she preferred *him* to anyone else. She *chose* him and now he would get to keep her for the rest of their mortal lives.

After that he was happy to simply hold her until she grew hungry and they were forced to go to the kitchens in search of supper.

Now, as he quickly moored the boat and hurried up the steps to his front door, he could not stem his excitement. Christine was not awaiting him in the sitting room, nor was she indulging herself in the kitchen by stealing biscuits from her tin. His mission demanded their prompt departure, and with that in mind he knocked firmly at her door—and although he should not even entertain such thoughts, suddenly wondered if after tonight it would remain *her* door. Could it possibly become *theirs?*

Any such wonderings left his mind when she opened the obstruction.

It was a dress he had never seen. Admittedly he was not well studied in women's fashion but he thought it a day dress—yet it was of a finer cut and quality than any of her previous garments. It was the softest shade of pink that merely highlighted her own feminine colouring. And though he did not know what she possibly could have used as he had provided her with so little, she had managed to tie up her hair in a becoming style befitting a bride.

Christine smiled at him timidly, and he was baffled by her bashfulness. "Will I do?"

His mouth was dry and for a moment he was simply overwhelmed that this beauty before him in less than an hour would be his *wife.*

"You will do perfectly, *mon ange*."

He could not bring himself to ask her the same question.

But Christine seemed not to care as she tucked her hand in his and smiled up at him, all traces of shyness a thing of the past. "I think you will do quite nicely too."

Thank God.

Erik cleared his throat awkwardly, and after quickly retrieving her cloak from his wardrobe. Once again he noted that he should either have to provide her a cloak of her own or hem this one so it would be saved from ruin. But he quickly dismissed such menial concerns, and focused instead on escorting her above.

It amazed him how closely she liked to keep to his side when they walked, and he relished the knowledge that she earnestly believed that he would protect her from all dangers.

Of course, he *had* given her ample evidence of his capability, as the very day they met had ended with the death of one of her abusers. But Erik decided not to dwell on such things.

Not on his wedding day.

The snow was falling softly and had he not been keeping a careful watch to ensure that no one waylaid them while they walked, Erik would have thought it quite beautiful. But he had someone to protect, and he would not allow harm to befall her simply because he was distracted by snow flurries.

However, it pleased him that Christine seemed able to do so, as she often lifted up her face and sighed as snowflakes would melt against her skin.

That was far more distracting than any nighttime snow scene, no matter how picturesque.

The walk was not very far, and soon he was ushering her through the heavy wooden door of the chapel which shut behind them with a loud thud.

Christine looked positively enraptured at the sight of the sanctuary glowing warmly in the candlelight, but after a moment he noticed that she was looking expectantly toward the direction of the rectory. "Should not the priest be coming soon?"

Erik sighed and grasping her hand softly in his, he led her before the altar.

The priest would most certainly *not* be coming, as a certain carefully placed drug was ensuring that he would sleep peacefully until morning, regardless of any late night visitors making use of his chapel. He would never be the wiser as he had not noticed the dark figure that had skulked into his room with a small dose of sleeping powder. If anything, Erik reasoned that he would be even more refreshed the next morning—though Erik begrudgingly admitted to himself that such reasoning might only have been a rather feeble attempt to assuage his guilt for having unwittingly dosed a man of God.

But Christine did not need to know such things. She simply needed to understand that someone willingly marrying them was not a viable option.

"*Mon ange*," It was only the second time he had used the endearment and from the way her eyes softened whenever he used it, he rather thought it would become his favourite. "I promise you that we will be married in the eyes of God, but certain limitations regarding my physical appearance," and lack of any true legal entity, he added silently to himself, "would keep us from being married by a priest. But that makes our vows no less important or binding. Is this acceptable to you?"

Christine looked hesitant for a moment, casting her eyes about the room once more before closing them tightly and bowing her head. He allowed her the time to think—and he assumed from her posture, pray— trying to quell his rising panic that she would demand there be witnesses and a priest to bless them and make the traditional pronouncement. To his great joy and delight however, she raised her head and practically beamed at him, squeezing his hand tightly. "This would be perfect." She nibbled her lip for a moment before adding quietly and almost to herself, "Adam and Eve did not need a priest."

Erik chuckled then, more from relief than amusement, and drew Christine so that she was facing him completely. He dropped her hands only long enough to remove his leather gloves, suddenly finding it terribly important that their skin be touching as they recited their vows.

He had never been to a wedding. He had attended Mass on occasion, but only when the music beckoned to him so enticingly as the pipe organ rang clear and true into the air. And even then, he would remain carefully positioned where no one could see him, and never had participated in the actual service.

And for the first time he realised just how important it was to *him* that he be bound to Christine by a covenant of God. Erik's birth had not been blessed, as his face was evidence of that. But if setting aside his anger and disbelief should somehow ensure that his marriage was consecrated from the beginning, Erik would gladly do so.

While learned in many things, Erik could not readily say that he knew the wedding vows by heart. So instead, he merely looked at Christine and recited what he knew were the most important words that she needed to hear. "I, Erik, take *you*, Christine, to be my living wife. I promise you my protection, to be faithful to you in all things, and to love you to the very best of my ability."

He should have said more—promised her the world and all of her heart's desires—but as he looked at her eyes welling with tears and happiness, he found that his throat had constricted too much for more words to be spoken.

And had both his hands not been occupied with Christine's, he would have given himself a small pinch just to ensure he was not dreaming.

When it was evident that he could not continue, Christine opened her mouth but quickly closed it again. "I... I do not know what to say!"

He meant to be encouraging and tell her he did not mind if she could not make him any promises, but before he could she straightened her shoulders and looked at him steadily. "I, Christine, take you, Erik, to be my husband. I promise that I will care for you, and be faithful to you, and..." Her words stuttered slightly and he braced himself for having to be contented with whatever word she substituted with the one he most desperately wished to hear, but she continued. "And I promise to *love* you to the best of my abilities, for as long I live."

And whatever control Erik had on his emotions broke with her sentiments, and he cried. He was comforted that Christine was crying as well. And soon he had pulled her into his embrace, knowing within his very soul that they were bound together in marriage.

It was quite some time before he found the will to pull back from her, but before he could fully extract himself from her arms Christine shifted her head from his chest in order to look up at him. "Are we not supposed to seal our marriage with a kiss?"

Erik simply gaped at her. She had suggested that she wanted a *proper* marriage, but faced with the prospect of physical signs of affection beyond embraces and holding hands, Erik felt wholly unprepared.

He had taken too long to react as her eyes began to shutter and *she* was pulling away, and he knew precisely what she was thinking.

He did not think her worthy.

Never was there a more insipid idea, so he yanked at her—*his*—cloak firmly, and brought her back into his arms. "My own mother never kissed me, Christine. You need not feel obligated."

She stared at him for a long moment, and slowly, *so* slowly, she raised her hand to his face. He would stop her if she tried to remove it completely, but she only skimmed his lip with her finger as her eyes held such compassion it nearly sent him reeling. "Then your mother was a stupid woman."

And then she was standing on her tip toes and her arms were around his neck as she pulled him closer, and with the softest touch he had ever known, her lips skimmed across his.

He had never known such joy.

She pulled away far too quickly, before he had even a chance to reciprocate the subtle pressure of lips. At first he felt a clench of fear that she was somehow repulsed by the action, yet he felt comforted when he noticed the crimson blush upon her cheeks as she look up at him shyly from beneath her lashes. "Was that all right?"

Erik did not know what came over him. He should have offered her words of comfort and adoration—that *anything* she chose to do to his person would be more than he had ever expected. But instead he found his hands tangled in her blessed hair, and his mouth was descending on hers before he had time to contemplate the consequences.

Her mouth was warm and pliant, and so wonderful he felt breathless. Belatedly he noticed the wetness—not from her mouth, but from the tears that mingled between their lips as they kissed.

As man and wife.

He pulled away from her abruptly, suddenly terrified that he had been too forceful in his exuberance and that he had inadvertently reminded her of all too painful memories.

She was breathing heavily and her eyes were nearly burning with intensity, but he could not detect fear in their depths. And when she caught him looking and her answering smile was so very bright and cheerful, he felt his fear begin to dissipate.

"Was that all right?" he mimicked.

Christine laughed and burrowed her way into his cloak with him, wrapping her arms around his waist once more. "More than all right. You make me feel..."

Oh how desperately he wanted to know how he made her feel. The way she was acting he knew that it must only be pleasant things, and the idea of her giving voice to the notion that *he* could make her feel the same throbbing tingles that travelled through his own veins was a heavenly torment.

His allowed his hand to push away a few of her curls that he had disrupted from their *chignon* with his enthusiasm, and tilted her face so he could look at her. "How do I make you feel?" He knew his eyes were pleading as he found that he *needed* to know, to hear it confirmed that she felt even a semblance of what he did.

"You make me feel like a wife. So many times I have felt..." Her eyes darted around the church suddenly, and she stopped. "Maybe I should not speak of it here."

Erik brushed his fingertips across her cheekbone, and he wondered if he would ever get used to the softness of her—his *wife.* "Where better to speak your thoughts and feelings?" He leaned down so he could whisper in her ear. "Tell your husband so he might know you better, Christine."

She shuddered, and tucked her head against his chest. "So often I have felt like a whore. Men wanted me, men took me and I did not have a choice." Christine sniffled, and vaguely Erik wondered if she was getting tears and other fluids on his coat. "I just wanted someone to love me for being *me*. To know everything that had happened and still...want me. But as a *wife*, not as just a..." She shrugged, and Erik held her more firmly.

He kissed the top of her head, and for a brief moment he wished that he could simply bury his naked face into her hair and live there forever.

Maybe in time...

But this was not the time for such thoughts. His wife had admitted something important, and it was his responsibility as a husband to assuage any such thoughts. His thumb began rubbing soothing circles into her back and he made sure his voice was soft as he answered her. "*Mon ange,* you are a gift. A gift from *God,* and I will treasure you for all of my days." It felt odd to recognise God so openly, but the longer he held Christine and felt her warmth seep into his cold and withered body, he knew that his words were true. He was thankful, so *incredibly* thankful that she had been given to him.

And he got to keep her.

Perhaps he could never confess to a priest as was the most traditional form of absolution, but even now he could not see the importance. If God was an all knowing being, giving voice to his sins to an elderly man of the cloth would only complicate matters, making the priest aware of things that would only cause trouble for Erik and his new wife. This was his business, and his repentance and gratitude would remain between him and his God.

Christine spoke so quietly he almost could not hear her, but her murmurs warmed his heart all the same. "I am still getting to know you, Erik, but I think I already love you... in my own little way."

And when he felt as though his heart would burst from the sheer outpouring of joy he felt, she added, "And I will learn to love you as a wife should love her husband, if you will be patient with me."

She was willing to *try.* While he knew they both needed more time to acclimate to one another, and there would be struggles and hardships and his temper would flair and her demons would haunt her, they would face such obstacles *together.*

Because they both were willing to *try.*

He found that words were inadequate to communicate just how much he loved the girl in his arms, so he only held her tightly, more than happy to remain in their cocoon of his cloaks for as long as possible.

But then when she whispered, "Take me home, Erik," he realised that perhaps home was the best place for them to be.

And he suddenly wondered precisely what their wedding night would contain.

XVII

There was only one more small detail that Erik felt was necessary to complete before they vacated the chapel. It was perhaps a ridiculous thing to do as they did not belong to the parish, nor did either of them pose as any serious legal persons, but he still felt that he should bind himself to Christine in every possible way available.

So with that in mind, he led her over to the large church registry that served as the record for all sanctioned marriages, and taking the fountain pen beside the large and ancient looking book, added his name with his childish scrawl. He knew he should have worked more diligently at perfecting his lettering, but he found little need. Erik could always read his own writing, and it was legible enough for the managerial fools at the Opera, so it seemed almost a waste of time to dedicate hours to his penmanship.

On this particular occasion he was rather glad for his lack of finesse, as while his first name was clear—if admittedly spidery—his last name was all but obscured. Erik had no family name to ascribe to, and while he would have enjoyed giving Christine a name for them to share, they could discuss the matter at a later date.

When Christine smiled at him and took the pen and signed her own name, he realised just how silly he had been to never have enquired as to her last name. Perhaps it was simply because he did not have one of his own, but seeing *Christine Daaé* written so clearly on the page served as a vivid reminder of just how much more he had to know about his new bride.

And when he took her hand in his and they began the walk back to their home, he was quite content to spend the rest of his existence getting to know these minute details that would only further their bond. *He* would know more about her than any other living person. Not some sweetheart in her childhood, but *him.* Her husband.

Erik did not think he had ever walked so cheerfully.

When they passed a few obviously intoxicated men, Erik remembered his responsibility and sobered immediately. They were in no true danger as they were both enshrouded in his black cloaks and Christine's head was nearly entirely obscured as she had her head tucked against his arm as was her favourite way to walk with him. But their drunken laughter served as an important reminder that he was all that stood between his wife and more horrors, and while he still appreciated Christine's presence—*and* her softness as his arm wrapped around her waist—he remained mindful and watchful. And he kept his other hand placed on his lasso, at the ready for any individuals who dared stray too close.

But their walk went unmolested, and soon Erik was lighting the lantern so that his wife's journey would be all the more comfortable as they descended to their home. He had not realised how tense she had grown, but as soon as the door was shut behind them and they were once more within his tunnels, he felt her relax noticeably. "I am glad you do not drink too much."

Erik turned to her. "I would not imbibe at all if it made you so uncomfortable. You should have said something." He grimaced slightly even as he offered, as there were few pleasures in which he indulged, and a glass of wine or port was most certainly one of them. But if it made Christine more secure that she was safe with him, he would never allow another drop of alcohol to pass his lips.

To his great relief she shook her head. "I did not say anything because you never became violent or ornery. Well, no more ornery than usual." She giggled softly, even as she tried to quiet the sound of it with her hand.

Erik stopped and turned to her, an eyebrow raised in question although he knew she could not see it. "Oh? You find your poor husband to be an ornery fellow who is impossible to please?"

His wife had the audacity to *grin* at him. "No, not impossible. Just very, very difficult, Maestro."

He scoffed openly but continued walking. "If you would simply obey your teacher and ceased your overindulgence in sweets, perhaps you would not have to work so hard to produce the required tone."

Now the insolent chit was the one scoffing. "I believe it is *you* who are the one always plying me with sugary confections too delightful to resist. So if anything you are merely enabling my 'overindulgence'!"

Erik sniffed but made no reply. For while he might protest, he knew it was true.

However, that did not mean he had to admit it—not to his cheeky slip of a wife that he happened to adore with all his heart.

But she seemed to have thought she won their little tiff already for she snuggled all the closer, and he felt a shudder run through him when he felt her place a soft kiss to the middle of his chest. "I love you for your baking."

Erik supposed he should be insulted, but instead he merely leaned down and pressed a kiss onto her curls. "I love you for your hair."

She stared up at him in disbelief. "You do? It is so... troublesome." She raised a hand to it self-consciously, tugging at the tendrils that were already demanding freedom.

He batted her hand away gently, patting where she had ill-treated in commiseration. "You are a foolish girl for thinking so." And while he had not meant for it to sound so petulant, he added, "If you were having so much trouble with it, you should have asked me to tend to it."

Never did he think he would willingly offer his services as a lady's maid, but with Christine he found that there was a tremendous pleasure in caring for her hair.

And if it made her appreciate her beauty all the more, then that was an added inducement.

Erik did not know what to expect when they entered their home. While his mind fought to add expectations of consummation and true wedding nights, he knew that to voice or act upon any such notions would lead to disaster. Just because his wonderful little wife was willing to kiss him did not mean she was prepared for any further relations.

Though he tried to prevent such thoughts from entering his mind for any duration, Erik had to admit that it would only be to Christine's detriment if he was unmindful of her past. He could not push her, and while he so desperately wished to communicate his love through touch and action, it would only be at his wife's express bidding that he did so.

But with a grimace he also acknowledged that with her innocence and beguiling naïveté, she might never gather the courage to instigate such proceedings.

Christine stood before the fire, warming her hands on the newly stoked flames, and he could readily see her thoughtful expression as she watched the flickering dance of power and energy. Perhaps it was better to leave her to her thoughts. But as was becoming common for him when it came to her, words escaped before his mind could process the potential consequences. "What are you thinking about?"

She seemed startled by his enquiry, but answered him all the same. "I am wondering what happens now."

If there was one thing Erik knew, it was that he had to tread very carefully so as not to frighten her. "If you are referring to our long term routine, we will resume your lessons and your husband will continue to be held in eternal servitude as your personal baker."

He was rewarded with a smile, but it was apparent that was not the *now* of which she questioned. "If you are speaking of our current doings..." He waited for her confirmation as he felt awkward and uncomfortable. If she did not need him to explicitly state his intention for their current happenings, he would gladly refrain.

But she looked at him so keenly that he knew she indeed wished for him to speak of his expectations.

He sighed.

Troublesome wife.

But she was his, and he would assuage her fears however he could, even if it meant being slightly discomfited. "I will be a husband to you in whatever way you need, Christine. While I am sure you know of my... *desire* for you," he paused, and watched her give a hesitant nod. It was not as if he had been overly subtle that he found her comely and appealing. "That does not mean that you must deny your own needs. If all you require is a cup of hot chocolate and a comfortable bed for sleeping, then that is the night you shall have."

He had meant the words as a soothing reminder that their marriage was based solely on what the other needed, not on any undo pressures and commands by societal influence and tradition. He felt quite dismayed when instead of smiling at him and retiring to the kitchen to sit on the counter as she watched him prepare their evening treat, her eyes instead welled with tears.

"What if that is not what I require? What if... what if I want to *try?*"

Erik froze. While of course that was what he wished—to know that she wanted to at least make an attempt at being together in such a way, he had never truly allowed himself the pleasure of imagining the prospect. But hearing the words from her lips and seeing how unsure and delicate she was in this moment, he realised with startling clarity that he could not afford to be the one plagued by demons. She had enough of her own and it was his responsibility to help her fight them, not force her to assuage his in addition.

So tramping down his doubts and his ingrained fear that at any moment she would bolt and scream in horror at the man she had just married, he instead went to her side.

He would remember that if she showed fear it was because of her past experiences, not because of him.

He would remember that she was just as new and inexperienced in the art of making love as he was.

And he prayed to God that he would be able to keep that promise to himself to *remember* once they were engaged in whatever acts she would permit.

"Christine..." He did not have to say more than her name before she was burrowing into his side, and he noticed with amusement that neither of them had removed his cloaks yet so they were all a swathe of black and cashmere—and with his wife positioned so, Erik thought an outsider would have difficulty determining where he ended and she began.

His hand began plucking pins from her hair, freeing it from its confines with relish. For each pin he removed he allowed his hand to massage her scalp, imagining that having such harsh ornaments tugging at such fine hairs would not be overly pleasant.

By the sounds his wife was making, his ministrations were very effective. He stooped over her, marvelling once more at just how petite Christine was in comparison to him, and leaned down to whisper in her ear. "What is it that you desire?"

If she said that she somehow desired *his* body in the same way that he longed for hers, he would know she had once more slipped into her ridiculous notions. He was no angel and he most *certainly* was not anything worth yearning for.

But instead she shuddered, and with heavy eyes she tilted her face to look into his. "I want to be a *wife.* I want to know the touch of a husband who loves me, and not..." Her face bloomed with colour, and although he half expected her eyes to continue overflowing with tears, they instead grew resolute. "I want to know how it *should* be, not simply be haunted by memories of how it should not."

That he could understand.

Ever since she had blessed him with her presence, his memories of horror and blood had softened. They were not gone—no, his dreams were just as poignant as they had ever been—but when he awoke he no longer had to face the harsh reality that nothing had truly improved. He was his own master now, performing only the tasks he found appealing, but that did not mean that he was *happy.*

Only Christine had provided that.

And if it was at all within his power, he would ensure she received the same. But he also knew a moment's hesitation, that within a simple word she could take it all away. "Please do not tempt your Erik if you do not mean it." He did intend for it to sound so much like a plea, but he realised just how much it would hurt if she rescinded her words. He would *never* hurt her, but he knew that if she mocked or spurned him once their seduction began, he was likely to lose his temper due to the rejection.

And he felt quite ill at the thought.

She did not answer him and he began the painful process of distancing his heart from her, no matter how loath he was to do so. It was the most precious gift to connect with her, and he did not *like* when her silences had the potential to wound.

But then he felt delicate fingers plucking at his collar.

It took every bit of self-control he possessed in order to keep from seizing her fingers and demanding to know her purpose. Surely she could feel how anxious he was beneath her hands, and when his collar and shirt buttons were opened—but only the first three—and when he felt the delightfully warm softness of her mouth press a kiss onto his chest, the tension he had known all but melted away.

His brave wife.

She had suffered through so much yet she was still determined to overcome her fears. And if he could feel such bliss from a simple brush of her lips, Erik grew all the more determined to set aside his cowardice and ensure that his rose—his *ange*—received her due.

But before he could reciprocate or even find the will and ability to move, Christine pulled slightly away. "Would you mind playing something first? I am a little nervous..." All Erik could think about was that there was a *first*. A *first* indicated that there would be something later to come. Belatedly, he realised that she had asked for something before the *first*. Her tone was regretful, and he almost reassured her that she was not alone in her anxiety. But before he could do so she continued, "Also, it seems wrong that there was no music to christen our wedding."

Erik blinked rather stupidly, trying to remember how to think let alone recall the functions necessary to play a wedding requiem worthy of his new bride.

She was fiddling with her fingers, looking the perfect picture of bridal innocence that sent many a bridegroom running to the bedroom, new wife firmly in hand. But Christine wanted a song and a moment to collect herself, and he would oblige—even if he felt as though his mouth was full of cotton and his blood had grown uncomfortably warm.

He wanted to kiss her again—was in truth nearly desperate for it—but he thought that would only worsen his condition.

Erik went over to the organ; more to distance himself physically from Christine than any desire to play it. But then he felt his wife settle herself on the seat beside him and she looked at him so expectantly, and he found that his fingers moved at her whim instead of his own.

He believed that his very soul was the one playing, not he. The notes appeared of their own volition and he knew that he was entirely lost in the rapture Christine had inspired, both physical and transcendental. It was joy and it was sorrow, and while he could feel the overwhelming nature of the music, he could not stop it. The longing and the yearning were nearly tangible in the air and he almost wept for it but then...

Then Christine rested her head upon his shoulder.

Erik did not think he had ever played something so sweet. His blood cooled and he thought that he would be quite contented just to live in that moment for the rest of his existence—only if it meant Christine would continue to be with him as she was now.

Eventually however his fingers stilled, and when the final note rang out long and clear in their home well beneath the surface of earth and the bumbling world above, they remained quiet even longer.

Neither moved nor spoke, and Erik wondered which of them would be the first to break the now poignant silence. To move meant that they would be travelling to the bedroom, and it would require courage—courage that he promised himself he would at least pretend to have so that Christine would not bear the full brunt of responsibility for tonight's endeavours.

He rose slowly, so as not to startle Christine at his movement. And though his first thought was to reach for her hand and draw her into her bedchamber, he felt a moment of pure whimsical need to tend to ancient tradition.

She looked at him in both wariness and amusement as he knelt down, and with slightly trembling arms, scooped her into his embrace.

Christine was far too light even now with all her meals and treats, and he knew that it would take much more of his attention and care to ensure she was of a healthy physicality.

But as he walked them over the threshold and he placed her down onto the bedstead—the very bed he had found himself thinking about as he laid in his own coffin—he suddenly wondered just what Christine looked like without her dress.

And while his first impulse was to banish any such lascivious thoughts from his mind, he realised that the girl—the *woman*—laid out upon the bed who looked at him with such nervous excitement was now his *wife,* and it was his right as a husband—his *duty* as a husband—to see that she was properly sated.

So with brave yet slightly quivering fingers, he moved her hair back from where it had shifted to cover her décolleté and mimicked her previous action—he released the top three closures of her bodice.

And they both gasped when her flesh was revealed.

XVIII

Their mutual reaction was born more of the affinity of the action than by what was exposed. There were scars, some red and puckered, others nearly matching the pale skin of her throat. But what drew his attention most was the subtle swell that only barely peeked from beneath the neckline of her chemise.

His breath was short and he found that it took great effort to tear his eyes from the sight of what *could* be exposed. But he did so, needing to look to his wife for permission. Her lip was firmly held between her teeth, and had his fingers not been holding tightly to the coverlet to ensure he did not begin unhooking more clasps before her acquiescence, he would have released it with a nudge of his thumb.

To his great relief she gave a small nod of agreement for whatever he planned to do next.

He held her gaze as he slowly lowered his head, pressing his dry lips to the skin of her décolleté, marvelling at the softness as well as the quivering sigh Christine emitted.

Erik froze, knowing that he should quickly remove himself from his position above her, but he allowed himself a moment to revel in the sheer intimacy of the moment. This was his wife beneath him, and she had not screamed or begged for him to stop—she had *sighed.* And from her expression it was one of surprised wonderment.

"You... you may continue." Her voice was breathy and uneven, and he felt comforted in knowing he was not alone in his nervousness. He pressed another kiss to her throat while his fingers made short work of her bodice, releasing each hook with tremendous satisfaction.

Of course, Erik was not wholly aware of the nature of women's undergarments, but he found that while he had appreciated and despised Christine's chemises in equal measure in the past due to their ability to both cover and expose, he now found the article quite annoying. Ideally, her bodice would be opened and he would be graced with his first view of her womanly endowments, but instead there was yet another barrier.

He wanted to *feel* her.

Erik stopped suddenly.

Impatience would get him nowhere. He had to be slow and he had to be mindful. His own pleasure could never be at the cost of Christine's, and she required more careful and thoughtful tending if he was to please her.

So with that in mind he quieted his impulse to simply tear into the impediment, and instead, oh so slowly, undid the small blue ribbon that held the neckline together. His fingers skimmed the tops of her breasts as he did so, and he was awed at the way her skin prickled and she shivered when the ends of the bow tickled her flesh.

It did not take much coaxing before the drawstring gave way, leaving voluminous material that could easily be manipulated to his will—or more specifically, pulled aside to reveal what he had so longed to encounter.

While her body had seemed quite underdeveloped when he had first stumbled upon her, it was obvious now that her tattered garments had hid the most beautiful of sights. Her breasts were pale and round, and as he regarded his wife, he found her more lovely than anything he had seen previously. The magnificence of the Opera House paled in comparison to her smoothness, and as he allowed a lone fingertip to touch the rosebud tips and heard her gasp at his boldness, he knew that he was the most fortunate of men.

Others might have tried to pluck her by force, but he was the one who received her freely and willingly.

And that moved him more than he could say.

He bent his head once more, intent on showering her exquisiteness in his adoration when he felt gentle hands at his shoulders, giving him pause. "Should we not... undress?"

Erik was at a loss of how to explain that while he would like nothing more than to have *her* undressed, the idea of disrobing in front of another was not something he found appealing. He was a private man and his body was nothing that would inspire her desire. But it somehow felt one sided to expect her to lie prone and naked while he remained perfectly dressed and dignified.

This was just as much about trust as it was about pleasure.

And she had been the one to undo his collar and shirt buttons, not he. If she had wanted him to remain fully clothed and shrouded as he would have assumed, surely she would not have done so—he never would have required it of her.

His first impulse was to darken the light, as he knew that it would diminish his view and appreciation of his wife only a little. But that also seemed unfair to Christine, as she had expressed her dislike of the darkness on many occasions.

Or conceivably he should not simply think such questions, but pose them to the one who was quite capable of answering for herself.

"Would you like me to douse the light? I promise I will protect you from whatever prowls in the shadows." He tried to keep his voice neutral so that she could not infer his preference. This was about her comfort, not his own—even as the idea of her seeing him fully nude sent him nearly fleeing from the room.

She blushed and looked to the lamp, considering it carefully. "Maybe you could dim it a little, but please do not put it out completely."

Erik sighed, though he steadfastly refused to be disappointed by her response. Having any light at all was not ideal, but he would merely have to settle for having less of it. She had already seen him with his shirtsleeves rolled up to the elbows, and the only consequence from that experience was that she now liked to touch his scars whenever possible.

Perhaps undressing when she could see him was not such a terrible idea after all.

He made no comment, yet he was rather despondent when Christine sat up from her reclining position so that she could shimmy out of her bodice and skirt, leaving nothing but her unmentionables—which in Erik's opinion were still far too many clothes. He wondered at other men whose wives also utilised corsets—yet another obstacle that would take far too much time to pluck and untie and manipulate until the bare skin was revealed.

His Christine did not need such contraptions in order to look pleasing to the eye.

Erik's attire was far less complicated, and while Christine had simply thrown her outer garments into a small pile on the floor, he carefully folded each of his, placing them safely on the sofa before turning back to his bride. He had left his trousers firmly in place, feeling that he was at the end of both his courage and his self-control.

Christine was trying to find a way to modestly release her garters and stockings without also removing her pantalettes, and all while trying to keep her shift from creeping up her legs. Erik was not entirely sure of the precise reason, but he found that her hands skimming up her legs and disappearing underneath her chemise to be strangely fascinating.

And distracting.

And arousing.

With a gentle grip, he wrapped his hand around her ankle, pulling it down flat against the bed. Suddenly wishing he had dedicated further study to the theory of lady's undergarments, Erik supposed that now was as good a time as any to become well trained in their removal through practical application.

Bows seemed to be the main source of closure. Blue bows if he was paying attention, and although he found that each small knot was fascinating in its own right, he was far more interested in the action of untying. His hands travelled into unknown depths hidden by her chemise, up towards his wife's most secret places and down towards her delicate feet.

Feet that he had seen naked, and would soon see again.

The pantalettes were moved first. They were a simple button at her waist, and while he would have been happy to have witnessed what was uncovered by its removal, Christine in all her shyness made sure to keep her shift covering her most personal bits.

Later.

Since she did not care that her day things were in a crumpled pile, with a casual toss of white linen they too met their fate upon the floor, and Erik's hands searched underneath the limpid fabric once more as he sought the ties of her garter.

It took nearly all of his concentration to focus on remembering how to untie something so simple, as he was nearly overcome with the knowledge that he was currently touching his wife's thighs. His task accomplished on the right he proceeded to the left, his hands shaking as he did so. Erik's fingers were trembling and he feared for his discipline until he felt the raised pucker of scar tissue that served as a vivid reminder of when he had last been exposed to this particular part of her anatomy. He rubbed it tenderly with his thumb, looking at her face for any discomfort.

She smiled at him sadly but showed little sign of pain. "You took such good care of me, Erik, and I know you will do so now." Her voice was muted, but her words filled him with such warmth he thought he might burst.

The only thing left was her chemise and her stockings, and he took each leg of silk and slid it down carefully. He would not be one of those brutish husbands that harmed any article of her clothing through his eager behaviour, and from the way her eyes burned as she watched him slowly roll down each leg and his finger skimmed her pale skin that was exposed in its wake, he knew that his ministrations were to her liking.

Finally his fingers fiddled with the bottom of her shift. "Christine..." He would not ask it of her. If she would be more comfortable with a covering he would of course allow it, but he felt nearly desperate to see her naked and wanting upon the bedclothes.

His wife—all perfection and beauty waiting for *him.*

She hesitated for a long moment, regarding him with a careful expression. He remained still as he reminded himself of his silent promise to be patient, and to his great delight with a shuddering breath she raised herself up and added her final garment to her growing pile of clothes.

Christine covered her breasts immediately with her hands and looked distinctly uncomfortable. While Erik found that his eyes were trying to absorb every expanse of flesh available to their view, he found that her distress was quite discomfiting. He would not like it if she had stripped him naked and asked him to lie upon the bed while she took her fill. Perhaps when their trust had deepened—when intimacy had become more familiar they would be able to be so open, but not now.

Now they could explore, but there was still shyness and awkwardness that spoke of their mutual inexperience.

So with a gentle smile, he pulled back the bedclothes and she dove under them gratefully. With her most private places covered she began to relax, and to his great pleasure she eventually took a bracing breath and pulled down the blanket, allowing him a very great view of the attributes he now so favoured.

"May I join you?"

It was her turn to smile in encouragement and she lifted the very corner of the bedding in invitation. "A husband need not ask." Her eyes belied her words, and he knew that she was thankful that he was providing her opportunities to refuse—even if she had not yet needed him to cease any of his actions.

With a shuddering breath and the last remnants of his courage, Erik fiddled with the button of his trousers and allowed them to drop to the floor.

Erik did not think he had ever hidden beneath the covers as quickly as he managed on his wedding night. It took him a moment to compose himself once he was once again hidden, and his breathing was ragged. He had tried to be quick but he had noticed that her eyes strayed *below* even though he had wished they had not.

In *that* regard he was a normal man, just as any other. He was aroused, ready and needy for womanly attention, but he tried most valiantly not to think of it.

His wife needed tending first.

But he found that he was trembling and was afraid to look at her, and he was quite startled when he felt a small hand rest upon his shoulder. "Erik, please look at me."

He shook his head resolutely, although he knew he did not need to fear his Christine. She had married him, and she would not do so merely to spurn him now.

She cuddled closer, and it sent shivers through his entire body at how different it felt now that they were both unclothed.

They were both lying on their backs, though Christine was trying to stealthily roll onto her side so that she could face him. What she obviously had not considered was the fact that her breasts were now pressed quite thoroughly against his arm.

He shivered.

Her fingers were tracing patterns on his chest, and he vaguely noticed she was smoothing over each of the scars that littered his own yellowed flesh.

He wanted her to stop.

He wanted her to continue.

But mostly, he just wanted to cry.

This was too much for him. He had been so concerned with ensuring that Christine was comfortable and unafraid that he had neglected to realise how vulnerable he would feel. He had wrongfully assumed that just because he loved her, it would mean that his insecurities would somehow have also vanished—that when she allowed his touch it would make him bold and passionate, when instead he was hesitant and fumbling.

She deserved a lover of the highest calibre, and that was anything but him.

Christine was touching his face, and before he could stop his hand it was gripping her small wrist. Not harshly, as he possessed enough of his faculties to remember that she would not wish him harm, but it was firm enough to stop her in case she tried to remove his mask.

"Husband..."

He did look at her then, for truly, how could he not? Her voice was soft and coaxing, and when he regarded her he noticed the slight smile that played at her lips. "There you are. I thought you had left me."

"Never," he rasped.

She traced his lips with her thumb, and his grip on her wrist loosened and drifted to cover her hand with his as he moved it so that she cupped his face. "I love you for your shyness."

He smiled at her ruefully; embarrassed that she should be burdened with the likes of him. "I love you for your patience."

She laughed then, and he knew it was not mocking as the sound was joyous and soothed some of his mortification. "Papa never thought me very patient! And I do not think you do either, as you have chastised me many times for complaining about how long it takes for scones to bake." She pulled herself even closer on top of him, her breasts now pressing deliciously against his chest as she leaned over to bestow his lips with a kiss. "But I thank you for the compliment."

Christine seemed content to remain reclining over him, but now that the initial shock and discomfort of being seen completely bare was beginning to abate, his attention once more turned to the currently nude body of his wife.

He cleared his throat awkwardly, unsure of how to reinitiate his investigation of her person after his little display of shame had sullied the mood. "May I continue?" he asked rather clumsily.

She pressed a kiss to the hollow of his throat, her fingers tracing his wrist as was her wont. "Oh yes..." Her voice was breathy, and he added that to one of his most treasured memories. He was the only one to hear her voice in such a way, as it was laced with insinuations of *more* that was rapidly reheating his blood.

Christine rolled onto her back but her gaze was expectant as she obviously intended for him to follow. Even though his mouth was dry and his hands were shaky, Erik obliged.

It felt rather rude to simply insinuate himself between her thighs and he did not think he could handle the excitement of being in such a position. So he remained at her side and ran his fingertips over her smooth skin, still wondering at the texture. Every so often he would feel the bump of a scar, and upon discovering the evidence her fortitude, he would lean down to place a kiss upon the mark.

And each time he was rewarded with a sharp intake of breath from Christine.

Eventually he found himself mesmerised by the rosebud tips of her breasts and slowly, with ample time for her to object if she found the action to not be to her liking, Erik placed a single kiss on her nipple.

Nothing could have prepared him for the soft moan that escaped his wife. It was similar to the ones he would earn when he provided her with pastries and other delicacies, but to know that he could cause such a reaction from simply his touch—from his *kiss*—sent him reeling.

He placed another and another, and soon Christine was squirming slightly against him. "Erik, please..."

Erik knew that women possessed the ability for pleasure from conjugation, and though he feared this next action more than any other, he knew it was an important step toward providing her fulfilment.

He kept his gaze focused solely on her eyes as he allowed one spindly hand to creep to her inner thigh, acclimating her to his touch as he rubbed slow circles into her skin until finally, almost in invitation, she parted her legs ever so slightly.

Erik drew a deep breath and waited.

Her eyes flickered open, and when she smiled at him in encouragement—although even he could see her slight trepidation—he knew what had to be done. He would show her that she had nothing to fear from his touch—that he was dedicated to her enjoyment. And that could only be accomplished through his courageousness.

She was perfection itself.

She was warm and slick and oh so *very* soft.

Each touch elicited either a sigh or a gasp, and when he found a particularly sensitive nub that seemed to be the source of greatest pleasure, he flushed with pride as she whimpered his name—and from her expression it was clear that the sound had nothing to do with pain or fear.

Eventually she shuddered and though he kept his hand still gently coaxing reactions from her body, she stilled his hand as she encircled his wrist, pulling it from her pink flesh with an apologetic smile. "Too much, my husband."

Too much.

Which meant he had given her *enough.*

He did not need anything else. This was bliss itself, knowing that with his own inexperienced fingers he had found a way to please his wife and provide her what none other had sought to do.

Erik had rolled onto his back, content to simply lie beside her while she drifted off to slumber, so he was entirely unprepared when he felt a shy hand lightly skimmed his stomach before creeping down to touch him so familiarly.

His eyes flew shut.

The memory of her satisfaction was too vivid, and the feel of her hand as she merely held him so intimately was his undoing. When she gripped him ever so slightly he felt the brink of nirvana, and to his complete horror and degradation, he found himself releasing upon the bedclothes.

But his bliss overwhelmed such thoughts of mortification, and his mind grew fuzzy in the aftermath.

The only energy he found as he still quivered and shook from the outcome of her simple touch was to curl himself around her, clutching her to his side as he fell asleep.

XIX

Erik awoke some time later with a start.

He felt disoriented—the room too large and the shadows unfamiliar. He was sticky and uncomfortable and he felt warmer than usual, and there was something tickling his face.

The something turned out to be hair attached to a head that was pressed against his chest in slumber.

It was a peculiar sensation.

But the more his befuddled mind began to awaken, the more he began to recall of the night before. The girl in his arms was his wife, and he had *pleased* her. And to his absolute astonishment, she had in turn pleased him of her own accord. He had not coaxed or beguiled, but had been fully contented to simply allow her to rest after experiencing her own gratification. Yet she had seemed determined that he should feel something as well.

He blushed even recalling his reaction to her touch.

How was he to ever hope of consummating their marriage if a simple grip of her fingers could affect him in such a way? His own fingers now knew the warmth and delight to be found between his wife's lovely thighs, and the idea of being fully within her was enough to awaken his desire all the more.

But Christine deserved her rest, especially after he had fallen asleep so rudely.

He had not been able to offer her assurances or more promises of his love, but had felt so overwhelmed and unexpectedly exhausted that he had succumbed with little protest.

Erik knew he had much to apologise for.

He shifted slightly, trying to determine just how fully Christine was using him as her own personal chaise. Now that he was more cognisant of last night's happenings, he dearly wanted a bath. And he noted with a grimace, the sheets would also require laundering.

He would find it mortifying to deposit the bed linens for service by a poor unsuspecting laundress who would see evidence of his overexcitement. No, it would be far better to take care of it himself. And though he would most likely feel skittish while doing so in front of Christine, she had been forced to show him the personal evidence of her bodily functioning and he supposed it was only natural that he would eventually have to return the favour.

To his great relief, Christine mumbled in her sleep and shifted to the side, releasing him from most of her embrace. As soon as he had thought it however, he chastised himself thoroughly. Every one of her touches was a gift, and his comfort did not matter. If she wished to sleep on him for hours to come, he would have to be contended to be her bed pillow and simply watch her. And perhaps play with her curls. And catalogue and compose while he did so.

But for now he was released, and while he was unhappy that he could not also take the top sheet with him as he crept to the bath-room, he still took time enough to ensure that Christine was properly warmed in his sudden absence and that she had sufficient pillows now that his chest was no longer available.

Yet no matter how much he enjoyed her presence and her attentions, Erik was quite glad that she slept and he could escape the room unnoticed. It seemed a kindness that she would be spared the sight of him rushing from the room entirely naked, and as he heated the water for his bath and entered the tub with a sigh, he allowed himself to bask in the lingering euphoria—this time mingled with the heat and cleansing powers of hot water.

He should have thought to check the hour before he began bathing. Erik usually was quite good at judging the time, but last night's events seemed to have muddled his abilities. The idea that Christine could awaken any moment and require the facilities made him hurry, even as he wished to soak and linger. He had been forced to remove his mask before entering the bath, as it had been on too long already. Now afraid that Christine would see him in such a state, both naked *and* unmasked, he forced himself to scrub thoroughly. Even as he did so he found that, quite shockingly and unhelpfully, he had a fleeting wish that Christine was there to wash him clean.

He was being absolutely ridiculous.

Last night might have been an anomaly—a temporary madness on her part to allow him access to her bounty and to wish to touch him in turn.

He would not allow his expectations to inflate out of proportion.

Resolute, Erik emptied the bath and dried himself, donning the mask even before he had secured the towel around his waist.

He chuckled darkly at the realisation that he would rather risk the possibility of her seeing his genitals than his face.

With a touch of his fingers he opened the hidden door that connected with his own bedchamber, looking at the coffin with a scowl. He could not remember the last time he had slept in a real bed. And he wondered if in some shadowy corner of his madness he would have once thought it more befitting that he enlarge his coffin and insist his Christine join him in it, but he now found it merely morose.

He knew now what it was to feel *alive* and suddenly the thought of wallowing in death only depressed him more. He shook his head firmly and turned to his wardrobe, not much caring what he selected. Just so long as he was dressed and his mask was in place, he would be satisfied.

His task completed, Erik felt much more comfortable. While he would not feel fully at ease until he knew Christine's feelings and the linens she currently slept in were scoured thoroughly, he felt more like himself.

It was later than he had thought, and it surprised him greatly that he should have slept so late. He had not done so in what felt like decades. But then, he had never experienced anything like last night before, and perhaps a deep and dreamless slumber was the expected result of being *sated.*

He would very much like to experiment with such a notion further.

But he should not allow such thoughts until he had spoken to Christine—even if having that particular discussion made his stomach twist uncomfortably with nerves. It would ruin him if she awoke and was disgusted. Or, he felt the stab in his heart even thinking it, if she regretted it.

To dwell on such things would only worsen his mood, and that would benefit neither of them. His bride would be hungry, and he should see about making her something special for the occasion. This was the morning following their wedding after all, and today would set the tone for the entirety of their marriage.

Erik's anxiety grew.

His perfect little wife deserved a fine breakfast, which would also possibly negate any negative feelings she might have once she awoke.

A *very* fine breakfast, then.

He actually found himself to be hungry also, which meant he was able to also consider his own tastes in addition to Christine's. A curious response to last night's passions, but one he did not begrudge.

Omelettes.

Omelettes and muffins and thick slices of ham...

And tea. Sweetened tea for his wife because she was a lovely thing and deserved to have everything to her exact tastes—even if her tone was slightly off when she indulged.

But no matter.

Over the course of his relationship with Christine there was one aspect that became very clear to him. With all of his baking—which in turn led to Christine's smiles and appreciation for she *loved* him for it—it became obvious that he would soon need to acquire an apron. All of his garments were black except for the occasional white shirt, and he found that wool and cashmere did not particularly care for being doused in the sporadic plume of flour that would explode from his mixing bowl.

He had grown more careful and definitely more skilled, but that did not make him immune to the periodic mishap.

Erik was growling at the front of his coat—he should have taken the damnable thing off before starting this venture—swatting at it petulantly as he tried to remove the flour from the hardy fibres when he noticed Christine watching him from the doorway.

He stopped shortly, staring at her with a wary expression until he could ascertain her mood.

Was she terribly angry with her poor Erik?

He had not meant to fall asleep...

She did not say anything but instead hopped up on the counter where she usually sat when she decided to watch him cook and bake for her.

Christine had always offered to help, citing that it was most traditionally a woman's duty to cook meals and tidy the kitchen afterward. He would have allowed it if that had been her wish, but then she had added in such a small voice that he had already provided too much and she was not contributing anything worthwhile.

That could not be allowed.

He should be offering her the world, and if the only thing she considered *too much* was his relatively few culinary skills and his abilities to do dishes, then he had quite a lot to make up for.

So eventually she stopped asking when he would give her a half-hearted glare, and happy herself with sitting on the counter and making little comments while he worked.

This morning however she was silent, which worried him more than anything. He had not said anything either, but he reasoned that it would be best to allow her to begin any discussions that were required, lest he apologise or further offend by mentioning the wrong item that had caused the upset.

With the aid of two spoons the muffin batter was conquered and placed into the awaiting oven, and Erik began preparing his omelettes and ham—while trying to covertly cast glances at Christine.

She was not dressed apart from having seemingly donned his dressing gown. He could not even detect a peek of chemise underneath, nor of pantalettes, and the idea that she was naked underneath *his* garment was causing an embarrassingly visceral reaction.

He turned his full attention to the rest of the meal.

Boiling water was next, and he could practically *feel* Christine's eyes watching his every move as he tended to all the critical tasks that would eventually provide them nourishment. While it should have given him confidence—perhaps he could even have impressed her with his fluidity and grace—on this particular morning he only felt clumsy and uncomfortable.

How he wished she would *say* something!

His anxiety had reached nearly unbearable levels, and he was afraid that if the unbearable tension between them was not alleviated soon, he would burst into a fit of temper merely to relieve the strain.

Erik forced himself to take some deep calming breaths as he added the boiling water to his tea pot, tucking the tea cosy around it carefully, then turned to plate the fluffy omelettes and sizzling ham. The muffins were last and each received a large pad of butter beside it to ensure optimal moisture, and then he set about placing everything upon the dining room table.

At this point, he firmly believed that he had felt more at ease when she had seen him naked than he did at this moment. Christine followed him silently, and besides the small smile and the quiet, "Thank you" he received when he placed her plate in front of her, she revealed no other clue as to her thoughts.

It was always awkward to eat with the mask on. It covered a small portion of his upper lip, and while it was by no means impossible as the leather used was pliant and was in no danger of slipping, it was not an easy task by any stretch of the imagination.

But he was startlingly ravenous, and he did not mind that he had to occasionally manipulate his mask in order to accommodate his appetite.

When his eyes finally left the food before him—which was surprisingly delicious, even by his standards—Christine was looking at him in near astonishment. "You have never eaten with me before."

Being naked was most decidedly less uncomfortable than this morning.

It was one thing to simply complete an action that had previously been unseen. It was another to have it commented on by the very woman he sought to impress with every deed.

"My apologies," he mumbled.

Erik set down his fork and pushed away his plate, forcing himself to be content with the cup of tea, even as the salty ham stared at him tauntingly.

Erik glared at it in return, but the impudent breakfast meat did not seem to notice.

But apparently his response was not satisfactory to his wife, for she rose quickly from her chair. "Oh, no, Erik that was not what I meant!"

He wanted to cry. He had felt the impulse many times since meeting Christine, but now it was raw and nearly overwhelmed him. Why could he not be like *normal* men who could make breakfast for their lady loves and enjoy it with them? Why did it have to be a novelty that he should be hungry and want to dine while watching his sweet wife take pleasure in the fruits of his labour?

Apparently he was still not reacting to her liking for she came around the table and got on her knees beside his chair. He hated when she did that, but he did not have the energy to scold.

"Erik, please say something."

He took a bracing breath. "What would you like me to say?"

To his absolute horror, her eyes began to water and her hands were nearly clutching at his trousers. "I want you to say that you do not regret last night. I want you to say that you forgive me for mentioning your eating habits." Her lower lip quivered and he subdued the impulse to still it with his thumb. "I want you to say that you love me."

Erik swallowed thickly, but obeyed. "I do not regret last night, and of course I forgive you for merely observing that this is our first meal together. And I love you." He tried to infuse his words with sincerity, but he found that the words sounded rote, even to his own ears. What was wrong with him?

She really did cry then, but nodded and returned to breakfast, pushing around her food absently as she struggled to compose herself.

Erik groaned audibly, cursing this entire morning. He should have stayed with her. Eventually she would have awoken and he would have kissed her while she still blinked at him sleepily. And then maybe, if she was very amiable, he would have been able to finish their consummation when the knowledge that she was still naked beside him stirred his blood once more.

But he was a fool and he had taken a bath and seen to their breakfast, and now his wife was crying over her teacup.

It was his turn to go to her side, and instead of kneeling on the floor—he did not think his knees would thank him for the action—he surprised himself and apparently his wife as well, when he scooped her up in his arms and placed her on his lap as he sat in her newly vacated chair. With her pressed against him and her arms circling his neck, he tried again. "I will never regret last night, Christine, though I admit that I fear your own feelings on the matter. I am not angry with you for questioning my eating habits, though I admit my embarrassment at you having done so." She opened her mouth in what he supposed would be an apology, but she remained silent when he shook his head. "And I *love* you, my rose. Even when you insist on sitting on the floor."

The arms that were once simply resting around his neck as she sought balance on his lap now turned into a vice as she practically crushed herself against him in an embrace. "I do not regret it. You were wonderful and gentle, and I have never..." Out of the corner of his eye he could make out the crimson blush on her cheeks, and he felt a moment's pride that it should have been his actions that made her colour so. "I have never felt that way before, and I liked it very much." She pulled back slightly, and blessedly her grip loosened so he could regain his ability to breathe unhindered. "I love you for your tenderness."

He smiled then, but he could not help but feel a tinge of sadness that he hoped would not be too obvious to his Christine. Although he appreciated that she could love any aspect of him, more than anything he wished that someday she could love him entirely. "I love you for *you.*"

She made to snuggled into his neck, but he tapped her nose lightly in reprieve. "No, no, my dear. Your husband has made your breakfast and you must eat."

Christine looked at her plate thoughtfully, before turning to him with a determined expression. "Not unless you eat as well. I am sorry for having made you uncomfortable."

Erik hesitated, no longer feeling hungry after it was brought to such attention. But Christine needed to eat and if she was going to be stubborn and refuse to do so simply to assuage her conscience, then he would not be difficult.

Well, not *overly* difficult.

He released a longsuffering sigh, and though it took a steady arm around her waist to ensure she did not topple over as he reached, he pulled his own plate and tea from across the table and brought it to sit next to hers.

Christine looked rather astonished. "You mean for us to eat like this?"

His eyebrow quirked although he knew she could not see it. "Yes, I do. You said you would not make your Erik feel more uncomfortable about his eating, and this is what I need to feel *comfortable.*"

That was not wholly true of course since he had been perfectly amiable in his own chair before this conversation had begun, but he found that he very much enjoyed the feeling of Christine pressed so completely against him. And if she would allow it, he would quite happily keep her here for quite some time.

She huffed, and he almost thought she was intent on abandoning him, but instead he was forced to suppress a groan as she wriggled in his lap to find a more pleasing position. His grip on her waist tightened and he willed himself not to react.

Perhaps this was not a wise idea on his part.

But his wife seemed unaware of his reaction and returned to her breakfast, though she looked expectantly at him every once in awhile, almost as if she was checking to be sure he would continue to eat—as if he had not been feeding himself properly for the entirety of his existence.

He huffed, while a very great part of him warmed at her concern.

Soon they had eaten their fill and Christine was now reclining against his frame, seemingly full and sleepy from her morning meal. His hand was petting her curls absently as he pondered her words from earlier. "Did you truly mean it, Christine? You enjoyed my touch?"

She smiled up at him, drawing small patterns on his coat with her fingertip. "Very much so." She frowned suddenly, and he could not stop the hand that rose to smooth the small line that formed between her brows. "Was that wrong?"

He chuckled, kissing her temple soundly. "Some might say it was wrong that you found pleasure from a monster. But as your husband, it pleases me greatly that you did so."

Her frown morphed into a scowl of affront. "You are not a monster, you are my loving husband." She kissed his lips then, swiftly and firmly, nodding to herself when she pulled away. "And I would not ever choose another."

His throat was dry, and he cupped her face gently with his long fingered hand. "Does that mean that you would not be opposed to completing our union?"

Christine simply stared at him with wide eyes before she nearly whispered, "No, I would not mind."

And Erik forced himself to relax, and kissed her once more before pushing her lightly off of his lap.

It would not do to consummate their marriage with a dirty kitchen, no matter how much he might wish to.

XX

Christine was currently napping on the settee. It perhaps had been rather devious of him to offer to play for her when he knew he could lull her to sleep so effectively, but he wanted things to be perfect for when they solidified their union.

And while it would not have been *too* terrible had she seen the mess in the sheets—even as he shuddered at the thought that she would have noticed it when she awoke the first time—he still would rather take care of things on his own.

He quickly stripped the bed, putting the sheets in the awaiting bath water and allowed them to soak.

Erik had not the faintest idea of how to remove semen from linens. As an adolescent he had suffered from nocturnal emissions just as any other pubescent male, but for those times when he did have access to a bed, he was not the one responsible for the laundering.

As for the other times...

It was simply best not to think of them.

He should have known that Christine had slept too much to remain slumbering for long. She entered the bath-room while he was still staring at the sopping bedclothes in contemplation, still looking rather sleepy as she did so. "Erik, what are you doing?"

He cleared his throat uncomfortably, deciding it was better to attack the problem instead of hoping that his gaze alone could make the stain disappear.

"I believe it is quite clear what I am doing." Erik did not mean to sound curt, but the twinges of embarrassment were still potent, and he truly had wished she would sleep through this.

It pleased him greatly that instead of being offended by his ill-toned comment, she instead rolled her eyes at him.

Impudent girl.

"I would have helped you do the washing. You helped me with *my* problem after all."

Erik removed his coat and began rolling up his sleeves, still amazed that even after he had performed the action many times in front of Christine, she still watched him so intently whenever he did so. "Your courses are beyond your control. Last night I should have had more... *fortitude* and I should have been able to complete our bond through actual..." He shrugged and plunged his hands into the water and assailed the sheets viciously with the soap.

He paused when Christine knelt beside him and placed her hand on his arm. Her touch was not insistent and he could have pulled free of her quite easily if he wanted to.

He did not want to.

"Erik, I want you to listen to me."

He huffed, mildly insulted that she thought he ever did *not* listen to her. Her words *mattered* and whether they wounded or made him feel like she cared for him, he remembered each of them completely for they came from her.

His scrubbing paused and he obliged her obvious intention that he cease his work and give her his full attention.

"Last night was perfect. While I was nervous, yes, you never made me feel afraid. You were careful and *so* gentle. And when you went to sleep so suddenly," his head dropped low and he found he could not look at her when she spoke so blatantly of his failure.

Her hand was at his chin and it was coaxing him to raise his eyes, and he was helpless to do anything but obey. "It gave me time to think. I knew it would be different with you, and it *was.* You did not have to actually..." She blushed then, and he thought she would leave her thought unfinished, but her shoulders straightened and she looked resolved. "You did not have to be *in* me for us to christen our marriage bed. I admit, I am still a little worried about what *more* will entail, but I know that as long as I am with you, you will take care of me. That is what last night showed me."

She kissed him then, slowly and sweetly. "And I will not have you looking so abashed about our wedding night anymore. You pleased your wife and," she lowered her eyes and fiddled with his fingers still in the water. "You were obviously quite pleased as a husband."

He snorted, and had his hands not been soaked he would have grasped her waist to pull her closer and kiss her thoroughly. But instead he could only lean forward and hope that she would meet him halfway, and to his great relief she did.

His perfectly wonderful wife.

Erik only broke away from her when his knees began to protest their position against the harsh stone floor, and he smiled at her apologetically as she fought to catch her breath. "You are married to an old man, my dear, and I must finish tending to the linens before my knees hatch a full on revolt."

She quirked an eyebrow at him, and he felt slightly discomfited by the intensity of her gaze. "I still do not know your age. Will you not tell me now? Because I do not think you so very old."

He shook his head and turned back to the sheets. "I do not have an exact age to give you, my dear. Birthdays were never something to celebrate during my childhood."

Erik glanced at her from the corner of his eye and he could clearly see that his answer upset her. "I do not like to think of how you were raised. It makes me hurt." Her lone dry hand went to her heart, and it touched him deeply that she should feel such compassion for him. He supposed that it was a dreadful way to be raised—with a mother that scorned him and who on more than one occasion had wished that he had never been born. He knew that other mothers were not so cruel and did not like to strike their toddlers for simply wanting a fond touch or affectionate word, but that was what Erik had been given.

And while before the pain of such memories used to leave him feeling despondent and angry at the injustice, he now felt a sort of detached sadness. He wished things had been different—he wished that about so many things about his past. But now that he had Christine to dote upon and care for him in turn, he found that much of his anger and resentment had begun to fade.

This lovely woman beside him had done that, and she was worthy of his trust—in *all* things.

He swallowed thickly, and although he addressed it to the bedclothes below him, he hoped she understood his earnestness. "You may help... if you wish."

Her smile was bright and beautiful to behold, and she rolled up her sleeves with far too much enthusiasm.

Ridiculous girl.

With Christine's assistance it did not take long to finish the washing, and with her cheery giggles as they strung up the linens over the bath and she managed to get water droplets over her face and hair, Erik found that actually completing tasks *with* Christine instead of merely doing them under her watchful gaze was a very pleasing practice.

It was fortunate that he had two sets of bedclothes; otherwise their nightly activities would have had to be postponed until the currently sopping set had finished drying. As it was, he pulled the second pair from the dresser drawer. Perhaps it was rather naughty of him, but he peeked into one of the other drawers to see if his wife had finally unpacked her trunk and thereby had accepted the room as hers. To his great relief and rather shameful excitement, he received an eyeful of pantalettes and chemises before he quickly closed it.

Christine pretended not to notice, though her blush belied her ruse.

The bed proved slightly more difficult. Christine struggled to pull the sheets taut, and she also did not seem to understand the importance of properly folded corners. "But they just get mussed anyway after you sleep in them!"

Erik sighed but demonstrated the proper technique yet again. "If you would like to wake up in a wad of linens and coverlets that are attempting to strangle you, then by all means, you may do so." He peered at her intensely. "I for one find that an unpleasant experience."

She nibbled her lip and looked at him unsurely for a moment. "Erik..."

He gave the blanket a quick flick, ensuring that it fully covered the other side. "Yes, Christine?"

Christine tended to the opposite side of the bed, yet he noted that she seemed more intent in tracing patterns on the covers than in actually smoothing out any wrinkles. "Will you be sleeping with me now? I mean... is this your room now too?"

Erik stared at her intently for a moment before holding out his hand. "Come with me."

She looked confused, but placed her hand in his quite willingly and he led her to his bedroom. She might have caught glimpses of it from when she was at his doorway, but she had never mentioned it if such was the case.

He led her into his bedchamber, and while the door was open and some light from the sitting room managed to provide some illumination, it was not until he released her hand and lit the lamps that she reacted with a gasp.

"What... what is that?"

She looked frightened and shocked, and though he had wanted her to see and understand what he was moving away from, he was not at all prepared for her to step closer to his coffin and allow one of her hands to trail over the interior. Her eyes were wide and when she looked at him it sent a pain through his very soul. "You have slept here all this time?"

He nodded hesitantly, not expecting her to be so horrified at the thought.

She practically flew into his arms.

"This is a terrible thing, Erik, and you must never sleep in it again. You will share my room."

He patted her head affectionately, if not a little bemusedly, and communicated what he truly had been trying to convey. "Christine, I did not show you this in order to play upon your pity so you would invite me to your bed." She reared back to retort in indignation, but he silenced her with a slight shake of his head. "I am a morbid man, my wife, and I am afraid one of my eccentricities led me to believe that this," he made a vague gesture towards his macabre bedstead, "was a prudent exercise in preparing for eternity."

Christine was shaking her head resolutely, and he knew she wanted to argue. But he found that he could give her a perfectly genuine smile as he realised that there was no *need* for her to argue with him—he now fully understood and embraced that he now had something to live for. And to dwell upon his death and the release from the pain and horror of the half-life had indulged for so long was unneeded.

"I will not sleep in it again, my rose, but that need not mean that you must share you bed with me every night. I could prepare my own *normal* bed in here for when you require privacy. Many married couples sleep apart." He grimaced as he spoke, as it was not at all what he envisioned for their marriage, but he felt it prudent to offer her the reprieve. He did not make it a habit of sleeping often, and when he did the idea of being so close and intimate to Christine was an appealing one.

Christine practically glared at him. "We are *married,* Erik, which means that you belong at my side." She took a deep breath, and her irritation seemed to fade and her voice quieted in confession. "You help keep the nightmares away. I had hardly any last night."

It seemed terribly ironic that it was only while sleeping next to a corpse that she would feel safe enough to slumber uninterrupted by nightly terrors—well, apparently hardly any terrors. He did not say as much to Christine, however, as such thoughts would only upset her.

"Then I shall have to do my husbandly duty and continue to dispense of anything that seeks to do you harm, even if it is only in your mind." Of course, like his own, her nightmares were steeped in memory and were not figments of an unsettled mind.

She sighed and pressed her face into his chest, and he revelled in the feel of her. Christine apparently was not as consumed with the feel of *him* for her clear and resolved voice was quite firm when she added, "I want you to get rid of the coffin."

He stiffened. While he had truly meant it when he said he would not sleep in it again, he saw little reason in dispensing of it entirely. After all, he would need it *eventually*—every person would need an eternal resting place at some point.

Erik opened his mouth to argue, but he closed it quickly from Christine's scowl. "You are not allowed to think about dying and seeing that is only a reminder. I have lost too many people, and I will not lose you as well!"

How was he to argue with that?

If it caused her pain, it would not stay within the house. He could lock his bedroom of course and forbid her entrance, but she would still know it was there, and she would most likely be ill at ease until she knew it had been disposed of.

And it was a husband's responsibility to please his wife—in *all* things.

So with a longsuffering sigh and a kiss to her temple, he promised. "I will dispose of the coffin, Christine, because you wish it."

She huffed softly. "I would prefer that you destroy it because you know that it is the right thing to do, but I suppose that will have to suffice. But perhaps..."

He supposed that he *did* know that such a dramatic gesture could be considered right, as it sealed away his past and allowed for them to embrace the future.

But what other rooms would they possibly need?

Erik was not allowed to ponder such things for long because Christine extracted herself from his arms and to his absolute *revulsion* scrambled her way into his coffin. "What are you *doing?*"

She looked nervous, but that quickly dissolved as she regarded him coolly. Christine lay down and folded her hands upon her chest and he moved closer so that he would not lose sight of her completely. "I want you to see how disturbing this is. At any point during my time here I might have walked in to ask a question or simply to talk to you and would have found you *here.* Would you like it if I pretended to be dead on a consistent basis?"

Erik did not like this. To further her point she had turned her head toward the ceiling and closed her eyes, and her mimicry of death was more than he could bear. "You will come out of there at once!"

He meant it to be a command but in his distress it sounded more of an anguished plea, and his hands were clutching at her skirt as he tugged, trying to pull her from the confines of his self-imprisonment.

She opened her eyes and her expression softened from the blank mask she had worn while pretending. "You will dispose of the coffin? Because you know it is right and that married people should not consider sleeping in such things?"

He nodded his head furiously, and to his relief she smiled at him. "Good."

She was not leaving it fast enough and though she was no longer imitating a corpse, he could not stand for her to be near it any longer. Resolved, he picked her up in his arms, too panicked to be amused by the slight yelp she gave at his sudden movement. "I was going to come out on my own!"

He shook his head and held her closer, striding from the room determinedly. She would not be allowed back into his bedchamber until the coffin was evicted from the house. Losing her was too painful to even consider, let alone have a visual before his eyes of what such a thing would *look* like. And while he knew it was not her intent, she had frightened him.

Erik crossed the sitting room to his reading chair, refusing to release his wife as he settled her once more on his lap, clutching her closer as he tried to calm his breathing and his racing heart. "Erik, what is it?" She placed her hand on his masked face and whispered, "You are shaking, what is wrong?"

He did not mean to glare. He wanted to kiss her until he forgot anything but the feel of her lips against his. But when he closed his eyes he saw her still in the coffin, and however irrationally, he felt the fear turn to anger that she should have put him through such a charade. "You will *never* do that again, Christine. That was beyond cruel to your poor Erik."

Christine gaped at him, clearly surprised that he should be so upset by her action. "I was merely trying to demonstrate..." He did not allow her to finish.

"It is not an accurate demonstration! You might be perturbed if you were to enter and see me sleeping in my coffin, but I *love* you. If you were to die..." He could not even complete the thought, the pain and sorrow was too acute. Instead, he buried his face in her neck and curls, trying unsuccessfully to stop his shaking.

Christine was quiet for quite some time. Eventually he felt her hands running gently through his fine hairs, and her voice was soft—and to his chagrin, full of pain that emulated what he felt all too well. "Is that what you think? That I do not love you as much as you love me? That I would not be equally devastated?"

Apparently the way he simply held her more tightly against him was all the response she needed. "Oh, Erik, I *love* you. I am sorry I have not made it more clear!" She was trying to coax him to look at her, but Erik was quite happy with the way her hair was absorbing his tears, and she would not be relegated to witnessing his joy and disbelief directly.

He did not like to see her cry...

That did not stop him from nuzzling his way to her ear and whispering his most desperate entreaty. "Do you mean it, Christine? You truly love your husband?"

She sighed, and he could hear the hitch in her voice that indicated she was close to tears herself. "Yes. More than I know how to express."

Despite his best efforts to keep her stationary, when he realised that she was merely shifting her head for a kiss he met her with equal vigour. His wife *loved* him, and if neither of them could find the words to express just how much they needed and appreciated the other, their bodies would have to find the way. And at this moment, Erik thought that her lips were doing a remarkable job of conveying her feelings.

His hands were caught in the curls of her hair as he pulled her closer, and her own were still petting the downy fine strands that resided on his own head. He marvelled at her passion, and when they eventually broke apart for breath, he delighted in the way her naturally rosy lips had darkened from his kisses.

He could not help but put one more upon them for their sweetness.

"I love you, *so* much, my rose. Let me show you how."

Christine looked at him then for what felt an eternity, but then she kissed him once more and appeared quite determined. "I would like that very much."

And then Erik carried her to their bedchamber.

XXI

Christine's confession of love had certainly stirred his passion, yet he found that he was no more comfortable disrobing than he had been before. Perhaps it was the way she stared, watching his every move as new bits of yellowy flesh were exposed that made him so uneasy, but he could hardly ask her to look away entirely.

And in truth, nothing terrible had happened the last time he was naked beside her—quite the opposite.

Memories of the previous night's activities made him ache to kiss her once more, and while he had only succeeded in removing his shirt, he still returned to his wife's prone form upon the bed. She had managed to remove her dress, and from the transparent quality of her chemise it was readily apparent that she had not thought to put on the rest of her unmentionables before joining him in the sitting room after breakfast.

His little minx.

Her lips were warm and pliant—just like the rest of her. Where he was yellow, she was pink, and while his skin had a thin rasp resembling parchment, hers was the finest of silks.

Especially at her breast.

One hand was delighting in the feel of her curls as they tangled around it, while the other crept down her throat until it slipped gently past the neckline of her shift and found the awaiting flesh that called to him so insistently.

He groaned into her mouth at the feel of her.

Erik made sure never to press too harshly against her tender skin, but he found that the most caring of caresses and kneadings produced a very pleasant mewl from his wife's throat. Her nipple pebbled against his palm and he revelled at her reactions to his touch. He would be forever grateful for her responses, and he swore that he would never take her willing acquiescence for granted. Each and every one was a gift, and he would not become one of those husbands that grew to expect such favours.

She seemed more responsive today. It did not take long before she was sighing and almost fidgeting. And when he looked into her eyes he could plainly see the desire for *more,* although she did not seem brave enough to ask for it outright.

As if he would ever deny her.

Erik knew that they were moving toward actual copulation. And while he knew his Christine was no longer a virgin in physicality and might therefore be spared the experience of pain during this endeavour—he *prayed* she knew no pain—he did not feel right simply *invading* immediately. She deserved to be pampered and prepared before he took his fill.

He pressed kisses down her chest, opening her chemise further as he did so. This particular garment was straightforward in its construction, and he found that the neckline was wide when he undid the drawstring. It could well accommodate her bust and hips if he chose to slide it down her legs instead of pulling it over her head, and he rather enjoyed the experience of kissing the newly uncovered flesh as inch by inch was revealed to his gaze.

By Christine's prickling skin and warm sighs, he knew she found it enjoyable as well.

Her stomach was flat and taught, and he realised unhappily that he could still plainly see her ribs without effort. He kissed them too, wanting them to know that he would do his best to ensure they were properly concealed by a healthful layer of softness that only further nutrition could supply.

He found her navel to be particularly fascinating. His time in Persia had afforded many glimpses at the female stomach, but he realised that just as with his wife's toes, this was a part of her that was for his eyes alone. No one else would ever see the little indentation, and he placed yet another kiss on it in approval.

Her chemise was now bunched around her hips, and if he pushed at it just a bit more, her most secret places would be quite within his view.

He pushed.

Christine wriggled.

Erik kissed.

With a moment of pure amusement he wondered if he would grow as fond of this particular patch of blonde curls as he had the others. He allowed a long finger to pet them and she moaned—not unlike how she did when he brushed her hair.

Curious.

He felt bold with the knowledge that he had already proven that his touch was pleasurable, so he afforded himself permission that he should also be allowed to *view* what he was satisfying. Erik looked up briefly to Christine and was momentarily distracted by the way her eyes were firmly closed and her hands clutched at the newly made bedclothes.

He pressed his lips to her thigh, and to his great delight they parted slightly in response.

She was so *pink.*

Erik had thought that of her before, of course, but seeing her most hidden places, he realised that she truly was capable of blushing all over.

He swelled with pride that once again this was a small detail of his wife that only *he* would know and appreciate.

He allowed his fingers to make languid strokes against her glistening flesh, and he celebrated her nearly visceral reactions when he petted the small nub that seemed to require the most attention.

And suddenly, he felt the intense desire to know what she felt like as she surrounded a finger.

He gently slipped one digit into her, and he knew that if it was at all possible, he should like to live there forever. She was so *warm,* and soft and silky, and he could feel his own imminent release at simply the *feel* of her—except Christine cried out loudly and nearly wrenched away from him.

Erik lay frozen and unfeeling, waiting for... something. "Christine?"

She blinked at him, seemingly coming back from whatever dark place had overtaken her. "Did I harm you?"

She shook her head thoughtfully, and her lack of conviction did little to calm him. He now felt timid and unsure, but when she reached for his hand and pulled him closer to her, he cautiously manoeuvred himself so that he lay beside her. "I am sorry, Erik. I just... I am not sure what happened." She placed a kiss upon his chest and he tried to push away the numb feeling that was settling over his heart.

Did she not want him inside of her?

Christine looked up at him, and where moments before she had been teary and shaky, she now seemed more sure of herself. "You did nothing wrong, Erik, I promise. You only surprised me and I was not prepared." She blushed. "Which I know is quite silly seeing as I *know* you were going to... eventually... *be* with me."

She must not have approved his silence for she prodded his side with a fingertip. "Please, say something."

Erik released a forceful breath. "I do not know what to say. I do not like that you would be... reminded of things when I touch you." He would *not* be angry. It was not her fault that her body reacted without her permission. He knew that she trusted him—she would not have let him touch her at all if that was not the case. But it still took a great deal of coaxing on his part to keep his mind from insisting that she had finally come to her senses and had recoiled from the monster who wished to bed her.

He would *not* think such things.

Christine grimaced, and distracted herself with tracing the scars that littered his skin. "I do not like it either. But please do not be upset with me if such things happen. I do not like when you are upset, especially not when we are like this."

He sighed heavily, but pressed his lips against her temple. "You cannot expect me to not be upset that you have known this sort of pain, Christine. That would be impossible."

She nodded and settled more firmly against him. "Perhaps," her tone was thoughtful and he could sense an underlying thread of heat that meant she did not wish to postpone their assignation completely. "Perhaps I should do some exploring first before we... continue."

While a part of his mind cried out with an insistent *yes*—that the prospect of having her hands upon him would be more blissful than anything he had ever known—the other part knew that to have her touching him in such a manner could only possibly lead to her revulsion. He was no beauty to look upon, and his scars only made things worse. Christine's were a testament to her resiliency, and while he wished he could but wipe them away with a tender hand, they did nothing to detract from her loveliness.

That could not be said for his.

"My dear, you will not be pleased by what you find." He tried to infuse his voice with a forceful air so that she would *trust* him when he said that it was better that she not, but instead it simply sounded sad.

Christine scoffed openly. "I am quite sure of that. Someone has hurt you terribly and I would never be pleased to see the visible evidence." She completely missed his point and he opened his mouth to further his claim but she silenced him with a finger pressed upon his lips. "But I love *you,* and you are my husband, and it is a wife's right to see and... *touch.*"

Erik groaned. It was so very difficult to maintain his position when she looked at him in that way, and when her words were precisely what he needed to hear in order to yield. She had but to call upon her title as a wife and he knew he would do practically anything to please her.

And for some, impossibly naïve reason, she thought that it was important that she explore him.

But perhaps if he considered how necessary he found it to learn every nuance of her body, it did not seem so very strange.

Afraid that his voice would betray his anxiety, he nodded his consent. Her touches were not so very different from ones she had given before—light brushes of fingertips against scar tissue and papery skin. What caused him to draw in a sharp breath was when he felt her lips press against each in turn, leaving behind warm patches of flesh that tingled from her contact.

Erik was not anticipating that she would move upward, her delicate fingers trailing over his throat until he met her gaze. "Do not be angry..."

Nothing good could come from such a beginning.

He eyed her warily, fully prepared to stop her should her fingers delve beneath his mask. "You have seen me naked, and I think it only right that we be vulnerable *together.*"

What on earth was she referring to? He had forced himself to disrobe the day before, and surely that was *vulnerable* enough for her tastes.

Until he felt her briefly skim his mask with her lips. "Trust me, Erik."

He lurched away from her. "How can you ask that of me? *Why* would you wish to look upon such a thing?"

Erik almost vacated the bed entirely, intent on gathering his discarded clothing and covering himself as much as possible. He wanted to hide, but Christine was gripping onto his wrist and was caressing those damnable patterns onto his scars with her thumb, and he could feel himself gentling at her touch.

"I am trying to overcome my fears in our bed, and I think it is important you do the same." Her words were not harsh, nor were they demanding. They were quiet and soft and he knew he was lost to her once more.

It took such courage for her to embrace the sensual after all she had suffered, and again he was the one who wished to flee.

And maybe—just maybe—if he was able to show her that he could be tender and kind even when his face was exposed, it would partly absolve the harsh treatment he had given her the last time he had forced her to look upon him. Perhaps if this was the memory she chose to dwell on, it would lessen her pain.

With trembling fingers he removed his mask, placing it upon the bedside table. He could not resist lowering the light. Not entirely, as the complete darkness would only cause his wife discomfort, but enough that there were some shadows that could potentially hide some of his most gruesome features.

It took a great amount of self-control in order to persuade his body to recline and relax, but eventually when Christine was once more pressing against him—in truth, nearly lying on top of him—his body felt not quite so tense. Her face was inches from his own and her fingers hesitantly began to trace fine lines upon his face, learning each harsh feature as they passed. "There now. That is how your face should be touched." She placed a kiss on both of his chiselled cheekbones and one onto his forehead, and he could not stop his hands from burying in her hair and pulling her to his mouth.

If possible, their kisses were even more satisfying now that his upper lip was not restrained by the confines of the mask. She opened her sweet mouth in a contented sigh, and he hesitantly allowed the same. Perhaps it was not so very dreadful if he allowed himself a taste.

She was tentative at first, but soon met the new sensation with vigour.

In their distraction she had straddled his torso, and Erik noticed that one of his hands had found her breast and was paying it all due attention, even as she pressed the rest of her body against his chest.

But when she began to wriggle against him, *seeking* as she did so, he knew that now was the time to join.

He *needed* her, and by her quiet whimpers and twitching hips it was clear that she needed him also.

Erik moved his hand from her breast and tried to unbutton his trousers, but discovered very intimate parts of his wife were keeping him from doing so successfully. She giggled and her breath hitched as his fingers brushed against her, mistaking his attempt for teasing.

Eventually she blushed and carefully moved off of him so that she could undo his trousers. He would have done it himself, but apparently she had not quite finished her exploration.

She was possibly overly cautious, although with that particular part of his anatomy he could not say that he minded the care in which she took of opening the placket and ensuring that his member was not caught in any material before she pulled off his remaining clothing.

And to his absolute mortification, she sat at his side and *stared* at him.

Perhaps someday he would find such perusal to be arousing—that his naked form could cause such interest in his wife and hold her fascination. At the moment however, when he was feeling so completely exposed, he wanted to do nothing more than cover himself.

What if he was not pleasing enough for her?

He had little to compare his size to, and he briefly wondered if she found him too large or too small, but quickly dismissed such thoughts. She had told him to trust her, and that would also mean allowing her to embrace him for all that he was—whether or not he was her ideal concoction of manly features.

Christine cast a glance at his face, seemingly seeking permission before she reached out a tentative hand and allowed her fingers to skim over him.

He hissed, the pleasure too intense and too wonderful, and he wished she would do *more*. Or, what he truly wanted was to be allowed inside of her—to be one with her in the most intimate of ways.

And though he tried not to think of it, he begrudgingly admitted to himself that he might simply wish to be within her as her small caresses were nearly enough to bring him to completion. And he would *not* do so again without first solidifying their marriage through consummation.

So he tugged at her hands and bade her straddle him once more, bringing her down for yet another kiss. It felt good allowing her to be the one to loom. He was the one prone and at her mercy, and while he wondered if this was not wholly traditional for the first time between a husband and wife, he thought that for their situation it might bring Christine some peace of mind.

He wondered if he should prepare her more. The last thing in the world he wished was to hurt her, but she had not reacted well when he had tried to do so before.

And, he noted with a grimace, his attempt had also led to the removal of his mask. And his trousers.

But when Christine moved her thumb to drift over the tip of his length and he felt the burst of gratification, perhaps he did not mind the absence of his lower clothing quite so much after all.

"Christine," he pleaded.

Her lip was firmly between her teeth and she looked at him for a long moment. He hoped that his expression remained neutral, as the last thing he wished was to pressure her in any way. She could stop at this moment and, while he would not be *pleased,* he would not resent her for it.

But her expression was one of resolve, and moving lower on his torso, worked to position herself upon him.

She was absolutely breathtaking.

She was everything that was warm and soft and welcoming, and as they both gasped and hissed at their connection as she guided him into her most intimate places, in that moment he knew that this was love.

Christine went so *very* slowly, almost tentatively as she tested her ability to adjust to him. And though he tried not to dwell too much upon it, he could tell from the covert glances she was giving him that she was trying to judge his reaction. Some part of him knew that she was watching to see if he would turn into a brute, flipping her over and pounding away at her until she was bruised and battered. And much to his surprise, he was not angry for her caution.

For while she felt nearly overwhelmed when she was fully upon him and he was nearly consumed by the heat and the *feel* of her surrounding him, he knew that the most critical aspect of this coupling was to show her that this too could bring her fulfilment.

If only he was brave enough to experiment.

He allowed himself a few moments to adjust to her as well, and it took many large calming breaths to ensure he would not release at the slightest of her movements. She shifted slightly which made him groan, but to his great relief he felt that he had enough control of his faculties that he would not embarrass himself further.

Christine's eyes were tightly closed, and he moved a careful hand to settle with hers upon his chest. "Are you all right?" His voice was close to a rasp, even as he tried to hold it steady.

Her eyes flew open and she smiled at him, even as her eyes flooded with tears. "It does not hurt."

He did not mean to, but perhaps when they were connected so thoroughly, it was all the more reasonable that her relief and joy would be felt by him as well. "My darling, Christine..." He rose slightly trying to meet her for a kiss while she also leaned forward, and they both moaned at the change in position. Their lips met and their fingers explored, and when Erik found that the tiny nub that brought her such pleasure was still readily accessible even now, he knew that she would see just how sweet and beautiful their marriage bed could be.

So slowly.

Tenderly.

Exquisitely.

They made love.

XXII

Erik awoke gradually. At first all he knew was warmth. Then he felt soft skin as his hand twitched in his almost-wakefulness. If this was a dream, he wished he would never fully wake.

But wake he did, and it took him a moment to assess how their night had ended. He could not keep the wide smile from overtaking his face at just how perfect it had been. To be certain, they had their false beginnings and had to overcome their own insecurities. But as he still felt the lingering contentment that could only be explained by their now fully formed marriage, he thought they had both done quite admirably.

Especially when he remembered how Christine had shuddered and her face had contorted in bliss, and he knew that he had pleased her.

That was all he ever truly wanted.

She was curled up against him, and to his wonderment, he realised that she was forced to do so because somehow he had managed to abscond with most of the pillows. He now had quite a mound about him, and she was forced to either sleep at the very edge of one, or content herself with using his chest for the same purpose.

He felt slightly embarrassed that she had been forced to do so, yet he could not help but be pleased that she looked so comfortable and peaceful as she slumbered. Erik shifted a little, again trying to ascertain just how much she was on top of him. This made the second morning he had been compelled to determine such knowledge, and he was already finding it an endearing habit of his newly married life. However, he did not wish to make the mistake of leaving her again too soon, as the last time he had done so caused only misunderstandings between them. But he needed to relieve himself, and he always preferred to do so when Christine was completely unawares.

He did still possess some dignity, as little as it might be.

Erik felt quite accomplished when he managed to wriggle himself free and shoved a pillow under Christine so she would be properly supported. He stood at the side of the bed for a minute to ensure she was still sleeping soundly, and he noted wryly that while he was grateful that she was easily appeased, she also did not seem to notice a great difference between his body and a feather pillow.

Deciding that she need not be overly modest any longer when covering her chemises, he reclaimed his dressing gown from her wardrobe and hurried to the bath-room.

His needs attended to, Erik crept back into their bedchamber. Christine appeared to still be sleeping and as he stood staring at her from the side of the bedstead, he contemplated his next action. His first thought was to don his mask and see to their breakfast, but that had not ended overly well the last time. It seemed decadent and wholly unproductive to simply lounge when he no longer required sleep, and even now his body felt sluggish and slow. He had slept more the past two days than he had ever before—childhood notwithstanding.

It was more difficult trying to slip back into bed than it was to vacate it. Erik had decided to keep the dressing gown on, as while he had managed to hoard all of the pillows, Christine had managed to take most of the blankets. He was never one to mind the cold, but he felt no great need to bask in it when it could easily be circumvented by blankets or garments. And in this case his greedy wife made it quite clear that he would be using his dressing gown.

He had nearly rearranged Christine to her previous position when she spoke to him, her voice still raspy with sleep. "I wanted to wake up first."

Erik froze, but decided there was little point in continuing his subtle movements of her body and tucked his arms around her and pulled until she was lying nearly on top of him. To his delight she nuzzled into the folds of his garment, and he idly wondered if his wife was part feline.

His hand started petting her curls affectionately, and at the way she shivered in apparent enjoyment at his attention, he decided that she was indeed.

"Why did you desire that?"

She blinked at him sleepily, refusing to move her head from his chest even to speak to him properly. "Because I am truly a wife now, so that means I take on some of the responsibilities."

Erik rolled his eyes. "I did not marry you for your domestic skills, nor did I intend for you to become my housemaid."

She hummed and he found the slight vibrations against his torsos to be exceedingly distracting. "A wife is not a maid. And I did not mean that I would have to do *everything,* I would just like to contribute." Christine's gaze lowered and she fiddled with the opening of his dressing gown. "Maybe make something for *you."*

He should protest. She had already given him *far* too much and now she was offering to change the balance of their relationship yet again. What did she receive if not sweet biscuits and tea and the occasional voice lesson?

Then he realised with startling clarity precisely what she received that she valued so highly.

His love.

He wanted to do those things for her because he *loved* her. In the marriage bed he wanted to ensure that she received her pleasure, not because he thought that his satisfaction would be all the more complete when he was able to feel the way she constricted around him, but because it was an expression of his care for her.

And miraculously, she must feel the same way.

His throat was tight and it took him a moment to breathe through what he knew was the beginning of tears. He placed a gentle hand at her chin and cupped it softly, bidding her to look at him. "You truly love me." It was a statement, not a question, as unbelievable as it was even now.

She leaned forward and placed a kiss where his garment had parted. "Of course I do. Just as you love me." Her smile was slightly drawn, and he felt terribly sorry that he could not infuse his words with more surety. "Someday you will not doubt it."

Though his revelation had made it clear that she *did* love him, there was still a small part of him that nagged and insisted that it was not at all the same way that he loved her. *That* was what would someday be silenced by her continued presence and actions.

And he felt a great weight lift from his heart that he could hope that such doubts would someday in future be permanently quieted.

He held her more firmly against him and pressed a kiss upon her temple. "I trust you, my Christine."

Her smile turned impish and to his great gladness and torment she parted his dressing gown even further, trailing kisses in its wake. "I was under the impression that this particular garment was now mine. It is terribly rude for you to steal it away again."

His tried to make his sniff indignant, but when she was plying him with such attentions, it sounded more like the sharp inhalation of breath that it truly was. "I believe it was meant as a temporary loan, not a permanent change in ownership. You have already deprived me of a cloak."

She somehow managed to look prim even as she settled her chin upon his chest and met his gaze. "I never *asked* for your cloak. I could have continued to use my own."

He glared back at her. "As if I would allow you to freeze in that monstrosity. The only thing it will be warming in the future is the fire." Had he not been so horrified when he had found her biscuits squirreled away, it would have already met its ultimate fate.

As of now he did not know its exact location. He had left it in the sitting room and intended to see to its demise once the shock had worn off, but it was not there when next he looked—which meant Christine had hidden it once again, just as she had done before.

She tilted her head in question. "Why would it need to be burned? I admit that it is rather worn," she glowered when he scoffed, "but it is hardly that offensive!"

He stroked her cheek softly, even as he allowed his voice to soften and turn into a coaxing lull. "It offends in the worst possible way. It is steeped in your tears and your abuses, and I will not allow you to wear it again."

She blinked at him owlishly, and he nearly gloated in his success before his triumph was negated. "Very well, we burn my cloak and we burn your coffin."

He had agreed to its disposal, but it seemed horribly excessive to *burn* it in some macabre semblance of a funeral pyre. "Why?"

Christine resumed her attentions to his flesh, tracing it with her delicate fingertips and pressing kisses in a pattern discernible only to her. "Because it is steeped in your loneliness and pain, and I will not allow you to sleep in it again."

Well.

It was terribly unfair that she should use his argument against him.

He groaned, and before he considered that his actions could cause her alarm, flipped their positions so that *he* was the one doing the pressing, and caressing, and the kissing in the same manner she had done. She stiffened for a brief moment before she took a deep breath and looked at his wary expression that had appeared when he realised what he had done. Her fingers pushed back his wisps of hair, tucking them neatly behind his ear. "I am fine. You just surprised me."

His lips found the delightful hollow between her two breasts, and he whispered his apology into it. "I love you for your resilience."

She smirked, and he found that it was both devilish and enticing. "I love you for your lips."

He decided that he was quite content for her to love that particular aspect of his person.

Erik paused in his ministrations, turning his thoughts from the loveliness of her skin and back to the original conversation. "I do not have a location that would properly contain the fire necessary to burn the coffin whole and it would be quite tedious to dismantle sufficiently so that it fit in our fireplace." He grinned at her. "For I would much rather use my energies for *other* pursuits."

She blushed prettily. "You are very naughty, husband."

His lips found her bare nipple, tightened and straining from the cold, and hopefully, for want of him as well. "I have plenty to inspire me, my rose."

Christine's voice turned solemn. "Erik, I was serious. I want your coffin to be destroyed. And if that means that you must also get rid of my cloak, then so be it. You cannot distract me so easily."

Erik briefly considered just what would be required to distract her *fully*, but decided to respect her wishes. For the moment.

He placed one last kiss on her neglected nipple, not wanting it to feel lonesome or unappreciated, before he rolled onto his back and allowed her to nestle against his side once more. "We do have a lake at our disposal. A drowned coffin and a sodden cloak would hardly be the worst things that had found their deaths in my lake."

Christine shivered. "Do not speak of such things. I want to think of it and remember how nice it was to sit on the shore with you and watch the light glisten on the water—not have nightmares about things drowning." She quieted, seemingly to ponder his proposal. "But I suppose that would be sufficient. I do not want to risk harming anyone or anything with a fire." Though her face increased in colour and her voice was barely audible she added, "And I rather like for you to use your energies on me instead of manual labour."

Erik did not think he had ever smiled so brightly.

He had not asked her for reassurances regarding his adequacies of the night before. He had been satisfied that her every moan, shudder, and gasp was evidence enough that she was pleased by him—and he knew that the words he had murmured into her ear as they lay together afterward was proof of his own gratification.

But that did not mean that he did not swell with pride that she could voice her own longing for his caresses.

As unbelievable as it seemed, she *desired* him.

He moved to kiss her soundly, to thank her for her declarations that he had not been forced to beg for. She pulled away quickly however, and before he could be hurt at her seeming rejection she hurried to explain. "I need to tend to some... needs first."

Ah. She had not had the opportunity to tend to her teeth and use the facilities as he had. So he kissed her cheek instead and pulled back the covers. "By all means."

She stared at him. "But you are wearing the dressing gown! And my chemise is..." Christine looked about the room, trying to locate the item that he had so carelessly tossed aside the night before. It was halfway to the bath-room door, proving itself completely unhelpful.

She appeared outraged when he made no move to offer her either garment.

"I quite like you as you are."

Christine huffed her annoyance before ripping the top coverlet from the bed, wrapping it around herself so that her entire body was obscured. "You are a wretch."

Erik rose from his mound of pillows and managed a rather elegant half-bow, even from his seated position. "At your service, Madame."

For a moment Christine forgot to be indignant and she looked at him peculiarly. "That is the first time I have not been called *mademoiselle.*" She bit her lip to contain her smile. "I think I like my new title."

He finally did exit the bed then, moving to her side. "That is very encouraging, as you will bear it for the rest of your life."

She beamed at him before placing a kiss upon his cheek and walking to the bath-room—tripping on the coverlet as she did so. She righted herself quickly enough and throwing him a sheepish look, closed the door behind her.

Foolish girl.

One moment she could be the siren intent on tormenting him with all manner of innocent seduction, and the next she was scampering about the room, tripping on bedclothes.

He would not trade her for anything in the world.

Satisfied that she would not be offended if he left the room, he gathered his discarded clothing and went to his own bedroom. He steadily ignored the large structure that would soon be settled on the bottom of the lake, focusing on the meticulous task of dressing—the only part of his appearance that he could control.

Properly clothed, he opened the secret drawer that held all of his masks. They ranged in colours and textures, and he knew them all well. He had his favourites, if any could be classified as such. None made him feel *normal*—that was asking too much of an inanimate object. But perhaps he should revisit the venture. His wife deserved to have the option of taking walks in the sunlight, and maybe carriage rides in the park on Sundays would serve as a delightful diversion.

And to do that, he would need to find a way to look like any other man.

But for now, he donned one of his most comfortable masks and turned to the coffin. He had built it in place, so he had never considered just how difficult it might be to take it out in one piece.

This might be a larger endeavour than he had anticipated.

Regardless of the difficulty, he would see to it that Christine was appeased. This was an important matter to her, and it was therefore worthy of his attention.

The coffin was on a raised platform, and though his first inclination was to carefully measure and ensure that nothing would be damaged if he was to attempt dragging it out alone, he snorted when he realised that destruction was precisely the point.

And he would not allow Christine to help him remove it from the house. She would never touch a coffin again if he could help it.

With a quick tug, it fell unceremoniously to the ground, protesting loudly against the floor. It had served Erik well but it was offensive to his wife, so it would have to be destroyed. He briefly wondered what other types of things would meet a similar fate due to Christine's whims.

The wood cracked slightly in one corner and the lid seemed damaged, but as he turned it on its side, he realised just how narrow the structure truly was. And with the help of his fine Persian rug, it was relatively easy to slide from the room.

He found a dripping Christine in naught but a towel, staring at him with wide eyes as he entered the sitting room. "I heard a crash!"

Erik gave the coffin another shove. "My apologies for worrying you, but apparently some things do not like the prospect of being drowned in a lake."

She huffed, and while he normally would have been amused, in her current attire all he could focus on was the way her breasts became slightly more visible, only to disappear again when she released her breath.

And from the way his blood heated, he remembered vividly exactly why he was dragging out the benighted object whole.

He had far more important things to see to. *Later.*

But the longer he looked at Christine, the more *later* seemed far better if it was *now.* But it was not until she shifted awkwardly and his eyes were drawn to her crimson cheeks that he realised she was uncomfortable. "Perhaps you would like to finish dressing. Then we may see to our funerals and also breakfast."

She shook her head in bemusement. "They are hardly funerals. We are simply... disposing of unwanted objects."

Erik hardly saw the difference.

Though according to Christine it was most likely terribly *naughty,* he did not continue his task until he had watched her walk hurriedly back into the bedchamber, enjoying the view of his wife quite thoroughly.

When she turned to look at him from the doorway however, she would only see him staring down at the coffin—but just barely.

His front door opened inwards and once it was sufficiently propped open, with one final burst of force the coffin rested on the shore of the lake. He turned it to its rightful position, trying to determine if he felt sorry for it.

The more he thought of the lovely bed he now shared with Christine, the more he realised he did not. This was perhaps a bit dramatic, but then, he always had a fondness for theatrical flair.

Christine emerged a moment later, lantern in hand. She was wrapped in his cloak—and though he would never admit it, he did peek to see if she was clothed *beneath* it.

She was.

And while he had to bend down slightly to allow it, she also clothed him in another of his cloaks before she knelt and placed her tattered brown rag and the rest of her old clothes into the coffin. Then Erik added a few loose rocks from along the shore and he pushed his casket and his wife's shabby articles into the murky depths of the lake beyond.

Standing with Christine as they watched their pasts dissolve into the blackness, he knew no sense of loss.

Not when her hand was neatly tucked into his own.

XXIII

After their impromptu funeral, they both were very quiet. It was not one of the horribly awkward silences they had known in the past, but each seemed to be caught up in their own thoughts. Erik allowed Christine to help with making breakfast—*and* to her astonishment, also permitted her assistance with cleaning the dishes afterward.

But now they were settled in the sitting room during the time that had once been designated for her singing lessons.

And as Christine read the sentence in her book for the fifth time with still so little comprehension, she closed it with a huff.

Erik was perfectly poised in his reading chair and from the way the pages rhythmically turned every few minutes, he seemed to have no trouble focusing—even with tumultuous thoughts and feelings.

"Erik."

His head rose instantly. "Yes, Christine?"

It always unsettled her when he looked at her so intensely—as if her every word was of the highest value. She dropped his gaze and fiddled with her book, trying to calm herself. "Are you still going to teach me to sing? We have not had a lesson for some time now." Her eyes strayed to the grandiose instrument looming beyond. "I miss it."

"You may have or do anything you wish. And you should never have to ask to sing for me." He rose swiftly from the chair and hurried over to the organ. When she did not immediately follow he turned to look at her expectantly, and she giggled while walking over to her usual place at his side.

"I see you are enthusiastic about it as well."

He did not deny it. "I merely assumed that you would care to *rest* after our activities last night."

Would he ever cease to make her blush?

"I never sleep quite so well as when I am with you." Her fingers trailed over some stray music, acutely aware of the way Erik's eyes followed her every movement. "I just feel restless, and I hoped singing would make me feel better."

Erik hummed noncommittally. "We shall try singing first, but I have a feeling you require something else entirely."

Christine had not the faintest idea of what he meant, but he distracted her from enquiring further when he thrust a few sheets of parchment into her hands and bade her begin.

She was fairly certain he still thought she needed rest for they did not venture into anything too difficult. Simple scales and melodies were all he required, and while she enjoyed his attentions as well as the opportunity to hear him play, she still felt quite out of sorts.

After over an hour, Erik stopped playing abruptly and she prepared herself for a scolding. Although she had been the one to request the lesson, she knew that she was hardly putting her all into the venture. Her thoughts kept straying to the significance of drowning her old clothes. And to her mortification, as she watched Erik's fingers glide over the keys, she remembered precisely of what else they were capable.

She felt hot and agitated, and the idea of dipping her toes into the lake seemed more and more appealing.

"You are looking at me quite peculiarly, my rose. Is something troubling you?" His mouth was quirked into what seemed to be an impish smile, and with startling clarity she realised that he *knew.*

He was not snapping at her for her inattention because he was merely waiting for her to vocalise her desire.

For she realised now that was precisely what it was.

Desire.

It seemed almost incredible to her that what had seemed like such a dreadful and horrible act could be so pleasing—that she could yearn for it. She had once thought it a wifely duty that would be required for babies, but that joyful notion had also been obliterated because of the cruelty of others.

When Erik had professed his love for her, she had realised that was all she truly wanted. It was a terrible thing to be alone in the world—to live within a crowded city and know so deeply that not a single living soul *loved* you.

But he did.

And she had wanted to try to be a wife to him. A true wife. He had made it quite clear that he had no such expectations, but she needed to know for herself if that was something of which she was capable. She had been frightened and nervous, but he had been so excruciatingly tender and gentle, and her fears had been abated.

On occasion his touch still reminded her of other times, but the more she embraced him and the ministrations he offered, her mind could not deceive her into thinking he was anyone but her husband. No man had ever touched her in such a way, and there was no comparison between the experiences.

She had felt the exquisite bliss he had offered twice now, yet she berated herself for not realising that was what she wished for yet again. Did that make her terribly greedy?

But Erik knew, and he did not seem to begrudge her impulses.

Now that she acknowledged what she craved, she did not know how to put it into words. It seemed too forward to lead him to their bedchamber, and it was hardly time for bed in any case. Should she not at least have the presence of mind to control herself until nighttime?

She was growing frustrated and embarrassed, and Erik seemed to realise it for he rose from the bench and pulled her into his embrace. "Tell your Erik what you desire. You may have anything you wish."

His words were low and soothing and they sent delightful shivers through her entire being. God had obviously not seen to bless him with physical beauty, but Christine did not believe she had ever heard anything as magnificent as his voice.

"Would you mind very much if we..." She could not look at him, but instead focused on the tiny buttons of his shirt.

He stroked her cheek lightly. "If we what? You may ask me for *anything,* my wife."

Christine believed him, truly she did, but it just seemed so improper to voice such things aloud! But he was asking it of her, and he was her husband and perhaps that meant it was not so very wrong.

"I would like for us to... lie... together again." Her face was hot and she nibbled on her lip as she worried over his reaction. Surely he could not be *offended* that she liked his attentions—but she could not help feeling nervous that he would be.

His hand lifted her chin and she finally met his gaze, and she gasped at the sheer *heat* she saw reflected in his translucent eyes. "Never doubt my willingness to be with you, Christine. While I admit to doubting your preference for wanting *my* flesh, I will forever be desirous of yours."

She tried to make her voice firm but all she could muster was a gentle whisper. "I have never desired anyone before you. Please do not ridicule me for it."

And that was the truth of it. She knew other women must have shunned him and he truly was nothing grand to look upon. But he was hers, and she was his, and she enjoyed his strength and his care of her. Many women had ugly husbands, whether in physicality or in their hearts.

And she would much prefer a man whose beauty resided within.

He kissed her then only briefly and she knew it was in apology. "You must forgive me, my Christine. Sometimes you just seem far more than I could ever deserve. There is *nothing* wrong with your passions."

She nodded her assent, and looked up at him hesitantly. "So we may... be together again? Now?"

He chuckled. And this time his kiss was exuberant as it stole her breath and made her heart quiver, and she knew that *this* was love—but then he pulled away and his whisper was devilish. "*Now.*"

His voice went straight to her very soul, and when their kiss began anew she returned it with equal ferocity. He was fumbling with the hooks of her dress, and the buttons of his shirt seemed almost as if they were on the wrong side. Eventually she pulled his hand to his own clothing as she began to see to hers, and he thankfully understood that she was too anxious for them to be together to allow time to be wasted by learning the intricacies of dress known only to the opposite sex.

She had half expected him to leave his trousers on as he had done the previous times, but he abandoned those too. And when she was in nothing but her shift, he picked her up in his arms and hurried them into the bedroom. She could not help the giggle that escaped when she saw all of their clothing strewn about the organ.

A music lesson *indeed.*

Unlike his attentions in the sitting room that had been nearly frenzied, now when he lowered her onto the bed he did so with the utmost care. He tugged at her shift yet he made no move to be rid of it. "May I?"

Perhaps one day asking permission would seem tedious, but for now, she adored him for it. He never took, he *gave,* and he received in turn.

She reached a hand up to his face and mimicked his question.

He hesitated, and Christine was well aware how difficult it was for him to be without it. She considered reprimanding him this morning when she had emerged and saw him once more fully covered, but she refused to be a scold. But in their bed, when they were at their most vulnerable, it seemed only right that he share *all* of himself with her.

She got on her knees upon the bed, even as he stood beside it, and she found that in this position she was nearly eyelevel to him. In amusement she realised that was more a testament to the height of the bed than anything, as Erik was of such great stature.

Christine found that when she pressed her kisses onto his dry skin and slowly took off the mask herself—laving attentions in its wake—he hardly gave protest to its removal. Perhaps it was the show that he disliked, as she always liked to watch whenever he removed something.

At first it had been a cautious act, but now it was merely out of fascination.

And he should hardly complain, for he most *certainly* liked to watch *her*.

With that in mind, she slowly divested herself of the rest of her clothing. She still felt shy and a little awkward, but there was no denying the transfixed expression on her husband's face. Whether or not she believed she was flawed or damaged seemed irrelevant. The man she wished to please most above all else found her attractive, and that was what mattered. At least, that is what she tried to tell herself, even as her arms nearly itched to cover her breasts in order to hide them from his unashamed stare.

She shivered when Erik reached over and ran his fingers lightly over her arm. Christine had never seen hands quite like his, and they were beautiful in their own unique way. They moved in a grace and elegance that was simply *Erik* and it left her feeling clumsy and childish in comparison.

It amazed her that something as effortless as the soft stroking of her arm could produce such tingles and *longing.* It was as if her body recognised the touch of the one who had inspired such feelings before and was awakening and nearly *seeking.* Soon Erik's attention left her limbs as his hand found the back of her neck. She knew a brief moment of panic as memories of harsh hands and frantic gasps for breath flooded her mind, but then Erik placed the slightest pressure and...

Oh.

She had not known how lovely this could feel. His fingers sought and found the tense muscles of her neck and shoulders, soothing them with his seemingly magical fingers until she felt languid and near boneless. She could not even find the will to be embarrassed by the mewling sounds that escaped her throat.

Christine opened her eyes when his ministrations slowed, and for a moment she felt quite guilty. He always worked so hard to ensure that she was properly tended to and prepared before he even thought about his own pleasure, and she wondered what she could do to inspire the same want.

But then her eyes strayed lower and she saw him, stiff and ready, and realised belatedly that such things were not necessary. Surely at some point he would require her more overt participation, but for now it seemed that his enjoyment and readiness was fuelled by her own.

The difference between her husband and her abusers was never more startlingly clear.

She pulled him to her, pouring as much of her passion and gratitude into her kiss as she possibly could. And though not so very long ago she was sure she never wished to feel a man press down upon her again, it suddenly felt like the most wonderful idea. Christine knew that if Erik had not acquiesced she could not have moved him, but he was amiable to her insistent tugging as she held him near and lay back against the pillows. He tried to move quickly to the side, but she wrapped her arms more tightly around him to cease his attempt. "No, it is all right."

He looked at her warily. "I do not wish to frighten you. Or squish you."

Christine could not help but laugh, and her amusement made her bold. It took a good bit of wriggling, but she managed to move the one leg he still rested slightly upon until she could wrap it around his waist, holding fast even as he shuddered and tried to pull away. "Erik, you said *anything* that I desire. There is no rescinding it now." Her reminder seemed to be the only encouragement he needed, and although he kept himself slightly raised by his elbows so as not to cause her discomfort, she still felt his presence looming above her as he covered her completely.

And instead of feeling stifled and trapped, she felt *safe.* Nothing could harm her when her Erik was so very near. But any thought at all flew from her mind when Erik shifted slightly and *that* part of him brushed against her most sensitive places.

It felt *wonderful.* She squirmed, trying to make him do it again, but he only nestled more closely against her. And with a gasp of surprise due to her sensitises nerves, finally felt him enter. He was watching her intently, and from the way she had wrapped herself around him she was acutely aware of how tense and effortful it was for him to keep still. It did not hurt, but it felt different than last night. She shifted her hips slightly as she tried to determine precisely *how* it could feel so different, but her attention waned when she heard the strangled moan from her husband.

"Christine... are you well?" His words were punctuated by gasps, and she felt a momentary triumph. Last night had been similar, but it pleased her immensely that even in this prone position he was still at the mercy of her actions—she could still be a willing participant instead of merely a recipient of another's act.

"Oh yes, Erik. Very well."

He groaned and let his head fall against her neck. "Thank God."

Her soft laughter turned into whimpers when he began to move. The sensations were not quite so intense this way, and she found that she rather liked that she remained sensible enough to appreciate how Erik's face so clearly showed his enjoyment once he had abandoned the crook of her neck. At times he looked nearly pained, but then he would smile slightly and she found that she adored that particular expression. He had never said so outright, but she knew with her entire being that she had been the only one to see that smile—and knowing it was because of *her* warmed her heart thoroughly.

He paused for a moment and looked down at her, his expression almost thoughtful. She raised one of her hands and cupped his cheek and he turned his head slightly and pressed a kiss onto the centre of her palm, and another on her gold ring. "I love you, my rose. So much."

Christine did not know why but tears pricked at her eyes and she brought him toward her for a true kiss. "I love you as well. More than you know." While his eyes had been soft they now burned, and his movements returned with vigour. This time one of his hands trailed over her heated flesh, skimming over her breasts before descending to the place where they were so intimately joined.

Each thrust and rub of his fingers sent a throb of pleasure through her veins, and soon she felt that wonderful rush of sensation that seemed to sweep over Erik in equal measure, and with a final plunge he stilled.

Christine had never considered him a heavy man, but as he collapsed from their lovemaking and used her breasts as his pillow, she noticed with some amusement that he was indeed a weighty presence. Eventually she would need him to move as her lungs were rather restricted, but for now, as they both tried to catch their breaths, she would never dream of asking it of him. His fingers were teasing over her skin and his face nuzzled into their makeshift pillows, and she smiled as she felt his lips nibbling softly.

"I do not recall being on the menu."

She could feel his smile even as he nestled more firmly against her. "Then you should cease being so delicious, though I would prefer you remain as you are."

Christine liked the way his head moved with her as she chuckled and she brought one of her hands to his hair, running her fingers through it mildly. "It was terribly mean of you to carry on with our lesson for over an hour when you *knew* what I was wanting." She also liked the way his body shivered when her fingers found a particularly sensitive spot by the nape of his neck. She would have to remember that.

Erik grunted, and placed one last kiss upon her breast before turning slightly to face her. "Sometimes anticipation is the greatest sort of inducement."

She huffed. "I do not think I like waiting."

He smiled, and she found it quite roguish—if her husband could ever be considered such of course. "I shall remember that.

The way his eyes shone with impish delight should have made her nervous, but she knew that whatever he had planned would only include pleasurable experiences for them both so she merely rolled her eyes before closing them contentedly. It was dreadfully indulgent of her as she had slept well the night before and it was *far* too early to be lazing and napping. But she felt sleepy and wonderfully sated, and she hoped Erik would not mind too much if she just rested for a moment...

And before she fell asleep she heard and felt his chuckle as he returned his head to her breasts and made himself quite comfortable.

Her marvellous imp of a husband.

XXIV

Domestic bliss suited Erik quite perfectly. They cooked, they baked, they sang, and although at one time he was sure that would have been his favourite activity, he found instead that making love held most of his attention.

It was very distressing at times having to divide his time so thoroughly. A large part of him wished to spend every waking moment with Christine, while the part of him that had once dominated his every action insisted that now was the time to *compose.* What time he did make for his music was tremendously productive, as his wife seemed to be the key to unlocking some hidden part of his genius. She inspired sweeter melodies and seductive refrains, and more than once his playing had induced her to tug insistently at his hand until he tended to her desires in the bedroom.

He always gave half-hearted protests that she was *interrupting* and that the music should always come first, but she would just give him that petulant glare and remind him that he had made vows to *her,* and not to some figment of musicality.

Which of course was simply insulting—as if *he* would ever forget his marriage vows.

What surprised him most was how enthusiastically Christine embraced housework. He knew she would tire of it eventually and he always made sure to help in some way, but he had to admit that he was rather glad that she could prepare meals and tea things while he wrote. It seemed a trifle ridiculous, but there was something rather sweet about *missing* her. There was a joy in her smile when they rejoined for a meal or for their evening hot chocolate and a novel, and her touches were always a little more enthusiastic as she insisted he sit with her on the settee and that she be allowed to use him as her personal footrest.

Not that he would ever complain. He would give a sigh of resignation to which she would merely laugh, and if he was in particularly good mood, he might even grace her with a massage. She was very ticklish along the delicate arch of her foot, and he would never tire of hearing the delighted giggles she would grace him with whenever he deposited light and teasing caresses on the area.

Her eyes would glow and her smile was bright, and he knew she had never looked so beautiful.

On this day however, it was time for him to work. He loathed leaving her—had not actually done so since their marriage, always taking her with him if they required food or other sundries. But the Opera had been neglected for too long, and it was time for him to reinstate his position as resident Ghost. It would not do for the managers to think he had vacated the premises entirely.

He had considered giving up the pretence completely and simply living in his little home with his wife, but he realised with a grimace that to do so would mean a lack of income. And while he did not consider himself a greedy man, he did firmly believe he deserved a stipend for all of his contributions over the years.

And besides, he now had a spouse to provide for.

He donned his cloak, gloves, and mask, kissed his wife at the door and told her to behave—to which she scoffed and gave him a light push out the door.

Impudent girl.

What he had not expected was how *lonely* he felt as he made his way to the stage. He was used to her constant presence now and it felt odd to be truly alone. He did not like it at all.

This would be a quick trip then. He would cause some mischief, see that his Opera House was not in shambles, and then he would hurry back down for tea. Perhaps Christine would even have made some lovely treat to welcome his return.

He quickened his steps at the thought.

The theatre itself was in the throes of a new production—if *Faust* could ever truly be considered new. The ballet rats were practicing in one corner while the chorus and lead singers rehearsed blocking and sent glares at one another when steps trod too closely to one another. It appeared they were in the middle of the second Act, and although the chorus *was* to resemble a carousing bunch of drunken villagers, Erik highly suspected that a few of them were indeed inebriated.

One particular dolt tripped over his feet and shoved one of the chorus girls as he fell. While Erik knew that it was not done purposefully—that much was evident—it still annoyed him greatly at the lack of professionalism.

Very well, *that* was where his mischief would be aimed.

Throwing his voice up into the rafters so it would bellow imposingly over the entire company, he allowed a sinister laugh to permeate the entire stage. A few sparks travelled down from what appeared to be the ceiling, and he was regaled with a full peal of shrieks and general hysteria.

Erik would not tolerate laziness or deficient coordination. From what he overheard as he skulked about the upper floors, they had been working on this particular scene for many days and had yet to show signs of improvement. How could he consider retirement when he was forced to work with such bumbling idiots?

He waited long enough to ensure they would resume the rehearsal and he was pleased when the chorus master did not allow them an interlude. Most of them would most likely turn to drink to steady their nerves, and that was the opposite of helpful. Instead, he demanded in a slightly quavering voice that they return to their positions, and Erik was satisfied that while most of them trembled and looked around the ceiling periodically, they were all much better behaved.

Suitably pleased at his work he turned to leave, but paused when he caught sight of La Carlotta. She would most certainly be playing Margarita and he nearly groaned. She had never been *magnificent,* but now that he had Christine's voice firmly imbedded in his mind he knew that to sit through one of La Carlotta's performances would now be simply agony.

He wondered if it would be possible for Christine to take her place. If he did not allow her to distract him as she proved so utterly capable, he would be able to prepare her voice by the time of the first performance. She was a wife now, and he knew that there were few married ladies who continued their singing career much past their honeymoon.

Erik could not help but feel excited at the prospect of displaying *his* creation upon the stage. Christine was her own person, he knew that quite well, but her voice had been nurtured and cultivated by him and he could not help but feel a tinge of possessive feelings toward it. It was a part of him, and it was not as though *he* could ever grace the stage.

But even as he thought it, he was nearly startled by an overwhelming jealously. The people of Paris did not *deserve* her, just as they did not deserve his art. While once he might have revelled in the idea of the audience being forced to acknowledge his genius, he now wondered if they could appreciate it even then.

The only answer he had decided upon by the time he reached his front doorstep was that he would have to speak to Christine. He would not compel her, and she always seemed to have a very strong opinion about most anything.

Headstrong girl.

He opened the front door feeling rather sullen, but when Christine came flying out of the kitchen and nearly attacked him with her affectionate embrace, he could not help but lose any sense of melancholy. He would have thought something wrong had she not immediately bestowed him with a smile and a wifely kiss. "I missed you!"

Erik tried valiantly to keep from smiling, but he could feel the corners of his lips quirk regardless of his efforts. "Indeed."

She merely cuddled closer and spoke into his chest. "I am going to pretend you missed me just as much, even if you did not."

Any pretence of teasing shattered and he laid his hand upon her curls and kissed the top of her unruly head. "There is no need to pretend when it is the truth."

She only hummed in response.

Content to simply stand with her but feeling his dilemma begin to gnaw at his consciousness, he pulled away from her with a sigh. "Christine, I need to speak to you about something."

She pulled away sharply. "Something *bad?*"

He shook his head and stroked her cheek lightly, chuckling despite himself. "No, nothing bad. Why would I trouble you with *bad* things?" Any such items would be quickly and permanently disposed of by *him.* She should be allowed to be happy.

Christine stared at him for a moment, and he could readily see that she was trying to decide if she should be offended by his declaration. He tugged at her hand, trying to distract her before she could make up her mind. "Come sit with me."

"Not yet, I have to get the tea things." She hurried off to the kitchen and Erik wondered if he should follow. He naturally wanted to go and offer his assistance—at the very *least* carry the tea tray—but she had been making it clearer of late that she wanted to do some things on her own. As she had put it, she wanted the opportunity to take *care* of him.

He still struggled with such a foreign concept.

But, he did not want the scolding she would give if he intruded so he sat upon the settee and waited as patiently as he was able. His comfortable reading chair called to him, but he wanted to sit with his wife, and he thought that trying to balance tea things while she perched on his lap—*distracting him*—would not lead to a productive conversation.

Christine looked immensely pleased with herself when she emerged from the kitchen. There were steaming scones and a bowl filled with preserves, as well as a white frothy substance that he could not immediately identify. "I used our new cookery book and made clotted cream. Now we will have a proper tea!"

A proper tea like the one she watched her *fancy ladies* consuming while she starved in the gutter.

He felt a pang in his heart at the thought, and quite ridiculously his throat tightened almost as if he was on the verge of sobbing. Would reminders of her torment ever cease to cause such reactions?

Erik held out a hand in welcome. "Come here."

She deposited the tray on the table, and though he wanted her to nestle into his side as was her usual habit when they sat together, she sat primly and set about preparing their tea and scones to her exacting standards.

He amused himself while she worked by playing with the loose ends of her hair. His fingers must have skimmed a particularly sensitive spot because she jolted, laughing as she did so before she turned to give him his plate full of now slightly mussed scone. "You have ruined my presentation!"

Christine tried to sound outraged, but her eyes were twinkling too much, so Erik simply leaned forward and kissed her cheek in apology. He had to remind himself at first that such things were allowed—these casual touches and caresses between a married couple who miraculously loved one another—but he was slowly growing more bold as it became their custom.

Finally, after what seemed an eternity, she had everything prepared and leaned back until she was pressed against his side.

Where she belonged.

"What did you want to talk to me about?"

He was momentarily distracted by the bite of scone that apparently was even more delightful than usual for she moaned and sucked prettily at her finger so as not to lose any of the clotted cream or sweet preserves.

Apparently she did not have to be sitting in his lap in order to drive him thoroughly to distraction.

Erik took a sip of his tea to brace himself before voicing his enquiry. "How would you feel about performing on the stage?"

He had timed it incorrectly for she had just taken a sip from her own cup and spluttered at his question, even as she pulled away to stare at him aghast. "Me? No!"

That was not the answer he had been expecting. She would have debated with herself and upon his assurances that she would be perfection itself, she would have deferred to his opinion—even though he was not entirely sure of his own at this time.

But his wife constantly surprised him. "You seem quite vehement. Why?"

It was a genuine question that was evidently the wrong one to ask. She *glared* at him, and put down her cup with a clatter. "How can you even ask that? I do not want all of Paris to be *looking* at me! I just want to sing for you!"

That was flattering and distressing all at once.

"You would still sing for me, but merely onstage. And as for people looking at you..." He dared not touch her when she was staring at him like that, even when he urged to soothe her in some way. "Why would that be such a terrible thing?" She was beauty personified, and she had nothing to fear of their ridicule or disdain.

But obviously he had forgotten an important detail. "I do not *like* people anymore, Erik. They either hurt you or ignore you even when you need help the most. Why would I want to allow them to hear me sing?" Her anger seemed to have abated and she now just seemed small and fatigued. "I just want to be with you."

He grimaced, and while his heart swelled at her words, intellectually he knew precisely why she felt that way. "You wish to hide."

She tried to regain her angry and imperious tone, but she only succeeded in sounding hoarse. "And why is that so wrong? *You* are hiding too!"

Erik would not get angry. She was merely using the same accusation against him, and he realised how painful it was once spoken aloud and directed at him. The whole purpose of speaking to her of this was to understand her feelings on the matter, and it was clear she had no interest in becoming the star of Paris. She would sing for him and they would continue their lessons, and maybe someday in the future she would change her mind. But for now he would not begrudge her, and he shoved away his ire resolutely.

"We need not speak of this anymore. It was only a passing thought."

To his absolute horror, Christine burst into tears. "I do not want to be a disappointment to you!"

Against his better judgement, he put his arm around her and pulled her back against him. To his relief she did not struggle, but to his bemusement he could feel her tears leaking onto his cashmere sleeves—although he decided he did not mind so very much, not if she found some comfort in his arms.

"Foolish girl. As if you could ever disappoint me. It is far more likely that I will do something horrid and you will be hard pressed to find it within yourself to forgive me." And that happened to be precisely why he had not revealed any of the truly gruesome details of his past.

Her tears abated and he leaned forward somewhat and brought her teacup and scone to within easy reach. She nibbled almost mechanically, and he cursed himself for even bringing up the subject as he wanted her joyful expression to return as she tasted the fruits of her culinary experimentation.

He had not the least idea of how to make it better.

Erik had thought she was improving. She seemed perfectly *normal* when alone with him. They still had their moments when engaged in intimacies where she would stiffen and tell him to be still, or he would make some gesture upon a scar that would make her flinch in memory, yet they were progressing together. He was becoming less shy and surer that his actions were pleasurable and well received.

But evidently her mind still required more healing.

The difficulty was that she needed it in the exact same way he did. To admit that shunning the world was unhealthy for her wellbeing was to admit it was the same for him also. And he did not think himself ready to do so.

Her voice broke the silence and he could tell that her tears had slowed for her voice was clearer than he had expected. "Do you think there is something wrong with me that I should like being *intimate* after everything that has happened?"

They had spoken of such things before of course, but the fact that she would still question it was also revealing. Christine was the only woman he had spoken to for any significant length of time, so he was certainly under-qualified to give an opinion. But she needed his reassurance and it would be cruel to withhold it. "I think only you can know what you need, and there is no one here that would complain about your *liking* of intimacy."

This time his fingers purposefully found the sensitive spot on her back and he was quite pleased with her giggling and squirming that seemingly shattered her despondency. When she settled however, she still looked at him with eyes tinged with worry. "I am sorry though, about not wanting to perform. I understand if you feel like you are wasting your time teaching me since no one would get to hear it."

He scoffed. "Providing you lessons will *never* be a waste of time. Music should be created for its own sake, not for recognition or fame." Although he often had to remind himself of the latter when he became frustrated by what was passing for musical talent.

"But if you ever change your mind and feel like it is truly important to you... I will try. Because I love you and I want you to be pleased with me."

She had joined their fingers and was staring down at them as she fiddled with his thumb, and he nudged her gently with his shoulder to get her attention. "That would be the worst possible motivation. I would not have you become a prima donna unless that was *your* express desire. If I forced you to do it from a manipulation of your affection that would only give you cause to resent me." He shuddered at the mere thought. "And the pain of that would outweigh any possible exaltation at your triumph."

Her eyes were glassy and he wondered what he could have said wrongly *again,* but then she smiled and he knew she believed him. "I love you for your thoughtfulness."

Erik squeezed her hand softly, and if both were not occupied he would have pulled her in for a kiss. "I love you for your smiles."

He was blessed with yet another before she settled down against his chest, nibbling at her scone and sipping her tea while he did the same.

Until the siren began to call.

XXV

It was not the first time someone had breached the lower levels of his domain, and he was certain it would not be the last. People were foolish and it was to be expected after his dramatics near the stage that new search parties would be coordinated as they tried to hunt down the Ghost.

Of course, as these imbeciles actually *believed* he was a ghost, he never could quite understand why they thought hunting him would be advisable. How exactly did one go about arresting a paramour?

But still, at times they felt obligated to look, perhaps thinking that he was merely a man posing as the great Phantom. And though he would not tell Christine, a few of them had lost their lives to the venture—either by his direct intervention or by one of the numerous traps that guarded his home.

However, while this had happened before, it never ceased to send his heart racing. He once would have delighted in the prospect of causing harm to the miscreants that so inadvisably tread where they most *certainly* did not belong, yet he now felt...

Fear.

Which was absolutely ridiculous.

There was no possible way they could find an entrance into his home, nor cross the lake without the safety of his boat.

But as he looked into the eyes of his frightened wife, he knew what the difference was. On the off chance that he was bested by one of the rogue trespassers, it was only his life that was at stake—something that had never mattered to him. But now he had his Christine to think about, and *she* valued his continued breath. And while he would quite willingly die to protect her, she would be left trapped and alone in the darkness of his home should anything befall him.

"Erik, what is that?"

Now was not the time for alarm. To embrace such feelings would lead to panic and sloppy work. He needed his mind alert and unencumbered by worry.

He placed his teacup calmly—or as steadily as he could manage with his tense fingers—back onto the tray and gave Christine's hand a reassuring pat. "It would appear that we have a visitor, my dear. Perhaps you would be so good as to wait here while I go and see who is ringing at our door."

Her anxiety was clear, and she opened her mouth and he was sure she would beg him not to go, but instead she simply implored, "Please be careful!"

He smiled at her wanly and kissed her forehead before rushing to fetch his cloak and lasso.

The small and cramped tunnel that allowed him to bypass the lake was created for this exact purpose. Erik was a firm believer in contingencies, and as he crept along the darkened tunnel, he prepared himself for what might soon transpire. If a person was in fact directly across from the lake, they would have to be disposed of. He could allow them to attempt at crossing and *that* would also ensure their demise, but his blood was warm and he felt a near desperate need to protect his home—and his wife—through action.

He exited the tunnel and closed the hidden door with a silent push, and he kept to the shadows as he regarded the intruder. It was obviously a man, and while he could only see the back of him from this vantage point, there was a striking feature that bespoke of the man's identity. Though the man had placed his lantern on the ground, Erik could clearly see that he kept a hand raised about his head, even as he prowled around the shore of the lake as he seemingly tried to find a way to cross.

"You are an idiot, Daroga."

The man in question whirled about, still keeping the hand levelled at his eyes. As if Erik did not know how to kill a man *without* the lasso.

He felt mildly insulted.

Erik had thrown his voice so as to confuse the direction, and he could tell that the Persian was having difficulty locating him. He would not kill this man, but that did not mean he could not have a bit of fun at his expense—after all, he had worried his wife, and that was unacceptable.

"Erik, show yourself!"

He remained unmoved, eyeing the man thoughtfully. "Why? What business have you here?"

The Daroga sighed and stilled, obviously realising how much of a fool he looked as he whirled about. "Do you not think frightening an entire chorus is a bit beneath you?"

Erik scoffed and took a final step forward. His body had been hidden by a large boulder, but as he moved away from his temporary shield he knew that his eyes would be visible as they glowed warningly in the darkness. "If they would behave themselves *without* my dramatic intervention, I would not be forced to take such measures." He waved his hand impatiently. "But surely that little event would not have been enough to send you scurrying down here—you arrived far too quickly for that. So what is *truly* your motive? And speak plainly, for I tire of looking at you."

He said it partly to goad his unwelcomed visitor and partly because it was entirely true. He was used to looking at Christine for most of the day and she was far more pleasing to look upon than the Persian—who now appeared rather angry.

"A very frightened scullery maid spoke about seeing the ghost and his *companion* in the kitchen pantry. Ever since then I have been trying to find your infamous home to see how you could have come upon a *young girl*."

The sting of the insinuation was lessened considerably at the knowledge that it had taken him so long to make it to the lake. The idea that his tunnels might have been so readily accessible that the Daroga should have stumbled down to his private lake in a mere hour had been quite distressing.

He must have taken Erik's silence for a confession of perceived guilt, for he grew even more upset. "Erik, tell me you have not kidnapped some poor girl. You have had your eccentricities in the past but I never thought you would stoop so low!"

Erik's irritation was rising. "Your faith in me is quite astounding. If there is nothing else..."

He moved to slip back into the shadows but he stopped when the Persian spoke once more. "Wait. I am sorry, my friend, I am simply worried. Do you have a girl with you? In the name of our past acquaintanceship I ask you to tell me clearly."

Damn him.

Erik turned around slowly, trying to decide if he would later regret his honesty. "You will not allow this matter rest, will you?"

He shook his head firmly. "I will not."

No, because that would be simple and allow Erik and his lovely wife to live in peace—which apparently was far too much to ask.

"*If* I take you to see my wife, you will not harass her. You will not pester her with inane questions about if she is with me willingly or how she came to be with me—to do so would only cause her pain." Erik gave him a withering glare when he noted the man's aghast expression. "*I* will not harm her, you *dolt*. The memory will."

The Daroga swallowed reflexively. "You have taken a wife then? And she..."

Erik did not allow him to continue. "I will have you know that *she* was the one to broach the subject of marriage. I found it perfectly acceptable to merely grant her asylum." He rose to his full height and took a threatening step forward. "And I *love* her, you stupid man, and by God's mercy she loves me. So you will *not* upset her!"

The Persian was silent for a long moment before he spoke again. "I should like to meet her. And rest assured, I will be delicate with any questions I ask."

That was not wholly reassuring but Erik decided to allow it. The only way to truly stop this man's inane enquiry was to kill him, and he did not relish the thought. "Wait here."

Erik slipped back through the tunnel and crossed back to the entrance of his home. He went to the boat but stopped suddenly. Christine was inside and undoubtedly anxious, and to simply walk in with an unknown man would only upset her further.

The blasted Persian could wait.

He entered his home cautiously, and while he enjoyed the way Christine flung herself into his arms as soon as he was fully within the sitting room, he did not like that she trembled slightly and clutched at him so fiercely in obvious distress. "Are you all right?"

He patted her curls in comfort and pulled her back from him so he could look at her face. "There is an old acquaintance outside, Christine, and he would like to meet you. Is that acceptable to you?"

Erik hated the way her expression shuttered, and she seemed wary and fearful once again. It reminded him far too much of how she had been when she first came to him, and it was startlingly vivid just how far she had come.

She pulled away from him completely and wrapped her arms around her waist in a sad semblance of an embrace. "If he is a friend of yours, I suppose I do not mind."

It was apparent that she *did* mind and he considered telling the man to leave them both alone. But perhaps this would be good for her—to know that even when a strange man was near she was safe and no one would hurt her.

With that in mind, after a short stop to procure an article from his wardrobe, Erik returned to the boat and allowed the Persian to enter, rowing them both across the lake. When they landed, he pulled forth the long, crisp tie of a cravat and held it out so it was visible to his *guest.* "You will put this on or turn off your lantern while I open the door."

The man had the audacity to look amused. "Really, Erik, is that not a bit excessive?"

"No."

His answer was curt and perfectly serious, and only after the Daroga blew out the lantern did Erik tuck the cravat back into his pocket and open the door.

Christine was standing where he had left her, fiddling with her fingers and appearing terribly nervous. A part of him wondered if it would be inadvisable to immediately go to her side and offer comfort as it could improperly be perceived as controlling behaviour, but he quickly dismissed the thought. This was his wife and she was uneasy in her own home.

And as her husband, it was his duty to set it to rights.

Erik went to her and she wrapped her arm through his, leaning her head against his shoulder as she gathered the courage to look their guest in the eye in greeting.

He put his hand on hers and patted it reassuringly. "Daroga, this is my wife, Christine."

"Hello, M. Daroga."

Erik could not help but smile and did not seek to correct her regarding the use of his title as a name. She would have no way of knowing the designations of Persian officials, so it was only natural she would assume he was addressing him by his surname.

The man in question gave a low bow. "A pleasure to make your acquaintance, Mme Christine."

Christine made a subtle dip of her own, and Erik could see how much effort it took for her to calm her nerves. And though her voice still betrayed her continued anxiety, she managed to play at hostess quite admirably. "Would you care for some tea? I made scones earlier."

Erik stiffened. He did not object to her offering of tea as it would induce them all to sit down and Christine could have a bit of respite as she took frequent sips from her cup, but he did not care for the idea of the man eating something of *hers.* Those were made especially for him after he had done his work for the day, and he did not appreciate her treats being disposed of upon unwelcome company.

"Just tea, my dear. Daroga is not one for baked goods."

The Persian glared at him, but wisely held his tongue until Christine had gathered their tea things and went to the kitchen to brew a fresh pot.

"I would have liked something to eat, Erik. I missed luncheon while looking for *you.*"

Erik shrugged and sank elegantly onto the settee. He would have preferred the more imposing figure he could have portrayed in his reading chair—and he grimaced slightly that another man should be seated in it—but there was no possible way he would allow Christine to sit with anyone but himself. He waved his hand in offering for the man to sit. "That was quite your own doing. I never asked for you to look for me, so you starve by your own choice."

The Daroga sighed but did as he was bid and sat. "She seems quite frightened. Is it of me or of her situation?"

Erik glowered. "It is none of your business. But as you will only press and I would rather you *not* hound us while she is present, I will answer your inane enquiry." He lowered his voice and cast a quick glance to ensure Christine would not enter. "She had some unfortunate dealings with men after her father died, and while she trusts *me,* she apparently does not feel reason to extend such courtesy to you."

The Persian blanched. "Unfortunate... *dealings.* Do you mean..."

Erik huffed angrily. "Do not ask me to speak of it so openly, Daroga. It would only unearth unpleasantness." A mild word for the rage that would come forth if he considered his wife's pain for any great length of time or voiced it aloud. When he spoke of it with Christine, he kept his temper properly contained for he knew how important it was for her to speak openly and plainly—that she could *trust* him with such details without fear of recourse.

To speak to another man about all she had suffered would be another matter entirely.

His guest's eyes softened, and when Christine returned and quietly asked how he took his tea—doing so while mumbling into the teacup—his voice was gentle and unassuming as he took the cup of simple black tea from her trembling fingers. "Thank you, Madame. You are very kind."

She nodded, and with more confidence made Erik's cup and then her own, nestling back into Erik's side for consolation.

Christine sat in her normal pose with her legs tucked up into her skirts, and with a covert glance from the corner of his eye, Erik was satisfied to note that her unstockinged feet were also concealed. Perhaps it was a bit ridiculous on his part, but he revelled in the knowledge that there were certain aspects of her person that were solely for him—and he would most assuredly not be sharing them with the Persian.

The Daroga took a sip of his tea, nodding appreciatively as he did so.

"You make a very fine brew. I am sure your scones would have been equally delicious." This was directed toward Erik with a raised brow, to which Erik sniffed and looked away.

The man chuckled, and Erik wondered if it was too much effort to rise from his seat and hit him soundly for his impudence.

"So, Mme Christine. How do you like living down here with Erik? You must want for female companionship."

Christine cast a worried glance at her husband, and he reached down to stroke her cheek lightly in encouragement. At one time he might have been distressed by any such enquiries, as they would have implied that *his* company or care of her was insufficient. But he was secure that his Christine was contented, and it was perfectly normal for ladies to desire the tittering of other women on occasion—no matter how repugnant that seemed to him.

But Christine shook her head. "I am perfectly happy here with Erik. I never had many girls my own age at home, so this is not so different from when I just lived with my papa."

She blushed then, deep and crimson, and although Erik's first reaction was to feel affronted at the idea that living with him was akin to a strictly *platonic* relationship, it was clear that as soon as she said it her mind drifted to the activity that made their arrangement completely *unlike* her childhood.

And from the way colour rose in the Persian's cheeks as well, he had also caught her unspoken recant.

To Erik's relief, the conversation remained civil. They all sipped placidly at their tea and Christine eventually began to lose some of her tenseness, and she even looked up shyly at the man once or twice when he asked her a direct question.

Soon however, it turned tedious, and he must have felt Erik's desire for his absence for the Persian rose, setting his teacup back on the tray. "Well, I must take my leave. Thank you for your hospitality, Madame, I hope to see you again soon." He bowed once more and then turned. "Erik, perhaps you would be so good as to see me out—and offer a light, as you deprived me of my own."

That was purely ridiculous, as it would have been dangerous for him to traverse the tunnels without a matchbook. But Erik saw it for what it was—he wished to speak to him alone without offending the mistress of the house.

Erik rolled his eyes but complied, knowing that at the very least he would have to open the front door in order for him to vacate the premises—a task that he was happy to oblige.

He had expected to be peppered with accusations and outrage as soon as the door was closed behind them and the abandoned lantern was relit, but to his surprise the Daroga was quiet and thoughtful. It was not until they were across the lake yet again that he spoke. "It is clear that she cares for you. If what you say is true," this received a scowl. Of course it was true. "She would not cling to you so if you did not hold her affection."

Erik wanted to growl something about how completely unnecessary it was to state what was obvious, but he remained silent when the man continued. "I apologise for my disbelief earlier. I am happy that you have found someone that... loves you." From his hesitation on the word, it was apparent to Erik that he still found it incredible that someone should be capable of such emotion towards *him.* He tried not to feel hurt by the notion that a man who knew him better than most could still think such things, but he failed miserably.

He wanted to go back to his wife. She found him worthy of love and capable of it in return and never questioned his affections.

Erik turned to leave without another word, but started violently when he felt a hand upon his arm. While their acquaintanceship was such that he did not feel the urge to kill him on sight, that did *not* give him leave to touch him. He pulled away fiercely, but before he could eviscerate the man for his presumption, he took note of the rather pleading look he was being given. "My intention was not to offend you. I meant that with all sincerity. I just find this entire afternoon to be quite unexpected."

Erik nodded, for *that* he could understand. "I never thought I would have a wife, but now I do and she does not like to be kept waiting."

There was no talk of the Persian ever returning or meaningless platitudes of how nice it was to see one another again—though he strongly suspected that the man would be making a habit of showing up on his doorstep.

Instead, Erik simply rowed home to his wife.

XXVI

Christine was restless.

She did not want to sing, she did not want to bake, and he dared not ask if she wanted to make love by the way she huffed and fidgeted whenever he touched her.

It mildly surprised him that he did not grow more offended by her seeming rejection, but he supposed that when they had grown so very close it was only natural that he would also grow more secure in her fondness—even when it dissipated for a time.

And did not *normal* husbands have wives who on occasion did not want their husband's attentions?

He was fairly certain he had read in a book that such was a part of marriage.

Though he was loath to admit that he was hiding, he supposed that was the most accurate description of the way he threw himself into his compositions. At first he had tried playing all of her favourites, but that did not even seem helpful as she mumbled something about seeing to the supper dishes—dishes that he had already washed.

So instead, he distracted himself from her ill temper by coaxing new melodies from hidden depths of his mind and soul, and he had so succeeded that he was startled when Christine placed her hand upon his shoulder. "Erik, I wish to talk to you."

That certainly did not bode well, and he felt intensely wary as he followed her to the settee, casting a longing look back at the organ. The organ never wanted to *talk* to him, nor did it sulk or begrudge his attention when it was offered.

He had assumed she would sit with him but instead she merely paced the floor, apparently unable to find the exact words she wanted to convey.

His worry grew and the voice that had been so silenced in the past idyllic weeks since their marriage niggled and whispered that she was going to confess that he had done something unforgiveable—that she had found some detail of his past that made her incapable of continuing as his wife.

"Christine, what *is* it?" His rising panic made his voice sharper than he intended, but she should *know* how much her agitation caused similar reactions from him!

She stopped short and cast an irritated glance at him before she released a long sigh and flung herself ungracefully upon the settee. "I want to go outside, but I am *afraid* to go outside, and I *hate* it."

Erik blinked. *That* was the cause of such a dither?

He was not certain if he should feel relieved or angry that she had concerned him so, but as he stared at her incredulously for a long moment he saw that she was genuinely distressed. Apparently this was important, and he would not dismiss her troubles when they were of significance—even if it was only imperative to her.

"Why are you afraid?"

She gave him an exasperated look and he returned it with a serious one of his own. She was verging on hysterical, and while he would gladly try to help assuage her fears, that did not mean he appreciated her ire—not when it was directed at him.

Christine noticed his shift and after a few deep breaths, her expression softened. "I am sorry, I do not mean to snap at you. I just feel... like my skin is too small, and I want to see the *sky.* But when I went to ask you I just felt this fear clawing at me that it is not safe, and it is foolish of me to even ask to go above because it could be dangerous."

"We have gone above many times together and you have not reacted so. What is different now?" Erik gave the cushion beside him an insistent pat, his intention obvious. She was leaning against the opposite arm of the settee, and even this short distance felt too far—especially when she was so plainly upset. She stared at him for a long moment, but finally relented with a huff.

She fiddled with her hands clasped in her lap, evidently finding them to be far more interesting to look at than her husband even as she answered him. "Because when we have gone before it was because we needed something. We *had* to go otherwise we would not have food. This is just me being selfish."

Erik could not help but scoff. "There is nothing selfish about it. You would like to go outside, and we shall go. Nothing will happen to you while your Erik is near. Surely you *know* that."

To his astonishment his words only caused tears to well in her eyes. "But what if something happens to you because of me? I could not bear that happening because I wanted to take a walk at night! We always go in the *day!*"

Erik felt completely lost. It was true; he had been trying to think of her feelings and had made sure that their little outings were restricted to daylight hours—although in winter that made their opportunities for productivity while the rest of Paris was not *also* awake to be rather limited. However, Christine's comfort was paramount, and while it meant he was greatly confined in what he could accomplish and where he could walk without being seen, she had finally grown comfortable being aboveground.

But apparently only during the daytime.

He could readily understand that she did not wish to be alone—and he would have strongly objected if she had wished for a nighttime interlude by herself as she traversed the streets and parks that Paris offered, but she obviously was forgetting that he had already proven himself capable against one of her attackers. A very large part of him wanted to remind her of this as she had almost maligned his pride as an assassin and protector. But as he watched her lip quiver and her eyes implore him for *something,* he knew pressing that particular point would be for selfish reasons alone.

"Get your cloak, Christine."

Her eyes widened and her hands clutched at him. "No! I am sorry, we will not go. I am being silly and I will go tend to..."

But there was nothing to tend and that was precisely the problem. Since she had instigated the touch, he placed a hand over hers and patted it softly, repeating the direction. "Get your cloak, Christine, and we will take a walk. Not because you asked but because you are looking a little pale, and some night air is *necessary* for your health. And because your husband would like to take a stroll with his wife."

She still looked like she was going to argue, but he felt as if this was an important step for her. There was nothing to fear when he was near, and he did not wish for her to continue to live with the burden of constant terror that the above was unsafe. She deserved to be able to walk freely and without care, and she had been robbed of that.

Erik would simply try to right the injustice by proving an able and willing guard so that she might regain her freedoms.

He extended a handkerchief—as he had found it necessary to have one always within reach when one had a wife so prone to tears—and Christine dried her eyes quickly before going to their bedchamber. Erik walked to his own, though it now served as a dressing room more than anything, as he had yet to replace the casket with anything suitable.

He had toyed with the idea of a parlour for Christine, as it was traditional for ladies to have their own separate apartments to do feminine things such as needlepoint and gossip, but he had swiftly dismissed the idea. Erik liked her within eyesight, not hidden away in an isolated room.

By the time he had fetched his cloak, hat, and gloves, Christine was already waiting in the sitting room for him. She seemed to have an aversion to his previous bedchamber, and that suited him quite well. Memories were harsh and vivid of her impromptu début as a corpse, and though her prop had been drowned thoroughly, the memories of her last visit into the room left him feeling nervous and displeased.

Christine had already donned her cloak, which had officially become hers when she had all but demanded for any of Erik's sewing supplies, and settled on the settee to see about hemming the garment. As he had predicted, the hem was quite abused, and he watched it rather woefully as she set about brushing the mud into the kitchen basin, then cutting off the excess once it had been freed from the lining. Her stitches were good, if perhaps a little uneven, and he was of course glad that she would not be cold when they faced the lingering chill of winter. But still, he was rather guarded with his items, and it pained him a little when he heard the ripping sounds as the fabric was shorn in two.

"Are you ready to depart?"

In addition to his other arraignment, Erik had also tucked away his Punjab lasso into the hidden pocket of his cloak. Christine had yet to mention if she had found the overly large pocket within hers, and he wondered if she would ever ask him about its precise purpose.

At her assent he tucked her hand into the crook of his arm, lit his lantern, and shut the door behind them.

What he did not anticipate was how positively *green* Christine appeared when they made their way across the lake. "Are you quite well?"

She nodded hesitantly—taking deep breaths as he steadily pushed them through the blackness of the water. Christine hurried to vacate the craft when they had reached the opposite shore, and if he had not quickly grasped her elbow to aid in the venture, she surely would have tumbled headlong into the lake.

It was easy to see how she had done so the one time he had not accompanied her.

But he would *not* think about that dreadful day.

"Should we return home? You look rather nauseated."

Christine placed a hand on her stomach and still continued breathing deeply, but she sent Erik a look of exasperation. "That is not a flattering thing to say to your wife."

Perhaps not, but he did not relish the idea of her vomiting on his shoes because he had not enquired. "You are loveliness itself, Christine, but if you are feeling unwell it might be more prudent for you to remain home."

She shook her head, and he could tell she was restraining the emphatic action so as not to worsen her uneasy stomach. "No, I think some crisp, night air will do me good. It is quite damp down here and I am sure the rocking of the boat only worsened things. I will be fine."

Erik did not believe her as he had a steady hand and his boat was solidly built, not some flimsy craft that threatened its passengers with rocking and bouncing. He had made it after all.

But he would allow Christine her fiction, so when she stopped breathing so carefully and gave him a nod that she was fit to continue, she placed her hand back onto his arm and they continued their journey above.

Winter was beginning to wane. The snow that had once blanketed the ground was now turning to an unpleasant slush that mingled with the filth that regularly coated the cobblestones. The wind was brusque and biting, and since he could still feel the chill upon his covered cheeks, he wondered if Christine would be warm enough.

She was looking about her with concentration and wariness, obviously intent on anticipating any would-be attackers before they had time to cause any serious harm.

Erik sighed.

He turned to face her and extracted his arm from her hold so that he could place both hands firmly upon her shoulders until she could do nothing but look at him.

"Do you remember what happened to the last man who hurt you?"

Though she had not yet regained her colour after her upset by the boat, she somehow managed to pale even further. "You... killed him. He did not even have time to look at you before he was dead."

He allowed one of his hands to creep up into her hair, finding warmth there that made his gloves seem entirely superfluous. "I did. He was not the first man I have killed, and most likely will not be the last. It was a profession of mine once upon a time." He stroked her cheek softly with his thumb. "Do you know why I am telling you this?"

Christine shuddered and tried to look down at his chest, but his gentle hand in her hair made that impossible. "You know the answer, my rose, just look past the horror of what your husband has done. Why would I confess that to you?"

How he ached to see the fear and confusion in her eyes! But she needed to *understand*, and if the Persian was ever to make a reappearance, Erik could not tolerate the uncertainty that a minor slip of his tongue could reveal what he should have admitted long ago.

But after a moment's silence the fear faded as quickly as it had come, and she stood resolutely before him. "Because I am safe with you. I do not have to be afraid of the darkness when you are with me because you will keep me from harm."

He could not help but bring her into his embrace, pressing kisses into her delightful curls, even as his eyes roamed the streets to ensure their continued safety. "Christine, enjoy your walks and your shopping, because the worrying and caution should come from the one charged with your defence." Erik pulled back and held her hand as he continued walking. "For you to continue to fear might insult your poor protector. Perhaps it means you doubt his abilities."

It felt so good to have her near once more. This entire day had been agitating, and it amazed him how quickly he could miss her touches after they had been absent for such a short while. "I do not doubt you, Erik. I just need reminding sometimes."

They found a park some short walk away, and Erik could easily see that Christine was searching out an appealing bit of ground for her to sit upon.

He would begrudgingly allow her to sit upon the floor of his clean and well kept home, but there was no possible way he was allowing her to rest on public property. This city was rife with dirt and illnesses, and sitting upon sludgy grass that still clung to the last of the winter frost was not something he could permit.

So instead he led her to a bench a little farther in, and while his wife lifted her face to the heavens and watched the stars, he in turn watched her with the same rapt wonderment.

Never did he think that he would tell her of his past deeds. She was so young and full of goodness and light, and it seemed impossible that she could understand what would have led him into such a life. But in that moment it had seemed almost a requirement, and he could not say that he regretted it.

She was sitting quite close to him—just as she should have been—and her hand was still tucked in his. He would need to get her some gloves of her own if she was going to insist on many more of these late night strolls, but for now he accepted the responsibility of being her personal hand warmer.

"Are you feeling better?"

Her nose was turning red from the cold, and it marred his ability to tell if her colour was returning due to necessity or because she was in fact improving. She did not turn to him but continued to gaze above, yet she smiled anyway. "Much."

They remained there for a long while, and it grew colder as the night grew darker, and Erik knew that it was time for them to depart. But before he could tell Christine so, she looked at him, her expression thoughtful. "Did you kill those men for pleasure?"

Erik rolled his eyes. He was surprised that he did not immediately feel cross at her question, but there was not a trace of anger to be had. There was no tone of censure or judgement, it was just asked from simple and understandable curiosity. "I did call it an occupation, Christine. That would imply I did not do it for any personal gratification."

"Then why did you do it? And who would have requested such a thing?"

Erik sighed, not truly wishing to delve into the details. "Persia is a very different place, my dear. It is not what you are used to, and a man of my *skills* was highly sought after." He hesitated a moment but decided to be honest. "As for the why, you must be able to comprehend why a man of my *physique* would have limited options as to how to raise funds."

Christine shivered, and he knew it was not solely from the cold. "I am glad you do not do that anymore, but I am grateful you can keep me safe." She looked up at him in alarm. "Is that wrong?"

He never thought of it in such a way. His past was simply that, and he had done what was necessary for survival—and he could finally admit, what was necessary for money and limited prestige. He had been so tired of the abuse and scorn and he wanted to be valued. Now he knew what it was to be appreciated for *himself,* and there was no comparison to how it made him feel.

It also pleased him greatly that she did not even consider the possibility that he could still maintain that as a profession.

The events of his life might have been filled with humiliation and pain, but they had brought him to this precise moment. And for the first time he knew with absolute certainty that it had been worth it.

Even when his wife was ornery and glared at him unjustly.

"No, it is not wrong. I find that I am equally grateful." It had meant he was able to save his Christine, and that would always be worth it.

She hummed slightly and her small fingers delved into the cuff of his glove to touch his scars as was her distracting habit. He started sharply at her touch. "You are chilled through!"

Christine shivered once again, and he berated himself thoroughly for not being more mindful of her wellbeing. In an attempt to provide her more warmth he opened his cloak and pulled her into his side, sealing her into a secondary cocoon of black cashmere. "You are going straight to bed when we return home. I will bring you a warm compress and make you some tea."

He felt more than saw her head shake in refusal. "Hot chocolate, not tea."

Of course.

By the time they had reached the tunnels she was shuddering violently. "You should have told me you were so cold, you foolish girl."

She glared at him petulantly, although it lacked any true ferocity. "You are no more plump than I am, so you should be just as cold."

Erik lost patience. Instead of arguing that their bodily compositions were not at all comparable, he merely picked her up and cuddled her to him. He was not naturally a radiator of any semblance of warmth, but he felt certain that Christine required any additional heat that could be provided.

The only oversight to his little plan was that Christine was forced to keep a hand out of his enveloping cloak in order to hold the lantern as they made their way home.

He made good on his promise. Though he briefly considered depositing her before the fire for more immediate relief, she needed a soft nightgown and a comfortable bed for true respite. Deciding that a compress would prove insufficient, Erik determined that a hot bath would be far superior.

Perhaps it was excessive, but he placed her gently on the bed and quite efficiently set about divesting her of clothing. She watched him with quiet amusement until he reached her unmentionables, to which she batted his hands away with a laugh. "If you would be so kind as to fetch my nightgown, I will finish the rest."

Erik shook his head as he walked to the bath-room. "A soak first."

Christine had bathed that morning, but she obliged him with an indulgent smile—which she promptly regretted when her toe touched the water. "It *prickles!*"

"That is generally the result of allowing yourself to nearly freeze to death," he replied dryly.

He turned to leave her to her bath, remembering his additional promise of indulging her penchant for sweetness and late night beverages, but he stilled when a wet hand grasped his wrist. "Come in with me. You are cold too."

Erik stared at her with eyes wide with disbelief. "You required your hot chocolate."

She gave another shiver though he could see the colour rapidly returning to her skin, and he supposed that must mean it was not purely from her chill. “I require that my husband also bathe with me. Hot chocolate after.”

Helpless but to comply, as he began divesting his own clothing he decided that *after* was a wonderful thing.

XXVII

Despite Erik's best efforts to ward off any chill or subsequent illness, Christine awoke the next morning with every possible symptom.

It had been a very new and exciting experience bathing with his wife. At first he felt his usual discomfort as she watched him undress with such rapt attention, but as soon as her fingertips began to trace those unknowable patterns, he was too distracted to pay much attention to any shame or embarrassment.

And then he had stepped into the bath behind her.

Christine had not been exaggerating about the prickly feeling that inevitably followed freezing appendages meeting hot water, and for a moment he could only release a gasp as he adjusted to the temperature. His wife bore a smug look of her own, which he purposefully ignored.

But once he settled into the delicious warmth of the bath he began to notice the firm and pleasant flesh of his wife as she began to nestle against him—once more using him as a personal *chaise lounge*. He was too distracted to feel insulted that she had only asked for him to join her so that she would not have to feel the hard planes of the tub against her back. Erik might have been bony, but he found that her head always seemed to find the bits of muscle that acted as a pleasant enough pillow.

But what held most of his attention was the way the curve of her backside was currently pressed so completely against his rapidly responding member.

He swallowed thickly, and set about washing his wife.

She mewled contentedly as his hands worked over any available skin, warming and pressing until she shivered with pleasure instead of the cold.

Eventually she had sighed and he was left with the distinct impression that she was growing more sleepy than aroused. However, her hand reached behind her all the same, and he suppressed a groan as her delicate fingers wrapped around him. "You may take me now, if you wish. Perhaps it would *warm* me even more."

He closed his eyes tightly, wondering if that was true acquiescence or if she was merely taking pity on his state. But then her fingers were stroking him tenderly and with a moan muffled into her neck, he had lifted her slightly and enveloped himself in her softness.

Never did he think he would enjoy the depths of his wife while in his bath. He had made it especially large because he relished a long, hot soak, but now he congratulated himself for the foresight to create such a wonderful place wherein he could pleasure his Christine.

They had remained together until the water began to succumb to the cooler air surrounding it, and then they had dried and dressed in their nightclothes, content to sleep and neither remembering about Christine's previous demand for hot chocolate.

But Erik had not awoken to the pleasing embrace of his wife. Instead, he caught sight of a ray of light from a partially closed door, and he was greeted by the sounds of her retching.

For a moment he felt frozen in the bed, unsure of how to proceed. There was nothing appealing about the idea of seeing Christine in such a position, and surely she would appreciate her privacy. *He* would not desire company if he was so indisposed, but then, she often scolded him for not making her feel better when she was upset. Did this count as upset?

He stood in the doorway, knocking timidly as he kept his eyes resolutely on the floor. "Christine? Do you require something?"

Surely he would have awoken if this was the result of a nightmare. She was certainly not the calmest of sleepers while in the throes of a night terror, and with her thrashing and mumbling there was no possible way he could have slept through it all.

Which could only mean she was truly ill.

When he received no reply his worry grew exponentially. Pushing aside any trepidation, he pushed upon the door and allowed it to swing open completely. And to his dismay saw Christine sprawled across the floor.

He rushed to her side, touching her with assessing hands as he tried to ascertain if she suffered any injuries from her apparent fall. She mumbled in response, pushing at his hands as she tried to curl up on the stone floor. "No, it is nice and cool," Christine muttered, pressing her face against the harsh stone—much to Erik's chagrin.

Despite her protests, he placed a hand upon her forehead, distantly noting the way his long fingers made her face look so very small. But such thoughts were dismissed when he took note of how unnaturally hot she felt against his own cool fingers.

He made to pull away but she pushed herself closer to his hand, seemingly finding that his somewhat pliant flesh was superior to the floor.

As he had told her on many occasions.

But he would not scold when she was ill. "How is your stomach? If I move you to the bed will you vomit on me?"

He loved her with his entire being but he *still* did not welcome the idea of that particular episode. He would much rather make her a nest on the floor where she could rest and have easy access for emptying her stomach.

But she shook her head. "No, I feel better now."

And then she lifted her arms and looked at him pleadingly. "I do not feel well. Can you please carry me?"

Perhaps he should have been uncomfortable with her nearly child-like enquiry, but all he felt was concern mixed with a quiet amusement at his wife's continued innocence.

"Yes, Christine. Let us return you to your bed, and then I will make you better."

It was far more cumbersome lifting her off of the floor than it was the settee, but he managed rather well. At any other time his impudent wife would have giggled at him for his less than graceful display, but in her current state she simply groaned at the slight jostle. "My head hurts."

Fever, headache, and nausea. Some sort of influenza then. "How is your throat?" He lowered her to the bed, pushing all available pillows around her as if to make up for her prolonged discomfort on the floor.

She raised a hand and pressed at it, almost as if she had forgotten about it completely. "It hurts too." Her eyes were glassy as she looked at him. "Are you angry that we will not be singing today? I am sorry that I broke my throat."

If he did not feel the compulsive urge to fret about her for each and every symptom, he would have laughed at her assessment. "No, I am not angry." Not about her throat at least. Her becoming ill was another matter, but even that he could not blame her for. If he had not taken her above...

Later. He could begrudge the world above *later,* when she was resting comfortably.

"Do not speak, Christine. You will only hurt yourself further." He rearranged her blankets so that she was properly covered, only to have her push at them petulantly. "No, it's too hot." Of course it was.

Her speech was slightly slurred and her eyes were already beginning to droop, and he knew he had to act quickly if he wanted to ply her with any medicines.

Erik went to his old bedchamber and pulled out his medicinal bag, rifling through the contents quickly. He was never one prone to fevers, but he kept a small bottle of extract of willow bark regardless. It aptly cared for those aches and pains that, while troublesome, did not require any of the more potent drugs that inhabited his coiffeurs.

He hurried to the kitchen, glaring at the water that seemed *far* more reticent to boiling than usual, until finally he was able to brew her a soothing cup of tea sweetened with honey for her throat, and infused with the willow bark so as to help her fever.

Lastly and without much thought to consequence— and despite his usual care of any of his items—he ripped a kitchen towel in half and soaked it in cool water, wringing it out so as to not drip all over Christine. Or his person.

Or his floors.

When he returned to her side she was nearly asleep. He set his supplies upon the bedside table and helped her to sit up, which seemed to amuse her greatly. "I stole all your pillows."

He touched her forehead again, noting that while warm, she did not seem desperately hot either. "You cannot steal what was freely given, my dear. Now drink your tea."

She moaned when he placed the cool compress against her forehead but she sipped her tea dutifully, even though she wore a small frown at the taste. "You did something to it. There is no cream." Christine glared at him accusingly.

Because even in her sickness she apparently believed that her tea should be made to her exacting standard and preference.

"Yes, I did. That is tea that will *help* you, not merely indulge your incessant need for sugar and cream. Now drink."

It must have helped her throat more than it offended her sensibilities as she obeyed. Erik felt much relieved when she drank the last of its content, for he knew that regular doses would help keep her fever from growing dangerously high and should also help her rest more easily.

She patted at him awkwardly and mumbled what sounded somewhat like, "Thank you, darling," before she rolled over and went to sleep.

Erik stared at her for a long while, the entire situation feeling rather surreal. His actions had been perfunctory and efficient and he was pleased that he could have made her more comfortable. But now as he watched her sleep, her cheeks ruddy from sickness and a slight sheen across her skin, he allowed himself to feel the panic and the worry wash over him in a dreadful wave.

He fell to his knees beside her bed, and although he dared not touch her in case she awoke, he still clutched slightly at the discarded bedding that she had deemed unfit for use, and shook with quiet sobs. *Normal* people grew ill, he *knew* that. Her temperature was not dangerous, and while all of her ailments were troublesome and discomforting, they were not life-threatening. Yet he still begrudged every one of them.

His little wife had suffered enough—she did not need any added burdens or pains or aches as punishment for wanting to take a nighttime stroll with her husband.

And what if he was wrong? Books on medicine did not provide him a doctor's experience. If she worsened, he would not have any idea of where to take her. And if she—he gasped, shuddering fiercely as he did so—if she *died* because of his lack of knowledge, he would surely follow her. The guilt would simply be too much to bear.

But he could not leave her to make enquiries now.

He decided then that as soon as she was well, he would find the best possible physician he could. While he would hope and pray—yes, *pray*—that he would never require that particular service, he would not be so careless with his wife's health again. It was irresponsible of him not to have pursued it before now, and he would not neglect it in the future.

Erik had not meant to wake her, and he did not know that he had until he felt gentle and overly warm fingers playing softly with the tendrils of his hair. "Why are you on the floor, Erik? You do not like the floor."

He could not help the bubble of nervous laughter that burst forth, and he took her perfect hand in his and pulled it down so he could place a kiss onto her palm. "You need the bed to yourself so you might get better. It was terribly unkind of you to become ill, my Christine, for it worries your poor Erik so."

She frowned, her eyes seeming to clear for a moment. "It is not anything serious, Erik. Papa always said I was prone to fevers, even for the simplest of things. I got sick like this many times when I was growing up. Did you not?"

Erik did not like to think of her being a little girl, plagued by fevers at every turn. She seemed so small and delicate even now when she was fully grown—he could not even imagine her father's worry when she was so young.

"I did not have a normal childhood, my dear. I must have missed such rites of passage."

Her frown deepened, and she patted his head awkwardly, her hands appearing too heavy for her to properly control. "It must be a terrible thing to be congested without a nose."

Her eyes grew wide and horrified, "Oh, Erik, I am *so* sorry! I should not have said that!"

Erik chuckled darkly, rising from his kneeling position on the floor. "Do not fret. I imagine that would be a dreadful plight indeed." He pulled up her blankets again and this time she allowed it, but he thought it was more of an attempt at apology than for true want of them.

When he moved to leave her to her rest as his continued presence was obviously keeping her awake, Christine stopped him. "Do not leave! Can you not... lie with me and maybe read me something until I fall asleep?"

Erik paused, considering. His voice could be soothing and would certainly lull her into a deeper sleep than even his tea had provided, and she needed *rest* if she was to recover quickly.

And he *needed* her to recuperate quickly.

So he nodded, and grabbed the novel she had left by her usual place on the settee, and hurried back to her. He did not pay attention to the story, and beyond asking her what chapter she had most recently completed, he did not make any more effort to engage with the characters. At any other time he would have made the voices and personalities come alive, but as it was he made his voice droll and quiet, urging her to sleep.

He did not make it three pages before her breath evened out and she abandoned her nest of pillows in favour of using his chest instead.

Erik supposed that he could not begrudge his wife her preferences—not when he had denied her proper tea.

He was not at all ready for more sleep, so he forced himself to be contented with Christine's trusting presence as well as testing out her book from the beginning. It had come from his library of course, but that meant little given the sheer eclectic nature of his collection.

But the next thing he knew, he was being awoken to Christine's whimpering and restless movements against him.

More tea.

Such was their routine for the next three days. He supposed she was getting better, but every morning she would either flee to the bath-room or simply hold her stomach and bemoan the nausea that still plagued her. The soreness in her throat had passed and her fever was finally broken due to Erik's diligent additions to her tea. And he begrudgingly admitted, time was also an additional factor.

The issue now however was that Erik did not think there were enough handkerchiefs in all of Paris to stem the sheer amount of mucus that seemed intent on escaping his wife. She was miserable and embarrassed that she could not wash all of the handkerchiefs herself, and she absolutely forbade him from doing it himself. She was too weak to leave the bed for any significant duration, and while he was uncomfortable leaving her, she all but demanded that he send all of her—*his*—handkerchiefs to his previous laundress for tending.

He did so without much protest.

By the fifth day she was all but improved. He was becoming increasingly troubled by the persistent nausea, and he had taken to providing her some dry toast as it seemed to help settle her stomach some if she ate it immediately upon waking.

Erik was not expecting a visitor, but now that he knew the Daroga could be the one lurking about when the siren called, he did not go into any significant panic. He still took his lasso in case he was incorrect as to the intruder's identity, but as he silently glided through the lake the lantern revealed the unmistakable countenance of the Persian. "And to what do I owe this unexpected visit? Have you not troubled me enough?"

The man rolled his eyes. "I have not seen you in over a month, Erik. That hardly seemed frequent enough to be considered bothersome."

Erik merely sniffed. "I do not have time for you today. My wife is in need of care and attention, and that does not allow time for me to fritter away hours with a guest."

The Daroga grew concerned, and even Erik could see that it was genuine. "Is she ill?"

He hesitated. It was not any of this man's business, and although his first instinct was to inform him of that quite forcefully, he realised that this was the opportunity for an ally. He had promised himself that he would find Christine a doctor for any future sicknesses, and this would mean he would not have to leave her side for any considerable duration.

And in truth, who else did he have to ask?

Erik sighed, still feeling rather perturbed that he had to ask this man for help of any kind, but his wife's health took precedence over all else—including his pride. "Christine has been unwell for almost a week. Her fever has broken, but she still has fits of nausea that seem no closer to abating." He did not mention her unfortunate requirement of nearly all of his handkerchiefs.

The Persian grew very still, and he seemed to be weighing his question carefully.

"Speak plainly, Daroga. I told you that I have a wife to tend."

He raised a placating hand, and Erik was briefly reminded of his absurd stance from before as he tried to ward off the sting of the Punjab lasso.

"Forgive me, Erik, I was merely trying to determine how to phrase this delicately. Was she nauseous before her fever or only after?"

Erik rolled his eyes. "Why should that matter? You have a magnificent way of trying my patience beyond reason!"

The Daroga chuckled, and it was not quelled by Erik's answering glare. "I assure you, it matters a great deal."

When he said no more, Erik allowed his mind to ponder the question—if only to finish this conversation at a more rapid pace. She had become dizzy and her stomach unsettled on the boat, far before she had been exposed to the cold for too long. There was nothing in his home or his craft that would have caused her illness, and his anger had not been misguided when he blamed the park bench and its cold temperatures for having stricken his wife with infection.

"Before." He still did not see the relevance, but he was not going to admit that so blatantly to the presumptuous man in front of him.

Just because he did not kill him before did *not* mean he was immune to Erik's temper and subsequent lack of mercy.

And if he knew something about his wife and he remained silent...

Erik did not even have to ask the man to see about finding a suitable physician for his answer rightly supposed that was why he had been told of her ailment originally. "Then I do not think it is a doctor I must fetch, but a midwife."

That was ridiculous. Erik knew *far* too much about his wife's menses, and with her irritation and restlessness that had been so pronounced the days before her illness, he had little doubt she was experiencing her monthly courses.

Except that she had not.

He never paid much attention to the calendar, but he knew it had been far too long since she had asked him for more supplies—and she had certainly not brought him any bundles of soiled linens needing his assistance.

Erik did not acknowledge his visitor in the slightest but walked quickly and silently back to his boat, intent on speaking to his wife.

But before the man departed he called, "I will make enquiries for her! She deserves to have proper care."

And as he drew the boat forward, Erik could not stop trembling.

XXVIII

Christine was propped up in her mound of pillows, precisely where he had left her.

It was a testament to her recovery that she could immediately sense Erik's agitation, for her welcoming smile quickly fell. "What is it, Erik? Was it not your friend coming to call?"

Erik drew to her bedside, sitting upon the very edge so that he could softly take her face between his gloved hands. "Tell your husband truly, Christine. Have you had your courses recently?"

Her eyes widened at his seemingly inappropriate question, and she blushed. He would have grown more upset but she began nibbling her lip and her eyes wandered as she carefully considered her reply. "It is very hard to keep track of the days down here. I would not say *recently,* so I suppose it is a little late. Why?"

Her question was spoken before her mind supplied the answer, and he could clearly see the colour drain from her face as her mouth opened slightly in surprise. "Oh."

He released her and watched her reaction warily. One of her hands strayed to cover her womb and she looked at him nearly frantically. "But, I was sick! Surely that was all it was."

Erik withdrew from the bed.

"The Persian is presently investigating a proper midwife. It seems you have not yet had your fill of potential pregnancies."

She stared at him for a long moment, and he could clearly see fear within her expression.

He *loathed* it.

Christine had been fearful when there was a possibility of birthing one of her abuser's babies, and although she had willingly submitted to being his wife, they had never discussed children. Obviously this had been a grave oversight.

Perhaps it was easy for her to accept him since he was the one who saved her and had given her a home. It took every fibre of his being to remind himself that she *loved* him, even as the dread at her certain rejection threatened to strangle him. Agreeing to have his child was entirely different than agreeing to be his wife.

There was a part of him that wanted to throw himself at her feet and weep his apologies into the bedclothes—that he would have accepted her as his wife *without* lying with her so as to save her the pain of bearing his child. But she did not like it when he had behaved thusly in the past, so he forced himself into stillness and tried to measure his voice so that none of his trepidation and dismay would be known to her. "I will fetch you some tea."

As if tea could solve anything. Its only great aid currently was in providing him a way to leave the room graciously.

There was safety in the kitchen. He had never taken her there, and it signified the *safe* parts of their relationship. Baking and tea, hot chocolate and suppers. Those were the things he should have provided, not his *seed.*

As he filled the kettle and he allowed himself to truly consider the matter beyond his self-loathing, he wondered if it was possible for him to be excited at the prospect of a child. Was it a child of Christine he feared, or simply *his* child?

Christine was not his mother. He *knew* that. She was beauty and goodness itself and surely if a child of his was plagued with the same blight, she could still find it within herself to care for it even just a little.

But the memories of his own dark childhood were overwhelming him—images of a mother who never spoke a kind word to her boy, and who had frequently touched him harshly when he had dared ask for even the tiniest of affections.

And perhaps one of his most painful memories was vividly seeing the disgust and revulsion the few times he had been foolish enough to remove his mask in her presence.

He was brought out of his recollections when he was startled by a tearful Christine standing in the doorway.

"You should still be resting." He tried to sound forceful, but even to his own ears he merely sounded tired. "Go to bed, Christine. We will not speak of it anymore." Not until he had his thoughts and emotions carefully under control. In addition, if they did not converse on the matter, maybe they could forget and things could return to normal.

Well, *their* version of normal—their perfectly wonderful normal that of course had to be interrupted by the unexpected.

He turned back to the tea things but was halted by Christine's emphatic voice. "No. No resting and no going back to bed. You do not get to be the frightened one, Erik. I know *nothing* of pregnancy, or childbirth, or babies! A mother always knows these things, but I can barely remember my *own* mother so how can I possibly be a good one?" Her arms were wrapped tightly around herself, and she looked almost deranged as tears stained her cheeks and her sleep rumpled hair fluttered around her.

His eyes narrowed. "And I know something of fatherhood? What have I ever implied about my childhood that would leave you with such an impression?"

To his intense irritation, she rolled her eyes at him. "Of course you will be an excellent father. You provide, you have patience," were they speaking of the same man? "And you are so *very* loving." Her words were sweet but her tone was verging on exasperated. "I barely know how to care for you as a wife, let alone care for your child!"

He reached out to her and while for a moment he thought she would draw away from him, she allowed him to touch her arm lightly with his fingertips—obviously sensing his need to feel her if only slightly. "You are a perfect wife, Christine. I could never ask for anything more." His words seemed to do little to comfort so he added, "It might not even be true."

She shook her head. "I... suspected, but I did not want to dwell on the implications so I ignored it. Now that you mentioned it," her hand strayed once again over her still smooth abdomen. "I can *feel* it."

From what little he had studied of human gestation, Erik was fairly certain that it was too soon for Christine to feel any movement. She must therefore refer to some sort of innate knowledge.

Erik did not believe in such things. There must be physical signs that a midwife was skilled enough to look for in order to determine if a life had taken hold, beyond a woman's claim at *knowing.*

But then Christine took his hand and pressed it against her, his own long-fingered hand dwarfing her slim form. He swallowed thickly and tried to imagine her rounded with child, and he found it nearly impossible. She had come to him as merely a slip of a girl, all skin and bones and large blue eyes that leaked far too much for comfort. And while she had begun to transform into a semblance of true womanhood, it seemed too strange to even consider that she could be *pregnant.*

By him.

Yet as his hand still rested upon her, he almost could believe he felt it too. "You are certain? This is not like... before?"

She shook her head. "If you would like for me to be checked then I will allow it, but I am quite certain." Erik pulled his hand back, suddenly feeling uncomfortable with touching her there when a small being was being formed inside—if his wife was to be believed of course. The logical part of him demanded she be examined just to be confident, but a greater part of him trusted Christine's intuition.

Surely it was possible for a woman to tell when something so monumental had happened to her body—was it not?

The water had begun to boil as cheerfully as ever, and he set about preparing the teapot and the rest of the essentials. So distracted by the topic at hand he laid out all of Christine's usual favourites, forgetting that he had disallowed her cream or sugar for nearly a week.

When all was acquired, he then attentively walked behind Christine to ensure she would not topple over from excess movement or excitement as they exited the kitchen. Even if her nausea could be explained away by pregnancy, she still had been quite ill. And though she protested, he knew she should continue resting.

The unforeseen consequence of his vigil was that he had to follow her—which did not seem such a terrible ordeal as he enjoyed watching her walk very much, probably more than was wholly appropriate. The issue occurred when, instead of turning into the bedchamber, she continued on to the sitting room—blatantly ignoring his bid for her not to do so. She was intent on her place on the settee, and she looked at him expectantly until he could do nothing but sigh and acquiesce. He did refuse to allow her to pour, and he resolutely refused to respond to her huff and irritable glare.

Cups of tea in hand, Christine settled with her back against the arm, her feet pressing into his leg as she regarded him. She remained silent, and was apparently waiting for him to continue their previous conversation.

Erik sighed.

"I will always be fearful of a child. Your confidence in my abilities as a potential father is quite flattering, but I have doubts in that as well." His throat tightened. "You could be hurt in the process. What if you perished during the birth and I was left alone with a baby? I have never even *held* a child!"

He took a sip of his tea in an attempt to soothe his suddenly parched mouth. "You did not think you could love the child of one of your abusers, who would have at the very least been *normal*. What if the babe looks like me?" His eyes were imploring and hers were wet with tears. "Would you grow to resent your poor Erik?"

They should not be speaking of this now. He needed time to think and time to process this new development. She had told him explicitly that she needed him to have the strength for the both of them while she too was frightened at prospective parenthood, and he was already failing her.

But he could not seem to stop voicing all of his deepest anxieties, even when her distress continued to grow. "Please do not blame me for what I said before, Erik. While I doubt my abilities as a mother, that does not mean I would not love our baby! For it was *born* of love, not my pain and fear."

Erik had been born of love—the love had faded *after* he had entered the world. Just because a child was conceived from violence did not necessarily mean it would be cursed because of it, but he had no way of expressing that to Christine. If she could so easily be frightened at the prospect of motherhood simply because of her lack of experience, it seemed impossible that she could grasp that there were far greater worries to be had.

She must have taken his silence wrongly, for she pressed on. "And I was more afraid that you would ask me to leave if it was true. I do not think I could actually begrudge an infant for the sins of its father, but you did not love me then, and I would have been back on the streets with a helpless newborn. Of course I was frightened!"

Christine was turning indignant, and he found himself rather mesmerised by her words. He had not yet admitted it to himself at the time, but he *did* love her then—and he had found himself feeling quite certain that he would be willing to support whatever child was born from her, *because* it was born from her.

Even if that meant the babe looked like him.

"You are my husband, Erik, and we should have both known that being married *properly* meant children. I cannot do this alone. We have had to learn to do everything together, and I need you with me in this of all things." She reached over and took his hand. "I know you will be frightened, as will I. But when you grow distant and refuse to talk about things, I feel as though I am back in danger of being without a home."

He stared at her in disbelief. "After everything, you would still doubt that? That I would someday change my mind and you would be left destitute?"

She smiled at him sadly. "I know you love me, and when you are affectionate and attentive those thoughts do not even enter my mind." Such ideas should *never* enter her mind, for they were the farthest thing from the truth. "But then you look at me a certain way, and I feel as though you are not *with* me any longer. And all the uncertainties come rushing back."

Erik shook his head. "There are... moments when I am reminded of my past. I require time to forget once more."

"But how am I to know? I do not know much of your childhood or your life before this became your residence, so I do not know when I have said or done something that has either offended you or made you sad. As your wife, I should be able to comfort you, not drive you away!"

She drew back from him again, and her tears fell heavily yet again. "And now I am pregnant and you will be constantly reminded of your mother! Eventually you might grow to resent *me* as I know you do her, and then you will wish to leave me."

Erik wanted to blame her reaction solely on pregnancy. Women with child were infamous for their moods, and although he had never come into much personal contact with a woman in that condition, enough books and whisperings from men throughout the world had made such perfectly clear.

But there was a grain of truth in her words that startled him. If his impulse was to draw away from her when memories of his past surfaced, then it was a logical conclusion that while she was within the throes of motherhood, he might find her company unbearable.

His mouth felt dry and he took a sip of his now slightly tepid tea, hardly noticing the temperature.

Erik set down his cup and cautiously moved to return her hand to his. "This is... difficult for me."

"I know."

He nodded. "What do you need of me? Do you require me to regale you with tales of my past dealings when they seek to overwhelm me?" There was no bite to his words, and the question was genuine. Erik did not know how a husband was to relate to his wife. Despite Christine's abuses, relating physically seemed to be the most natural form of communication that came relatively easily to them.

Speaking was not.

At least, not for him.

"Only if that is what *you* need in order to feel better."

"*Not* thinking of it makes me feel better." He sounded petulant, even to his own ears.

Her thumb was moving gently over his knuckles, and he allowed himself to focus on her touch instead of the subject for a blissful moment. *That* made him feel better.

Touching always did.

No.

Not merely touching.

Touching *her.*

And her touching him.

Perhaps that was the key. She did not need to be burdened by his past, but there was a significant chance that his traditional method of coping with the encumbrances of his memories was no longer the most effective. And Christine had all but admitted that his current process *hurt* her.

"Maybe..." He continued to stare at their entwined hands. "Touching you softens the memories."

Her face brightened into a wide smile. "As it does for me." She had mentioned that, but he had never reciprocated.

And perhaps such was a necessity.

"I have nightmares. They are more memory than fiction, and they used to visit me each time I tried to sleep—so I stopped. My body never required much sleep but it grew used to even less, and so for years I would go for days without eating or sleeping."

He looked up at her briefly. "And then when we married and I slept beside you..." Erik shrugged, suddenly feeling uncomfortable by the intensity of her gaze. "You need me as much as I need you."

He had told her as much before, but she acted as though this was a new revelation.

"Then do not turn from me. We have to support one another, Erik. In *all* things. That includes with babies."

He swallowed, his eyes straying to where he knew a baby would eventually begin to swell and grow. "Erik will... I will... love and care for you and whatever children you may have. Please do not doubt that."

Christine leaned over and kissed his masked cheek. "I will try."

Erik felt exhausted. He had done relatively little that day beyond caring and tending for Christine when she required it, which was no more strenuous than amusing her with a book or preparing toast with far too great a helping of preserves.

He was therefore unprepared for when she settled against his arm, and in a quiet yet sure voice remarked, "Tell me something nice from your childhood."

He blinked. There were so few *nice* things that happened, and they were hardly the most readily available of his recollections. At any other time his first inclination would have been to snap at her—to retaliate in some vindictive way until she never returned to the subject. But now he just felt weary, and if she felt it important to know these minute details of his life that seemed beyond any semblance of relevancy, then so be it.

That made it no less difficult to scrounge for something that fit her description.

"When I was about six I... spent some time in the attic of our home." He paused, assessing if she would scold him for speaking of a time when he had been locked in an attic for three days.

She did not.

"While I was there, I found a dusty old trunk. Inside I discovered some discarded sheet music—though I did not know what it was at the time. And at the bottom, there was a violin. It had a broken string and when I fiddled with the peg another snapped," he unconsciously smiled. "It startled me dreadfully when it broke, and it gave my finger quite a lashing." Erik showed her a faint scar on his left index finger.

"At first it sounded like the most dreadful screeching, but after a good deal of coaxing it started to sound rather lovely." Of course now he knew what a properly maintained instrument sounded like and the simple tunes he had managed to persuade from the ancient strings and bow now made him cringe. But he had been proud of his accomplishment at the time, and that had been the beginning of a lifelong affair with the violin.

He decided that it was a bit easier to forget about the *actual* lashing he had received when the noise he made reminded his mother that he had been locked up there. Before she had arrived however, he had hidden the instrument away, and though she had raged at him for tampering and meddling with things that did not belong to him, she could not find evidence of his intrusions.

Christine was still looking at his finger, and after a moment of silence she raised it to her lips and placed a small kiss on the barely noticeable mark. "You will teach our baby to play some day. But you most certainly will *not* allow them to have strings snapping about their fingers."

As he held his wife, and realised he had spoken of his childhood with a tinge of wistfulness instead of resentment and anger, he found that he could picture the happy fantasy she described.

Perhaps fatherhood would not be so very dreadful after all.

XXIX

Fatherhood was going to be a terrible thing.

At least, that was what he determined if pregnancy was any reflection of what he would be enduring for the rest of his mortal existence. For he would be damned before he allowed any child of his to perish before himself—not when he had to endure so much during their gestation.

His beautiful, wonderful wife was now an entity to be feared. Their singing lessons could not be established in any semblance of routine, for there was the distinct possibility that he would speak too sharply and reduce her to tears or growls of frustration. Not that he actually *did* speak at all harshly towards her. At best he had attempted to keep her voice relatively tuned through exercises, and he had no great expectations of her range or dedication.

That even proved too taxing.

He was perpetually reminded of the few occasions he had experienced before her courses had arrived. Temperamental was a kind word for the way her moods would fluctuate so rapidly, and he felt certain he would say or do something displeasing at any moment that would begin the vicious cycle of placations and apologies once again.

And she had not yet even begun to show.

When her *moods* began, he had insisted that she see a midwife. After about a week of searching, the Daroga had provided the information for a discreet yet reputable woman that had been informed of Erik and Christine's unusual situation.

Erik had nearly lost his temper when the Persian revealed that particular detail, but the man calmly informed him that he would not be held responsible if the woman had some sort of fit at seeing a young lady appear at her door within the arms of a masked individual who could be intent on seeing either of them harm.

It was due to that particular explanation that the Daroga did not receive even a word of gratitude before Erik left him upon the shore.

They did not make use of her for another month. Both of them required more time to reconcile the mere *idea* of a pregnancy, and though Christine had recovered fully from her illness, Erik still utilised that as an excuse to keep her from wandering above.

For the most part Christine was content to allow him to dote and fret as he pleased. She had taken to sleeping for even greater lengths of time than was her usual wont. When she would awaken, it was to fierce bursts of energy that would have her baking and cleaning until she collapsed from exhaustion in mid-afternoon, and would only wake long enough for Erik to ply her with tea and biscuits.

Erik had not actually been certain she could make the journey to the midwife given her strange periods of wakefulness and fatigue.

However, there was one particular occurrence that made it perfectly clear that they required the services of someone far more knowledgeable of gestation than either of them.

Over the month since their discovery, they had not once been physically intimate. Fond kisses were shared, but Christine had never initiated anything more passionate and Erik was wary of doing so. Although his attraction to his wife had not in the least waned, it seemed almost presumptuous to consider doing what *begot* a child in the first place when one was already maturating within Christine's womb.

And in any case, he found himself frightfully worried that if they *were* to engage in such activities, that he would somehow harm the tiny babe.

But one morning, Christine had awoken early. It was a rarity that she was even aware of his presence in their bed for he would arrive late and leave not necessarily prematurely, but far earlier than she would usually consider rising from her nest of pillows and blanketry.

With sleep still clinging to his eyes, he could feel soft kisses lazily being placed over his exposed chest—a chest that had most certainly not been exposed when he had fallen into bed the night before.

His mouth went dry and he felt his body preparing rapidly for what it had for so long been denied. "What are you doing?"

Christine blinked at him. "I am being your wife. We have not done this in *so* long."

And there was *reason* for that. Her body was now being used to accommodate another little living thing, and he would not be selfish or greedy with it.

He did not want to deny her—not when her hair tickled at his sensitive flesh and she looked at him so sweetly. But he would not risk the child, and he would not risk Christine. "I do not think we should."

Christine gaped at him. "Why?"

He realised how it had sounded, and knew that if she had ever rejected his blatant advances, he would feel hurt and embarrassed as well. So pushing at her shoulder slightly so he could rest over her—not allowing any of his weight to become bothersome—and he placed his large hand over her womb. "*This* is why, my rose. I will not see either of you harmed."

She nibbled at her lip, and to his dismay her face crumpled. "But I *want* you. Please do not deny me for much longer."

How was he to keep his resolve when she pleaded so?

He sighed and pressed a kiss above her covered navel and looked at her seriously. "I wish to deny you nothing, Christine."

She sat up abruptly, and he had to move quickly to allow her movement. "I want to see the midwife."

He had asked her numerous times if she would like to go. It was true that he had been trying to encourage her to remain below for as long as possible. As the more the weather yielded to spring, the more comfortable she would be—and the lesser chance of her catching another chill and subsequent sickness.

But it was *her* lovely body that was undergoing such changes, and he had wanted to ensure she had access to someone who could offer her answers regarding precisely what was happening. And though he was a learned man, that unfortunately could not be him.

At the time, she had protested that it was unnecessary given the fact that she was so certain she was pregnant. She had known nausea was to be expected, and so far there had been little else that had seemed worthy of a visit. She did not appear to notice her fatigue or her frequent naps—and he did not feel safe mentioning the sharp contrasts of mood that seemed to strike her at the oddest of occasions.

He felt oddly flattered that it was the denial of lovemaking that would lead her to finally wish to see the midwife.

To his surprise, Christine rose quickly from the bed and began dressing. "Now?"

She gave him an exasperated look. "*Yes,* now. I told you, Erik, I want you, and you are being troublesome. Perhaps a more experienced woman will be able to talk sense into you."

While there were parts of her garments that were once too big in places, they now were filled out nicely. In fact, the waist on the one she was currently shimmying over her head was even beginning to look a touch strained while she fastened the clasps. If he provided her a corset she might have been able to continue wearing it for at least a bit longer, but that most certainly would never happen—not when his child was growing inside. He would obviously need to procure more dresses for her.

Perhaps this time from a proper dressmaker.

But for now, she was standing with her hands on her hips, his cloak already about her shoulders. "Are you going to lounge for the rest of the morning or will you be dressing also?"

Impudent girl.

He dressed with deliberate slowness, which was conceivably rather petty and childish of him. The Daroga had said that the midwife did not require an appointment as, in her words, "Babies do not keep to a schedule." For impromptu visits that would prove a blessing, but there was always the possibility that she could be out tending to a birth in another location when they arrived.

Erik did not know how they would see to Christine's delivery. He thought that midwives usually went to the couple's home, but that was decidedly out of the question.

Yet another thing to be discussed.

He hesitated when it came to selecting a mask. He had been so preoccupied that he had still not fashioned one that made him appear normal, but if ventures that required coming into contact with more people was going to become commonplace, he would need to do so with haste. But for now he picked one of his least offensive, and with that, he was ready.

Christine must have been truly irritated with him for she did not cling to his arm as was her usual method of walking with him. Her hand rested lightly and she held her body slightly away, and he pretended that it did not sting as much as it did. He had to begrudgingly acknowledge however that her lack of closeness was directly due to his own action—even if he was truly trying to see to her wellbeing. And that of the baby.

However, when she tripped and he caught her by the waist and she nearly lurched away from him, his reasonableness faded. "Christine, has it occurred to you in the slightest that the midwife might agree with *me*? I am *trying* to care for you in your pregnancy—*as you insisted*— and you seem to take it as a personal insult!"

Immediately, he knew his tone had grown too sharp. Her lip quivered and while to his great relief she did not in fact begin to cry, he was quick to placate. "I am sorry, my dear, you must forgive your poor Erik. I am not used to having to deny you anything, but we have to be mindful of someone else now. Can you understand my reticence?"

She sniffled and moved closer to him so she could rest her head against his arm. "I know, and I am sorry. I do not know what I am feeling half of the time and I *know* I am being unfair to you." Her eyes glowed in the light of the lantern, their usual brightness increased by her unshed tears. "I just miss you."

Carefully he raised a hand and touched her cheek softly. "No more than I miss you."

She walked closer to him from that point on, and Erik was pleased to note that the cool morning air was crisp but not chilling. Christine seemed to grow more cheerful the longer they walked, and he realised that although she still seemed to have a lingering fear of being aboveground by herself, she did in fact require time to enjoy the sun and fresh air.

The midwife was located not far from the Opera House. She lived in a relatively clean building, whose architecture was neither impressive nor offensive. The markets and shops were in the opposite direction so the streets were relatively empty as they traversed them in the early morning hours—for which Erik was quite grateful.

For the fourth time he checked the little scrap of parchment that the Persian had provided which gave the woman's name and address. He knew it by heart by now, but he still felt the need to check and verify yet again. Just to be certain.

A middle aged woman who was closer to elderly than to her prime opened the door. She looked tired but was fully dressed, her clothes slightly bedraggled and her hair mussed.

She inspected both of them shrewdly, her eyes lingering on Erik for only a moment before turning to Christine.

"You must be Erik and Christine. I thought you would come to me sooner."

So, this was the illustrious Mme Aida Bertrand whom the Daroga assured was one of the very best of her trade—if soothing mothers and catching babies could be considered a *trade* of course.

Erik only nodded, feeling rather lost. He had not actually considered what it would be like to interact with this woman, and he was already finding it uncomfortable. Precisely how much had the blasted Persian told her about them?

"Well, don't just stand there all day, come inside."

Erik gently pushed Christine through the front door first with a hand at the small of her back, and she looked as wide eyed and nervous as he felt.

Hopefully his mask concealed his trepidation a little more efficiently than his wife's open expressions conveyed.

"You will have to forgive my appearance, I just arrived home from a birth. It lasted three quarters of a day, and the poor mother was pushing for nigh on four hours. But, the babe finally came." Mme Bertrand was leading them through her small apartment even as she spoke, and Erik felt quite horrified by her description. She looked back at him and laughed. "Men do not usually pay much attention to such things, but births are a long business, especially the first ones."

They were led into a small parlour and Mme Bernard sank into a worn chintz chair with a weary sigh before gesturing them to sit in the other available seats. There was a small sofa and yet another chair, but Christine held Erik's hand and silently bade him sit with her.

He was not going to refuse.

"I am sure you are bubbling with questions. Your little foreign friend gave me the impression you were uncertain you were even with child, so I was under the impression you would need to be examined. Is that not so?"

Christine shook her head slowly. "My courses have not come and I feel... different. And I am sick most mornings."

The woman nodded. "I could manually confirm your pregnancy through manipulation of the uterus," Erik opened his mouth to vocally protest, but she dismissed his outrage with an unconcerned wave of her hand. "But I hardly think it necessary. I am certain your husband here could provide me with even more details than your morning unpleasantness, am I correct?"

Christine looked at him sheepishly, and he cleared his throat awkwardly. "She has... not been herself for the past few weeks."

Mme Bertrand smiled indulgently. "What a kind way of stating that." She turned to Christine. "You have been rather hard on your poor husband, haven't you?"

Christine fidgeted and seemed torn at whether she should be addressing her husband or the midwife. "I do not mean to be. Honestly I do not, Madame..."

"Oh, how foolish of me! You may call me Aida, my dear. There is little point at keeping to formalities with subjects such as these."

Erik shifted uneasily. He had forced himself to question Christine about her menses because she was so terribly frightened, and at the time he did not have even an acquaintance to go about finding a female to which Christine could converse. But now that there *was* such a woman he felt that he was intruding on some kind of feminine coup that no man had business overhearing.

Yet Christine's grip on his hand tightened slightly all the same, and she took a bracing breath before voicing the intention of their visit. He winced as she did so but voiced no complaint. "Aida, I was wondering if you knew about... *intimacy* during pregnancy. Erik is worried about harming the baby."

The woman laughed—long, loud laughter which made the couple across from her blush deeply at her reaction. "Forgive me, I am afraid the sleepless night is catching up with me." Erik was not at all convinced that he *could* easily forgive her, but he wisely remained silent. "Monsieur, you are not the first husband to be concerned, nor will you be the last. As long as you are mindful of your wife, all shall be well." Her eyes were still sparkling with mirth, and she lowered her voice to a mere whisper. "And I should also warn you that some women become rather... *voracious* as their pregnancies progress."

Erik did not think he had ever seen Christine reach that particular shade of crimson, and he was certain that his own cheeks would have matched should they have been visible. Never had he been more grateful for the concealment of his mask. "Thank you, Madame. I am confident that is... quite enough detail on the subject."

Was it not time to leave yet?

She smiled at him again and it was one full of knowing and experience that made him feel a foolish schoolboy, and he begrudged her mightily for that—even more so when he saw Christine's rather smug expression.

Erik did not lose his temper. He considered himself fairly calm when he pulled his hand away from Christine and resentfully looked at her and uttered, "Pardon me for thinking of the welfare of our child. I am new to this experience as well."

It seemed that his quiet declaration was far more effective than one of his rages, for instead of becoming frightened, both women appeared chastened. Christine cautiously took his hand once more, and although he briefly considered pulling it away so that she could truly understand just how hurt he was by her attitude, he decided to allow it. "I am sorry, Erik. You have been *so* good to me and it is wrong of me to gloat." Her thumb was wheedling its way to the scars on his wrist and with a gentle tug she bade him look at her. "We are both new at this, and I will try to learn how to better see to your needs, just as you see to mine."

That was all he wanted. He *tried* to be a good husband to her, but it seemed that when she was with child nothing he could do was sufficient. He felt a failure and it made him withdrawn and sad in ways he could not adequately express.

Aida spoke softly and Erik was appreciative that she decided to forego making either of them continue specific enquiries and instead informed them of major symptoms. She encouraged Erik to be patient and loving, and readily acknowledged that pregnancy tended to make a woman slightly mad.

Not that he had any personal experience of being *mad.*

She only spoke for a moment about illness and worrisome signs to be cautious of. Erik knew that if she spent any significant amount of time speaking on such matters he was likely to spiral into his own despair. Having babies was of course a natural process, but it was also a well known fact that many women died in the endeavour— with or without a highly experienced midwife.

Aida must have seen his growing agitation at the subject and smiled at him kindly. "I only speak of it so you may be prepared. Christine is a young, healthy woman," only because he had recently made her so. What if there were lingering issues from her malnutrition? "And I encourage you to have *faith.* Stress is harmful for both mother and father, and your relationship can bear the brunt of your worries. Enjoy this time you have before the baby comes, as I can guarantee that you will both be quite consumed by your little one once it arrives."

Erik was not very good at sharing.

To Christine's visible relief there was no physical examination, and as they began their walk home—a slightly different route now that more people were beginning to mill about—she turned to him seriously. "I love you, Erik. I have not been saying it enough. I want our baby to be born into a happy home, so I will do my best to be more mindful of my moods and to take your needs and feelings into consideration."

Erik doubted that while in the *midst* of her moods she could do so very effectively, but he kept such misgivings to himself. Yet he still took her hand and tucked it firmly into the crook of his arm, and with a kiss to her temple whispered, "I love you as well."

Her grip on his arm tightened and quite placidly she responded, "I still want you."

His minx of a wife.

XXX

Despite his reservations, life was slightly better after that. Christine still had her moments, but she seemed to catch herself in the midst of a mood before she could snap at him too harshly or cry too fiercely. She would hold up her hand and ask him to give her a little time, and while he waited with bated breath to see what she would do, she would eventually walk over to him, place a kiss upon his cheek, and tell him she loved him.

Well.

That was far more preferable.

And although he was intensely grateful for her efforts, he was rather suspicious that it was their resumed lovemaking that greatly improved her mood.

Not that he was one to gloat about such things.

But still, ever since they had returned from the midwife and she had all but dragged him to their bed, she had been smiling and cheerful once more.

The only thing that chagrined him about that particular assignation was that she had been so hurried to *have* him, that she had not allowed either of them to undress fully. His shirt had been opened, and her pantalettes pulled down, but that had been the extent of it.

Later, though he was almost fearful of her wrath, he had awoken her by undressing her completely so that their reunion could be one of sweet words, soft touches, and naked flesh—everything he had missed so acutely during their mutual abstinence.

To his amazement, she had awoken before him the next morning. His first thought had been that she was once more plagued with nausea and he hurried to the bath-room. Most mornings she no longer was physically ill but would only complain of a lingering feeling of *sickness* that made her sullen and miserable if he did not bring her enough toast to settle her stomach. But despite having overslept, she must not have felt overly ill as he blessedly did not find her there. And satisfied that she would not immediately require his assistance, he completed his morning ablutions.

He instead found her in the kitchen preparing their breakfast.

Her kiss had been long and deep, and then she had chastised him greatly for so distracting her that she nearly burned their toast.

Impertinent girl.

He told her so, and wrapping his long fingers around her waist lifted her onto her favourite bit of the counter so that she could sit and rest while he finished their breakfast preparations—but not before kissing her once more, simply because he wanted to.

This morning however was not so pleasant.

Christine awoke with a start, gasping and gulping for breath even as tears flooded down her cheeks and her hands clutched at his nightclothes with near desperation.

He blinked, trying to awaken his mind so that he could properly tend to Christine, but he could hardly tell if anything was seriously the matter. "My love, you have to tell your Erik what is wrong. Are you injured?"

She shook her head, burrowing into the crook of his neck even as he tried futilely to disengage her so he could assess her body for any damages.

But she told him it was not an injury. If something had been wrong physically with her or the baby, surely she would have demanded to see the midwife.

"Did you have a nightmare?"

While once they had been a nightly occurrence on both their parts, they now were a rarity—something that still surprised him even now. But apparently his lovely wife was not to be spared forever.

She started to sob and he felt that was sufficient answer. He could do nothing but put his arms around her and hold her close until she was calm enough to explain what had distressed her so.

It took quite a bit of time before her tears abated, and Erik had to provide much coaxing with calming touches and hummed lullabies before she sniffled a final time and pulled back to look at him. "Oh, Erik, it was so awful."

He was not certain that he wished to know what had reduced her to hapless weeping, but according to Christine *talking* about such things was an important part of learning to share each other's burdens as a proper husband and wife.

So swallowing thickly he replied, "Tell your Erik what you dreamt."

Christine took a shuddering breath and nestled down so that her head was resting upon his chest, and she stared at her fingers as they drew patterns on his nightshirt.

"I was walking along a dark alley, and I had our child with me. She was about six years old and I was trying to find my way back to the Opera House but I kept getting lost." She went silent, and Erik hoped that was the end of the dream. Yet he knew while frightening, that would not be enough to cause such hysterics. One of his hands settled in her hair, and he worked his fingers soothingly through her curls as he offered what comfort he could.

"And?"

He could feel her tears making small puddles upon his shirt, but he could not even find a bit of irritation that she was once more maiming an item of his clothing.

"Some of the... men..." she did not even have to specify *which* men, "found us, and they grabbed our daughter and made her watch while they..."

Her words cut off as her sobs renewed, and Erik's hand froze from its work in her tresses.

They had no way of knowing the sex of the baby before the terrifying day of birth, and of course her dream could not be any kind of premonition. The midwife had mentioned that strange dreams could be a common occurrence during pregnancy, but Erik doubted many women she had encountered had experienced the heartache and cruelty that his poor wife had suffered.

She looked up at him with tears streaming down her cheeks, and he felt such pain bolt through his very soul at the sight. "You cannot let that happen, Erik. Our baby must never know what that is like."

For a moment he could imagine that very thing—his beautiful wife and a little daughter of their own, a mirror image of her mother. In time Christine might feel comfortable wandering the streets on her own, doing small errands and amusing herself with their child in tow. Two such lovelies would draw the attention of the same nefarious thugs that had so brutalised her before, and without his protection his small family would always be vulnerable.

Life was uncertain. Perhaps he could not promise Christine that her dream would never come to fruition, as he could not predict the future. But if the child growing in his wife's womb was a girl, there was little doubt in his mind that he would be the most protective of fathers. No daughter of his would ever know the hardships and brutality that could befall a woman—not while he drew breath. He would shadow their every outing if necessary, but he would keep them safe.

"You have my word, Christine. Our child will be raised with love, and will not know of such things. You will have a home and so will they. Always."

She sniffled once more, and he noticed the way she still trembled. "Was there more?" If even in a dream they had touched his daughter...

Christine shook her head. "No. I just... I can still feel them touching me."

Erik hesitated before removing his hands from her person. "Would you like me to draw you a bath?"

She released a shuddering breath and turned so she could reach his hand that had fallen away from her back and tucked it around her in an embrace. "No, I just want you to remind me of sweet touches. I want you to talk about our baby and what preparations we still must do."

Distractions, but pleasant ones, and he was happy to oblige.

"We neglected to arrange with the midwife where the baby will actually be born. I can hardly bring her down here."

Christine chuckled then, a short breathy sound that was more in relief at the change in subject than actual humour. "I would think not. She might be understanding of your face, but I doubt she would appreciate being dragged through the tunnels merely to tend to me."

If that was what it took in order for Christine to be cared for, Erik was fully prepared to do just that. He wisely did not voice that to his wife.

"We need baby things. Clothes and bassinets and diapers," Erik grimaced slightly at her mention of diapers. He would not burden Christine with the sole responsibility, but he could not honestly say he relished the notion of caring for that particular need.

The only thing they had truly taken care of was Christine's need for new dresses. Always wanting to be prepared, Erik had insisted she order an entire wardrobe in varying sizes and styles that could accommodate her growing frame—each of which he also insisted must be worn without a corset. She had almost begun to protest that particular requirement as she reminded him that her breasts would also grow along with her stomach. And though his eyes had drifted to her décolletage for perhaps longer than was appropriate, he stood by his pronouncement.

Christine began to nibble on her lip, and while Erik was grateful that she seemed to be successfully immersed in their planning, that particular look never boded very well for him. "Yes, my dear? What is flitting through that pretty head of yours?"

She blushed and plucked at one of his nightshirt buttons. "Do you think..." She took a bracing breath. "I was wondering if perhaps your dressing room should become a nursery."

Erik paused. She had never referred to his old bedchamber as such, and he supposed it was its proper title now. Many men had dressing rooms, some even fitted with beds in case the mistress of the house should tire of his company. That had been his original intention, but far more pressing things had happened and not once had she complained about his continued presence in her bed.

He had not even begun to think of where the baby would sleep—where the child it would someday become would rest its head.

"Please do not be angry. They can sleep in our room while they are little, but eventually they will need a room of their own."

"You... you do not wish to leave here? Once the child is born?" He felt choked and slightly panicked, fearing her response.

Erik had never once considered that he would leave this place. It had been fashioned just for him. It afforded privacy and solitude, and though perhaps it was inconvenient for the larger trips to the market for food and sundries, he still found that he had no desire to leave it.

Christine looked at him curiously. "I had never thought about it. I did not think leaving was an option."

He wanted to tell her that it was not—that he would live forever in his little home, and that was that. She could fill it with however many babies she wished, but they would remain safe and secure in his personal fortress.

But he could not.

If Christine wished to leave and asked him to procure a little cottage somewhere—or even a sprawling château in the country—he would not refuse her. He would protest, pout, and perhaps even connive as he attempted to change her mind, but he knew the truth of it. He would follow her anywhere.

His hand felt thick and heavy, but he still managed to touch her cheek lightly, revelling in the way she leaned into his touch. "We do not have to remain here, Christine, if it is not your preference. I want you and the child to be comfortable."

He would make that sacrifice for her, even if it meant once more hiding in stuffy rooms and only being allowed outside when it was dark and no neighbours were awake to possibly see him.

Erik shuddered slightly just thinking of it.

But his wonderfully perceptive wife must have seen that the offer was not wholly willing, and her eyes softened and then it was her hand touching *his* cheek. "You are sweetness itself for offering, Erik, but I would not manipulate you so. I do not think either of us are ready to rejoin the real world just yet. Maybe someday, but not now."

Thank God.

His hold on her tightened and she giggled as he pressed kisses into her curls. "You do not mind raising a child here with your Erik? Truly?"

She grew serious again. "I can think of no safer place for our baby to be. There are doors that no one but my genius of a husband could ever dream of opening, and I have been so happy here."

Christine snuggled further against his side. "And we will go to the park in the evenings so that they can run and play and you will be *very* watchful of all of us so that nothing bad could happen."

He should have reminded her that even he had his failings. He was not perfect, nor all seeing. And though he hated even the idea of allowing something to happen to his family, he knew that there was always the possibility that something beyond his skill could circumvent their happiness.

But in that moment he knew to what she referred. The monsters that prowled his wife's mind and heart were the very same kind that he had dispatched on the day they met. *Those* mindless thugs would always feel the sting of his lasso, and as he whispered his reassurances to her that all would be well, he knew that there was little harm in doing so.

He kissed her then. It was long and languorous and promised of *more.* But as his hands crept up her thighs and pushed slightly at her nightgown, she stopped him as she pulled back and put a hand on his wandering fingers.

Erik froze, suddenly remembering that he was to be distracting her from her nightmares, and surely she would not appreciate to be preoccupied in *that* way. She had asked for sweet fantasies about their future, and so lost was he within them that he had temporarily forgotten that *he* was to be the one providing the diversions.

He pulled his hands back shyly. "Forgive me."

Her smile was thin and she kissed him once in forgiveness. "You did not answer my question, you sly thing. Can you fashion your dressing room into a nursery?" Her tone was deliberately light and teasing, and he noticed how much effort it took for her to make it so.

His poor wife.

Perhaps at any other time—and if his rose had been any other woman—he would have felt more upset at her quiet rejection of his advances. But not with his Christine. She was all that was strength and love and beauty, and while it was to be expected that he could lose himself in all that was *her,* he would not begrudge her when she kindly reminded him that he had to be mindful of her demons—just as she was of his.

So he played along with her little game. His expression turned woeful, and he sighed piteously. "Would you have me dress in the sitting room then? I hardly think that appropriate."

She smiled slightly, evidently knowing his words were in jest and she placed a kiss on his cheek in gratitude. "No, I doubt children would much like seeing their father dress each morning. You will just have to move your wardrobe in here with mine."

His eyes widened in mock disbelief. "With you, Madame? Where you could so easily ogle?" He sniffed indignantly.

Perhaps he had gone too far, as the niggling voice in his mind reminded him sharply that she would never actually *ogle* him. She did like to look at his body whenever he undressed, but he could still hardly find it within himself to believe that it was from any type of desire.

His playful countenance must have faded, for Christine frowned a little and smoothed her fingers over his unmasked face. "I like to look at you, Erik. I know you do not yet believe me that I find you to be pleasing, but I do." To his surprise, she stopped leaning over him with her elbows and instead moved to sit upon his stomach—a much better position in his opinion, though it was effortful to keep his body from expecting *more.*

Her hands ran over his chest and down his arms—light touches that were more hints than actual contact.

Christine's fingers skimmed tantalisingly over the muscles of his chest and he suppressed a whimper. "You are so strong, yet so very gentle. I like how tall you are and that I have to go onto the tips of my toes in order to kiss you unless you bend down." This particular compliment was punctuated by another kiss, this time more prolonged and it made his heart ache.

And when she blushed her eyes grew heated, and her voice lowered until she was merely breathing the words into his ear. "And you have such *lovely* fingers."

He could not help but groan in response.

It was possible she did not mean it the way he took it—that she was referring to the way he could pleasure her so intimately. It was equally feasible that she meant something as simple as the way he would rub her tense shoulders after she had spent an afternoon kneading bread dough into the little rolls she liked so much. Yet in either case, she was speaking to his ability to bring her enjoyment. And though he tried to firmly remind himself that she did not wish to engage in congress, his body had very different ideas. "Christine," he nearly pleaded.

She slid down his body slightly so that she could access his sleep trousers more readily, pushing them down as she did so. This seemed to be her favourite positing for lovemaking when she had a difficult day coping with her memories. She could control the rhythm and the depth, and while he had not thought it wholly appropriate to do so, once he had even choked out the question outright.

Christine had been quiet for some time afterward and he had nearly recanted the enquiry. But eventually, in a quiet voice that was filled with pain and memory she replied, "Because no one ever took me that way, so it can be solely between us."

He was brought out of his remembrances when Christine lowered herself onto him. He threw back his head at the intensity of the feeling of her, yet he dimly realised that she still managed to have the presence of mind to be able to undo the buttons of his nightshirt. Her fingers tickled his flesh, and it took every ounce of control he possessed to tear open his eyes so he could look at her.

Because no matter how much he wished to merely surrender to the sensations, her needs, her emotions, and simply *she* mattered far more.

"Do you believe me?"

She was looking down at him with so much love that it nearly brought a sob from some hidden depth within him. How could he not believe her when she was embracing him so intimately, and the proof of her affections was so very vivid?

He brought one of his hands to cup her chin, and she placed a soft kiss on his palm in response. "I believe you, my rose."

Their lovemaking was soft and slow, and at one point Erik had to remind her that she was safe and loved because she began to tremble and had that haunted look that he hated with such a passion.

But when both were sated and languid in each other's arms Erik whispered into her ear, "You may have my dressing room, Christine, to fill with all your things for the baby."

She hummed in contentment and pressed a kiss upon his chest. "And you will have to become used to being ogled."

Perhaps there were far worse fates for a husband than to be desirable to his wife.

XXXI

There was one particular subject that Christine did not know how to bring up to her husband. When she had first come to live in his home she had briefly thought it odd that there were no mirrors—not even above the basin in the bath-room, yet she had dismissed it readily enough. At the time she had no supplies for doing her hair in any case, so beyond seeing to whatever tangles she could with her fingers there would be little help with a mirror.

When he had brought the trunk full of clothing, at the very bottom was a small pewter hand mirror that she now used to try and tame her curls into somewhat appealing fashions. She supposed that fancy ladies had maids who helped them with the elaborate styles she saw through the windows of the tea rooms she had once coveted. And while she tried to replicate them herself, she generally grew frustrated and forced herself to be content with a simple braid or the occasional *chignon*.

But now she wanted a mirror. A full length one that would allow her to actually see and reconcile the physical changes she noted as she looked down at herself. For quite some time she began merely to look plump. Her lower belly had begun to protrude slightly just between her hip bones, and she would catch herself rubbing it absently throughout the day.

And catch Erik touching it when he thought her asleep at night.

But now there was no denying that her shape now lent toward pregnant instead of merely fleshy. When they had ventured to the market the day before, she caught herself eyeing the few women they happened to pass with a touch of wistfulness as she looked at their tiny waists and slight figures.

Which was absolutely ridiculous.

Despite her fears that she would be an inadequate mother, she found that she *wanted* this baby. Erik assured her many times that she would learn along with their little one, and that eventually the nuances of life and routine would be commonplace and not nearly so frightening. She tried to believe him.

But she still thought it might be a easier to adjust to her changing body if she could see it—not simply take Erik at his word that he still found her lovely and desirable.

She pulled out one of her most comfortable dresses, although on more than one occasion she had decided that there was little point in dressing at all. Nightgowns and chemises became far more favourable, but she did try to preserve her modesty by stealing back Erik's dressing gown.

Today however, she wanted to dress. She wanted to cook a proper supper and make herself look nice for him—as nice as she could with nothing but a small hand mirror and her own two hands.

As she fastened her petticoat she felt the strangest feeling in her abdomen. It was not exactly a cramp, but it made her gasp and pull her hand to the not so subtle protrusion of her stomach. With her hand pressed firmly against the swell, she felt it again. It was nearly a flutter against her palm, and she realised suddenly that it was her baby pressing to meet her.

Intellectually she knew there was a baby inside. She had certainly grown and suffered the multitudes of symptoms that Aida had warned her about, and she had made plans and spoke for long hours with Erik about what they hoped their child would be.

But to actually *feel* that there was a living thing inside her was one of the most peculiar experiences of her life. And suddenly she felt a surge of elation.

"Erik!"

In her excitement she had forgotten that a shout of that volume would accomplish little beyond causing him great alarm, and the sheer speed in which he managed to fly to her side was a testament to his concern. Perhaps she should have felt guilty for tearing him away from his composing in such a manner, especially when he took such little time for himself these days. Mostly he doted and saw to her every whim, but this morning she had insisted that he needed to do something purely for himself—to which he had begrudgingly agreed.

"Christine? What is it?" His eyes were wide and frightened, and his gaze roamed over her form quickly as if assessing for injury.

She smiled at him and took his hand, placing it against her swollen belly.

"I felt it *move.*"

It did not occur to her that someone else might not be able to feel it, or that the tiny babe could have already tired from its first stretches and might have returned to slumber. But just when she thought it would not move again, she felt the small flutterings from within and saw Erik's look of shock as he stared at his hand. "Does it hurt you?"

Of course his first thought would be regarding her comfort. Her loving husband.

She shook her head, unable to contain her large smile. "No, it is just a bit odd. You felt it too?"

Erik nodded hesitantly. "Just a little nudge."

Christine patted his hand that still remained covering her womb. "I wonder why he picked today to say hello."

He looked at her sceptically. "He? Why do you think it is a he?"

She shrugged. "No particular reason. It just does not seem right to continue to call him an *it* if he is now capable of moving."

Erik did not seem so certain. "I would be terribly insulted if I discovered my parents had been referring to me by the improper sex for the entirety of my gestation."

Christine rolled her eyes at him and bestowed a kiss upon his cheek for his ridiculousness. "You know what this means. We have to begin talking of names."

Her husband grimaced, plainly visible as he had forgone the mask at her insistence—although she was quite sure she would awaken in the morning to see it firmly back in place.

"How can you name something without seeing it first?"

She sighed, but refused to give in. He wanted to call their baby an *it* which was distressing enough, but to also deny her any discussion regarding potential names was not going to be tolerated.

Her dress was put back into the wardrobe, and thoughts of fixing supper and dressing prettily were temporarily forgotten. She was still in her shift and petticoat, and that was surely enough clothing to not be *too* distracting for her poor husband.

But as she saw his eyes straying to her blossoming bosom, she realised with amusement that her assessment had been mistaken.

But regardless of her ever distractible husband, she did not desire the weight of his dressing gown upon her shoulders, and she knew she would easily grow overheated by what she had in mind.

Erik was looking at her strangely as she took quite a few of their bed pillows and walked to the hearth of the fire, arranging them in a small nest before the warmth of the flames. She assessed it shrewdly, and after she had added some of the cushions from the settee—and though he protested, one of his favourite pillows from his reading chair—she settled down into her makeshift lounge approvingly. The only thing currently missing was her husband.

She held out a hand and tried to temper her voice so that while pleading, it would not sound whiney. "Come here."

He seemed doubtful even as he settled in beside her, shifting and prodding pillows all the while until they conceded to his much longer frame. "Why is it that you always insist on being on the floor? Do you find something lacking in my furniture?"

Christine smiled and cuddled up beside him, quite glad that between the fire and her husband she found the temperature to be pleasing. "I do."

Erik looked affronted. "Do enlighten your poor husband as to precisely *how* our furniture is so inadequate."

She did not give in to his tone, although it was bordering on sulky. She liked the way the flames danced from this angle, and while she knew she should be engaging her husband in conversation—she *was* the instigator of it after all—the longer she watched the sleepier she got.

It took a great amount of sheer determination to keep herself from succumbing altogether, but when she glanced up at his face she noticed that he truly seemed bothered by her complaint. "We have not yet furnished the nursery. That was all I meant, I promise." She allowed one of her hands to skim the fine silk threads that comprised his Persian rugs. "And if you did not want me to enjoy the floor so much, you should not have chosen such lovely rugs."

"Quite," he responded dryly, yet she could easily feel him relax against her. "We will furnish your nursery, Christine. I do not want for you to worry."

She smiled at him, and knew that it would be done. She did not know if he would take her shopping for all the precious little items that would make up the future home of the tiny baby that was still fluttering about her womb, or if she would simply awaken one day to see his dressing room transformed. But either way, she knew that if she gave voice to its importance, Erik would oblige her—he always did. And she would not abuse him for it—would not wheedle and connive to get what she wanted. She would have to remember to be thoughtful and caring in all that she asked, for she knew very well that he disliked ever denying her.

"Have you given any thought to names? Even you must have *some* ideas, even if you deny it."

He shifted beneath her and she felt momentarily victorious until he evaded her enquiry once more. "I believe the mother is the one who should rightfully do the naming. She was the one who suffered all of the discomfort after all."

Christine huffed. "I believe you have done your own bit of suffering over the past few months, Erik. I know I am not the easiest person to live with." She was *trying* to be better, honestly she was. It was far better now that they had resumed their intimacies, as she could always be sure to at least meet those needs—at least, when she did not feel as though her skin was stretched too tightly, and her mind would settle enough to allow her to feel pleasure at Erik's touch.

He had surprised her one day by embarking on a mysterious errand. She had offered to accompany him but he had simply looked sheepish and made his excuses that he was going too far for her to comfortably follow. She did not believe him as Erik had stated on numerous occasions that he never went too far from her side—especially not in her current condition. He would go to the market or their regular shops, but beyond that he would send a currier or one of his street rascals.

Erik had returned not an hour later and after her evening bath had approached her cautiously, holding out a jar full of what appeared to be a pale paste. "You had complained of your skin itching. I was told this would help."

She had not meant to burst into tears at his thoughtfulness, but she could not help herself and her wonderfully patient husband took it with grace. He was getting better about comforting her during these episodes. In the past he would pat her back awkwardly while seemingly trying to escape as he leaned away from her, but now he would hold her truly and hum softly, and on more than one instance she had fallen asleep on him.

On this occasion however, she had pulled away from him with a smile. And while he was shy and a touch bashful, he had offered to apply it for her.

And Christine felt as though she had never loved him more.

She had lain upon the bed, and although she tried to cover her most private bits with the towel, any considerations of modesty were quickly abandoned by how *good* it felt for him to massage the soothing balm into her skin. He had focused most of his attention upon the swell of her abdomen, small though it still was. While many women remained confined during the lasts of their pregnancies, Christine had still seen enough of the poorer folk to know that she would be growing much larger still.

She could admit that it frightened her.

Ever since that first application—that had soon turned into fervent lovemaking when Christine had decided she desired Erik's ministrations on *other* places— Erik had taken it to be his personal responsibility to ensure that her skin was well moisturised.

And Christine was not complaining in the least, especially now with a warm fire and her husband's arms around her, one hand resting protectively over their little one. A little one that needed a *name.*

"I find that I have no objects to living with you."

She hummed contentedly, not wishing to quibble with him but finding it dreadfully important that they speak on the subject. Perhaps there were better methods to be utilised in order to draw her husband into contributing. "Well, we could name him after your friend. Daroga is a very nice name." It was said in jest as she did not think it a very nice name at all. She had nothing against the man as he had been nothing but cordial to her when they had tea, but she certainly would not be naming her firstborn after him.

But as she had hoped, Erik scoffed. "Firstly, that is not actually a name, but his title. And there is no possibility that I would allow my child to bear that man's name."

Christine looked at him quizzically. "Then what is his name? And why did you not correct me before?"

Erik glanced at her drolly. "Because that would have been rude."

She continued to wait for him to supply the name, but he remained silent. "That does not answer my first question."

He sighed and closed his eyes. "Well, I shall not be telling you of it now. You might name our child after him."

No matter how much she cajoled or huffed, he would not be moved. Finally having enough of her wheedling, he distracted her by kissing her soundly. And when her thoughts had all but melted away he pulled back and asked, "What would you name a daughter?"

"Lotte."

The name was spoken even before she had truly given it any consideration. That was *her* name, the one that was used with such affection and tenderness from her girlhood. And she realised suddenly that if she was ever blessed with a girl, that was indeed what she would wish for her.

"Little Lotte thought of everything and nothing..."

She had not thought she had spoken the words aloud, but when she opened her eyes and saw Erik gazing at her questioningly, she blushed. "It was a story my father used to tell me. She had hair like the golden rays and her eyes were blue like the sky. They called me Lotte after that."

Raoul was in those memories—her teasing and cheerful playmate that she had been so very fond of at the time. Looking back at the incident all those months ago she truly could not blame him for not recognising her. She had been drenched and filthy and more greatly resembled a street farer than the girl he had once known. During the episode she had thought it was further evidence that she was unworthy of any good man's attention, but now she knew that it was simply a mistake.

But while she no longer felt hurt and angry at the error, that did not mean she felt the same fondness for him that she once did. Still, it did not seem wholly appropriate to speak of one's childhood friendship with another man to one's husband. Erik had little cause to be jealous since she so rarely ever came into contact with anyone else, but she did not think *she* would like to hear tales of him cavorting with another woman.

She scowled slightly just thinking of it.

Christine never gave much thought to his age. With his face it was nearly impossible to gauge, and his body was lean and firm to the eye and touch, so that was also not a very helpful indicator. But she did realise he was a good deal older than she, and suddenly she had a powerful urge to know if there was anyone he loved before her.

"Erik..."

She was not entirely sure how to pose the question without immediately making him uncomfortable. He had already stiffened at her tone, even while she had tried to keep it as unimposing as she could manage.

"Yes, Christine?"

She fiddled with the buttons of his shirt. "Did you ever love a woman before me?"

No matter his answer, she would not resent him for it. She had thought long ago that she fancied Raoul, but that paled in comparison to the feelings that Erik had instilled within her. She could extend him the same courtesy, even if he admitted that he had pined for another.

At least, she would attempt to do so.

Erik placed a fingertip below her chin and pushed at it gently so she would look at him. "Why would you ask such a thing?"

She nibbled her lip and felt very silly. He was *her* husband, and his past infatuations did not matter.

"I was only curious, that is all. You do not have to tell me."

He was silent for quite some time. "I would like for you to know first and foremost that you are the only woman I have ever loved." She should have felt comforted, but instead she was filled with a sense of unease. "There was a girl once... long ago that I thought I cared for. I was wrong."

His voice was soft and full of pain, and she felt dreadful for having brought up the subject at all. He did not press her for information on past loves, and here in a fit of childish wonder she had hurt him.

"I am sorry if I upset you, Erik. I should not have spoken of it." She kissed his cheek and tried to assuage her guilt by embracing him tightly, but she only felt worse. "Forgive me; I do not want you to be sad."

Erik released a long breath, and with it seemed to go his tension. "You surprised me, that is all. I have not thought of her in many years." His eyes narrowed slightly as he regarded her. "Would that have bothered you? If your husband had loved another?"

Christine was certain that the mature young woman would have been able to say no and been entirely truthful. She blushed and tried to find the ability to lie.

She failed.

"Yes."

Erik laughed. He did not laugh but rarely, and even then it was usually small chuckles that seemed to be pried from him against his will. This however was loud and mirthful, and she revelled in the way his chest moved against her ear as she lay against him, although she felt her blush rise steadily at his amusement.

"I have a jealous wife, I see. I suppose there are far worse traits for you to exhibit. I love *you* Christine, and if you would like to name a daughter Lotte, then that shall be her name." He had not pressed for any more details as to the name's origins, but must have known from the wistfulness of her tone just how significant it was to her.

How she loved him!

Erik did not make any enquiries about her own romantic past, for which she was grateful. She regretted having brought it up at all, and was content to simply return to their afternoon of gazing at the fire and speaking of names.

Until her husband spoke once more.

"Christine, would you do me the honour of attending the theatre this evening?"

XXXII

She blinked at him in surprise. "We cannot go to the opera! There will be *people.*"

Erik rolled his eyes. How startlingly observant his wife could be. "Yes, there will be *people,* it is a theatre after all. I would think the managers would be very disappointed if the seats remained unfilled."

Christine huffed at him, sitting up suddenly. He slowly mimicked her movement. "Their production of *Faust* is ending in less than a week and I thought you might like to see it before it closed. Was I mistaken?"

She looked flustered, and he could see the indecision clearly on her face. "But... what shall I *wear?*"

He could not help but snort at that being the extent of her true concern. Now that she was not forthrightly refusing his offer, he could relax slightly. Erik took her arm to assist her from the floor, and with her help they righted the settee cushions—though he ensured that he was the one who perfectly placed the pillow back on his reading chair. It was precisely the size that offered maximum comfort to his lower back, and it had to be positioned just *so* for it to fulfil its greatest potential.

Satisfied that the sitting room was set to rights, he took Christine back to their bedroom and stalked purposefully toward the wardrobe. It would not truly matter what she wore as she would be going as the companion of the Ghost. She would be seen from afar—that was part of his entire scheme—but by no means would anyone come close enough to take note of the cut and fabrication of her attire.

But still, he pulled out one of her finest gowns that could still accommodate her pregnancy. All of the dresses he had commissioned did not require a corset as his strongly worded letter to the dressmaker had all but censured the wearing of the contraption entirely. The one he helped her don was a fine silk, purchased for the occasional suppers where she insisted they dress the part.

He always was formally attired, and though she had her moments where nothing but chemises and petticoats would be donned for the entire day, other times she insisted that she could at least match him in ceremony.

Perhaps it was silly of him, but he had been planning this evening for quite some time. He had not known that it would be *this* evening—instead it was a vague figment of fantasy that he hoped would one day come to fruition.

It was far too early to actually ascend to the theatre above, but he had an idea of how to fill the next hour or so. Christine seemed satisfied with his choice of dress, and when she informed him rather primly that she would request his assistance later when she needed to do up the laces at the back of her bodice, Erik took his leave.

His own clothing was never troublesome to see to. There was no reason to actually change except for the fact that he wanted to ensure that he looked especially nice while wooing his Christine. Not that she particularly *needed* to be wooed since she was in fact his wife and reminded him nearly daily that she loved him, but he did not want her to feel as though he took such things for granted.

He donned a mask as the last part of his apparel. Christine had made it very clear that if he chose to wear one in their home it was for his sake, not hers. He had been doubtful for quite some time, eyeing her surreptitiously to make certain she was not merely saying such things out of a false sense of duty, but she truly did not seem disturbed.

And he did so love the way her lips felt against his bare flesh.

So for most of the time he went without, although there were still occasions when he felt overly exposed and vulnerable without what was once his most important article of clothing.

But for this event, being without his mask was not an option. Christine would be seen by many, but he would remain carefully hidden—unless of course, he felt a sudden urge to show his visage so as to further the illusion of a Phantom skulking about.

While he had given thought and consideration to how this evening would further his reputation amongst the patrons and workers of the Opera, this was first and foremost a treat for his wife. She deserved to have her fanciful evenings full of musicality and delight—and dare he say, romance—and it seemed a waste to have her locked away for the entirety of her days. As of yet that was her preference, and he trusted her to tell him when she needed a reprieve from the tedium of life lived belowground.

But tonight, she would be his lovely companion at the theatre—just like any other couple with enough intellect to realise that the arts were worthy of their time, attention, and funds. Not that he had actually purchased tickets.

He made his way to the kitchens, pulling out a small basket from a hidden cupboard. Ever since Christine had convinced him to sit with her on the banks of the lake, he had whimsical notions of a picnic upon the water.

Tonight it would become a reality.

He had purchased a small basket, enough for a bit of bread, cheese, roast chicken, and the first fruits of the season that he had been delighted to find at the market only that morning. Erik had emptied one of his flasks that had once contained spirits, and now filled it with water. He took a small sip, and was pleased that the strong aftertaste of its previous inhabitant had not contaminated the container.

Satisfied with his spread, he now had only to wait for his wife.

Erik was not kept waiting long. Christine entered the sitting room, a shy smile on her face—as if she could ever be considered anything but beautiful.

The colour of her gown was a deep blue, and it contrasted the paleness of her skin and hair to perfection. She seemed quite womanly as this particular dress was slightly lower than most of her others, and he felt rather dry mouthed and inadequate as she came towards him.

"Could you help me, please?"

She had turned around, and he was given the great pleasure of lacing up the bodice. While on many occasions he would much rather *unlace* such things, tonight he found that he was looking forward to enjoying her company in another way.

Christine shivered each time his fingers brushed against the sensitive flesh of her neck, and she giggled when they skimmed the ticklish part of her upper back that he generally only found when he was playing with her curls.

That was the one element of her attire that he was quite certain he would like to undo. She had bound them in a becoming manner, but he found that he much preferred them bouncing and free and lively—and oh so teasingly awaiting his touch.

But no matter. Having her hair thusly allowed for a tantalising view of her neck and shoulders, and he would appreciate that until they were once again home—and he could amuse himself with finding all of the little pins that kept her hair so carefully contained.

With a final tug and flourish, her bodice was closed. He could not help but lean forward and place a kiss upon her shoulder, and upon feeling the softness of her skin, that might have turned into a slight nibble.

She laughed lightly and turned to him. "Erik, much more of that and we will never make it to the performance!"

He sniffed indignantly. "One would think you simply did not want my attentions."

Christine rolled her eyes and tucked her hand into his. "No one would say that, not after they had spent more than a few moments with us."

That was true. While the Daroga had been wary of Erik's explanation that he had taken a wife, after only a cup of tea and not even a scone, he had been quite convinced of Christine's affections.

His wife caught sight of the small basket and looked at him curiously. "What is that for?"

Erik placed a hand over his heart in mock horror. "Did you think I would starve my poor wife? I believe our babe distracted you from supper, and I must be the one to rectify its oversight."

Christine beamed at him. "I will fetch my cloak!"

He watched her hurry back to the bedchamber, feeling ready to scold that she should not have thought to bring it before.

But she was back before he could begin his reprimand, and the way she smiled at him and looked at him so expectantly, any type of admonishment died before it could even be formulated.

"Would you care to join me on the lake, Madame?"

It struck him suddenly just how different a man he was now. He could tease and be kind and gentle, and it was all because he knew his affections were reciprocated. He could hold out his arm without fear or trepidation, because he knew that a temperate hand would be placed in the crook and a warm smile would be bestowed upon him for the simple gesture.

Yet with his wife tugging at him and practically trembling with excitement, he could not take much time to ponder such drastic changes.

He offered her a choice of carrying the lantern or the basket, and she held out her hand for their supper with a greedy gleam in her eye that made him chuckle.

Erik had thought her a voracious eater *before* her pregnancy, but now he could plainly see that her previous habits paled in comparison.

Not that he would ever tell her so—he knew enough of his wife's current temperament to know that even moderate teasing on *that* particular topic would only lead to disaster.

Erik placed the lantern on the small hook that protruded over the bow of the craft, allowing for a warm glow to surround the boat. The light shimmered off the murky depths, and with their cloaks warding off the cooler temperatures, the lake was truly a pleasant atmosphere for a romantic supper with his lady love.

He helped settle Christine, ensuring that nothing dreadful would befall her as she entered the craft. She had already proven capable of capsizing if left to her own devices, so he made sure to keep a steady hand at the small of her back and another clasped tightly around her hand as he lowered her into the vessel.

She looked up at him with eyes wide with excitement. "Are we having a picnic on the lake?"

"Obviously," came his rather droll reply. But apparently his eyes shone with his own excitement that belied his tone, for she smiled all the more and waited anxiously for him to enter the boat himself so he could steer them into the middle of the small lake.

He chuckled at her enthusiasm and did exactly that, noting that she began setting out their supper before he had even managed to push the boat away from the shore.

By the time Erik felt comfortable allowing them to drift upon the waters, Christine had opened the flask and was sniffing at it delicately. "You are not trying to ply me with spirits are you?"

He stared at her incredulously. "It is water, Christine. What kind of husband do you take me for?" He leaned in to her closely, as though divulging a very great secret as his voice lowered. "I do not need to inebriate you in order to press my advantage."

Even in the lantern light he could clearly see the blush blossoming on her cheeks and her eyes lowered to the small feast between them. For a moment he worried that he had deeply offended her, knowing that she had often asked him for reassurance that her enjoyment of their marital relations was not in fact a poor reflection on her character.

But after a moment she smiled at him demurely. "No, you do not. And I am quite glad of it."

Then she popped a bit of cheese into her mouth to end that particular conversation.

That did not stop her from supplying another. "We have yet to speak of boys' names."

Erik sighed and took small pieces of each of the items and chewed thoughtfully. "I have not met many men that I have found agreeable, so I admit that many male names are rather tainted by association."

That was truly at the heart of the matter. Erik had never been in much contact with *girls.* They avoided him—for good reason—and those he did know were generally from foreign nations that had little relevance to the naming of their child. If Christine wished to pick a name that her father had supplied—though it was perhaps unusual that a mother bestow her daughter with the same name she had grown up with—but he had little objection.

And there was also a pressing matter that he had yet to even broach with his wife.

He took a sip of water from the flask before taking a bracing breath. "Christine, I would like to explain something to you."

She looked at him steadily and nodded that he had her full attention.

Erik briefly wondered if other couples discussed important issues while on picnics, or if they simply lounged and nibbled—both on food and one another.

He supposed they were not like other couples.

"I do not have a family name. My mother was not the one to provide me with my given name, and though I am aware of their surname, I refuse to ascribe to a house that scorned me from birth."

Christine's eyes grew sad as they always did when he mentioned his upbringing. While he could be grateful that she had enjoyed a happy childhood before the world's cruelties had brutalised her, she had no such comfort regarding him.

"I had no name to provide you when we wed, and I have none to give a son."

A daughter would take on her husband's name, but how would a son enter into the world without a surname? Assuming he was healthy and *normal* and capable of such things.

But Erik would not consider that issue now.

Christine was looking down at her lap, and when she regarded him again after minutes of silence, she had tears glimmering in her eyes. "I do not need a new name, Erik. And I would not want to burden you with a family name when they were so unkind to you. They were not a *true* family in any case. But our baby will have one." She reached across the short distance that separated them and took his hand. "Would your mind be more at ease if our children took my father's name? My name?"

Perhaps he should have been upset. It was certainly one of the least traditional suggestions she had ever provided, but all he felt was overwhelming relief. Christine's father had been a good man. While he had his faults—most notably dying and selecting an elderly woman as guardian for his young and innocent daughter—he had loved his child dearly and seen that she was a happy, healthy girl for as long as he was able.

"I would like that."

She still seemed sad, and her eyes continued to be lowered as she tried to formulate her next reply. "You could use it too... if you wanted. A family should share a name."

This was not how this evening was supposed to go. He would shower her with pampering, and she would smile and laugh and think that she had the greatest husband in all the world. But instead he was fighting back tears as his lovely wife haltingly offered him a family name—something that his own progenitors had not even allowed.

Because *she* loved him, and they did not.

His silence must have been misinterpreted for she hurried to fill the silence. "Papa would not have minded. His family was not very rich or important, but they were a kind one."

As if money or prestige ever made people more kind.

Erik found that he could not find the words to thank her, so he tugged at her hand instead and pulled her close, and while still mindful of the fact that they were floating upon water, he kissed her. She was hesitant for a moment, obviously surprised that he was so pleased instead of scolding her for potentially threatening his masculinity, but soon she responded with fervour. When they parted, her eyes were glassy, and she brought a finger to skim over his lips softly. "You are pleased?"

"Foolish girl," he retorted and kissed her again before she made any more inane enquiries.

He could feel her smiling against him, and perhaps this was not so unlike how other couples had their lakeside picnics after all.

It took quite a bit for him to pull away and decide whether or not he should forgo the evening's performance completely. He had a wife to pleasure, and suddenly the physical aspect seemed all the more pressing.

"Are we going to be late?"

She appeared worried at the prospect, and her excitement was clear.

Later.

There would always be later.

Erik steered the boat so that it would cease its mindless drifting, and soon enough they were on the other side. He exited first and all but lifted Christine from the craft.

There would be no tumbling this evening.

The rest of the food was tucked back into the basket, and then they began their journey above.

There was one particular aspect to this trip that he had not divulged, and now it made him uneasy. "Christine, I am afraid that with so many people milling about due to the performance, I am going to have to forsake the lantern."

She appeared frightened and he knew that was entirely his fault, and he quickly tried to placate her. "I will *not* leave you. I can see perfectly well in the dark and you are safe—safer still than when we have a light. Others cannot see you, but your husband will see them."

It truly was too dangerous to keep a lantern with them for this venture. The walls were thin and there were far more prying eyes as the last few performances sent more patrons into the theatre.

But all would be well if his wife would trust him.

Christine took a deep breath and put her hand in his. "Please do not let go."

Erik gave it a comforting squeeze. "I will keep you safe."

XXXIII

He had never taken her along this route. Once they passed the tunnels along the cellars, the walls tended to be wood instead of stone, and it was far less depressing an atmosphere. Many times the passages were too narrow to walk alongside one another, but he always ensured that he kept her hand clasped within his.

A part of him would have liked to be a normal man who could enter through the grand doors with his lady, and be ushered through the large and luxurious staircases to their private box. She would be seen by all and many men's eyes would leave their own finely bedecked companions in favour of looking at *his* most beautiful rose.

But a larger part liked the mystery.

It had been born of necessity, but his ability for secrecy and obscurity became a personal challenge that had flourished by his own affinity for it. And whether he chose to admit it or not, he did so enjoy terrorising the management.

They entered the final chamber. This was a false room, built especially for this purpose. The only door was to his tunnel, and while there were functioning rooms on either side, no one seemed to question the discrepancy of space.

He pulled a cord from the ceiling above, and an iron ladder descended.

Christine looked at it incredulously. "You wish for me to climb?"

Erik rolled his eyes. "I wish for you to hold my hand."

He ascended quickly, and though she still eyed him rather warily, she placed her hand trustingly in his as he hoisted her above.

It might have been prudent to mention that *she* would be watching the performance from the actual seat in Box Five, while he maintained his usual position within the large column. It opened towards the back, in the shadowy part of the box, and Christine was able to exit the hidden space without any undue attention. He remained within, and he hesitated before closing the façade.

She appeared positively captivated. "Erik, it is beautiful!"

Christine had the good sense to whisper, though it was not wholly necessary given that the theatre was already beginning to become crowded. Their voices tended to carry upward, and he knew from experience that the higher his vantage point, the louder they became.

She tore her eyes away from the magnificent theatre to look back at him, still swathed in the shadows. "Are you not going to sit with me?"

He shook his head slowly. "I will remain right here, Christine. I can hear you, and see you, but it would be impossible for me to be seen in such a way." He lowered his voice and whispered into her ear, though he remained carefully hidden away in the shadow of the still open column. "This evening is for *you,* my rose. There is nothing to fear."

She looked uncertain and very close to protesting. It touched him deeply that she would want his presence beside her so acutely, but he knew that there was no way he could keep his *profession* and also remain visible within the box.

And although he was rather loath to do it, he sealed the column and waited for the performance to begin.

Christine must have lived with him for sufficient time to no longer be wholly surprised by his ability to disappear into seemingly solid walls and furnishings. Her eyes widened briefly, but she soon settled and appeared contented to return her attention to the theatre about her.

He grew uneasy when she rose from her seat and peered over the edge, apparently wanting to garner a closer look at someone in the crowd below. She did not wave or give any other sort of recognition, so she must not have been recognised by anyone—and he could rightly suppose that her attention had simply been drawn by a particularly impressive gown.

Erik wanted to tug her back to her seat, but that would have required leaving his hiding place. He was saved from having to make such a decision when the performance began.

He was quite certain the Opera House itself could have gone up in flames and Christine would not have noticed. La Carlotta did not even compare to what he knew his wife's vocal talent to be, but Christine did not seem to notice. Her face was alight and her gaze only flickered occasionally to where she knew him to be hiding before it would return to the stage once more.

The orchestra was performing surprisingly well, though the first violinist needed to restring his bow at the next possible moment. Erik would be mentioning that in his next letter, as there was little excuse for improper maintenance.

His own attention was distracted from the performance by the sound of footsteps rushing up the staircase that opened into Box Five.

Erik had written a rather scathing reminder to the new managers of his terms of employment, detailing that this was *his* private box and that his monthly payments were to continue without fail.

Apparently they had taken his warning to heart and disapproved of Christine's presence in what they considered a cursed compartment.

Excellent.

He moved quickly, opening the column and pulling a bewildered Christine from her chair, and disappeared once more into the pillar. She made to protest—and by her previously enraptured expression it was going to be quite a loud objection—but she remained silent once she saw two gentlemen burst into the box.

She did not seem frightened for which Erik was glad, as he found the entire episode to be particularly amusing.

"There was a woman here!"

"It must have been a figment of your imagination. This is the Ghost's box and he is most certainly *not* a female."

Erik recognised the men as the managers, Moncharmin and Richard, and he was mildly surprised that they would see to the sanctity of his box themselves instead of sending some underling to do their bidding.

Delegation did not appear to be their forte.

He gave Christine a reassuring pat, and he could see her surprise was giving way to irritation.

"I heard that the Ghost now has a companion. A kitchen maid saw them together in the lauder. How can phantoms be multiplying?"

This was not the place for their debate, and he wanted his wife to be able to return to her enjoyment. It was quite dark within their confined space and together it was rather cramped. While he was able to see from a peephole he had installed for precisely this purpose, it was far too tall for Christine.

It was not very difficult to throw his voice at the two managers, though his wife looked at him curiously while he did so. "*Leave,*" he hissed, infusing his voice with the promise of bodily damage should they linger. He could have been more verbose he supposed, but the way they blanched at the lone word he knew that he had handled the situation effectively.

They scurried out and shut the door behind them, giving each other frightened glances as they did so.

"Are they gone?" she whispered.

He kissed her cheek and opened the hidden panel. "Quite gone, my Christine. They shall not bother you again."

Her eyes flickered to the stage, and she pouted prettily. "You will have to tell me what I have missed. I have never seen this before."

Erik chuckled and regaled her with the very limited details she had missed, and promptly rolled his eyes when apparently he had spoken too long and was shushed so that she could listen to the music once more.

Such impudence from his little wife.

But he did not begrudge her, and when the final curtain closed she practically floated to his side. "That was wonderful!"

He hummed noncommittally. "They were adequate. You would have made it exceptional."

Erik had only meant it as a truth spoken aloud, not because he had wished to scheme or encourage her to enter the stage.

Christine however, thought differently. She took a step backward, her expression one of hurt. "Is that why you brought me here? To show me what I was missing? I told you I was not ready..."

As if she could become his prima donna while pregnant with his child! And she could hardly take to the stage with a newborn in tow.

Erik reached out a hand and patiently waited for her to put her hand in his. She looked at him suspiciously for a moment before cautiously conceding. His thumb traced over her knuckles tenderly, and though he knew this conversation would be much more appropriate in the confines of the chamber below—or better yet, their own home—he would not have her doubting him for any significant duration.

"I wanted for you to have a pleasant evening, Christine, nothing more." His hand covered her middle, and his eyes grew imploring. "You have enough to think about with our little one. At a time like this I would never put you through the strain of rehearsals and practices and petty jealousies—for they *would* be jealous of you, my rose."

She was quiet for a moment before she nodded and gave him a small smile. "I believe you."

He allowed himself to scoff a little, although he kept a careful watch of her mood to ensure she would not take true offense. "Of course you do, for it is the truth."

Erik moved to lower her back down to the chamber below, but she stopped him. She was nibbling on her lip, which never boded well. "You wish to remain in our box?"

She shook her head slowly. "I was wondering... the stage is so beautiful and the entire production defies the senses," Erik would hardly go *that* far in his description, but he allowed her to continue. "But I was wondering what it was like backstage. Do you think we could look?"

There was an unspoken challenge in this. Whether or not she had intended for it to be so—which he rather doubted given that she did not possess the shrewd nature necessary for outright manipulation—he still found that the prospect of sneaking her backstage was rather an exciting one. It was never a very difficult thing for himself as he possessed the agility and stealth necessary to remain unnoticed, but his wife was pregnant and every action would have to be well thought out before it could even be attempted.

He did so love a challenge.

Erik bowed low and with possibly more flourish than strictly necessary, but he made her giggle so it was worth every showy bit of it. "As you wish, my lady."

It was at times like these that Erik appreciated that he had never procured a new cloak for Christine. Ladies' fashions dictated luxurious fabrics in bright and showy colours, while his were specially designed for their ability to fade into shadows.

Though he admitted it was still as luxurious as anything a dressmaker would provide the most snobbish of women.

He was grateful for this because on numerous occasions it became necessary to forego his tunnels in favour of treading actual hallways. There were numerous alcoves that provided a modicum of secrecy, and on normal occasions it would not be uncommon to find lovers engaging in passionate trysts in just such places. If their cloaks had been anything but black they could have easily been spotted by the tittering and performance-drunk ballet girls and singers that fluttered about, half out of their costumes even as they walked.

"This is terribly exciting," Christine breathed into his ear. He glanced down at her and indeed, instead of the fearful expression he had half-expected, she was positively glowing with barely bridled excitement.

Who could have predicted that his wife would find his profession so thrilling?

He smirked at her and nodded his head, but made no answer.

Once the dancers had departed, Erik made his way to his desired passageway and pushed at it firmly in the small crevice that opened the panel. There was a tunnel available of course, but it very cramped and not at all suitable for Christine in her condition. He instead selected a stairway that led directly to the scene changers platform above—the perfect location for spying nearly all of the backstage workers as they flitted about, setting their respective departments to rights before retiring for the evening.

He looked back often to ensure Christine was not having too much difficulty on the steps, and if she tired he would immediately demand that he be allowed to carry her back home. But each time she met his eyes with a bright smile of her own, and he was at once struck with the level of trust she had in him. Before she would not have voiced her desire to see the backstage goings on as it could have been considered an unnecessary risk.

But now she had faith that her husband could protect her, and since it did not in fact also include allowing her to be exposed to the cold for too long a period of time, Erik was more than happy to oblige her.

He opened the door at the end of the hall, and after leaning his head out to confirm that the individuals still seeing to their work were properly *engaged* in their work, he ushered Christine through the door.

She seemed utterly fascinated by the people scurrying about, laughing or snapping at one another when a foolish person performed their task incorrectly. Erik also noted that quite a few were sneaking swigs from bottles of what he was certain were alcoholic beverages.

Such professionalism.

They were at the highest point, and what scene changers still milled about where far below them. It was possible that they could look up, but it was impossible for them to be able to catch either Erik or Christine before they disappeared once more into his tunnels.

He was rather horrified when Christine tried to sit down on the platform, obviously intent on staying a while to watch them as they worked. Why did she always insist upon sitting on things that were most decidedly *not* furniture?

But he helped her all the same for he would not have his pregnant wife tumbling down below just because her husband disliked her penchant for sitting on flooring. "You do not fear heights?"

He said this as he settled down beside her, eyeing the wooden structure with distaste. He would have continued standing, but this way he could keep a careful arm wrapped about Christine. And he did not care for *looming* over her.

She shrugged. "Maybe if I was by myself, but I know you will not let me fall."

He felt that warmness in his heart whenever she voiced her absolute confidence in him. "No, I would not."

Christine tore her eyes away just long enough to place a kiss on his masked cheek, and wrinkled her nose slightly as she did so. "I like kissing *you* much better."

He hummed. "I am quite glad to hear it. Perhaps you will have to settle for my lips when we are in public."

His insolent wife rolled her eyes but conceded, and he perhaps coaxed her into a more lingering kiss than she had originally intended.

Erik did not feel the least bit guilty for it. Just because Christine was above manipulating and *persuading* to her advantage—at least not blatantly so—that did not mean he was against utilising such methods himself. Especially when it led to tasting her sweet lips for a little longer.

Eventually however she pulled away from him, and while breathless and blushing from his attentions, somehow managed to put on a look of sheer petulance. "You are distracting me."

"I am doing nothing of the sort," he replied, his tone one of absolute innocence.

She rolled her eyes but the gesture was softened as she leaned her head against his shoulder. Things were beginning to settle down below as many had finished their tasks and would either be going to bed or travelling to a nearby spot for multiple rounds of libations.

Erik tried to remind himself that the performance had been passable so they should be allowed their late-night amusements, but it still seemed inappropriate. They should be dedicated to their work and their art, and should not be like common craftsman who after a long day's labour would try to drown themselves in a bottle of swill.

Christine's attention was drawn to a loud and boisterous laugh, and he recognised Joseph Buquet as the culprit. He was the head scene changer and quite inept at his job—a point which Erik had pointed out numerous times in his letters to the previous management. He liked to bluster about, chastising the actual workers for some perceived slight or unaccomplished task, and it was known throughout the entirety of the Opera that he had wandering hands and peeping eyes toward some of the younger ballet rats.

His wife stiffened and looked closer, her face blanching as she did so. "Who... who is that?"

Her voice was a mere whisper, and Erik seemed torn between assessing his wife's condition and seeing if he could glean the cause of her distress from staring at Buquet alone.

"He is employed by the Opera. Do you know of him?"

Erik wanted to hear that she had seen him from one of the windows she liked to peer through while she was living on the streets. Or that she might have even stumbled upon him if she had come here when her father auditioned so long ago.

But as he felt her begin to tremble and he saw the tears begin to glisten in her eyes, he knew she would not be telling him any such thing.

"I want to go home."

Her voice was a breathy plea, and he could clearly hear the strain as she tried to hold back her sobs. If she began to cry in earnest here, the sound would most definitely carry down below, and the last thing she desired was to draw *that* man's attention.

Erik was currently trying to assess the physical damage that would be done upon his person if he leapt from this height down to the unsuspecting man. There would be witnesses of course, but they could be disposed of as quickly and rapidly as their supervisor.

So focused was he on the demise of the entire stage staff that he was rather startled when he felt Christine's hand clutching at his arm. "I want to go *home. Please,* Erik."

He tore his eyes from the man who had caused his poor wife such agony, and when he saw the tears that fell unimpeded and the way she was so deathly pale, he knew that murder would once more be on his hands this night.

But first, his wife desired the safety of their home.

Erik cast one more glance on his victim and then helped Christine rise from the platform before they began their descent. She clung to his arm and tried to burrow into his cloak, and eventually he simply carried her as her sobs were muffled into his chest.

There would be no mercy. Not for Joseph Buquet.

And as he tried to soothe his wife as her heart broke once more at the horror of being in such close proximity to one of her abusers, Erik felt the righteous anger burn hotly through him, and knew no remorse for what he would soon do.

XXXIV

Christine did not want to release him when they finally entered the safety of their home. While Erik wanted nothing more than to return upstairs as quickly as possible in order to dispatch the man who was the cause of so much of her pain, he realised that his wife's need must be paramount to his own desire for vengeance. She was the one reliving her past horrors. And if she would rather have him to cling to than know he was going to ensure that man could never harm her again, then so be it.

At least, he tried to accept that. But the anger was still flowing through him and his hands twitched for the feel of the smooth lasso as it caressed his palm, and his mind readied for the calculations of the perfect trajectory that would make the kill easy and swift.

As if the man deserved such a fate.

He should be made to suffer—to feel his life's blood trickle away just before the life left his sorry excuse of a body.

But she was still clinging to him, and as he settled them down together in his reading chair and she sobbed into his neck, he was able to push down his anger enough to provide what she needed of him. "He will never touch you again, my rose. *Never* again."

She took his hand and pulled it to her thigh. For a moment he was perplexed, but then through her tears she whispered, "He was the one who cut me."

He would die slowly. There would be no quick death or opportunity for leniency.

Erik rubbed at the healed mark soothingly, and while he wanted to lift her skirt and press kisses to it as a reminder that it did not matter, that she was *loved* even with her past afflictions, he knew that such touches would not be welcomed.

The memories were too close and too vivid, and the last thing he wanted was to provide her more discomfort. "He will die for what he did."

He said it solemnly and almost without thinking. He braced himself for the pleadings that would be sure to follow—that every life was sacred and that he should not sully himself with the taking of another.

But it did not come.

"You will not be hurt? I do not want you doing anything that could put you in danger."

At any other time he would have scoffed and reproached her for having so little faith in his abilities. But as he regarded her, he could tell that she was being perfectly sincere. She would rather this man be allowed to live if it meant she could continue to have her husband, whole and alive and unharmed.

His lovely wife.

"He will not touch me, Christine. I will be perfectly safe."

She was quiet then and he again waited for her plea to stay his hand. She was nibbling at her lip and the tears were finally beginning to stem, and she now simply looked tired.

Tired was perhaps too small a word. She looked weary and world-wizened, and Erik realised he would give anything to rekindle the enraptured expression from earlier. "Would you like to speak of it? Would that... help you?"

Christine sniffled, and she begrudgingly allowed him to manoeuvre his hand from around her so that he could retrieve his handkerchief from his front pocket. She grabbed at it hastily and dried her eyes, suddenly looking embarrassed.

"I ruined our evening. If I had not asked to go backstage we would have gone home and had such a lovely time..."

Her tone was wistful, and oh so very sad that it made his heart hurt in sympathy. "You are not to blame, for any of this. You believe your Erik, do you not?"

Clearly she did not.

She shrugged noncommittally, and he knew this was important. He could not in good conscience leave this house while she could possibly think that a man's blood was on her hands. He would not allow her to think that he blamed her for the many assaults upon her person.

And although he had tried to make all these things clear over the course of their marriage and time together, perhaps just as he occasionally needed to hear that he was loved and cherished above all things, she required the same kind of reassurances.

"I would not put you through the trauma of a trial, *mon ange*. He will face justice, not revenge," though in this matter, was there truly a difference? "And your husband loves you *no less* for anything that has or will happen. I love you, Christine, *so* much." He brought her hand to his heart and stared into her swollen and glistening eyes. "Nothing will ever change that."

His eyes flickered down to where her belly brushed against him, and her eyes followed his gaze. She looked stricken then, and she took the hand not clasped in his to cover it protectively. "If he was capable of doing that to me, he could have done so to someone else's daughter."

Erik did not mention that with his reputation at the Opera, *could have* was more akin to *very likely.*

Her eyes grew fierce and her jaw set with determination. "You must not allow him to hurt anyone else, Erik. It was no excuse that he was drunk, or that I was poor and alone and unprotected. He had *no right* to do what he did. None at all."

He stroked her cheek softly. "None at all," he repeated.

She nodded, and it was with great relief that she leaned forward and pressed a firm kiss against his lips. "I believe you."

Despite her proclamation, Christine did not move from his lap. She appeared resolved and he braced himself for whatever was next to come.

"I told you when we first met that I was not a whore, but I confess that I was beginning to believe it." She gazed at him steadily. "Tell me truthfully, Erik. Were you going to propose marriage to me that day?"

Erik stiffened, not at all prepared for her to ask such a question. This was dangerous territory, and with the burning need to *kill* still pulsing through him, it took a great amount of energy just to quell it long enough to think through his answer in a way that would not insult her terribly.

For he had not.

He would never have argued with her about it, and since he *loved* her it did not matter if it had originally been his idea or her own. So little of their brief courtship and marriage had been traditional, so why should the original proposal?

Erik shifted awkwardly beneath her and she gave a small, sad smile. "I see."

She moved to release him, but he held her fast. "I had not allowed myself to even consider the possibility that you would agree to be my wife. I was going to offer you a ring that would symbolise my promise of protection and that I would always care for you." He smiled briefly at the memory. "But then you enquired if I was asking for your hand, and you seemed so... enthused at the idea."

Christine was studying her fingers down in her lap, and Erik had to coax her with a finger under her chin to bid her look at him. "You have no concept of what that meant to me, my Christine. I did not have to cajole or threaten. The idea came from *you.* How could I doubt that it was your true desire when I had not even broached the subject?"

She took a deep breath and looked at him in entreaty. "I thought that if we married, there could be no possibility that I was a whore—I would be a wife. Everything we did would be blessed by God and it could not be the same as before."

Erik grew cold, and he stared at her in horror. "That is why you wished to marry me?"

Her hands were skimming over the seam of his mask and he could tell from her movements that she was silently asking him permission to remove it.

He could refuse her nothing.

She peeled it away slowly, and he shuddered at the feel of her lips and fingers as they smoothed over his thin flesh. "That is why I *thought* I married you. Looking back I know it is because I love you. *So* much."

He tried to tell himself that the moisture pooling in his eyes was a reaction to some unexpected plume of dust—never mind that his wife kept their home relatively immaculate.

"I will never regret any of the things we have done, but I realise now that I did not truly understand what it meant to be a wife. And I am still learning."

His voice resembled a croak. "As am I."

She smiled at him and kissed him just as softly, and that time when she pulled herself off of his lap she was met with no resistance. "Go. Go and make the world a safer place for our baby."

Erik had a deep suspicion that she was not quite ready to move on from the experience, and she most likely would climb into their bed and weep for a while longer. Perhaps she would even take her tin of sweet biscuits that he still made for her on a consistent basis, and he would grumble and protest the crumbs that made their way resolutely between the bedclothes.

And he could not blame her.

She had received a shock and memories were still too fresh, and she had to grieve for what part of her soul was harmed by the unthinking actions of a man who was now doomed to die.

While she had bid him go for the sake of their child, he was also going for her sake. She deserved to know that her home was not a prison, with one of her abusers five floors above. This was her asylum, and her refuge, and her *home,* and Erik would return the sanctity of that title once more.

There were a few provisions he required just to ensure the ease of the execution and the safety of his person. He had promised his wife that he would not be harmed, and he intended to keep his vow.

Lastly, he replaced his mask, this time settling on one of his most frightening.

Christine did not seem pleased by his chosen mask, but still managed to give him a watery smile as he went out the door. And as he traversed the dark passages that would lead him to his prey, he felt the righteous fury that had been temporarily quelled by her presence rekindle to its full potential.

Joseph Buquet was not hard to find.

Erik was well aware of the run down establishment many of the less important staff members frequented, a mere four streets over from the Opera. The stress of the performances often led to a lingering feeling of giddiness once the final curtain had been drawn, and he supposed that intoxication was one way of coping with the excess vigour.

Not that he approved.

Drunkenness should be confined to one's own home, as indignities were a common by-product of inebriation.

As he took in the carousing, the drunken laughter, and the bawdy groping of the tavern girls, he realised with sudden distaste that he too had entered into his marriage with a misapprehension about his character. Christine thought she was cleansing herself of her perceived wantonness, and he had thought that by his wedding a young, innocent angel, he would somehow prove that he was not the monster he had for so long believed himself to be.

But he was only a man.

And a man who was far more a gentleman than any of these mindless miscreants.

Joseph Buquet was the loudest and most obnoxious of all the drunkards. Each time a scantily clad girl would bring him another drink, one of his hands would sneak to her rump and pinch at it harshly. While obviously used to such behaviour as she tried to laugh and gently scold, Erik could plainly see a hint of fear and anger at such treatment.

She would not have to suffer through it for much longer.

Erik's main dilemma was in deciding whether or not he should enter the establishment. It was ill lit to be sure, and if he kept his head down, his hat would do an adequate job of hiding his face.

And if this man's intake was any indication, he might remain within for a very great period unless he intervened—and Erik never did much care for waiting.

Not many paid him attention as he slithered his way beside Buquet. He did not intend to stay long in any case—just long enough that when the man was distracted by a rather busty woman that showed far too much of her endowments, Erik was able to place a few drops of tasteless liquid into his unsuspecting drink.

Then he returned outside.

He did not have to wait long, as Buquet staggered out less than a quarter of an hour later, yelling to the other patrons all the while that he was going find a nice girl on the way back to his rooms and show her the true meaning of being with a man.

Erik's eyes burned as he watched him from the cover of the alleyway.

He imagined a night just like this, where his poor Christine had tried to find meagre shelter beneath the cover of a shop. A heavily intoxicated Buquet would have been itching for the company of a female, willing or not, and stumbling upon his lovely wife unprotected, had taken full advantage.

The fact that he kept a knife upon him would indicate that his brutalising of Christine had not been the first time he had taken a woman by force.

He did not strike immediately.

Erik wanted the advantage of his own domain, and as long as the man kept walking back toward the Opera, the less effort he would have to expend dragging him back into the cellars. There could be no evidence and no witnesses. And if anyone saw a staggering scene changer returning to his workplace for a few last minute tasks, it would be quite reasonable to believe he had suffered an unfortunate *accident.*

Or, as Erik also would allow, that the Ghost had struck again.

Either scenario suited his needs quite well.

To his great fortune, Buquet's rooms seemed to be on the opposite side of the theatre, so he passed right past the side of the grandiose building. And unfortunately for him, this particular side housed one of the tunnels leading to the cellars below.

The catgut was smooth in his palm and he felt the sudden thrill as it found its mark around the bastard's neck. He did not pull it *too* taut, as there was a bit of movement that was required before he met his ultimate end.

"Move."

Erik came up behind him, pulling the rope tight around his hands and shoving the man forward. He was too busy unsuccessfully attempting to dislodge the cord about his neck that he met with little resistance. And between the effects of the drug Erik had administered and the lack of oxygen, he stumbled forward obediently.

There was no pressing need to conceal the entrance to the tunnel, as this man would never be able to divulge its location to anyone. It was black as pitch within as Erik moved without a light, and as they trudged through the cool passageway, he noted how unpleasant it was to be near Buquet. He reeked of alcohol and unwashed flesh, and every so often as Erik allowed small breaths of air to be allowed by loosening the lasso ever so slightly, he noted that his breath was equally rank.

That was what this villain had subjected his wife to? A filthy body bearing down on her as she struggled and pleaded for mercy?

He could wait no longer.

He felt defiled just being *near* the man, and he could hardly imagine how his poor Christine had felt being forced to have him *inside* of her.

And in any case, to take him any further below would be taking him far too close to his home. In actuality, Erik *wanted* the man to be found, as he did not want him befouling his domain any longer than necessary.

They were within the third cellar, amongst the forgotten props and sceneries that had once been so tirelessly perfected in order to be worthy of the Opera's magnificent stage. Now they were little more than dust collectors.

And while once they had been for the delight of the audience of the theatre, they would not serve audience to an execution.

With a final push, Erik placed him between a farm-house and what appeared to be a scene from the *Roi de Loire* and climbing upon the former structure, pulled the rope through a hook located in the wooden beams above.

He leapt down silently and drew the catgut so that the man was only barely able to keep his toes balanced upon the floor. "Joseph Buquet, for the maiming and rape of Christine Daaé I hereby sentence you to die. Any final words?"

It was more than he deserved, but Erik wanted him to *know* why he was about to perish.

He allowed the lasso to slacken slightly, and the man spluttered and coughed for breath. "Who?"

Erik rolled his eyes, expecting the question. While it seemed impossible to him that anyone could *not* remember his beautiful wife, this man was not one to appreciate true loveliness and goodness. Christine was naught but a warm body to him, and what was meant to be a beautiful act consecrated by the marriage bonds, was a sullied and violent act in the darkened recesses of the Paris streets.

"My *wife.* You brutalised her, made her bleed with a knife and she will forever bear the scar. And now you are going to die."

He was shaking his head furiously. "I never touched no man's proper wife. Only whores and tavern wenches."

"And that somehow makes it *right?"* Erik snarled, giving the lasso a firm pull, and he relished the gurgling sounds that erupted from the mongrel's throat.

"My wife was no whore. She was a scared, penniless girl without protection, and you took full advantage of her state."

Even as he struggled to keep his toes upon the ground, the man desperately tried to shake his head in denial—his thick fingers scrambling to pull away the noose digging into his throat.

With one final heave, Erik had him elevated in the air. And within moments the man stilled, his face purpled in death and his hands falling limply to his sides. Erik tied the end of the lasso to the farm-house and looked at the corpse.

Perhaps another man would have felt remorse, but he suddenly just felt tired. This man could harm no other, and his wife had one more demon put to rest. She would continue to bear the scars as she always had, but she would not have to be wary the Opera above, fearing that she would once more see the face of one of her attackers.

Perhaps someday he would ask precisely how many there were so he could hunt each of them down and ensure that *every* man who had lain with his wife against her will would face eternal judgement.

But for now, all Erik wanted to do was to join his wife in their bed and hold her until he fell asleep.

XXXV

News of the apparent accident—or murder, depending on which scintillating story was to be believed—travelled quickly.

Erik did exactly as he had wished, and when he had returned home immediately sought his wife. As he had expected she was curled up in their bed, her eyes finally dry though still red and swollen, and his handkerchief clutched firmly between her clenched fingers.

She turned over as soon as he entered, her eyes travelling his form in assessment. "You are not hurt?"

He shook his head, having no energy for games of false indignation. "Not at all."

Erik did not undress. Perhaps he should have taken a bath or changed into his nightclothes. But as he collapsed upon the bedstead and pulled Christine close and felt the silk beneath his fingers from her evening dress, he noted wryly what a fine couple they made—still bedecked in their best clothes, but neither having the will to scrub away the horrors of the day.

She was facing away from him and he allowed himself to savour the feel of her pressed against the curve of his body—a greater comfort than he had ever thought he would be granted.

"Is he... is he dead?"

Her voice was hollow and it sent an ache through his heart as he heard it.

"He is." He placed a kiss at the back of her neck. The once elegant arrangement of her hair was now crumpled, and he absently thought that he should very much like to pull out all of her pins and brush it so that it was soft and gleaming once more.

Later. After he had held her for a while longer, and felt sure that she was whole and well within his arms and that no man would ever touch her in that way again.

She began shifting, and at first his hold on her tightened so that she would not leave him, but he quieted when she murmured a gentle, "Hush."

Christine rolled over so that she could look at him, and she gazed at him for a long while without saying a word.

That was all it took.

He did not mean to cry, and for a while he did not know what prompted him to do so. He had killed many men, usually without much emotion of any kind. It was a task, a necessity for his wellbeing, and this did not feel so different.

Except that it was.

His wife pulled him close but not before she had peeled away the mask that had so disturbed her, and he found that he did not mind it so very much that she did not ask as soon as he felt her hands smoothing through his hair.

"Are you all right?"

He had already assured her that he was physically well, so she must mean something deeper. And at this moment he was not entirely certain that he *was* all right.

A part of him wanted to keep it from her—that she had known too much of this man already and should not be burdened with any more.

But if he told her such things she would surely chide him, reminding him that sharing encumbrances was what married people *did.* And perhaps along the way, he had come to believe it as well.

"He did not even remember you. How could any man not remember *you?* You who are sweetness itself, and after what he did..."

Erik could not continue as he felt as though his throat could no longer produce sound. Her hands had stilled, and for a frightening moment he worried that she would turn away from him. It was one thing to have knowledge that her husband was about to end a man's life. It was something else entirely to hear the gruesome details.

"And you will remember him for the rest of your life. And no matter what I do, you will *remember.*"

How he wished that he could wipe away her pain!

In tales from afar there were always stories of wish fulfilment. He had always scoffed, knowing precisely what he would demand. Riches or fame would all come of their own accord once he could appear as a normal man, and until he had met his Christine he had always known that would be his one wish.

Not anymore.

Now he would implore and entreat that she could be released from her memories and that only sweet and gentle things could take hold within her mind.

Christine was silent for a moment longer until she took a deep breath, her voice still hoarse from her own earlier tears. "I do not know if I mind that so very much."

Erik lurched his head away from the softness of her neck. "*Why?*"

She smiled at him sadly, her fingers skimming under his eyes and the hole where his nose should have been.

"Because I do not know who I would have been without those experiences. What if I was not ready to be your wife? I would not be expecting our baby, and I would not have the lovely life I have now." She nibbled at her lip and her eyes pleaded that he be able to understand. "I do not know if I would risk it."

And perhaps he did understand. She had met true monsters and while she had survived the encounters, it was those experiences that made her ready to understand *him.* She had not been afraid of his face, but she could have been if she had not learned to trust him beforehand.

Erik had already decided that he would willingly go through every painful lash and mocking glance once more if Christine was to be his reward. It was now obvious that his wife felt the same.

It seemed almost too much to be believed, but as he held her and was held *by* her, he found himself to be very glad.

"Would you like me to brush your hair?"

He supposed he should also suggest they change for the night, and maybe take one of those charming baths together she had insisted on before.

She hummed, and burrowed her face into his shoulder. "Only if you stay close."

As if he would choose to ever be elsewhere.

Neither moved for another few minutes, but eventually Erik tore himself away only long enough to fetch her comb and a ribbon.

He was never one to remove his shoes without first seeing to the laces, but on this occasion he felt nearly panicked when he was not touching her in some way. So he merely pushed them off hurriedly before reclining on a mound of pillows that she had carefully crafted, then pulled her up against him so that she was nestled between his legs and nearly reclining on his chest.

With each pin that he removed and every curl that he watched bounce back after his comb had skimmed through it from beginning to end, Erik felt more and more calm. Their lives would never have been perfect, but it had led them to one another so perhaps there was no need to complain.

Christine began to release contented little sighs whenever the comb would skim over her scalp, and every so often she would shiver slightly from the sensation. "I should ask you to brush my hair every day."

He hummed, and pressed his lips to the curve of her shoulder, simply because he could. "You would demote your poor Erik from husband to maid."

She sighed once more, and with deft fingers he began plaiting her hair until it was tied with a flourish with one of her extravagant ribbons.

"Somehow I do not think you would mind so very much."

Pressed so completely against him as she was, she could easily feel his rather visceral reaction to her closeness. Neither felt prepared to do anything to assuage the matter—not tonight— but she still felt saucy enough to tease him for it.

Little minx.

They had fallen asleep a short time later, after nudging and wriggling until they were both in their preferred sleeping arrangements without actually having to break way entirely.

Erik felt fairly groggy the next morning. Though he had spent many a night in his evening clothes, it was not usually also within the confines of the bed linens. He felt bedraggled and heart-sore, and he was glad that Christine was able to sleep for a little longer.

The tea things were calling to him quite loudly, but at the moment all he truly desired was a long hot soak.

He tucked in Christine and nestled some additional pillows around her, and briefly wondered if he should attempt undressing her in her sleep. She would be dismayed by her gown once she awoke, and she might appreciate that he could already tell her it was being taken care of and that no permanent damage had been done.

At least, he hoped it had not.

If the laundress was unable to remove all of the creases that had been pressed into the fabric over the course of the evening, Erik would have to decide if purchasing a replica would be beneficial. He did so like the colour on her...

But no. She needed her rest more than she needed to know that her gown was not as wrinkled as it was. He grimaced as he looked down and noticed just how his suit had fared.

To his dismay, just when he was about to turn the taps that would begin the wondrous flow of hot frothy water that would wash away the horrible night, the siren called.

And Erik pitied whoever was keeping him from his bath.

It was possible that a party had banned together to once again scope out the lower levels of the cellars in order to ascertain if the resident Ghost was an actual phantom or merely a man in disguise. They had done it before and each time their resolution only grew that a paramour *did* indeed haunt the bowels of the Opera.

Or it was another visit from his supposed friend coming to scold him on the improprieties of dispensing with men's lives.

Erik was far too tired and had too little patience for dealing with either.

Casting one last forlorn look at the abandoned tub, he went in search of a mask and yet another lasso, and left the house.

Since there was reasonable doubt that it was in fact the Persian across the shores, he forwent the boat and utilised his most obscure tunnels.

There was no angry horde on the opposite shore, and it was with no small irritation that Erik saw the Daroga pacing the embankment, casting not so subtle glares across the lake as he did so.

"What do you want?"

Erik tried to sound forceful, but even to his own ears he merely sounded weary.

His tone seemed to surprise his visitor, and though he clearly had been rehearsing a rather biting speech during his trek below, he now hesitated. "What happened to you?"

Erik huffed in annoyance and crossed his arms. "Last night was rather trying, and *you* are interrupting my morning ablutions. What do you *want?"* There, that sounded better. The more his irritation grew, the less tired he sounded—and perhaps that would be enough to convince this troublesome man that he should leave.

But apparently nothing could be easy for Erik this fine morning.

Instead, the man's own frustration returned and he took a menacing step towards Erik, despite how foolish such a move would be in normal circumstances. "I am certainly glad to hear that it would be *trying* for you after having killed a man!"

Erik felt the fury beginning to roil within his blood yet again, drowning out any previous exhaustion. "Forgive me, Daroga, for dispensing of one of the men who *raped* my wife!"

He had said the words last night as part of the execution, but he felt it all the more acutely now that the initial bloodlust had been sated. "He *raped* my wife," he whispered.

Whatever indignation the Persian had come with faded, and the self-imposed need to act as Erik's conscience seemed to weaken just as quickly. "Erik..." He took another step forward, this time in what he supposed was meant to be comfort. And when he raised a careful hand and tentatively placed it on Erik's shoulder, he felt his faltering hold on his emotions dissolve.

He had thought that after spending the night with his wife it would have been sufficient. He had held her close and known she was safe. But speaking the words aloud to an impartial bystander—someone he did not have to think of comforting but could simply *feel*—it was nearly overwhelming.

"I did not know. I am sorry for my presumption."

It seemed almost bizarre that he was apologising. For so long he was the one trying to keep Erik's morality in check—to remind him of his humanity and his need to relate well with others.

But as Erik looked at the Persian's face, he merely saw understanding. "If I was confronted with a man who had harmed my wife in such a way..." He looked far away for a moment as he gazed into the darkness of the lake, but then he turned back to Erik and there was such conviction in his tone that he could not help but believe him. "I would have killed him too."

Erik nodded. Perhaps that was the natural reaction of a husband who loved his wife. Others might not have had the means or skills necessary to actually perform the action, but the desire would have been there all the same.

"How is little Christine?"

Erik took a shuddering breath. "Resting. She was... quite devastated last night."

The Daroga moved away from him slightly, obviously preparing for his ire once he voiced the question. "Did she not approve of your actions? Was she angry with you?"

"No, it was seeing him again that caused her such distress. Even if it was only from a distance."

He realised belatedly that he had not told his wife that he would be checking his traps after the siren had called, and undoubtedly the noise would have woken her. It was a tremendous oversight on his part as she was prone to worry—especially after last night.

"I must return home. I neglected to tell Christine I was leaving and she will be... upset."

An understatement to be sure.

The Persian nodded and hesitated, but seemed to decide to ask despite his momentary reticence. "Might I accompany you?"

Erik eyed him suspiciously. "Why?"

The Daroga sighed. "Because I want her to know that not everyone will disagree with what you did. That she has my sympathies."

He could not fathom why that would be so important, but the tired feeling was returning and he did not wish to argue. He did not want to go all the way back to retrieve the boat, so without asking the man's opinion, Erik doused the lone lantern that had accompanied his guest and grabbed his arm, pulling him through the cramped tunnel that bypassed the lake.

As he walked, it occurred to him rather sharply why it was so important to the man. The Persian was forever devoted to his now deceased wife, so there was little cause for true jealousy, but Erik realised he *cared* for Christine. She could inspire the hardest and grumpiest of men to bow to her whims just by her sweetness, and through their brief introduction, she had apparently ensnared the Daroga as well.

Perhaps that should trouble him more than it did.

There was not even the smallest shaft of light surrounding them, so Erik did not worry overly much about his secret tunnel being discovered. The Persian's intentions were becoming clearer, and Erik knew that the more he saw of how married life had changed him, he suspected that his visits would be more friendly in nature instead of accusatory.

However, that did not mean he would allow him to enter before he had seen to Christine.

He opened the door and was practically assaulted as soon as he stepped into the sitting room.

His wife was still clad in her bed-rumpled gown, although her hair had survived much better within its long plait. She was clutching at him and mumbling into his chest, and even he could not make out the words. "Christine, you shall have to come up for air if you would like for me to understand you."

She tilted her head only slightly. "Was it a mob coming to take you away?"

He smiled down at her sadly, wishing he could assure her that such would never be. Instead he could merely offer feeble assurances. "Nothing of the kind, my rose. The Persian has come to ensure we are both well after he heard of last night."

She blanched and peeked behind his arm to the slightly open door. The man in question took that as his cue to enter, much to Erik's annoyance.

"Mme Christine, I hope you are feeling better this morning."

Nothing about her seemed *better,* at least not to Erik. She was still trembling, and while he wanted a bath more than anything, he realised now that Christine required it far more than he.

She was silent for a long moment and simply stared at the man. "Do you know why he did it?"

Erik sighed and pulled Christine until they could sink onto the settee, and he made a vague gesture at his reading chair in offering to their guest.

All seated—Christine practically in his lap—the Persian replied, "I do now."

She nodded, still looking at him with a curiously blank expression. "Do you think he made a mistake in marrying me?"

He leaned forward in his chair, and his sincerity was clear. "I think you saved this man's life when you married him. And I do not begrudge him for what he did. I admit that I came here to scold, and while he has not given the particulars of what was done to you, I do not blame either of you for what has transpired."

Christine's lip quivered, and Erik pulled her more firmly against him in an effort to comfort. "Thank you."

Perhaps he should have been insulted that she required absolution from a relative stranger when he had offered the same promises, but that seemed rather petty when he found such relief in it as well. They were too close—too emotionally involved—and while he barely considered this man a friend, Erik had come to find that he respected his opinion on what was right.

In addition, the Persian had been happily married for many years before his wife had died, so he must have some knowledge regarding proper behaviour.

And it appeared murdering men who had abused one's wife was not wholly objectionable.

Christine tilted her head and whispered, "Erik, I am hungry."

Of course she was. Crying was exhausting work, and although their picnic had been sufficient for a light evening supper, his wife always liked her titbits in the morning.

"My wife would like some breakfast." As he rose he eyed the Persian pointedly, silently informing him to behave himself in his absence.

The man must have caught the look for he raised his hands in supplication. "I would not object if you would like to bring me something as well."

Erik ignored him and strode from the room, surprisingly grateful for his attempt at levity—even if he would not indulge it himself.

Though he did not feel any particular worry beyond the slim possibility that the Daroga would say something that would upset his wife, Erik still hurried through the process of preparing their morning meal. Thick slices of ham sizzled in one of his cast iron frying pans, and another housed eggs that were poaching in a pool of simmering water. A bit of toast and a large pot of tea finished the ensemble and everything found its way to the table.

The only thing left was retrieving his unhelpful companions—though he much more begrudged the Daroga than his wife. *She* was with child after all, and had suffered a trying evening. The man had no such excuse.

They were murmuring softly when he walked in the room, and he eyed them both suspiciously when they quieted at his near silent entry—obviously taking careful note for when he made an appearance. "If you two have finished with your secrets, we may eat."

And for a moment he seriously considered taking back the third plate and dumping its contents into the bin.

XXXVI

Breakfast was a quiet affair. Though Erik had been quite tempted to deny his guest food, he realised he was more grateful for the man's understanding than he was angry for his whisperings with his wife.

And besides, once he had Christine to himself again, he could easily wheedle their topic of conversation from her.

He could be *very* persuasive.

As Erik and Christine cleared the dishes and set them into the basin to soak, she looked up at him and touched his arm lightly. "I am glad you have a friend. I should like one someday."

What hurt most was that she was perfectly serious when she made her declaration. His first reaction was to rankle and resentfully make a case for how *he* was her friend, and also inform her that the Persian was nothing more than an annoyance.

But as he looked down at her his ire melted away, and he began to recognise that a husband could not be all things to his wife. She needed her ladies to titter and giggle with, just as a husband needed other gentlemen to fondly bemoan the actions of their wives. Perhaps, if he would allow it, that could be the man still seated at his dining room table.

It was worth considering.

And when they both felt more secure—surer that the world could allow for good and sweet things instead of merely pain and horror—they would venture up above with their children underfoot, and Christine could make friends with all the wives that would be their neighbours.

It was a lovely dream, even if he felt a bit odd and frightened when he thought of it too long.

Not now, but maybe someday.

He took her hand and gave it a gentle squeeze, and leaned down to kiss her cheek. "Someday, my rose. When you are ready."

Her answering smile was slightly sad, but she returned the gesture all the same. "When we are *both* ready."

The Persian coughed quietly at the doorway, obviously tired of being abandoned by his hosts. "I will take my leave now, little Christine. Thank you for the lovely breakfast."

"You are welcome, M. Daroga. My husband does love to spoil me."

Erik was a bit affronted that his gratitude was directed at his wife when *he* had been the one to provide their bounty, but he remained silent—although he did still glare at the Daroga for his impudence. However, his Christine was infinitely worthy of praise and Erik allowed it with as much grace as he could muster, though that was mainly due to the fact that Christine had bestowed such admiration upon him.

As Erik rowed the man across the lake he considered interrogating him about what he and Christine had been discussing. Apparently his dilemma did not go unnoticed for the Persian laughed at him softly. "If Christine wants you to know what she asked me, she can tell you. I will not betray her confidence."

Erik growled lowly in this throat, but relented. He would rapidly lose respect for the man if he proved incapable of keeping his wife's divulgences. And Erik rather looked forward to hearing it from his wife's lips.

The Daroga grew serious. "It would be unwise to leave your lasso in the possession of the magistrate, Erik. Catgut is not a common item, and it could raise enquiries that you do not want."

He groaned, knowing the man was correct. "I do not relish the thought of leaving Christine at this time, even for such an important errand."

The Persian sighed and rubbed at his temples. "I would consider *absconding* with the evidence myself, as long as I have your word that the only murders you commit will be those that are directly related to your defence—both of your wife and yourself."

Erik was insulted. He wanted to rage and remind him that he had never killed merely for amusement and he hardly needed to make such a vow now. But the weary feeling was returning even after his morning nourishment, and as he looked at this man he remembered Christine's words. Perhaps he did want this man for a friend. And friends required reassurances, just as wives did.

"You have my word."

The Daroga sighed and nodded. "Good. Then I shall take care of it. You tend to your wife."

As if Erik needed to be told such a thing.

They exchanged awkward farewells and Erik hurried back across the lake, feeling confident that the issue of the lasso would be taken care of post haste.

Christine was in the kitchen taking care of the dishes. "You do not need to do that, my dear. It is your husband's responsibility to dote upon you when you are expecting." He came up behind her and wrapped his long arms about her middle, a hand straying to cover the swelling of her womb.

She hummed in contentment and leaned back against him, her hands soapy and already slightly pruned from their toils. "But my husband already cooked for me. He needn't do the washing up as well."

Christine tilted her head back and closed her eyes, obviously expecting a kiss.

He sighed deeply in resignation even as his heart warmed to see such trust, and she smiled as she felt the feather-light brush of his lips upon hers.

He kept his lips firmly closed and the kiss chaste, as he would allow her to be the one to press for *more.* On the days when her nightmares would return she would be rather withdrawn, flinching at any unexpected noises or actions, yet still would all but demand that she be able to keep him within eyesight. But she was improving, and as she opened her mouth and went up on her tiptoes in order to keep their connection as he began to pull away, he realised just how much.

"I am not going to let that man keep us apart, Erik. He already took enough from me. He is not going to make me cower from my husband and fear your touch."

She looked so sincere, and there was a ferocity in her gaze that left him almost breathless. Erik had always assumed that it was the man that held the most interest and sheer *need* for physical intimacy. But as his wife fumbled for a towel to dry her hands so as not to drench him in the lingering water, he realised that his little minx defied all of his previous assumptions.

Christine pulled away eventually, panting for breath as she did so, and Erik was behaving similarly. Her smile was rather triumphant, and she turned and wrapped herself in his arms, burrowing into his coat as was her wont. His fingers found their way into her hair and she sighed and nuzzled further, happy with the contact. "You are trying to distract me, but it shall not work."

In truth, it *had* almost worked as a very large part of him would like to completely forget the little interlude with the Persian and take her to their bed.

But he wanted to know of her conversation with the Daroga and he knew it would niggle and torment him until he did so.

She tilted her head up and her brow was furrowed in genuine confusion. "Distract you from what?"

He tapped a finger lightly on her nose and was pleased that whatever the subject was, she was not wilfully keeping it from him. "What did you speak of while I was fixing your breakfast?"

Erik put special emphasis on *your* so as to prick her conscience. If she had not requested nourishment—not that he would ever have denied her—he would not have had to ask.

Christine looked rather sheepish and began fiddling with his shirt buttons, her eyes downcast. "I merely wanted to know how you two had met, and if he considered himself your friend. I do not like the idea of you being alone, and I wondered if you were *truly* alone or if it was because you simply felt that way."

He could not help but bristle. "Is there such a significant difference?"

Her voice was soft and her touches meant to soothe, and when she placed her head against his chest and closed her eyes before responding, he wondered if he could ever manage to remain angry with her when she behaved thusly. "He worries about you. He says that ever since we married he has felt a tremendous relief that you had finally accepted someone as your companion—that you would not have to be alone."

Erik opened his mouth to retort that it was never by *choice* that he had remained friendless and loveless. People had spurned *him,* not the other way around.

But as he thought of her words earlier, he realised slightly begrudgingly that perhaps in his bitterness he had not been overly open to the idea of a companion either. Christine had been an enigma, and had she not related to him in such a fundamental way through mutual pain and agony, he doubted he would ever have intervened.

They shared a love for music, and despite his greatest efforts to the contrary, she had coaxed her way into his heart. He had no choice but to accept her, for to reject her in the slightest would be to shove away the remnants of his very soul—and obviously he proved incapable of doing so.

And as he allowed his arms to pull her closer once more, he realised he ached faintly even considering the pain that would have caused.

"And does he? Consider himself my friend?"

He could not explain why he felt so nervous at her possible response, but as she held him a little firmer, he felt comforted all the same. "He does.

He would not come to check on you if he did not."

She peeked up at him and seeing that he was no longer looking irksome, she smiled and patted his chest lightly. "And now, I think I should like to see to something we have been delaying."

Erik braced himself.

"We have a baby coming, and I am only going to grow bigger and more uncomfortable as time goes on," Erik grimaced, "and I should like to have the nursery sorted before that happens. May we go shopping?"

He hesitated, remembering that it was midmorning and that all of Paris would be up and bumbling about as they went about their daily routines. He briefly thought of all the shadowy doorways he would be forced to contend with, trying to keep Christine safe while also keeping out of sight of any other patrons.

But then he remembered his surprise.

Erik had not wanted to raise her hopes so he had not mentioned one of his many projects that he had tended to while she slept. Regardless of the fact that he was sleeping more, it was absolutely impossible for him to continue sleeping as long as she did—for even in normal circumstances, she was fostering a new life, and he was most certainly not.

He took her hand and they went to his dressing room—that as of today would apparently be his no longer. The secret compartment opened to reveal the shelves of masks that ranged in colour and texture, and Christine looked at all of them with a sort of sad wonderment. On the far right was his newest creation, and she gasped as she beheld it.

It would cover his entire face all the way to his neck. It more resembled a prosthetic than a traditional mask, and as her fingers skimmed the flesh-like feel of it, her eyes welled with tears. "I am so sorry that such a thing should be necessary."

He placed a kiss upon her temple, feeling strangely touched at her words. She did not try to deceive him by offering false platitudes and wrongly trying to convince him that it was not needed and people would accept him for who he truly was. She too understood that people were cruel and that he would never be able to walk amongst them normally without blending in as inconspicuously as possible.

"As am I, my rose. But if it means that I may accompany you while we shop for our little one, then I am glad for it."

She nodded, and as her eyes strayed downward, she must have realised she was still in her gown from the previous night. "Oh! I must change!"

If she had not noticed soon on her own he would have nudged her toward doing so himself. While there was nothing overtly risqué about her attire, it showed far too much of her décolleté than he would like the everyday shopkeeper to be privy to.

Christine insisted that Erik bathe first, and by the slightly haunted look that overtook her features as she took in his crumpled appearance, he could do nothing but relent. After he took the first step into the warm water he knew that he was in appalling danger of refusing to ever vacate his tub again, and it was only knowing that his wife was waiting on him that made him scrub quickly and see to the rest of his ablutions before vacating the bath-room.

While she had insisted that she was not going to shy away from his touch, Erik did not wish to press. At any other time he would have mischievously suggested that they share the bath in order to prove more efficient. But that surely would lead to more *intimate* activities that required far more time than they could afford—especially as he intended to savour his wife very thoroughly when next she allowed it.

So instead he dressed and tried not to think about his naked beauty luxuriating a mere doorway away from him.

Clad in his trousers and shirtsleeves, Erik braced himself for the most important task. The left wardrobe door had a compartment that when pressed revealed a mirror. It would have been his preference to keep all looking glasses from his abode and for the most part it was unnecessary to check his appearance, but sometimes it was an obligatory evil.

Especially when he created a new mask.

It was one thing to work with a sculpted replica—it was another thing entirely to apply it to oneself.

This one in particular required much attention, and though he kept his eyes as focused as possible on the minute details of the task, it was unavoidable that he should catch the occasional glimpse of his own corpse-like appearance.

Memories assaulted him of the first time he had seen his own reflection, and to his surprise he did not feel the overpowering revulsion that used to accompany it. He was ugly, and that was the truth of it. But he no longer thought himself a monster. A monster could not love his Christine, and his Christine could not love a monster.

So simple, yet it still amazed him that it could be true.

What did startle him was his appearance with the new mask. He looked, not exactly handsome, but comely enough. Erik could not help but allow his fingers to glide over the dignified nose, and he assessed the reflection from all angles. Once his collar was buttoned and the rest of his attire set to rights—especially his hat—he would not be worth taking note of.

It was a curious feeling.

He must have been wholly preoccupied by his reflection that he was alarmed at the gasp behind him.

Christine was freshly pinked from her bathwater and she had donned one of her light summer gowns. She would be too warm for one of his heavy cloaks once they reached the above, and Erik decided that it would be far more sensible to simply tuck her into his side during the walk in the tunnels than having to carry hers while she shopped.

But any such thoughts were interrupted when she took a hesitant step forward, her eyes wide and slightly glassy. "You do not look like you."

He grimaced. "I look as I would have if I had not been cursed."

Christine nibbled at her lip and stepped closer still, her hands reaching forward to gently feel the texture of his superimposed flesh. She frowned, and he had to remind himself to allow her time for exploration and not interrupt it by smoothing out the small pucker between her brows with one of his fingertips.

"Will I do?"

She tilted her head to the side and stood on her tiptoes and waited patiently for him to lean down slightly so she could bestow him with a kiss on his covered cheek. It seemed more experimental than affectionate, and he watched her with bemusement as she pulled away. "I like the feel of your own skin much better."

And that was all. She took his hand and was happy to cuddle into his side as he took her up onto the sun-warmed Paris streets.

The only thing that seemed to draw people's attention—and even that was few and far between—was that Erik was wearing a cloak and kept his hat drawn low over his eyes. Christine garnered far more attention, and although he had to occasionally pat down some of his jealousies, Erik could rightly understand why.

She was glowing.

Each shop they entered seemed to only excite her further, and on more than one occasion she would thrust impossibly small items at him and exclaim at how *perfect* they would be for their baby.

Erik had not the slightest idea of why particular items seemed superior to their counterparts, but he wisely remained silent.

"Do you have a book on how to knit?"

He had momentarily lost track of her as he was distracted by a wooden carving that was either trying to be a horse or a bear—and failing miserably at either attempt—and when he looked back to his wife she was holding a pair of new knitting needles. "This mademoiselle says that I should learn to knit baby things for the winter, and I have no one to teach me."

That was one area that he could not assist her, but at the prospect of entering the bookseller he realised he did not mind admitting that something was beyond his repertoire. "I am certain we will be able to locate one of your liking. Are you finished?"

Erik had given her a small purse filled with coins, and while at first she had looked rather aghast at the amount, he noted wryly that she now had little difficulty parting with them.

By no means was she extravagant, and she often looked to him in order to approve the amount or an item in question, but Erik even found that to be completely unnecessary. If it made her happy and would prove useful when their small one came, he would voice no objection.

He would merely charge the managers more for his services.

It might be wise to do so in any case since they *had* disrupted the sanctity of his private box.

Christine was not in fact finished, and it was only after Erik had been laden with a few skeins of yarn in varying colours—he was intrigued by the few in inky black—she declared herself properly prepared and allowed them to leave.

They spent quite a bit of time at the bookseller's, much to Erik's enjoyment. Christine found many subjects that interested her, including one on the many techniques used for knitting and darning alike. Eventually she turned to him and asked if he would spend a few hours each evening teaching various subjects. "I would like for you to have an intelligent wife, and our baby should have two knowledgeable parents."

That was of course ridiculous as he valued her awareness and talents to no end, but he agreed all the same, only huffing for a short while so she would not think him too easily persuaded.

Lastly, and perhaps most importantly, they stopped at a woodcarver and commissioned a bassinet, a chest of drawers, and the rest of the furniture that would make up their baby's nursery.

Christine was delighted by their purchases and she hurried them along, regaling him with her many ideas of how to move his large wardrobe into their shared bedchamber.

Feeling terribly harangued and equally joyful at their uneventful outing, Erik pulled her close and silenced her with a kiss.

XXXVII

Life in their little home was not always the most pleasant.

As Christine's pregnancy progressed, she often complained of aching joints and that she was leaking *everywhere.* Erik did not try to think on such things too closely, and decided instead to believe she was referring to the fact that she seemed perfectly capable of crying at absolutely anything.

He would fix her breakfast and she would cry that he was too wonderful to her.

He would read to her from one of his many books about fantastical stories from far off lands, and she would cry that he was a better teacher than she had ever known.

And then there was her knitting.

When she first began, she seemed absolutely determined to knit every possible item for their child. Of course, since neither could possibly know the sex of the baby—ignoring Christine's daily declarations that were all equally adamant—each of the tiny items were made in the neutral styles and colours befitting a newborn.

Her first attempts were abysmal, though Erik never would have said so. On more than one occasion she would hurl both knitting needles and her chosen skein across the room, and declare that it was a stupid method when cloth was so much nicer. That was usually preceded by tears of frustration and Erik would surreptitiously gather up her supplies and return them to her basket until her mood shifted once more.

As close as they could figure, she was expecting in November, and while Erik occasionally felt overwhelmed by the fear of whether or not their tiny babe would prove deformed, those were quickly being overridden by his desire for the baby to simply *appear.*

The nursery had finally been furnished to Christine's exacting specifications. This simply added to Erik's desire for their newest addition to arrive, as it felt terribly wasteful to dedicate an entire room to a person that as of yet had no need of it.

Getting each of the small pieces down to their home had been challenging, but after a rather large bribe to the woodcrafter to deliver the furnishings to the entrance of the Rue Scribe, Erik was able to manage rather well—though he begrudgingly noted that it would not have been quite so easily done without calling upon the aid of his *friend.*

The Daroga had been happy to oblige, yet Erik thought that was mainly because Christine had been the one to contact him about the, "Tremendous favour that was critical to the wellbeing of our baby." During his last visit he had slipped her a calling card with his address written in flourishing script, and while Erik was not overly pleased by knowing the exact whereabouts of the man, he would not resent it either.

The only drawback of the Persian's increased visits to their abode was that he was dropping none too subtle hints that a subterranean environment was no great place for raising a child. Erik had borne each with equal parts incredulity and irritation, but it was Christine who had eventually silenced him on the matter.

"All I mean to say is that a child requires places to play—to run freely about without fear of falling into a death-trap or a lake!"

Erik had rolled his eyes, perhaps a little more dramatically than necessary when accompanied by the heaving sigh. "Children live by water often, Daroga. And do you truly think us so negligent that we would allow them to *drown?*" He rose up a little higher in his chair. "And no child of mine would be foolish enough to be caught in one of my traps. Surely they would have more intelligence than that."

Christine's expression grew slightly alarmed. "They will not have the opportunity!"

He looked at her in surprise. "Not at first, of course. They will be little more than a lump for quite some time. But eventually they will need to begin to roam my tunnels, and I will ensure they know how to do so safely." Erik narrowed his eyes at her pointedly. "As I do for *you.*"

She did not appear wholly convinced but eventually nodded, returning her attention to their guest. "What our baby needs most is the love of a mother and father. We feel safest here and while maybe in the future we will feel comfortable finding a home above," she glanced at Erik in confirmation. He merely grimaced. "For now, we will have our little one down here."

With that she had poured more tea, and her eyes clearly dared him to continue making any protestations.

The Persian wisely remained silent.

As Erik had rowed him across the lake once more, he could not help but pause before reaching the furthest shore. "Was your wife quite so... unpredictable when she was pregnant with your son?"

He knew he was bringing up a sensitive subject, as the man had clearly never fully recovered from the loss of those he held most dear. But on this occasion, there was only the faintest twinge of pain in his expression and his chuckle was genuine. "A woman with child can strike fear into the heart of even the bravest of men. As a husband, your only hope is to survive and remember that it is all worth it in the end."

And although doubts that such could ever prove true still threatened to consume him, Erik only nodded and returned home to his wife.

When he returned to the sitting room Christine was reclined on the settee, absently stroking the large swelling of her womb. She was looking towards the fire, and for a moment he allowed himself to stand in the doorway and revel in this moment of peace. She was not upset, and while she seemed not exactly *happy,* there was nothing in her expression that implied she was discontented.

He had thought she remained unaware of his presence, but her voice cut through the silence even as her gaze remained firmly upon the flames.

She had both teased and thanked him profusely for the fact that the fire remained a constant necessity throughout the summer months. The heat of Paris in combination with the errant humidity made their infrequent trips above to be nearly unbearable for Christine, and whenever they would descend yet again into the chilly depths she would insist upon lying in front of the cheerful blaze in order to fully appreciate the pleasant temperature.

"I do not want our child to be afraid."

Erik blinked at her, finding the statement a bit ridiculous. Of *course* they would not wish their child to feel fear, but a healthy dose of trepidation was important for proper behaviour. Even he, with all his genius and curiosity, still found it necessary to remember that self-preservation was important and steps must be taken to ensure one's continued longevity.

Especially now.

"Are you speaking of something specific?"

Surely *asking* would beget better results than dismissing her declaration.

She sighed, and finally she looked at him. "I was just thinking of what M.

Daroga said. Will we do our child harm by staying down here?" Her lip quivered, though she seemed to be determined not to allow another bout of tears to overpower the conversation.

Erik hesitated before crossing the room and sinking into his reading chair with a heavy exhalation. "We are going to make mistakes, Christine. I will lose my temper, and you will fill their heads with too many stories that make them believe that fairies and wood nymphs roam the forests."

She glared at him, but did not respond.

"But you were right in your assessment. We will *love* them, my wife, and we will learn through experience. Perhaps by the next one we shall not be so nervous."

He did not know what possessed him to say it aloud. Many days he was barely able to process the concept of *one* child, let alone a second. But upon seeing the small smile Christine produced, perhaps it was not the worst thing he could have said.

"We still do not have a boy's name. And since I think it is a boy today, I believe we should discuss it once more."

Erik groaned, only partially in jest. They had agonised over every conceivable name for a male, and each time they disagreed on what constituted a potential candidate.

"Why do we not agree that our little one is a girl since you have already selected a name? Surely that is more efficient." It would bother him of course that there was the possibility that he would be whispering his greetings and using a name that was not proper to the sex, but he would make that allowance if it meant they could cease this discussion.

It only led to arguing, and they had done quite enough of that.

She shook her head determinedly. "No. Besides, if you keep protesting I may just name him after *you.*"

He scowled. That had been one of his first forbiddances when the subject had originally been brought up. Simply because he now did not think of himself with the same self-loathing as he had during the majority of his life did not also mean he was prepared to saddle a *son* with his father's legacy.

Although he could admit to himself that he was already looking forward to taking his child around the Opera with him and performing all kinds of mischief—he just hoped that Christine would not protest too vehemently.

"We could name him after your father. Certainly that would be more than acceptable."

He offered it as a diversion, not as a true suggestion. He had not ever asked her father's Christian name. The last name of *Daaé* had been vaguely familiar from his reputation as a violinist, but that did not mean he had retained the full name of the man after all this time.

Her smile became more genuine, and for a moment he was both afraid and relieved that the matter had been settled. "I love you for suggesting it, Erik, but I think we are honouring him enough by keeping our family name. I would like for him to have something special."

Special.

As though the child of the Opera Ghost and his illusive wife would not be unique as it was—especially since there was the very great possibility that he would bear a striking resemblance to his father.

Erik pushed away the thought and found that it was getting slightly easier as time went on.

"Keane."

Christine looked at him, startled by the suggestion. "Keane? What is that from?"

Erik began plucking at a bit of lint that had suddenly decided to attach itself to his coat sleeve, feeling embarrassed for even having mentioned it.

"I believe the tale is Irish in origin. I heard it once as a boy and while I do not remember all of the particulars, there were plenty of fairies and wood nymphs within it to entice even my lovely wife."

This did not seem to satisfy her. "*You* do not remember something? Perish the thought!" He took her teasing with as much grace as he could, but she must have sensed that this particular name meant a bit more than she had first assumed. "Why do you remember the name, Erik?"

He sighed, not intending for this tale to be unearthed so unexpectedly. "I met a man once. A funny little man whose accent was so thick you could barely make out what he was saying. I did not know English at the time, but I found him rather fascinating as he struggled with his French."

"I did not know you spoke English," she remarked in surprise, though he sensed a chastisement as if he had been withholding something important.

Erik gave her a bemused smile. "I speak many languages, but that is not relevant to the story."

She looked properly abashed for her interruption, and motioned for him to continue. "The circumstances surrounding our meeting are not relevant nor are they pleasant, so I shall not trouble you with the details. In any case, it was the myth from his native land that stayed with me most."

It was after he had fled his mother that he had been found by the man. He had left without any provisions, and he was completely inexperienced in how to survive on his own. Stealing had become his primary source of nourishment, as well as foraging through the wooded areas. It was during one such venture that he was found by the Irishman, a wayfarer himself.

He was kind, in his own brusque sort of way, and though he had stared at Erik's make-shift mask for a long while before speaking to him, they had spent a few days in each other's company before parting in their respective directions—the man in search of work, and Erik trying to escape civilisation entirely.

But on one night as they sat a good distance away from each other while still about the same small fire, the man had told him a story from what he said was a common tale in Ireland.

"There once was a boy named Keane. He was a sad little fellow who liked to hide away in forests and shrubberies because his da' was mean to him—liked to beat him with a leather strap when he had too much of the drink. He had heard rumours that there was a wood nymph that would grant a single wish should she ever be caught, and he was determined to find her.

Keane searched for years, growing sadder and more desperate and he had almost given up hope of ever finding his nymph. But then one day he found a stream and just when he was about to doff his clothes and take a swim, he heard the most cheerful laughter.

Sure enough, the nymph was behind him, the most beautiful creature he had ever seen.

'You have searched long and hard for me, young one. What is it you seek?'

The boy, who now began to more resemble a man than a child had dreamt of his wish. On some of his da's more violent days, he thought he would wish for his death so he would never be harmed again. On others, he thought he would wish for money enough that he could move far, far away and be free. But as he looked at this nymph before him, he knew he could not ask for such a thing. She could be tainted by it, and that he could never allow.

So with tears in his eyes, the boy fell to his knees before her. 'I wish to be loved.'

The nymph was moved by his plea, and took him with her back to her woodland realm, and when he came of age they married, having many spritelings between them."

Finished with the tale, Erik looked up at his wife and saw tears in her eyes. "That was not an actual myth, was it? He told you that to give you hope."

Erik had scoured many books on the subject, and none even resembled the tale. "Yes, though I did not appreciate it fully at the time."

"Keane Daaé," she murmured.

Christine said it in the same accent he did, emphasizing the Irish origins instead of the traditional French inflection. She smiled at him then, brightly and happily. "I like it. I like knowing that you had someone be kind to you, even if you were too hurt at the time to realise it." She reached over as best she could to pat his hand. "Thank you for sharing that with me."

Erik felt suddenly shy and wanted nothing more than to escape to his organ for awhile. His composing had dwindled of late, and while he did not begrudge his wife for that as he fully appreciated that she needed her rest and undisturbed quiet, he knew that he missed the process.

But instead his attention was drawn as his wife tried to raise herself from the settee, apparently intent on retrieving her afternoon nibbles from the kitchen. He rose instantly to help her, visions of her tumbling form flooding his mind. "Are you all right?"

She released a pained grunt and gave up the effort, using his arm as a balance as she sank back into the cushions.

Extra blanketry had been one of the most noticeable additions to his home since their marriage, as Christine insisted that they lent a more homey feel to each of the rooms—and he often caught her snuggling into the warmth whenever the fire grew too low and she was too lazy to tend to it or ask for him to do so.

But since her pregnancy, pillows had become the other large superfluities. She wanted some on the floor in case she decided to lounge about the carpets, and she would not listen to Erik's indignant complaints. She also requested more upon the settee, as that had become one of her favourite napping places while Erik read to her in the evenings.

But as she huffed and still looked pained even against her excessive mounds of cushions, Erik grew more concerned. It was too early for her to have begun labour safely, for either her or the babe, and he fussed over her until she took his hand. "It is nothing Erik. My ankles are swollen and my feet hurt. That is all. You needn't fret so."

He sat down beside her and eyed her with disbelief. "If you are in pain, my rose, I will always worry." She was pushing at the pillows petulantly, seemingly unable to arrange them in a pleasing position. Erik reached over and helped, and she finally sank back with a sigh of relief.

"You always know what I need most."

He most certainly did *not* know such a thing, but he did try his best, and he hoped that counted for something.

Christine was pulling one of the many coverlets over her and Erik assisted in that as well, much to his wife's amusement.

"Would you..." He braced himself, realising the absurdity of the offer before he had fully spoken it aloud.

"Yes?"

Erik took a breath and started again. "Would you like me to rub your feet?"

Never did he think he would make such an offer. In theory it was subjugation itself, but in practice...

This was his wife.

For better or worse it was their child within her womb that was causing her such discomforts, and as she sighed and looked at him with an expression of sheer gratitude, he knew he had offered rightly.

"You always know."

She had forsaken stockings almost entirely except for when she claimed that non-existent drafts would sneak under her skirts and give her a chill—and even then she was more likely to steal a pair of his cashmere socks from his wardrobe than don a pair of her silk stockings.

So now as she lay upon the settee, she placed a pale pink foot upon his lap and looked at him expectantly.

He was tentative at first, not having the slightest idea of how precisely one aided swollen ankles and sore feet. It pained him a little to look upon the evidence of her hurts, and as his fingers trailed over the delicate sole and pressed firmly, she released a moan of pleasure.

His mouth went quite dry as he beheld her expression of delight and the way her head lolled to the side as she closed her eyes in contentment. "It is adequate then?"

Christine did not even bother to look at him, but simply smiled softly and burrowed more deeply into her nest of pillows and blankets. "Oh yes, Erik." She opened one eye then and he could easily tell that at any moment she would give way to sleep. "I love you for the way you spoil me."

As he pressed a little more firmly and she whimpered again, Erik allowed himself to place a kiss upon one of the troublesome ankles. "I love you for your fortitude."

She released one last happy sigh and fell asleep.

XXXVIII

It was time.

Though they had spoken at length with the midwife about what that precisely entailed, Erik felt more fear than he had since...

He had not ever felt such fear.

It was ridiculous to think they could somehow manage to bring the midwife back down into their home, yet Erik found that was precisely what he wished. While in the calm of their seldom afternoon chats it had seemed perfectly reasonable that Erik would usher Christine to her doorstep when her pains were at the proper durations, but it now seemed like the most ludicrous suggestion.

Their morning had begun smoothly enough. He had been tending to his composition, as Christine assured him that when he played the violin it was more likely to lull her further into slumber than to cause her to awaken unduly.

He had been working diligently on a lullaby for their baby for some time now.

His wife had assured him that the melody her father had played for her was sufficient enough for their little one, but Erik was not in the least convinced. Although her father had been proficient at his chosen instrument, he was not a composer.

Other children had heard the same lullaby, and Erik's child deserved a song of their very own.

Christine had not been exactly herself when she finally did awake. Her hands rubbed at her back, and she resolutely refused to dress, citing that her body was protesting viciously to any thought of moving.

Breakfast in bed it would be, as was common these days. Her belly had swollen greatly during her final months, and while she tried to insist that Erik take her for walks in the crisp autumn air, she could hardly make it to the doorway above. He had begun to carry her through the tunnels as her slow gate seemed exhausting in the extreme, and in that way they had managed a few strolls that ended with a sleepy Christine firmly returned to his arms as she murmured her thanks for him being so strong.

Even with the changes to her body throughout the duration of her pregnancy, she was still no great burden. She had filled out to be sure, but not in an unpleasant way—he had to admit, he had a growing fondness for her breasts and would have enjoyed them with far greater frequency if they had not become the source of such discomfort for her.

Later, after she had consumed her breakfast, she had insisted on walking to the kitchen. "Perhaps it will do me good to move a bit—work out some of the soreness."

He watched her warily as she trudged along, each step heavy and cautious. She had scolded him fiercely for *hovering* as she called it, so his careful observances were now far more subtle—though he still remained ever at the ready to catch her should she stumble.

Satisfied that there were no pending disasters, he allowed her to hurry him from the kitchen, citing that this was *still* her domain and that it would remain so until she was too large to function.

In Erik's opinion, such a time had already come.

But he obeyed, casting only two worried glances behind him as he returned to the sitting room to continue with his violin.

That was until he heard the cry.

He nearly damaged the instrument as he hurriedly thrust it back down into its case, not caring in the slightest if it was harmed if only it meant returning to her side all the sooner.

She was hunched over the basin, clutching at her middle with tears of mortification streaming down her face. "I think I wet myself."

Erik's eyes wandered down her nightdress, nervous of what he might see. He was distracted when a pain hit her low in the back and she fruitlessly tried to massage it away with trembling fingers.

He gulped, not at all feeling prepared for what was to come. "Christine... I think it is time."

She shook her head furiously. "No it is not. I will clean the breakfast dishes and in a few hours you will make me a lovely luncheon and then you shall read to me all afternoon. Perhaps you will even finish your song!" Tears were escaping and Erik had never felt so helpless in his life. "I am so frightened."

Christine could not be. She was to be the one who assured him that all would be well—that their baby would be born whole and healthy and she would never dream of leaving him through some sort of child birthing tragedy.

But instead he found himself moving forward and taking her into his arms, trying to calm both of their fears through sheer force of will alone. "I will not leave you, my rose. But we are going to meet our little one today, and we need to get you to the midwife." He took a shuddering breath and tried to keep his own tears at bay. "Your Erik does not want to deliver our child."

She huffed out a tearful laugh, burrowing her face in his shirt as she tried to calm herself.

Erik cleared his throat awkwardly. "Would you like to change before we depart?"

She nodded, though unenthusiastically, and he guided her back to their bedchamber so she could remove her wet garments and exchange them for something more suitable.

Christine slowly lowered her pantalettes and to Erik's relative surprise she did not don another pair. She pulled on a chemise and reached for one of her loosest maternity gowns—one especially fashioned for the later days of confinement. She picked out a pair of her plainest pantalettes and stuffed them into an overly large pocket, evidently for later use. The dress itself more resembled a dressing gown than a day dress, but as Christine closed it with the simple ties and shuddered as another pain seemed to rip through her, Erik was grateful that even the most ridiculous fashions took pity on a woman so close to giving birth.

He pulled on his own cloak and carefully secured hers about her shoulders, feeling terribly inadequate. It was so unfair that she should have to go through such pain! While he would be suffering through the knowledge *of* her pain, he would never compare the two.

His wife was rubbing at her back again, her breathing strained and slight whimpers emerging. "Bring some of the baby's clothes. I do not want to bring her back naked."

So it was a girl today.

It seemed surreal that in a few short hours they would *know* and could finally stop supposing. Erik hurried through to the nursery and stuffed some of the impossibly small clothing that Christine had so thoughtfully selected and ordered into one of the large pockets in his cloak. At the last moment before he returned to their bedchamber he spotted the small cap she had worked so diligently on. It was the first item she had been successful with, and though she had made many other articles once practice had honed her skills, this misshapen lump of cashmere was meant for their newborn's head to keep his—or her—ears warm on the journey home.

Erik had a lump in his throat when he added it to the pocket.

Christine had walked into the sitting room and was standing by the door. She had become unable to sink onto the settee without his assistance as it was far lower than was comfortable, and he felt another pang of ineptitude that he had left her waiting. "Are you ready?"

She sighed and seemed to steal herself, and slowly nodded. "I suppose so. As long as you are with me."

As if he could bear to be anywhere else.

Helping her into the boat was an absurd notion, but a necessity that could not be circumvented. His tunnel around the lake was far too small for her in this state, and he would not subject her to such close quarters in any case.

He nearly pulled the boat completely onto the shore so he could ease her in without fear of capsizing the vessel, and soon he was able to carry her unimpeded. They had no lantern as he had not wanted to take the time to light one, but as Christine huddled in his arms and occasionally gasped and hummed her discomfort into his neck, he realised she had far more pressing matters to focus upon than the encompassing darkness.

After the wave of pain had waned, he felt her gentle fingers upon his face, and he looked down at her without slowing his gait. "Your eyes glow in the darkness—little golden orbs."

She sighed, and rested her head against his chest. "I hope our baby has such beautiful eyes."

Erik did not scoff, but he was able to contain it only barely.

His eyes were not *beautiful.* They were unnatural. Their child should be blessed with her own blue eyes that sparkled so strikingly when she was happy.

Their baby would be happy.

The trek to the world above had never seemed so long before now, but finally they emerged. Erik initially froze, not in the least having thought about the fact that it would be daylight. He was not wearing the mask that would make him look like any other, and the idea of carrying his wife through the streets of Paris in the sunlight suddenly seemed ludicrous.

Except there was no bright sunlight. The streets were rain-soaked and the air was cold. He muttered a prayer of thanks at the brief respite from the rain as Erik hurriedly walked the now familiar route to the midwife's door, and he encountered barely another human being.

Perhaps this birth would be blessed after all.

Numerous times however Christine would beg him to stop—to let her down for a moment until the pains had temporarily abated. And although he simply wished to *get there,* he was helpless to do anything but oblige. She would lean heavily against him as she panted and whimpered, and he would try to soothe as best he could.

It seemed an eternity but he they finally arrived at Aida's door, just as the heavens opened once more and torrents of rain poured down about them. Thankfully there was a small eve that protected them from most of the downpour, but as he knocked he noticed a small note pinned to the door.

Out for a birth. Back soon.

Erik looked at it in disbelief.

He put Christine down and tried the handle, only to find it locked.

Perhaps it went beyond the proper behaviour of expectant fathers, but there was no possible way he would allow his wife to remain out shivering in the rain while she gave birth to their child.

From another pocket that did not house their baby things he pulled forth his lock picks, and though Christine seemed torn between gratefulness and disapproval, she made no protest when he ushered her through the newly unlocked door and into the small apartment beyond.

When they had first presented the problem to Aida about their lack of available space for the birth, she had been rather sceptical. "Surely you have a bed. That is all that is really required."

Erik had shaken his head resolvedly. "We do not live within the city, Madame, so using our bed would be out of the question." He cringed inwardly even thinking of using their wonderful marriage bed for something as messy as childbirth.

Aida had raised her eyebrows and looked at them both shrewdly, but did not press further. "I have a small room here we could use. It is nothing fancy but it will serve its purpose well enough."

She had shown it to them then, and it was indeed a small room. The bed more resembled a cot than an actual bedstead, but Christine had nodded and assured her that anything would be better than trying to do it themselves.

Erik had heartily agreed.

But here they were, and there was no midwife to be seen and no evidence as to when she might be returning.

He walked her into the back room, and as soon as she saw the bed she began ripping off her clothing.

Erik watched this with bemusement and would have chided her lack of modesty—as he refused to believe that the midwife would *not* return in time—but when he saw how agitated she was he prudently remained silent. "This was not how it was supposed to go!"

He was very much in agreement.

The hours passed slowly. There was no sign of Aida and Christine's discomfort was growing by the minute. There were times when she would allow him to sing to her softly and pet her hair as she tried desperately to rest after her bones shifted and her entire body ached. But other times she would snap at him that *he* was the cause of this and that she did not want his touches.

Erik tried to tell himself that pain caused all kinds of hurtful words to be spoken, but he still felt wounded and frightened—so *very* frightened—yet he remained in the corner of the room, unable to leave her even when she shouted.

She would cry soon after and beg his forgiveness as she held out her hands in welcome, and sob all the more when she noticed how hesitant he was to return to her side. "I am sorry! I just... I did not know it would be this bad!"

Though the sun had never managed to break through the clouds, what dim light there was began to fade. Candles and lamps had to be fetched even if it meant leaving her for a moment, and when he returned Christine was lying upon the bed, panting desperately and crying.

Erik nearly joined her.

"I wish we were at home. If we were to be without a midwife, I would," another pain hit her and she cried out, clutching at Erik's hand until it felt as though she was going to break all of his fingers.

He grimaced, but knew that his discomfort was nothing in comparison to hers.

"You would what, my rose?" He said through clenched teeth, although he managed to keep his tone soft.

She released a breath as the clenching of her womb temporarily abated, and she looked at him with teary eyes. "We are safe in our home. Nothing can harm us because it is just the two of us. Maybe it was a mistake trying to have our baby aboveground."

Erik's heart clenched and he pushed away her sweat-drenched curls that clung to her forehead and caused her such agitation when they fell into her eyes. "It is the fact that we are *together* that makes our home a safe haven, *mon ange*. Not the shelter itself." He tamped down his panic and willed her to believe him. "You are perfect, and you can do this. If any woman in the world can overcome this, it is you."

Just then they heard the latch of the front door, before hesitant steps moved toward them. Erik rose to his feet in preparation of defending his wife, but felt a wave of relief as the soaked midwife entered.

She blinked at them both in surprise, but gave a tired smile all the same. "It figures you two would pick today of all days. I just came from delivering twins. Took over a day for her poor mother to push those younglings out, and I am worn through."

Erik rather thought that the mother who was forced to deliver not one but *two* babies would be the one who rightfully could complain of tiredness, but even as she spoke she was shedding her outer garments and rolling up the sleeves of her rumpled dress. Erik could see that it was slightly damp and the hem was soaked completely, yet she put aside her own fatigue and saw to Christine.

He was not sure if he was more grateful for her attentiveness or simply for the fact that *he* would not be the one to catch the babe.

"How long as it been?"

"We have been here since before noon."

Aida was pulling up the lone shift that covered Christine, and though Erik grew intensely uncomfortable as knowing fingers probed and apparently discovered what they were looking for, it still unnerved him that someone other than himself was touching his wife in such a way.

Not that the two experiences were in the least bit comparable.

Christine did not seem to mind, and looked at the woman expectantly. "Well?"

"I can feel the head. It seems your little one is quite anxious to meet you."

His wife beamed at him, but it was overshadowed by another contraction and Aida was urging Erik to hold her hand and keep her steady as she ordered Christine to push.

And push.

And push.

Erik did not know why he thought the entire process would be over quickly, but time seemed to drag as his wife laboured and cried and insisted quite passionately that their baby hated her—hated her *very* deeply.

Aida merely produced a nearly inaudible chuckle that only Erik caught because he was looking, but his attention soon went to his wife. "That is not possible, Christine. Just a little bit longer."

With one final cry and a push that bespoke of sheer desperation, a small slippery body emerged into Aida's waiting hands, and was quickly wrapped in a towel and placed upon Christine's chest.

"My congratulations, you have a son."

Keane did not cry but gulped in a large breath as his lungs expanded, and he crinkled his face as though the oxygen had offended him.

He was perfection.

Christine was weeping as she took in his tiny features and she allowed a lone finger to trace over his skin, entirely enraptured.

Little Keane.

Erik was not sure what he should be doing. Aida was busy with the rest of the birthing, and Christine had yet to tear her eyes from their new little bundle. It seemed wrong to intrude while mother bonded with son, so he slipped away from her side so he could stand watch by the door. He was not being petulant—truly he was not—but as he watched his wife coo and fawn over their little boy, he suddenly felt a pang of uncontainable worry that she would somehow manage to replace him in her heart.

"Is he not wonderful?" Christine turned her head to look for her husband's agreement, and her brow furrowed when he was not where she had last seen him.

"Why are you all the way over there? Come meet your son."

He wanted to shake his head—to tell her that he could see Keane perfectly well from his current spot and that he need not get any closer. But she looked devastated at his apparent rejection, and that he could not allow.

Erik stepped forward slowly.

Aida had apparently finished with the rest of the birthing and was clucking away as she nipped at the cord and swaddled Keane more firmly, this time in a warm blanket instead of a towel. She wiped away the excess fluids that clung to his skin, and hummed her approval when she handed him back to his mother.

Christine was still looking teary, and when he came close enough she moved him ever so slightly in offering. "Hold our boy, Erik. He needs to know his papa."

And with a shuddering breath he did so, and knew he would never be the same again.

XXXIX

He had never imagined this part of it. There had been a vague idea of a *baby,* but Erik had never been around one to truly know what that meant.

Keane was impossibly small. Erik was quite confident that he could hold him in one hand, but he would never actually attempt to do so. Instinctively, he kept his boy's head supported as his neck seemed terribly limp and lacking in any kind of strength.

He had little wisps of brown hair that were just a few shades lighter than Erik's. He lacked the pinkish hue of Christine's complexion, and instead appeared to take after his father's yellowy tone.

But what Erik found most fascinating was the tiny button nose that graced his son's face. He allowed one finger to gently stroke at it, assuring himself that his boy was whole and perfect, only to have the babe scrunch up his nose at the contact.

Erik drew away quickly; waiting for the harsh cries he had imagined would come from their newborn. But Keane only opened his eyes and blinked curiously at his papa.

"Is he not beautiful?"

Erik could not tear his attention away from the small being staring at him in order to answer her properly. "A son is not *beautiful,* Christine. But I admit, he is a fine little fellow." His eyes were nearly colourless, and he thought of his wife's earlier declaration that she would like for him to share his father's shade. At this point it was impossible to determine what they would become, but for now it did not matter so very much.

Aida got his attention with her soft laughter. "You'll be needing to give him back soon enough, M. Erik. Your little lady needs to learn how to feed him proper before you three may return home."

It amazed him how *empty* his arms felt as soon as the light weight was deposited back in his mother's arms. He told himself that he should not watch as Aida showed Christine the proper method for coaxing milk from her breasts when it was troublesome. And as Keane began to burrow as he sought his first taste of nourishment, a lone arm appeared from the loosened blanket.

So intrigued by the baby's face, Erik had not paid much attention to the tiny hands with their perfect fingernails, and he rather thought that they were very long fingers for a newborn.

Not that he had much experience with infant hands, but he was relatively certain that his boy would prove quite apt at the organ or perhaps even the *pianoforte.*

He wondered at the feeling of pride that swelled within him, but such thoughts left him when he noticed that Keane had grown tired of waiting for his meal and had instead reached out a clumsy hand and pinched at Christine's nipple, causing her to squeak in surprise.

Aida merely chuckled and brought Keane's face closer to Christine's breast and soon he was happily suckling while Erik watched his wife smooth out his boy's downy hair.

After a few moments she looked to her husband and smiled at him tiredly. "Perhaps I will not cry so much anymore."

He sniffed, and moved the wooden chair that Aida had previously been utilising closer to the side of the cot so he could be near his family.

He blinked back tears at the thought.

"One can only hope, my rose."

Aida had gone to clear up most of the soiled linens but returned shortly. "I assume you walked here, but I can assure you, your Madame will not be up to any walking tonight. I suggest you go fetch a carriage."

Erik blinked at her, not at all wishing to leave them. But it was obvious the woman was exhausted and having two relative strangers within her small apartment as well as a newborn must not have been conducive for proper rest. And while he had not as of yet tested his lungs to full capacity with wailing, he was sure to begin doing so soon.

Christine looked at him in alarm. "Can you not carry us home? I am certain you would walk more smoothly than any carriage on the cobblestones." She shifted slightly and grimaced when the soreness of her body made itself known.

Aida shook her head in apparent disapproval, but made no further comment.

Erik hesitated, unsure of the proper course. He would have to carry her down to their home in any case, and it was not *that* long of a walk to the entrance of the Rue Scribe. He nodded haltingly. "But if it proves to be too much for you I will hail a carriage."

It was an empty promise as that would most likely require actually depositing her and the babe somewhere as he sought one out for hire, and that would never be considered an actual option.

But Christine seemed relieved in any case, and while she set about reinstating her clothing—and Erik noticed, adding quite a bit of padding to her pantalettes, much as she did for her courses—Aida set about showing Erik how to properly diaper and dress the baby with the garments produced from his cloak pocket. "Will you have a nurse? If so, she will usually tend to such things herself, but it still might be useful to know."

Erik stared at her blankly. "Is that not the parent's responsibility?"

Aida shrugged. "I would say it is, but it seems people who can afford to like to hire a wet nurse to care for their little ones. If you do not, I would suggest becoming quite proficient at diapering. Many mothers can get a bit grouchy if it is all left to them."

Erik listened attentively to her instructions as he was quite determined that however distasteful, he would be an active participant in his boy's care. He would not be one of those aloof figures that barely paid attention to their offspring. No matter how much he feared being a disruptive influence or that he would somehow harm him with his inexperience, as he looked at Keane's obviously bothered face as his limbs and body was manipulated into the strange new garments, he knew that it would hurt him too deeply to remain unattached.

Lastly, and possibly most importantly, Erik placed the small, misshapen cap upon his head and pulled it down so that it covered the tiny curve of his ears so he would be well protected from the autumn chill. That at least seemed to be less disagreeable to Keane as his face smoothed slightly and he fell asleep with only the least of frowns.

A few coins were given to Aida along with many thanks. She hugged Christine softly and murmured how well she had done before giving Erik a warm yet tired smile and departing to her own bedchamber. "If you were able to unlock the door on your own, I am certain you may lock it on your way out."

Such impertinence.

Christine was holding their baby, and although she grimaced when Erik initially picked her up, she nestled against him comfortably and did not protest too much when he had to gently set her down briefly in order to ensure the midwife's safety by securing the door.

The rain had stopped and the clouds cleared, leaving bright stars and a nearly full moon to light their way home. Christine's breath was warm upon his neck and for a moment he thought she had fallen asleep, until her soft voice whispered into the otherwise quiet night. "I would have loved him, you know. Even if he shared your face. I want you to know that and believe it."

Erik had not the slightest idea why she was bringing it up now—not when there was evidence sleeping in her arms that they did not have to dwell on that particular unpleasantness any longer. "Is there a reason it is of such importance to you?" The Opera loomed welcomingly, and his pace quickened.

Christine sighed, and he felt her press a kiss upon what little of his neck was exposed. "Because even after all the pain, once I saw his little face I knew that I would gladly do this all again. And the next time I fall pregnant I do not want us to have even a glimmer of fear. We will embrace it from the start and treasure every moment—even when I am being unreasonable and you regret ever having met me."

This last part was added in a teasing tone, but Erik still felt pained at the speaking of it.

"That is not true. Even at your most... temperamental, the most I ever wished for was a door and a separate music room. I would never wish to go back to a time before I had met you."

He felt more than saw her smile as she was nestled so completely against him. "You love him, do you not? As soon as you held him, you loved him."

Erik's throat tightened at the memory, but he shook his head resolutely. "No, I loved him far before that for he was a piece of you. But now I think I know what it is to love him for himself."

"I am so glad."

Foolish girl—as if he would ever be able to keep himself from loving anything so small and helpless and so entirely dependent upon him. He had come to love her, had he not?

She really did fall asleep then as they passed through the entrance to the Rue Scribe, and Erik shifted to ensure that his family was properly enshrouded by cloaks and blankets so as to not catch a chill.

It felt odd entering the house.

So much had changed since they had departed only that morning. No longer would he sneak a careful hand over her womb while she slept to feel a nocturnal baby squirm about inside. No more would he have unreciprocated conversations in the darkness as he poured out his worries, his hopes, and his prayers to the lump that grew with each passing day.

Now there was a real, living human being that he could hold and protect.

And it terrified him.

He deposited Christine in the bed and watched her nestle and fuss even as her eyes remained closed. He debated about removing her clothes and cloak, but when Keane opened his own eyes and appeared terribly unhappy to be awake, Erik knew that keeping the babe satisfied was more important than divesting his wife of clothing.

Hopefully.

Erik did not like being inexperienced.

He liked knowing how things worked and precisely how to fix them should it be required, and especially how to intervene before disaster would strike. But in this—in *fatherhood*—he knew nothing.

"Hush, little Keane. You must not wake your mamma. She worked very hard for us to meet you."

He picked him up gingerly, and the baby blinked up at him once more, obviously still trying to work out who the man was that kept pulling him away from his mother's breast.

Christine was stirring and Erik was anxious to allow her to rest, so he placed a light kiss upon her temple and left the room hurriedly.

He briefly wondered if Christine would want to be there when their boy was introduced to his nursery, but he decided that it would be rude to keep him away from his allocated bedchamber any longer than strictly necessary.

No matter which item he pointed out to Keane, the babe seemed far more interested in the man holding him. Erik finally halted in his identification of each of the carefully selected items and hand crafted articles that would adorn his small body until he outgrew them, and sighed in resignation. Perhaps newborns were not capable of so much on their very first day outside the womb.

He stared at his boy a moment longer, and holding him safely in one arm, he removed his mask with his free hand.

If he was going to study the face of his father, he might as well see him for what he truly was.

Nothing remarkable happened. Keane looked up at him sleepily, and a tiny, yet long fingered hand reached up and made small grasping motions until Erik indulged him and placed the mature version of the same finger within reach.

Satisfied that he was being held and cared for, the babe fell asleep.

And Erik felt his heart swell in response.

There was one particular item that would remain covered—much as it had been for the past month. It was a gift to Christine and though she had wheedled and cajoled—and even *seduced,* which was perhaps Erik's favourite method of interrogation—he refused to allow her to uncover it until the baby was born.

It sat in the far corner of the room, covered in the same white cloths that once protected the furniture in their shared bedchamber.

Tomorrow. When Christine had rested and was once more alert, he would take her into the nursery and show her what he had especially designed and ordered for her.

He was too proud of his creation to feel any of the nerves that once might have plagued him. If there was anyone in the world that would appreciate his genius, it would be his lovely wife.

For now however, he contented himself with holding his son in his reading chair—but only after experiencing the difficulty of stoking a fire one-handed with a sleeping infant in the other arm.

He must have drifted off himself for he was rather startled by the anxious call from the bedroom. "Erik?"

He looked down and saw Keane still sleeping in his arms, and after a quick glance at the mantle to see the time, hurried to his wife's side. "Yes, Christine?"

She released a deep breath at his entry and held out her arms beseechingly. "I woke up and no one was here and I felt so... empty."

That must have been a terrible feeling indeed. She had fostered their boy for nine months and to wake up suddenly alone...

He knelt beside the bed and handed Keane over carefully, though even as he did so their son awoke and protested the movement with little mewls of displeasure.

"Oh, I am sorry, my little Keane. I do not like to leave your papa's arms either."

She struggled to sit up and it took Erik's assistance and the manipulation of quite a few pillows to see her upright. The babe was still expressing his upset, although it could hardly be called outright *crying.* It was more a combination of a whimper and a grunt, and it was not at all how Erik expected a newborn to sound.

"Do you think he is hungry?"

Erik shrugged. "You have been sleeping for a few hours, so he might be. Do you not have any... motherly impulses that might guide us?"

Christine looked at him incredulously. "I have no idea what a *motherly impulse* might entail, so I would suggest we simply try and see if he latches."

But Keane did not want to eat, much to his mother's dismay, and after they checked to ensure that his diaper was still dry, Christine returned him to Erik's arms with a desolate sigh and a roll of her eyes. "I do not know why I thought any child of ours would love me best—not when you are around. You are quite irresistible you know."

A lump settled in his throat as he stared down at the now calming baby, finding it utterly incredible that anyone would choose *him* over the loveliness of Christine.

"He has spent the whole of his life with you, my rose. Perhaps he would just like to get to know his father a little."

She smiled at him then and he could tell she did not truly begrudge him for it and he was very glad. She shifted again and grimaced, and glanced at him sheepishly. "Could you help me to the bath-room?"

He nodded, and was rather amazed at how quickly he was adapting to doing things with only the use of one arm. Keane was peering at his parents curiously, his little brow furrowed and his mouth slightly pinched as Erik held out his arm and helped Christine ease over the side of the bedstead. "Would you like me to carry you?"

It seemed important that he offer, for even if his son proved displeased to be out of his arms, by no means would he allow his wife to unduly be in pain by making her walk if it caused her to much discomfort.

She took a hesitant step and hissed, holding her middle as she did so. "No, I might feel better if I move a little."

Erik wondered if he would later find bruises on his forearm from the way she clutched at it for balance, but he made no complaint as Christine shuffled forward. Before they reached the lavatory however, she took off her cloak and dress that Erik had chosen not to remove, and stopped before the wardrobe. To Erik's bemusement she took the time to place them on their proper hooks and she donned a fresh nightgown, leaving her soiled things in a pile on the floor before taking his arm once more and continuing on her way.

He exited the room as soon as she bid him do so, though he did not stray far knowing she would require assistance on the return journey. Sure enough, she called for him, but she did not immediately begin walking back to their bedchamber. "When will I get to see my present?"

Physically exhausted and requiring much more rest and recuperation, his little wife's mind still drifted to the forbidden item residing in their boy's nursery.

He chuckled, and while he was sure he should scold and make her go straight back to bed, a part of him was quite glad that she was so insistent.

Erik opened the hidden door in the bath-room and watched in amusement as Christine's mouth popped open, although he quickly schooled his uncovered features when she turned to glare at him. "That was there the entire time? You could have intruded on me!"

He raised his eyebrows in indignation. "I would have done no such thing. And besides, I would think you would be rather grateful for its existence as it shortens the amount of required walking considerably."

She huffed but nodded her assent.

They proceeded to the nursery, but not before Christine turned so she could look at the other side of the doorway suspiciously, evidently trying to determine how she could have missed it while transforming Erik's bedchamber into the nursery for their boy. "There were no peepholes were there?"

Her husband sniffed indignantly. "Of course not."

As if he would have wanted to see *that.*

Of course, watching her bathe unawares would not have been so very unappealing, but he would not mention that to Christine. He might be a Ghost, but he was also a gentleman.

Most of the time.

Christine tried to undo the covering on her gift but it proved too taxing on her abused abdominal muscles, so Erik reluctantly handed her Keane who this time made no protest as he was already sleeping soundly.

Beneath the cloth was a chair of his own design. It would rock smoothly when sat upon, but unlike the hard wooden creations that would prove taxing for long durations, his invention more resembled his comfortable reading chair. Christine gasped and though she sat rather gingerly, she sighed in contentment when her back met the ample cushions.

"I thought you might like a special place to nurse."

He looked at her expectantly, trying to assess if she found the fine chenille to be pleasing enough against her skin. "Oh Erik, *thank you.* It is perfect!"

She began to rock softly and this time when Keane opened his bleary eyes he happily latched onto his mother's breast, soothed by the lulling of the chair his father had provided.

And that was how they welcomed their boy home.

XL

Christine was exhausted.

Even with her husband's abundant assistance, she found that motherhood was a tiring business. Erik would do all he could to ensure she could sleep throughout the night, but even with his lullabies and stories and his efficient method of changing diapers when necessary, he could not provide nourishment.

Keane did not like large meals. That she had learned within the first two weeks since his birth. Christine ruefully acknowledged that he was very much like his father, where small nibbles throughout the day—and night—were far more preferable.

In the beginning she would rouse herself to go to her special rocking chair for the mere ten minutes of suckling. But when she was awoken for the third time, nearly in tears as Erik passed her their whimpering son, she had taken to simply remaining reclined and holding him close, trusting that Erik would ensure she did not squish him if she fell asleep while he fed.

Her husband was a godsend.

She would never fully understand what it was about his body that functioned so differently from other people, but never had she been more glad of it. He did not seem to require regular sleep, but instead the short naps he would take periodically kept him cheerful and well-functioning—even as she grew teary and despondent that she was a failure as a wife, even as she tried to learn how to be a mother.

It had been three weeks since she had given birth. Her body had finally stopped aching so fiercely, and she did not have to change her gauze so very often anymore. Her stomach had also begun to flatten, though not nearly as much as she would have liked. She supposed that was one positive of not having a full length mirror in the house. While she might grow frustrated that her body did not immediately return to its previous state, she also did not have to look at it in its entirety.

Christine walked into the sitting room, and she could not help but smile as she saw Erik seated before the organ, giving Keane his first music lesson. Of course, the baby was barely cognisant of anything his father said, and in truth, his eyes were barely open, but Christine was always touched by Erik's confidence in his son's future abilities.

Her papa had always been attentive and nurturing, and she had often wondered if that was simply because her mamma was not there to be so. But their boy had both of his parents, and it gladdened her that Erik was not afraid to care for him as he deserved.

"May I speak to you for a moment?"

Erik turned to her in surprise. "Of course."

He finally seemed to notice that his son was already half asleep for he chuckled softly and placed a kiss upon his forehead before tucking him in his bassinet near the fire. Not *too* close, for both were paranoid that he would somehow be singed by the flames. But he seemed to enjoy the warmth, especially when napping.

That was something new for Erik. She had taken to practically showering her little boy with kisses on a regular basis, but her husband had always held himself rather aloft. He would dote and tend and coo whenever necessary, but it was only a week ago that he had actually bestowed a kiss.

She had confronted him that day, and he had bashfully confessed. "What if he grows up and does not like that I had done so when he was too helpless to protest?"

Christine had been aghast at the mere suggestion. "Erik, he *loves* you. I am sure there will come a time when he will rebuff *both* of our kisses, but not for a good long while!" At least, she hoped so. In his current state he was a perfectly bony lump that was amiable to any of her attentions, and she would like to relish that attribute for as long as possible.

He was not built like other babies she had seen. While admittedly, she was not at all experienced with little ones, the ones she saw in prams, bedecked in layers of white lace and small rompers were all plump and rosy. Her boy on the other hand was all long and skinny limbs, and she knew they would only grow longer and skinnier if she did not ensure he ate sufficiently throughout childhood.

And the more she considered her son's body, the more she wondered if her husband's frame was not solely due to his deplorable eating habits, or if he was simply destined to be thin and so deceptively strong. And if so, no matter how much she nursed and eventually plied with biscuits and other tempting treats, he would remain tall and slender.

Erik had tried it then, though it was the so light and so quickly done that she doubted that Keane had even felt it. He had pulled away quickly and eyed the boy suspiciously, apparently waiting for some sign of displeasure or protest.

There was none.

And ever since that day he had been more than happy to bestow his little affections, but perhaps not quite as often as Christine managed to do so.

But now she sank onto the settee with a tired sigh, pulling one of the many coverlets that were scattered about so that it wrapped fully around her. Erik came and sat beside her, glancing at her worriedly. "Is something troubling you, my wife?"

Christine did not mean to do it. When she had first given birth he had teased her that he hoped she would cry less once she was no longer with child, but she feared it was becoming entirely the opposite. She started to cry—not the dainty shedding of a few tears, but deep heaving sobs that could very well threaten to wake their boy. "I *miss* you!"

Erik blinked at her in surprise, and gingerly placed his arm about her shoulders. "I have been here with you, Christine, this entire time. I only ever leave to bring supplies."

She sniffled into his coat and she knew him well enough to know that he was grimacing as her tears once more stained his cashmere.

"I am so *tired.* And there is nothing more you can do for me, so please do not think I am finding you lacking. But I miss when you would read to me and I could actually *learn.* But when you do it now, it just lulls me to sleep until Keane wakes up and demands another feeding!"

She hiccupped and she was keenly aware of how unladylike she was being. And she felt even worse for begrudging her baby who could not help that he liked to eat every two hours.

His voice was low and she could not quite place his emotion. It seemed pained and yet steeped in wariness, and it hurt her even more to hear it. "Are you so terribly unhappy?"

Christine shook her head furiously and shifted in his arms so that she could look at him fully. "Truly I am not. I just find that I... miss sometimes when it was just us. Life was so simple and I..."

Her guilt and shame was growing as she realised what was truly the trouble. "You spoiled me greatly, Erik, with your love and attention. I was never very good at sharing because I had all of my papa to myself. I *love* that you are such a devoted father but I..."

The tears burned in her eyes and she could not bear to look at him anymore. "I am selfish. The mother of your boy is a selfish woman and I am so very sorry!"

She should not have tried to speak to him of her feelings. She should have prayed more and kept them to herself so she could have worked through them on her own. There was nothing he could do in any case, and surely it would only hurt him to know that she suffered these occasional bouts of melancholy.

Erik sighed and seemed uncertain for a moment before drawing her closer to his side and kissing her temple. "You are not selfish. You are new to this just as I am. Aida asked if we were to have a wet nurse to do most of the daily care for Keane but it never occurred to me that you would like something like that. Would it... help you if we were to live above with a nurse?"

The offer was there but everything about his posture and tone made it clear that he was suggesting it only for her sake. And as she pictured a stranger nursing her son and cuddling him as his tiny mouth finally stilled as he fell asleep, and another woman stroking his downy head as she lowered him into his bassinet, she knew that no matter how tired she was, or how she no longer felt as a wife should, Christine would not give up motherhood for anything.

She sniffled once more and leaned her head against his shoulder. "No, I do not wish that. You mustn't mind me; I just must not be my old self yet."

Erik sighed. "I have been reading about infant development. While I consider most of it to be absolute drivel, I would tend to believe that eventually he will sleep through the night." He looked down at her worriedly and coaxed her chin softly upward so he could assess her feelings. "I know that does not help you in the *now*, but perhaps you might be encouraged that this will not last forever."

She was not certain why, but he seemed almost pained by the suggestion. "You love this age, do you not? Even when your wife is little use but as a milk cow?"

She felt horrid that she had no energy for tending to the dusting, and she felt even worse when she caught Erik doing it himself. He had tried to hide the rag immediately and feigned innocence, but she had been so sad and felt so *useless* that he had confessed. "I know that you like a tidy house, my dear. I do not blame you for being too tired to see to it yourself."

Christine had nodded and had allowed him to continue, but inside she felt even worse.

But now Erik was looking at her in sheer astonishment. "Is *that* what you think?"

She shrugged, realising that such was indeed how she felt most of the time. Erik saw to nearly everything else in the house from the cooking to the cleaning, and even took care of most of the diapering. What lovely balance they had struck during the first portion of their marriage was gone. She had grown to love caring for Erik since it was so apparent that no one had been there to do it before. And now she was just so *tired.*

Erik shifted and took her by the shoulders so she could not help but look at him. "Christine. That is the most ridiculous thing that has ever come from your pretty pink lips. You are being the perfect wife by *being* a dedicated mother to my son. You have given me the ultimate gift of a child who is healthy and well loved, and meaningless nonsense about housework and who tends to the meals does not make you insufficient as wife. This will pass. But as you reminded me, he might not like to be kissed and cuddled later in life."

He kissed her then. Not the simple peck on the cheek or temple that had become his most usual method of affection, but a searing kiss that she felt in her very soul as his approval and devotion to her, no matter how sleep deprived and grumpy and weepy and..

One hand was buried in her loose hair while the other gently cupped her cheek, and she found that thoughts were not very important things, not when her husband was kissing her so.

Erik pulled away eventually, and her eyes were glassy and she felt short of breath. He *smirked* at her in triumph and pecked her once more on the lips before rising from the settee. "I am going to make you some tea and then you shall have a nap. Perhaps you should like to feed our boy in the meantime so he might allow you to rest for as long as possible."

She blinked, not at all ready to begin the tedious process of thinking or protesting that he was telling her what to do, so she merely nodded when the words finally sank into her befuddled mind and went to retrieve Keane from his bassinet.

There originally had only been one in the nursery, but as they began to truly *live* with him, it became clear that while he eventually would need a room of his own, it was wholly impractical at this point in time. He usually spent the night with them in their bedchamber, occasionally sleeping in their bed when Christine was too sleepy to take him back to his cradle.

Erik had another commissioned for the sitting room, and she thought this was because he got rather tired of moving it wherever it was needed.

"Not so," he had retorted. "I simply do not believe in locking him away. He should be with his parents."

He had said this with a faraway look in his eye and she knew he was referring to his own upbringing. *He* had been locked away in darkened chambers, waiting and wishing that he might have even a few seconds of love from his parents, only to be left wanting.

And apparently he was determined that his son would never feel such things, even at this young age.

But for now she returned to the settee and looked down at Keane thoughtfully. "And what do you think of your mummy? Your papa says I do nicely, but you seem to like him much better than me."

He appeared disgruntled to have been disturbed from his nap, but when she undid the neckline of her shift—she had not taken to dressing most days as it seemed troublesome and fussy for having to nurse so very often—he seemed perfectly amiable to suckle.

She looked down at him and noted the way his little face could scrunch in such intense concentration, his mouth working so hard to keep a steady flow of milk that only *she* could provide. This was something Erik could not do, and while she had begun to resent it for it would allow her the blessed respite of a full night of sleep, she realised that this was a special connection that she could share with her boy. He might find comfort in Erik's arms and like the way he sang to him and talked to him of all the ways music was important for a proper education, but when he was hungry it was only at Christine's breast that he would be sated.

When Erik returned with the tea things and she was still holding Keane in her arms, unwilling to put him down, she smiled at him in gratitude.

"How do you always make me feel better? I was the one raised in a loving household, so I should be the one to comfort *you.*"

Erik grimaced and set about pouring her tea and placed a sweet biscuit on a plate for her to nibble on. "I most certainly do not know what will console you, but I suppose I just tell you what I would need to hear."

He sank onto the settee with a sigh and pulled her close, balancing his own cup of tea on his knee. She took a sip and looked down at the cup in surprise. "What is this?"

His fingers began combing through her hair soothingly, and she nestled against him in contentment. "A special brew. It does not contain any *caféine* so you should have little trouble falling asleep."

She took another sip and found the flavour to be quite nice, though different from the robust tea he would make her in the mornings. The warmth of it was quite relaxing, and she felt safe and cosy and most of all loved as she bit into the biscuit that was obviously freshly baked that morning.

"We do not have to be like everybody else you know."

Christine turned to him, wondering where his mind was going. "What do you mean?"

He was not looking at her, but instead was staring intently at her hair, and eventually he took a lone tendril and it tickled her skin as he slid it over her exposed décolleté. "Other people have servants and nursemaids and cooks. The husband would dabble in business affairs while the wife would see to the running of the home and any social engagements." Erik watched as her skin prickled from the sensation of her hair drifting over her skin.

"I am happy with the way we live. Are you happy, Christine? That is all your Erik wants for you..."

He finally did look at her then and his eyes were imploring. She suddenly understood that her unhappiness would have been his greatest fear once their baby was born. There was little doubt in her mind that he would have loved and cherished their baby even if it had proved to be deformed, so his insecurity had been that *she* would have been unhappy with such a child.

"I am happy, Erik, I promise. You just have a foolish wife that does not know what to do with herself sometimes and needs your reassurances."

He hummed and to her amusement did not deny her foolishness, although he did kiss her so she supposed she forgave him for it.

She glanced up at him though, and while her first impulse was to tease him—to ask him if he thought she was too plump to ever be desirable again—he still seemed a bit tense and she knew that any such enquiries would only hurt him.

And that she could not bear to do.

So instead she placed a kiss on his chest and murmured, "And what is it that you need to hear?"

Erik glanced down at her, perfectly serious. "That you love me. That I will always need to hear."

Her eyes watered even though she told herself firmly that she was being completely ridiculous and that his words did not need to inspire tears. But she felt them prickle all the same and she gave him a smile and reached up with her free hand to pull him down for another kiss. And this time the heat and the passion was initiated by her, and it felt good to allow herself the simple respite of feeling like a *woman* again, even if her body could not yet allow them to go further. "I *love* you, Erik. I love you for your devotion, and your kindness, and your tea things."

He smiled then, almost impishly, and it warmed her heart to see that the pain had faded from his features. "As I love you. For your kisses, and your caring, and your breasts."

Christine's mouth fell open and he had the audacity to merely kiss her forehead and take a sip of tea.

Her rogue of a husband.

XLI

Life seemed a little easier after they had talked.

The true turning point of course was the first night, five weeks since his birth that Keane decided it was time to sleep for four hours without interruption. Erik had been concerned as he could practically schedule his entire day into the two hour intervals that made up their son's entire existence. And when he missed one of his feedings, he had hovered and fretted, though did not stupidly attempt to wake the baby to ensure his continued health.

Christine had stopped trying to remain awake throughout the day and was not so distressed when she caught her husband tending to household chores. She would roll her eyes or smile in gratitude, but she no longer appeared guilty that she was somehow lacking.

She was tired still, that much was plain, and he remembered how young she was. Even during his adolescence he had required more sleep than his adult counterpart, and he had to remind himself frequently that his Christine was merely exhibiting the same behaviour.

But she was happy, that much had become evident. He no longer found her weeping in their bed, trying to console Keane herself so that she could offer him a few minutes of personal diversion through music. She stopped accusing the baby of hating her, which was in itself absolutely absurd. And most of all she was smiling more and more—and that was all he truly wanted.

He would have thought that he would have grown resentful by how much time was taken away from his compositions. His long abandoned Don Juan Triumphant had been niggling in his mind for quite some time, but once Keane was born he could feel the melodies and the libretto slip away into the void. It would have been passionate and entirely written to suit Christine's voice, and he had even fantasised about her singing it upon the stage when it was complete.

But instead he changed diapers and made tea for his wife and did not find anything to complain about.

Aside from one particular issue.

It was not so much a complaint but more of a wistful remembrance. Seven weeks had now passed since their little boy had graced them with his presence, and he found that he missed his wife. He would never be the one to broach the subject of resuming their marital relations. It was not even the physical aspects that he missed most—it was the *oneness* and completeness that was shared.

Though the absolute bliss that it also offered was not such a dissuading characteristic either.

What he noticed most was that he lost track of time—they both did. He had to remind himself to check the calendar in order to chart their son's growth, but it never truly seemed important.

It was late December, and Christine had begun hiding herself away for the last few weeks. He had grown concerned at first and often went to check on her to ensure that she was not unhappy or distressed, and had even grown more so when he found the door to the nursery *locked.* Keane was with her and although he could hear no signs of crying from either of them, it still sent a pang of worry through his being.

He tried the handle once more just to see if he had been mistaken, and just when he was about to abandon the door to fetch his lock picks, his wife's calm and slightly muffled voice came from beyond the barrier. "You will *not* break in, Erik. A wife is allowed to surprise her husband sometimes and you will respect that."

His first inclination was to have been deeply insulted. She could have merely *asked* for privacy and not actually *bared* the door. But then, she must have realised that locks truly did not mean much if he truly wished to go around them, so it must have been only so she could hear his attempt and warn him away.

Erik had sniffed indignantly and left her alone, and when he went to investigate later he was disappointed not to find any evidence of what she had been working on.

Keane was now sleeping through most of the night with little complaint, and both of his parents were relieved—Christine for she was finally appearing less haggard and was able to resume some of her lessons with her husband, and Erik because he did not feel the horrible stab of guilt when he had to gently shake her awake in the middle of the night in order to feed their whimpering boy.

It was late evening and Christine had hidden herself away again, and he was growing a tiny bit perturbed. It was not that he begrudged her solitude if that was what she required, but he did not like that she was not within eyesight, and he found that he was terribly lonesome when neither she nor Keane were with him.

How things had changed over the past year.

It did of course give him an opportunity to work on Christine's birthday presents, which he was quite pleased about. A few of the things were purchased items that he had hidden away in the tunnels so she would not come across them before it was time. But there was another item that she would hopefully appreciate that was solely from him. He had just finished it that morning and was feeling rather content with it, though as with most of his creations he was never *truly* satisfied. Her actual birthday was not for another week, but it felt good to be prepared.

He would not allow this one to pass unnoticed.

Christine finally emerged from the nursery, a small parcel under one arm and their son in the other. She was dressed, and it briefly startled him to realise that such was a novelty. Aside from their few trips into the chilly world above, she still preferred her chemises and dressing gowns to any of her dresses.

He was seated in his reading chair and although he was acutely aware of her entrance, he remained staring at the book that he had been pretending to read for the past quarter of an hour, steadily ignoring her.

Erik heard her sigh and she passed him in order to deposit Keane in his bassinet, kissing him softly as she did so.

Not that he was watching.

He told his eyes to remain on the page before him with absolute resolution, and he maintained the posture valiantly even as he could feel her coming closer.

What he did not expect was for her to pluck the book from his hands and settle on his lap.

"No sulking, Erik. I would not have stayed away if there had not been a reason, and I can assure you it was not because I did not desire your company. So please do not be cross."

He most certainly was not *sulking* and his crossness was only because she insisted on taking a period of time each day and holing herself away. Did she not fully understand how *wrong* it felt to be alone now?

Erik knew he was scowling, but apparently his facial features were just as pliable to Christine's touch as his heart, for as soon as she started caressing and coaxing with her fingertips and lips, he softened. "I just do not understand *why.*"

She smiled at him and presented her little bundle with a sudden shyness that surprised him. "There are two of them—one for tonight and one for tomorrow. I just thought this would be useful tonight after I ask you."

His eyes narrowed suspiciously. "Ask me what?"

Christine took a deep breath and seemed to gather her courage—as if she ever needed to fear that he would deny her something. "It is Christmas Eve, Erik. I should like to go to Mass."

He stiffened, though not because her entreaty in the least surprised him. Of course she would wish to go to a Christmas service, as even he had been drawn to the warmth and radiance of the candlelight when he had dared venture above during the holiday season.

What troubled him was that he had given no thought to presenting *her* with a gift aside from the ones allocated for her birthday.

And it made him feel dreadful.

"Christine..." he began, only to be cut off by her hurried words.

"I know we did not speak of it, and perhaps I should have given you time to prepare. I just wanted to do something for you since I know my birthday is coming up and I..." she looked down at her lap and fiddled with the ties on the package still sitting there, neglected. "I do not know your birthday and this was the only opportunity I could think of that I could give you a gift without you protesting."

His mouth felt dry and he swallowed thickly, trying desperately to determine how he could convince this lovely woman on his lap that she and their boy were far beyond any gift he could ever have imagined.

"You must know that is not necessary. I have everything I could have hoped for." His arms went around her waist and he held her more firmly to him, and she bestowed him with one of her bright smiles.

"Gifts are not about necessity, Erik. They are about wanting to do something for the one you love." She leaned in close and whispered, as though confessing a very great secret. "And it just so happens that I love *you.*"

How could he argue when she was so utterly perfect?

So he simply nodded and accepted her proffered gift, wrapped in the same brown paper that many of their groceries arrived in. "I am sorry that the covering is not prettier. I was going to draw something on it but apparently my skills have not improved in *that* area." She was blushing and he swallowed again, realising with a startling clarity that he was about to open his very first Christmas gift.

His fingers trembled as they plucked at the string, and he stared at the black item within that had been so carefully folded.

It was obvious she had knitted it herself and that each of the small baby items she had laboured over for all those months had honed her skills considerably. With great care he lifted it from his wife's lap so he could better see her handiwork, and by the length and width it was apparently a scarf befitting his great stature.

It was no wonder she required so much time to complete it.

Tears prickled at his eyes even as he tried to keep them from falling. But his wife saw them anyway and she brushed at the few that escaped with her thumb, and she was smiling at him so sweetly. "Do you like it? I decided you were not the type of man who liked fringe."

He had no words to describe how he felt when she took it from his hands and wound it around his neck until it was just *so,* and she patted it in approval. "I think it suits you." She glanced at him from beneath her lashes, and though he was still struggling to find the words of gratitude that were so firmly lodged in his throat, he could easily see that she desired some reassurance that she had done well—that he *approved*.

So he kissed her.

It was long and languid and so full of *need* that it left him breathless. He pulled her impossibly closer and she was forced to straddle him otherwise she surely would have fallen. One hand was trying to coax its way into her hair while the other was holding her firmly against him, and *why* did she have to choose today to begin dressing once more?

She was even wearing shoes and stockings, and those were only worn when it was absolutely necessary—which could only mean she was quite serious about attending tonight's service.

He might not have a gift prepared for tonight, but he could allow her that.

With great reluctance he finally pulled away, yet he allowed himself a moment to relish in the sharp intakes of breath and the colour in her cheeks that revealed she was just as affected as he. "We may go to your Mass if you so wish."

She blinked, obviously trying to regain her senses, and he felt an irrational sense of pride that such a thing should be necessary. If he had continued his ravishment he was certain he could have driven any such thoughts from her mind, but she had exerted a great deal of effort to prepare him for the possibility of an evening in church, and he would not deny her.

He picked her up by her waist and set her down on the floor and gave a gentle squeeze of reassurance before slipping out into one of the tunnels. He might not have prepared specific gifts for Christmas, but surely she would appreciate opening *something.*

She was waiting for him when he returned, and he could tell she was trying not to be miffed at his sudden departure. But when she saw the cleanly wrapped parcel, any hint of lingering irritation dissolved and was replaced by a look of anticipation.

He sniffed imperiously. "You now have one less present to open on your birthday, so on your head be it."

And if he had ever needed a reminder of just how young she was, she began bouncing on the balls of her feet, her greedy hands held out for her package in excitement. "That is all right!"

Erik could not help but chuckle as he presented her with his gift, feeling surprisingly warm and satisfied by her reaction. She settled on the settee and carefully undid the wrappings, although he had half expected her to tear into it with voracious enthusiasm. There was a plain box within and inside was a new gown. It was entirely frivolous and he knew she had hardly a need for it, but his wife deserved something decadent and lovely simply because it was for *her.*

She gasped when her hands touched the velvet of dark blue. It had a high collar and long sleeves and was especially commissioned so she would have something warm and practical—yet an indulgence at the same time—to wear when she demanded one of her snowy, nighttime walks.

Christine nearly assaulted his person with her fervour.

He had settled in his reading chair so he could better judge her response, and while his first thought was to be concerned that she was crumpling her new garment, as her lips met his and her hands caressed any bit of flesh they could find, any use of his mind quickly faded.

This time it was she who pulled away first and he was relatively surprised to find that she had returned to his lap. His little minx of a wife did seem wholly capable of driving him to distraction.

She pressed one last kiss upon his cheek and exclaimed, "Thank you!" before disappearing into their bedchamber, her slightly rumpled gift clutched within her hands.

Keane decided at that moment that he did not like being ignored for so very long and he gave his usual whimper of protest. Erik tried to convince his body to quiet as it would *not* be appropriate to enter a church in his current state of stimulation, and he was grateful that as he walked over to his son his body decided to cooperate.

Their boy was dressed warmly and Erik supposed that was the most pressing reason why he demanded attention. They kept him sufficiently dressed as their home was generally on the cool side, but Christine currently had him bundled for an excursion into the frost. "Soon, little Keane. As soon as your mamma is ready. We must be patient when our ladies take time to primp and dress."

Christine cleared her throat from the doorway and although she was attempting to look stern—apparently it was not yet time to teach their son the intricacies of living with women—he could still see that she was waiting for his approval. "Well?"

His mouth was dry and though he had been the one to select that particular fabric in memory of the silk gown she had worn when she had accompanied him to the theatre, he had not truly imagined it would look so comely. The contrast with her fair hair and eyes was still breathtaking, and his fingers itched to run over the fabric that was now accentuating her new curves to perfection.

"You are perfection itself."

And he meant it.

When she had first come to him she had been all skin and bones—an emaciated shell of her potential beauty. Under his care she had filled out some, obviously enough to support a child, although with little spare reserves. She had remained delicate even to the last of her pregnancy, but certain endowments had flourished under the increase of diet and womanly work and she now was simply breathtaking.

And she was his.

And he was hers.

And he did not mind so very much that such might be unfair to her, for she *loved* him.

He held out his hand, and as he suspected, the velvet skimming across her curves was exquisite to the senses, and he wondered how he would survive the walk to the church when *this* was pressed so tantalisingly against him.

It had not been very difficult to provide the seamstress with her new measurements. His eye for scale and dimension that was so useful for architecture was similar in principle, and evidently had proven accurate.

Christine had brought both of their cloaks with her and she waited patiently for him to bend slightly so she could secure his for him as he still held their boy in the crook of his arm. She tugged at his scarf a little until it was positioned to her satisfaction once more, then smiled at him shyly when she was finished. "Thank you for my dress. It feels heavenly."

Perhaps it was inappropriate right before they departed for a church, but he could not help but lean over and whispered in her hear, "*You* feel heavenly in your dress."

She blushed and he chuckled, and they departed.

They returned to the chapel from which they married, and even Erik was overcome by the feeling of warmth and fellowship that the Mass inspired. The entire sanctuary was aglow with candlelight, and as they slipped into the very back—to a darkened corner that none of the other parishioners seemed to favour—he decided this was not a dreadful way in which to spend Christmas Eve.

Not when his wife was pressed against him, singing cheerfully the carols of the season, and his son was in his arms and blinking at more people than he had ever seen in his short weeks of life.

And as Erik adjusted him slightly in the crook of his elbow to afford him a better view, he realised with an astonishing lucidity that he and his boy were both celebrating their very first Christmas.

All thanks to his Christine.

And though he would have been satisfied with what had been gifted to him already, when the song ended and they were seated, Christine leaned over to him and whispered, "When we get home I should like to issue in Christmas properly." Her hand strayed just a little bit onto his thigh and gave it a light squeeze, so there was little escaping her meaning.

"I have missed you."

The service could not end quickly enough.

XLII

There was a twofold reason that Erik hurried them away right as the service ended. The first was that he had neglected to put on his most concealing mask, and while a part of him doubted anyone would make too large a scene on Christmas Eve, he was not about to take any chances.

The second, and perhaps the more pressing, was that Christine's whisper still echoed through his mind with distracting resonance.

She *missed* him.

Erik was not certain why, but he had rather thought that a woman's appetite for her husband would have all but disappeared once the baby was born. That had certainly proven true for the first seven weeks, but he had thought it would continue on for much longer. He had visions of distressed husbands as they were shunned for months on end, and tearful wives who did not think their bodies were worth treasuring any longer once the marks of pregnancy had taken hold.

Erik did not think he had ever been so grateful for being mistaken.

Christine had only laughed at him softly when he had taken her hand during the final benediction and hurried their little family out of the heavy doors and back into the night air.

He had specifically ordered her dress to have a trimmer skirt than some of the more elaborate fashions of the present time. Erik liked to be close to her, and the last thing he desired was an impediment to that proximity.

The fact that he had not purchased a new cloak for her was a matter of great consideration. Very early into their relationship he had gone to a reputable cobbler and ordered a few pairs of shoes—slippers for when at home, and sturdier fare for the streets. But a cloak was another matter.

He had tried to be objective about whether or not he should procure her a new one, but selfishly he *liked* the way she was swathed in something of his. The shoulders were too big and she looked more a wraith than an actual woman when it was bundled about her so, but it was something of his all the same. But ladies did not usually wear black cashmere unless they were in mourning, and he wanted to be sensitive to her fancies—even if they disagreed with his.

So he had finally asked her outright.

She had shaken her head determinedly as soon as he had broached the subject. "I do not need something more feminine, I like yours." Her resolve faltered however when a thought crossed her mind. "Did you want it back? Is that why you ask?"

He had chuckled and taken her hand and pressed soothing little circles into her palm. "I wish for you to have everything you desire. If that meant a new winter cloak then that is what you should have."

But she did not and so even when he made his purchases for her birthday, a new cloak had not been among the orders.

He had been walking quickly, trying to get them home as quickly as possible when he finally felt a tug at his arm from Christine. "Erik, slow down please. You will tire me out before we even return!"

That was a rather horrifying thought.

His gate slowed immediately. "Forgive me. Would you like for me to carry you?" Supporting her weight would be little trouble for him and if it meant they could be secluded in their own little room all the faster...

She chuckled at his enthusiasm but shook her head. "No thank you, husband. I would just like to enjoy the night air with you before we are home."

Erik sighed and looked forlornly at the rest of the streets before them and the way the looming presence of the Opera House seemed so far away.

Calm.

He needed to be calm and have patience.

It would bring her no pleasure to have an overeager husband when they were trying to resume their intimacies. While he did not like to think about the specifics of what her body had undergone during childbirth, it was still his responsibility to be mindful.

So he tampered down his yearning to simply get home, and enjoyed the feel of his wife and son about him. Occasionally he had to tuck Keane's cap down more securely over his tiny ears as he was moving his head this way and that so as to better watch the snowflakes as they tried to attack him. His eyes were narrowed and it seemed that each and every chilly speck was bent on personally offending him—especially when one had the audacity to settle on his nose.

He gave a horrified cry that turned into a whimper and Erik brushed it away with the side of his cloak, deciding that perhaps it was better to just keep the boy within the confines of his outer garment so he could not be molested by the distasteful flurries.

Christine watched it all with a bright smile, and he realised just how right she was. Anticipation was a wonderful thing, especially when it meant enjoying each moment for its own sake.

They did finally manage to return home, and the flickers of desire and excitement flared to life once more.

Christine extracted Keane from his arms and instead of moving to their bedchamber, went to the nursery instead. "While I get him settled for the night, perhaps you could make some hot chocolate? I will meet you at the fire to warm up."

Her eyes sparkled with promise of *more,* and while he would be perfectly amiable to warm up by a different method entirely, a fire and a hot beverage while cuddled with his wife was an excellent diversion as well.

Just as long as there remained the possibility of *more.*

He nodded in agreement and went to put on the milk before returning to their room in order to prepare his own person for bed. If his wife was intent on lounging before they retired he would like to be comfortable, and he was wearing far too many layers to be able to appreciate her thoroughly.

Although he took excellent care of all of his things, he paid special attention to his new scarf, folding it attentively before tucking it into a small cedar lined drawer to ensure that nothing dreadful could befall it while it waited to be used once again.

And so bedecked in his nightly attire he returned to the kitchen and finished the preparations of the hot chocolate, and even went so far as to make a few slices of toast slathered in butter, just in case his lovely wife decided she wanted something to nibble—before hopefully allowing him to nibble upon *her.* He tried valiantly to keep such thoughts from appearing as it would do no good to allow for expectations to form that could sadly be unfulfilled. But when he thought back to her delicate hand on his thigh and her whispered words, it did not seem as if she intended to leave him wanting.

When everything was settled upon the tray he returned to the sitting room. She had wanted them to warm themselves before the fire, and in his wife's language that generally meant lounging upon the floor. He could refuse of course and set up their little midnight rendezvous on the settee, but that would not be in keeping with her request. And he did so wish to please her.

So with a begrudging sigh he placed the tray on the side table before divesting their furniture of cushions and spreading a generous amount of the coverlets and blanketry that had scattered themselves about his rooms. The last time they had lain so it was before the fateful night when he had taken her to the theatre. She had wanted to speak of names for their little one, and he could recognise now that he had been far more uncooperative than was necessary. Keane would not have known the difference if they had indeed referred to him as a girl before his birth—just so long as Erik made it perfectly clear to Christine that by no means was she ever to reveal such things in future.

That evening had ended in disaster, but this one would only hold sweet things, he was certain of it.

Satisfied that the nest he had made would prove sufficient for protecting them from the floor—even though Christine regularly insisted that his plush Persian rugs were adequate cushioning by themselves—Erik placed the tray upon the floor and lay down.

And he felt absolutely ridiculous.

It was one thing to do so when his wife was smiling at him and tugging her encouragements, but it was another thing entirely to *wait* for her in this way.

But before he could scold himself too thoroughly and rise to wait for her in his reading chair, she emerged from the doorway of their bedchamber.

The light was just so that he could plainly see that she was wearing nothing beneath the thin muslin of her shift. It outlined her every curve and for a moment he was wholly glad that he was already reclined, otherwise he felt certain he would have toppled by how breathtaking he found her. She had released her hair and it was loose and wild about her, and at her brief chuckle his eyes finally went to her face, a teasing smile gracing her features. "I am glad you approve, husband."

Feeling shy at being so easily caught at his gawking, he felt the colour rise and looked away completely, rearranging a few of the pillows self-consciously. "If you did not want your husband to look then you should have put on a dressing gown." Perhaps he was being a bit petulant but she did not have to *tease* him—not when they had been without physical intimacies for so long.

He was startled when he felt the sudden brush of her lips against his cheek as he had not heard her approach. She was kneeling beside him and her eyes were soft, as was her touch as she smoothed down wisps of his hair. "You need not be embarrassed. It pleases me to know that you still find me attractive."

Erik looked at her sardonically. "Was that ever in doubt?"

She shrugged and moved to her side of their makeshift *chaise lounge,* and it was very evident that such *had* been in doubt—at least by her.

But before he could press the matter she began pouring their hot chocolate into the awaiting cups, and she settled back into the pillows with a sigh of contentment. He watched with bemusement as she took one of the buttered slices of toast and swirled it around the cup, and she hummed in delight as she bit into the now sodden bread.

Trying to find a distraction from his tantalising wife he took a sip from his own cup, ignoring his toast completely. Just because he did not begrudge his wife the occasional crumb did not mean he would add to the problem himself.

He remembered his earlier resolution that he would enjoy each moment instead of focusing on his desire for the next, and in that way he found that lounging with his wife as they sipped and simply enjoyed being alone together was a very pleasing way to spend the night. They talked of Christine's lessons, and she assured him that her muscles had healed nicely and that more vigorous vocal demands would not be overly taxing—though she reminded him firmly that she would not be parting with her teaspoon of sugar and dash of cream in her morning tea.

When their hot chocolate was gone and everything returned to the tray, Christine rested with her head upon his chest. And Erik decided that he would be quite content to simply sleep here in the warmth of the fire with the comfort of his wife nestled beside him.

But then her fingers began to fiddle with his buttons and he could feel her fingertips as they found what little slivers of skin they could reach, and any thought of giving into the languid feeling fell away. She turned her head slightly so she could look at him, and her eyes were dark in the shadows of the room. "You will have to be gentle with me, Erik. I do not know if it will feel... different. But I would like to try."

It hurt somewhere deep inside of him that her voice was almost pleading—as if he would somehow turn from her and inform her that he had no interest in once more resuming their intimate relationship. So he took the hand that had stilled upon his chest and he kissed her palm. "I will be so gentle, my rose. You need not worry on that account."

Christine smiled at him then and stroked his cheek, and he noted that she was relieved. He knew it was not that she was truly concerned he would be boorish with her—he never was—but only she knew how her body felt as it still recuperated, and it was her mild way of communicating her need.

As he looked at her, Erik discovered that he did not know quite where to begin. He had tried to keep himself from imagining their interludes as it would only stir up desires that could not yet be fulfilled, and now as he found himself finally faced with the possibility, he felt lost.

When had they become such strangers?

He rolled his eyes to himself, knowing precisely what had transpired that made everything so different.

Erik did not resent his boy—*never*—but he was certainly a monumental change.

Christine huffed loudly and buried her head in his chest with a groan. "Why do I feel so awkward? We were so good at this before."

He allowed one of his hands to weave itself into her hair, and he massaged tenderly in comfort. Erik could not deny that some of his masculine pride swelled at her words, knowing that she had thought them *good* together. His only aim had ever been to please her, and to hear her give voice to her satisfaction—even in frustration—was gratifying.

He did not like her feeling *awkward.* This was to be a night of reconnection, and his Christine feeling uncomfortable and ill at ease would please neither of them. So with firm hands he grasped her waist and pulled at her until she straddled him, and with her eyes still wide at the sudden move, he reached up and coaxed her down for a kiss.

She sighed against him and her body turned to liquid and each muscle loosened as his hands plundered and massaged, reminding her that there was no cause to be uneasy when she was with him. He had missed her mouth—her welcoming mouth that reminded him first and foremost that she thought him a worthy husband.

Eventually however, she pulled away with a gasp, her hands travelling over his chest as his hands kneaded at her thighs. Her lip was firmly embedded between her teeth and she looked down at him shyly before climbing off of him entirely.

Erik did not realise how quickly he could feel abandoned, but that move alone was enough to leave an ache in his chest, and before he could stop them his hands were grasping at her for reassurance. He had forgotten how vulnerable he felt in these moments—how any seeming rejection could lead to hurt feelings and misunderstandings.

But she smiled and she tugged, and soon it was obvious that she wished for him to cover her with his frame. "I have missed you like this."

While their lovemaking had continued until late into her pregnancy, the positions available had been rather limited. Her growing womb had made this particular option impossible, and as he felt her small and delicate form beneath him, he decided that he revelled in this particular contact most of all.

Their kisses resumed, and his fingers found the ribbon of her chemise and began coaxing it down her body, Christine mewling her consent all the while as his fingertips and the ribbon itself tickled and teased as it descended. Her fingers made quick work of his buttons, and he was rather amused to find that particular skill had not waned, even by their prolonged abstinence.

They both gasped as he allowed his chest to settle upon hers, though he was careful to keep his full weight from crushing her. How he had missed the feel of her skin against his! Somehow her flesh felt even silkier than it had before, and he savoured the softness of her new curves as they brushed against his bony frame.

He broke away from her lips, determined to meet these new wonders for himself with more complete attentions.

His lips skimmed over the swell of her breasts, large and round from their new employments as nourishment for his son. He pressed only the softest of kisses to their peaks, worried that she would find it discomfiting for him to linger for any significant duration. He pressed downwards, his hands skimming over her sides until she squirmed. Erik glanced up at her as he reached her middle, and while he hoped she would be looking at him in naught but desire, instead he saw traces of trepidation and worry.

There was evidence to be sure. No matter how much balm she smoothed into her flesh, marks still managed to invade from where her skin had struggled to accommodate their growing boy. He kissed each of these in turn, much as he had done when she was still with child, pressing his love and adoration into her flesh with every pass of his lips. "You are so beautiful, my rose."

The scars from her past horrors had begun to fade and these would as well. But while those had been born of pain and fear, these had been the result of something wonderful.

She smiled at him, but even he could see the thinness to it that belied her remaining discontent. His hand spread more completely over her stomach, and he once again marvelled at how much larger he was than she. "I love you for your softness. I love you for your courage, and I love you for giving me my boy."

Christine hiccupped then, and he looked at her in alarm only to see tears in her eyes as her chest heaved in barely contained sobs. "I love you *so* much, Erik. For you love me as I am."

Silly girl. As if he could ever love her for anything less than her entire being.

He held her then as she soothed, and he was content to do so until she pulled him down for a kiss once more, and that time he allowed his fingers to seek out her most intimate places—carefully, and tenderly, watching her face anxiously so he could cease any ministrations that caused her pain.

She felt different he supposed, but no less wonderful. His wife was still silken and warm, and as she nodded her consent and he divested himself of the last of his clothing and oh so gently rediscovered her hidden depths, he felt the utter completeness of being with her wash over him once again.

There were frequent pauses as she asked for a moment to adjust to him, or even whispered for him not to thrust quite so deeply. And those he filled with kisses and other attentions that would distract and relax her as he whispered away the hints of a grimace that occasionally flittered across her features.

But when he allowed a hand to find the source of her greatest pleasure, stroking and coaxing until she whimpered in completion, he soon found his own.

After, when Christine once more lay across his chest and his hands were smoothing out what tangles his fingers had wrought in their passions, he noticed himself waiting to hear Keane's jealous protestations at his father's monopolisation of his mother. His covetous little boy.

But all was silent and the fire was warm and he still felt the lingering euphoria that could only originate from lying with his Christine, and soon husband and wife fell asleep.

XLIII

They were both awoken at the sound of Keane's distressed cry.

It was a rarity that he would actually *wail,* as his parents usually tended to whatever need or perceived annoyance proved troublesome before he had cause for such dramatics. But as Erik blinked awake and took in the dying embers of the fire and the slight twinge in his back that protested a night upon the sitting room floor—settee cushions or no— he realised that his son was also not accustomed to sleeping without either of his parents near.

The clock upon the mantle assured him that their boy had actually slept a very admirable length of time, and as Erik glanced down at his still naked wife surrounded by dishevelled blanketry, he could plainly see that this particular call was for nourishment.

She blinked up at him sleepily and stretched languidly, her arms held out partway for a babe that had not yet been retrieved. Christine blushed as she realised her mistake, habit being such that Keane was often handed to her immediately upon waking as Erik had long since been up and capable of handling any such upsets.

But Erik had slept the rest of the night away with his wife, and as he hurried to don his sleeping garments—he refused to hold his child in the nude—he followed his son's cries until he found him looking positively irritated at being left alone in his nursery for the first time since birth.

Whether or not Christine had intended for them to spend the evening in the sitting room, she had apparently planned on them having a night of privacy all the same. They had never discussed the possibility of marital relations while their child was in the room—infant or not—but he felt relieved that she seemed to be of the same mind as he. That was still their *baby,* and when he treasured his wife through physical intimacies, he most certainly did not want an audience.

"Hush now, Keane. Your papa did not forget you."

Despite his boy's hungry pleas, Erik did not feel proper in providing his wife a son to feed who was in the possession of a wet diaper. So before he had even tended to his own morning needs, Erik performed his fatherly duty of cleaning up his son—who protested vehemently all the while.

Christine had not even bothered to don her chemise when they finally emerged from the nursery, though she had pulled one of the coverlets to conceal her most private places. Erik supposed that she was merely being practical as she would have to expose her breasts immediately in any case, but as he caught sight of her shift a good distance from their little nest, he quickly amended his supposition.

His lazy beauty of a wife did not want to move from her encasement of pillows and blankets in order to retrieve any semblance of her modesty. Erik did not have any particular recollection of flinging it quite so far the night before, but he still felt amused that the bed he had constructed obviously pleased her so much that she did not wish to vacate it.

Keane did not settle until Christine pushed a rosy pink nipple into his mouth, and even then he still gave little hiccups of discontent between otherwise quiet sucklings.

His wife cuddled back into her mound of pillows with a sigh, and looked to her husband beseechingly. "Could you tend the fire?"

Erik sighed perhaps a bit dramatically before doing so, knowing perfectly well that he had no desire for either member of his little family to catch cold.

Christine shifted a little and her nose wrinkled. "We are going to have to do laundry today, husband. I had almost forgotten how messy...it... could be." He found her stuttering to be rather endearing, though he felt a modicum of embarrassment himself since it was *his* mess to which she referred.

He made no reply, knowing that to do so would only lead to more blushes from both parties.

Satisfied that for the moment his family had no immediate needs, he retired to the bath-room to see to his morning ablutions before dressing for the day. His wife might enjoy lounging about in naught but her skin, but *he* preferred the security of actual clothing.

But perhaps if he was as beautiful as she, he would not mind it so very much either.

Such thoughts did not have the same bitterness as they once did, and as he looked at the compartment of his wardrobe that held his masks, he decided against donning one—although he tucked one of the simplest into his pocket in case of emergency. While he was comfortable in his home and in showing his wife and son his face, it was still imperative to be prepared.

And as he entered the sitting room and heard a knock upon the door, he was grateful for his forethought.

Christine looked positively frightened, a surprisingly still nursing Keane clutched to her breast as her gaze flew to the door.

There was only one man who could possibly have known of the tunnel bypassing the lake.

And he actually had the impertinence to use it.

Erik donned his mask with a growl, casting a glance at Christine to see her huddling down in the covers with an expression of pure mortification on her face. Her movement had dislodged Keane and his tiny features scrunched in displeasure at his meal having fallen away. His greedy hand was already pinching at her breast, but his mother was too distracted to notice.

He threw open the door with a dramatic flourish, making their unexpected guest take a hurried step backward to avoid being struck by Erik's flamboyant display. "I believe you are to be on the *other* side of the lake, Daroga. I would then retrieve you when it was convenient." His eyes narrowed and in the dim light of the tunnel he knew they would glow menacingly. "And I assure you, it is *not* convenient."

The Persian's eyes flitted into the sitting room curiously before Erik moved to obstruct his view.

"That seemed a terrible hassle, especially when you should be with your wife and child. I would have come to meet your little one sooner but I was unwell and did not wish to spread any illnesses when a newborn was about."

They had not actually seen the man in over two months. Erik had made it perfectly plain that he was to keep away during Christine's final weeks as she was completely miserable on most days and was not at all suited for company or playing hostess. He begrudgingly acknowledged his gratitude that he had extended his absence to include sufficient time for them to adjust to their new addition, and Erik suspected that it was the man's personal experiences that gave him such prudence.

But that did not mean he should be on *this* side of the lake without invitation.

Erik eyed the man shrewdly, his gaze assessing for any outward signs of sickness that might still be visible on his person. He might not wholly resent the intrusion since apparently he was a *friend,* but he most certainly would not allow for any manner of disease to enter their home if at all preventable.

The Persian chuckled good-naturedly, holding his hands out in supplication. "I have been well for nearly a fortnight. I was not going to take any chances with your child."

Erik sniffed, but grabbed him by the arm firmly when he made to enter his home. The action was too late however, as the Daroga had already caught quite an eyeful of Christine, though to his credit he rapidly cast his gaze to the floor. "I beg your pardon, I did not mean to interrupt."

"Which is why you should have alerted the siren to your presence and I would have *collected* you."

It was only because Erik knew the man to be so faithful to the memory of his deceased wife that the jealous feelings did not overwhelm him. He still gave the man a shove backward and away from the entrance, and closed the door on him resolutely before turning to his wife. "Perhaps you would like to dress?"

She nodded furiously, and he felt a pang of guilt and sorrow that tears of mortification were pooling in her eyes. What was meant to be an easy morning of teasing glances and unhurried breakfasts had all but shattered due to their visitor. And he had been fool enough to open the door.

Keane had finally finished his own breakfast and was content enough to be given over to his father, although he did not appear to wholly appreciate his mother fussing over the bit of milk that clung to the corner of his mouth.

Christine refused to look at him, and as she bundled up one of the blankets as a makeshift covering before fleeing to the bedchamber to dress, Erik could not help but grab her shoulder gently and turn her to face him. "Please do not be angry with your husband, Christine. I should not have risked your exposure by opening the door."

She took a shuddering breath and still kept her eyes lowered to the floor. "I am not angry. It would have been terribly rude to keep him standing on our doorstep, and I do not object to his visits." Her voice lowered to such an extreme that he could barely make out the murmured words. "But I must have looked like such a trollop."

It was difficult to make her look at him when one arm was occupied with his fussy boy, but he still managed to coax up her chin with one long-fingered hand. He tried to temper his irritation and dismay, but he knew that he was still a bit too forceful. "Do not return to such dark thoughts, my wife. *He* was the one who intruded, and you are allowed to lounge about your home in whatever manner you see fit." He leaned down and placed his forehead upon hers as he felt the weight of her past demons hovering about them both. "Please do not mar what we shared with such judgments. Not when it was so beautiful."

She nodded then and he released her, hoping all the while that she would believe him. He watched her scurry off to their bedchamber with a heavy heart and tried to find comfort in the small smile she offered before she shut the door behind her.

Erik stalked toward the front door and opened it roughly. "My congratulations, Daroga, you have managed to make my wife feel like a wanton in her own home."

The Persian had the good grace to look chastened. "I will apologise to her at once if she will still see me. That was never my intention."

He still felt the overwhelming urge to *hit* something—or perhaps more realistically, strangle *someone*—but the man's contrition was genuine, and he would know better from now on than to ever come so close to Erik's home without first making his presence clearly stated.

Erik waved him in with a frustrated gesture and the Daroga entered mildly, apparently aware that he had trodden on his friend's generous nature. "You had a son then?"

He sniffed imperiously. "Obviously."

Erik truly looked at the Persian then, and he felt his lingering vexation wane. He was looking at Keane with such sadness, though the hints of a smile still tugged at his lips. This man had lost his entire family—now lived with only memory and pain with little hope of respite except in death. Erik had finally been granted the bliss of love and contentment, and it must be a painful thing to witness indeed.

Perhaps he had stayed away for so long not simply because of his sickness.

"Would you care to hold him?" It felt a very personal thing indeed to make such an offer. Except for Aida's brief touch on the day of his birth, Keane had never been held by anyone but his parents. And while a part of him wished to selfishly keep it that way—he had struggled and hurt enough over the years to deserve to hold firmly to his boy's attentions—he realised that somehow living with his Christine had softened him.

The Daroga swallowed thickly. "May I?"

Erik tampered down the retort that he would not have offered only to rescind it a moment later, and instead nodded his assent and allowed the man to seat himself in the reading chair—the only seat available with a cushion—and passed over his son.

"Hello, little one. What is your name?"

Keane stared up in him with a furrowed brow, evidently unconvinced about this new person staring down at him.

"His name is Keane. Keane Daaé."

He could not explain why but he suddenly felt nervous waiting for the man's reaction. Erik knew the importance of a name, and it was not to be mocked or ridiculed.

But the Persian merely smiled and allowed the little boy to grasp his finger in greeting. "It is very nice to make your acquaintance, M. Keane. You are a very handsome boy." The Daroga tore his eyes away for a moment to glance up at Erik, and he did not think he had ever seen quite that expression on his friend's face. "He truly is perfect. You have been blessed."

Erik did not know why this man's approval mattered. He already knew that his boy was perfect—he had known so since the day he entered the world. But to hear it spoken aloud, by someone who did not love him so completely and was therefore prone to bias...

It meant something.

And although he chastised himself greatly for it, he could feel a rather sizeable lump in his throat.

"Tea," he managed to choke out. "My wife has not had breakfast yet."

He looked at the man thoughtfully, trying to determine if he trusted him enough to leave his son in his care, even if it was only long enough to boil water.

The Daroga smiled at him ruefully. "I do remember how to hold a young one, Erik. He will be safe in my care."

Erik hesitated a moment longer but ultimately relented. He was quite certain the Persian knew that his life was forfeit if anything should befall his boy, and surely that would lead him to be on his best behaviour.

He turned to leave, but the sound of rustling made him pause. "I almost forgot. I was not certain if you would remember to celebrate Christmas with your lovely wife, so I thought I would bring you something special for breakfast."

He held out a small parcel, making no move to vacate the chair long enough to walk it over to his host.

Erik sighed dramatically and accepted it, feeling wary of whatever was kept inside. It was not like the Daroga to celebrate such holidays, and it was a testament to his fondness for Christine that he would take special notice of it for her sake.

The tea kettle set for warming, Erik opened the package slowly and suspiciously, lest anything nefarious be lurking inside.

Pastries.

And from the amount of them, the Daroga was awaiting an invitation to breakfast.

Impudent man.

They ranged in number and variety, and as Erik placed them all on a plate he found himself wondering at what had become of his life. It was a rarity that he ventured above to haunt the Opera and tend to the music. *Faust* had long since closed and they were on to other productions, all without his careful guidance and attention. His salary continued to be deposited each month, and while he did steal away to oversee *that* particular exchange, he almost felt guilty since he had offered little to deserve his consultant fee.

But he had a family that required funds, so he would tuck it away in his cloak all the same and hurry back down to his wife and son.

And he had no regrets.

Music had been his family when there had been none other, and while it would always hold a portion of his heart, it no longer was the only thing. His heart belonged to Christine and to the squirming boy that was now beginning to protest his position with the stranger who held him.

He would trade them for no other.

Erik strode back into the sitting room purposefully. "Pray tell, what are you doing to my son that is causing all this commotion?"

The answer of course was obvious. The Daroga simply had the audacity to be neither of the boy's parents, and Keane was protesting this fact quite thoroughly.

The Persian grimaced, and rose to surrender the infant to his father. "Apparently I am not as amusing as his progenitor."

Erik sniffed. "I would think not."

The door to their bedchamber suddenly opened, and a dressed yet demure Christine emerged.

The Daroga rose swiftly and made a slight bow. "Madame, please accept my humblest apologies. It was never my intention to intrude or cause you any embarrassment." He waited for her to look at him, and Erik noted with a small degree of amusement that he could be waiting a very long time. If Christine did not wish to look at something or someone, only the most tender of coaxing could bid her do so—and *that* would most certainly not be accomplished by anyone but himself.

But soon enough she glanced at their guest, a blush still gracing her cheeks. "You may be a new mother, little Christine, but you are also a newlywed. I remember what it was like to be young and in love once."

That was something Erik did not particularly want Christine to dwell upon.

Christine smiled softly and made a small dip of a curtsey herself, and Erik rolled his eyes at their formality. "I accept your apology, M. Daroga. But perhaps you should wait across the lake next time in case we are... indisposed." Her voice was quiet yet firm and the man had the decency to appear abashed.

"You have my word. I will not intrude so boorishly again."

Erik cleared his throat. "Our guest has brought you some pastries in apology, Christine. Would those interest you?"

Her eyes lit up instantly, and her gaze drifted to the dining room door. "Is there *frangipane*?"

Anxious to please the woman he had so mortified, the Persian quickly assured her. "I was not sure of your favourites so I purchased a variety, but yes, there is an almond." His eyes flickered to Erik. "Unless your husband ate it while he was preparing the tea.

The traitor.

Christine looked at her husband in dismay, and he narrowed his eyes warningly at their guest. "Do not make me regret allowing you to *live*, Daroga. You will not turn my wife against me."

Erik walked over to his wife and kissed her temple. "Your confection is quite safe, my rose."

Their breakfast was a merry affair, and Christine and Erik were both rather pleased with having company for Christmas—even if neither actually voiced their approval aloud. As soon as the pastries were gone and the teapot emptied the Persian took his leave, once more making assurances that their privacy would be respected in future.

Now that they were once more alone and their sitting room had been put to rights, Erik turned to his Christine. "I believe you had a gift for me."

He would not become a greedy man, but now that their day had quieted, he could acknowledge to himself that he quite liked receiving gifts when they were from his wife.

Her answering smile was bright and obviously pleased that he was so enthused, and after a quick trip into their room to fetch the package, she returned to his side upon the settee. "I hope you like it."

This parcel was smaller than the last, but he opened it just as carefully. She had made more use of her black yarn, and as he held it between his fingers he could not immediately ascertain its function. He looked at her imploringly for an answer, not wishing to appear a fool or hurt her feelings by his lack of recognition.

She laughed and he was relieved at the sound. "I thought you might appreciate a more masculine tea cosy."

He kissed her then, firmly and meaningfully, and decided as he covertly moved his present to the side table so he could make use of both of his hands, that he quite liked Christmas with his wife.

XLIV

Christine awoke the morning of her birthday with a smile on her face.

Erik had given her a whimpering boy a few hours before and then told her quite strictly that she was to go right back to sleep after he had breakfasted. She had smiled at him incredulously as *she* was the one who should be giving orders on this particular day, but the idea of sleeping the morning away with little care for anything else was a delicious one. So after Keane had been satisfied and Erik had whisked him away, she had curled back up into her mound of pillows and blankets and drifted back to sleep.

Now she felt utterly refreshed and decadent after having slept so long. The only thing that would have made the waking sweeter was if her husband was lying beside her, but she supposed the knowing he was up and caring for their boy was comfort enough.

She stretched languidly as she hummed in contentment, and was quite happy to see the door open a little and her husband peek inside. "Ah, the birthday maiden awakens. I shall fetch your tray."

Before she could protest and tell him that she would rather he come lie with her for a moment, he was gone. Deciding that she would coax him into bed with her by any means necessary, she rushed into the bath-room to take care of her morning needs before slipping back into bed. He obviously wished to keep her there, and she was not going to argue—but only if he would join her.

He returned a moment later, his eyes narrowing suspiciously and she knew he could tell she had moved. It was *good* he had noticed for she had hurriedly brushed and braided her hair so that she would look all the more comely for him.

"Your breakfast, my lady."

Erik placed a footed bed tray upon her lap, and she could not help the feeling of warmth and love that flooded her at the sight. There were pastries and a bit of omelette, as well as a steaming cup of tea that beckoned to her. But what touched her most was the lone rose that stood proudly in a vase, its fragrance drawing her to its petals most efficiently. "How did you find one? It is freezing outside!"

Her husband sniffed and looked very pleased with himself. "Your Erik has his ways. My rose must have a rose on her birthday."

She bit her lip to keep the tears at bay. He did so hate to see her cry, but this time it was solely *his* fault for the welling of her eyes for he was just so *wonderful*.

Christine was about to beg him to join her but there was a sharp and loud protestation from the sitting room that delayed her entreaty. Erik sighed and offered her a rueful smile. "It seems our boy wishes to see his mamma."

As soon as he returned with Keane she patted the bed beside her. She was not going to take even a bite until her little family was cuddled up with her. "Please join me."

He deposited their son at her side, and he smiled at her happily.

Christine firmly believed that Keane was a duplicate of Erik when he was young. The long limbs, the way his face would scrunch just *so* whenever some new stimulation was near, it was all too like his father. But his neediness was genuine, and what he hated most was to be away from either of his doting parents. He would submit to napping in his bassinet, but only if he found something particularly objectionable about his parent's arms—and while at times she thought it to be a trial, she found that she could not complain.

If that attribute was also similar to Erik, her heart hurt whenever she considered how much he had been neglected from such a base need. Touch and companionship were so important, and nothing on this earth would make her begrudge her little boy his desire to be held.

But for now he was content to smile and gurgle, nestled between his two parents.

Erik produced another teacup seemingly from nowhere and poured himself a cup. He was sprawled out atop the bedclothes, already fully dressed for the day. "Did you take Keane with you to abscond with my pastry?"

Her husband took a deliberate sip and poked at his boy's belly with a long finger. "He might have woken you if I had not, and you deserved to sleep in." He sniffed. "Besides, he must learn how to be stealthy."

Christine rolled her eyes, not finding it necessary to chastise her husband for teaching their infant the art of covertness. "Of course."

Erik peered at her from over his teacup, and he appeared almost doubtful. "Am I doing an adequate job for your birthday? I have never had a wife to pamper before."

With a tray on her lap and a baby between them she could not roll over to kiss his doubts away, so she instead reached over and took his hand in hers. "You are *so* good to me, Erik. I could not ask for a more perfect husband."

And it was true. He might not be handsome, but he was pleasing in every way that mattered. He squeezed her hand in thanks before pulling it to his lips so he could place a kiss upon her palm. "I am glad you think so. But if you do not begin eating your breakfast soon I shall be horribly insulted."

She laughed and did as she was bid, not wanting to waste the delicacies he had afforded her. Though she had consumed a *frangipane* a week ago at Christmas, she was all too ready to indulge in another. The sweet almond paste was pleasure itself upon her tongue, and she observed with amusement how Erik watched the flaky exterior tumble onto the tray below.

Her fastidious husband.

The omelette was also delicious, and she was grateful that he had been mindful of her appetite and kept it small.

When she had finally completed her meal he whisked away the tray, ignoring her protests and assurances that it would be fine waiting upon the floor as they continued to laze and lounge.

She was about to pout and perhaps have a bit of a sulk that he would not listen to her, but any such thoughts died away when he returned, arms laden with packages.

Christine had forbidden him from giving her any gifts on Christmas Day. It was her own whimsy that had made them celebrate to begin with, and she still felt slightly guilty for it when he had obviously taken such pains to prepare for her birthday. So instead she had consoled him with assurances that she did not want to take away from today's gifts, and he had finally relented with a wearied sigh.

But now, as he piled her presents about her, she realised that she could have opened any number of them a week ago and he still would have outdone himself.

"Erik, there are too many!"

Her husband rolled his eyes and straightened the one at her feet, apparently intent on creating a sarcophagus of gifts in which to enshroud his wife. "Nonsense. There will never be too many for my Christine."

He would not look at her and as he continued to fiddle and fuss, she realised just how vulnerable he was in that moment. Christine knew with certainty that his main priority in life was to please her, and he must be feeling awkward and unsure. It was her responsibility to accept his efforts with grace, not make objections that his overtures were too extreme.

She took his hand again and was grateful that he allowed her to draw him closer. "Thank you, Erik. For everything. I love you for your generosity, but I just want you to know that even if you did not provide all these things, I would love you no less. *You* and your attentions are a gift." She grasped his hand a little more firmly and her smile grew mischievous. "But I would never complain about you indulging me."

Some hidden tension seemed to ease from his shoulders, and he huffed good naturedly and mumbled about his greedy wife.

But when he moved to his rightful side of the bed and lay down once more, pulling Keane upon his chest so he could be all the closer to her, she did not mind his endearing name calling.

He had apparently arranged them in some kind of order, and for the next half an hour she was delighted by all kinds of gifts. There were some beautiful new hair combs that would allow for some of the more womanly fashions that could not be accomplished by pins alone. She blushed when she opened one package to discover not one, but *two* new chemises that where of the finest silk she had ever seen. They were almost completely transparent and had the most exquisite lace about the necks. And each was fastened with a small ribbon drawstring that would allow for easy removal.

She caught Erik smiling at her roguishly from the corner of her eye, and carefully tucked them back into the box.

Later.

There were other pretty trinkets that would make beautiful additions to her bedside table and other places about their home. It touched her quite a bit that he would allow such feminine figurines to grace their rooms, and she kissed his cheek for each one.

But what meant most to her was the very last one.

Feeling the need to tease her husband she made a very great show of trying to identify the item by touch alone, to which he rolled his eyes and huffed petulantly at her silly game. It felt like a book, and she immediately thought it was a compilation of his compositions. She had complained on many occasions that his works were treated unjustly scattered about as they were, but he merely informed her that they were all still residing within his mind so their written form served little purpose in any case.

She argued of course and he smiled at her indulgently, but obviously with little intention of ever taking more care with his work.

But it was not a book of compositions.

Christine should have known that her husband could draw. With all his other creative outlets it seemed only natural that he would also be perfectly capable of recreating the moments that meant so much to them throughout their marriage.

The first was a picture of them standing before the altar in the church. She in her blush coloured dress, and he looking so dashing in his cloak and formal attire. It was their first kiss, and she felt the remembered warmth upon her lips and the stirring of nervous anticipation that had kindled at his touch.

"Oh Erik, it is *beautiful.*"

This time it was he who rested his head upon her shoulder, and he tapped the page meaningfully. "There is more."

She was relieved that he had not drawn any of their more explicit moments, and instead had catalogued the sweet and tender happenings that had made her love him so very deeply. She saw how her stomach swelled, and it truly amazed her how much *attention* her husband paid to her in order to capture every detail so completely.

"The final entry is new."

Christine slowly turned the final page and her breath caught in her throat. There were many of her and Keane, but this one held particular significance. It was from Christmas morning while she was nursing him in the lovely nest that was still rumpled from their lovemaking. Her hair was tousled and wild, one breast nearly completely exposed while the other was hidden behind Keane's downy head. She was gazing down at her boy with such an expression of love and affection that it nearly overwhelmed her.

Erik shifted slightly against her shoulder, and she only barely was able to keep from staring at the page in rapt fascination in order to glance at him. "Does she look like a trollop to you?"

His voice was soft as was his touch when he reached out a fingertip to wipe away the quiet tears that fell, and she shook her head determinedly. "No. Not in the least. She looks like a wife and mother who is well loved."

He pressed a kiss upon her collarbone. "I sincerely hope she is. Her husband tries very hard to show his love in every way he can."

Abandoning the pretence, Christine turned so she could face him fully, careful not to disturb Keane in the process. "You have given me more than I could have ever dreamed of." She leaned over and kissed his lips soundly.

"And since it is my birthday, I forbid you from doubting it."

Erik looked at her solemnly for a long moment, and she willed him to accept her words for the truth they were. Finally his lips quirked and he made a flourishing gesture with his free hand. "As you wish, my lady."

Keane suddenly scowled in his sleep, and Erik patted his back comfortingly. Christine always wondered what her boy could possibly dream about as his world was mostly confined to their little underground home, but by the faces he made it did not always seem pleasant.

Maybe he dreamed that his mother was not always quite so quick to uncover a breast at his whim.

She reached over and brushed her fingers through his soft, fine hair and prayed fervently that his worries would remain so inconsequential for many years to come.

"And how should my rose like to spend the rest of her day?"

Christine gasped in mock surprise. "You mean my doting husband has not planned the entire day away?"

He hummed and fiddled with Keane's toes, making them scrunch up further into his little body. "I thought you might like to be able to contribute something in the endeavour of creating your perfect day."

Erik kept giving her unsuccessfully clandestine glances from the corner of his eye, obviously trying to reassure himself while keeping to her earlier declaration that he was to stop being so uncertain that he was pleasing her.

So instead she sank back into her pillows with a sigh and cuddled up against him, rubbing her leg against his as best she could while she was confined to the bedclothes and he was not. "I think I could grow used to being your lady and having you to do my bidding." Her tone was breathier than she had originally intended and even to her own ears it seemed almost... sultry.

And remembering how she had looked in his pictures, she did not feel the least bit sorry for it. She was a married woman and it was her prerogative whenever she wished to seduce her husband.

Perhaps it was a bit too early in the day to begin utilising her new chemises, but that did not mean she could not reveal some of her intentions for later in the evening.

Erik swallowed thickly, evidently aware of her suggestive tone. "I believe I have been your willing slave for almost a year now, Madame." He tried to sound droll, but there was a heat that entered his eyes that belied his tone. Perhaps at another time to hear him use the word *slave* would have seemed harsh, and she would have thought to ensure he did not truly feel she was taking advantage. But when he was looking at her like that, his eyes full of *wanting* and *needing*, she could find no cause to do so.

He had once told her that if she would but love him, she could do with him what she pleased.

And it pleased her that he be happy.

And in that moment, she did not doubt that he was so.

She kissed him then, because she could simply not bear to go any longer without feeling his cool lips against her own, though she found the position slightly awkward with a babe fast asleep on his chest. Regretfully she pulled away, stroking her son once more before climbing from the bed. Erik appeared rather forlorn at her departure, but *he* was the one trapped by Keane's sleep-warmed body, not she.

It was her birthday.

Since he could not occupy her most satisfactorily in their bed, she would luxuriate in the bath. "I am going to bathe, and then perhaps you would like to read to me for awhile. And then maybe we could sing."

Erik sighed but waved her away to her soak.

The rest of the day was lovely. There were more treats and pastries to be had, and she felt quite plump and decadent as she ate her own fill, while also ensuring that Erik indulged sufficiently as well. It was not nearly as rewarding to indulge by oneself, which she reminded him consistently throughout the day.

He had asked her if she would like to dine elsewhere, perhaps at one of the finer restaurants that Paris had to offer. She had hugged him for offering, but assured him that she was perfectly content to eat at home. Erik was visibly relieved at her answer, and she grasped him a little more firmly for the sacrifice he was willing to make should she desire it.

But she desired other things far more.

After their evening meal she had taken Keane into the nursery for his own supper, and tucked her already sleeping boy into his bassinet for the night.

She was both grateful and relieved at his cooperation as she wished to celebrate her first birthday as a wife properly.

And that required consummation with her husband.

Christine smiled at the thought.

Before she had gone to Keane's room she had changed into one of her new shifts, always finding it far more comfortable to nurse unencumbered by the extra fabric of her gowns. Now, as she entered her own chamber and saw the candlelit room and her husband in his own nightclothes waiting for her upon the bed, she was very grateful she had done so.

He was fiddling with the rose he had provided at breakfast, but his attention drifted to his wife standing in the doorway.

As it should.

The light from the lingering fire in the sitting room must have provided an ample view of the limpid state of her shift, and from the way her husband's eyes darkened, he must have been well pleased by his gift.

He swallowed and once more toyed with the stem of the rose, and she finally noticed that he had carefully removed each of the thorns. "What would you like to do now, my lady?"

She did not know from where the depths of her boldness came and even when the words were spoken she did not blush, nor did she falter. "I would like for my husband to ravish me."

Erik groaned at her words, obviously not displeased by her forwardness. And before she could even move to aid the process, he was striding toward her with a determined gate. She yelped quietly when he suddenly picked her up, and she prepared herself to be flung upon the bed. But ever her gentle husband, he softly lay her down atop the bedclothes before allowing his long frame to cover hers.

He hummed as he felt the silk of her chemise against his palm, and she released a hitched gasp as his long hand covered her breast through the fabric. "I find that I quite like your birthdays."

Slowly, oh so slowly, he undid the tiny bow that kept her covered, and while she waited for him to pull it off of her completely, he simply opened it to reveal both of her breasts to his view. Ever since their lovemaking on Christmas Eve, they had steadily begun to reengage in intimacy. Her breasts however had remained carefully limited in contact and attention, as she was partly worried that she would leak on him, and he was concerned that she would somehow be discomfited.

But when he took the rose still dangling in his fingertips and skimmed her rapidly heating flesh with its petals, she could not help but whimper at the delicious tickles and the ghost of contact that threatened to overwhelm her.

He languorously drifted the rose over the very tips, brushing lightly and almost teasingly. "And you, my rose? How do you like them?"

Not caring in the least that it would disrupt his little game she reached up and brought him down for a kiss, *needing* to feel the press of his chest against her as it grounded her within the moment.

"I like them very well, husband. Very well indeed."

And she also decided that she liked these chemises very well, for they inspired her husband to very thoroughly apply his attentions.

And when they finally slept, too exhausted for more than off-centred pats of affections as they nestled against one another, she felt meticulously sated and ravished.

She had never been quite so fond of birthdays.

XLV

Theirs was a quiet life. The Daroga visited them on occasion—slightly more often now that they had a baby boy to draw his affection, but not so much that they felt he was an intrusion. He minded their privacy quite well and always purposefully triggered one of the traps so that Erik could come and collect him on the other side of the lake should his visit be convenient. On more than one instance he had been left waiting, but he did not begrudge their lack of response.

When winter waned and spring began, both Erik and Christine were introduced to the joys of colic. No matter what they did or how comfortable they tried to make their boy, he would cry and whimper at all hours of the night, leading to *both* of his parents appearing haggard and harangued. But that too passed, much to the relief of all.

Keane was never a very cheerful baby. It was a delightful day when he released his first laugh, but it took quite a bit of coaxing in order to get him to repeat the action. He did like to smile, much to his parents' enjoyment, but mostly at his mother—which Erik understood perfectly. In general he was of a sombre disposition, and Erik and Christine could already tell he would be of a thoughtful nature. But it made his smiles and his laughter all the sweeter for its scarcity.

Their anniversary was celebrated in a befitting fashion. Erik had cooked them a delicious meal and they had feasted upon the lake. Keane was kept in his bassinet a safe distance away from the shore in case he wriggled too much, and he slept through most of their supper. The new Opera had yet to open, but Erik did manage to take all three of them up so they could spy on the rehearsals. Christine had been rather wary at first, but had soon lost herself in watching all of the scampering performers and very much enjoyed herself overall.

But both were in agreement that what was best was when they had tucked Keane back into bed and enjoyed the more intimate side of their marital union.

Erik had held her close when they were finished, running his hands through her curls as was his wont, his expression thoughtful. "I think we have made a mistake."

Christine turned to face him, already feeling the trepidation take hold. "What do you mean?"

He kissed her temple softly, and she could not help but relax, although she still waited for him to expound. "Christmas, your birthday and our anniversary are all within a month of one another. We should have spread it more evenly throughout the year so I might have something to look forward to."

She had wanted to smack him for worrying her, but found she could not—not when he was so sweet.

But now spring was giving way to summer and Keane had grown considerably. His favourite new trick was rolling about on the floor, and no matter how Erik tried to persuade him that such was not dignified nor appropriate, Keane continued to do so all the same.

Christine found her boy's newfound abilities to be highly amusing, and she was thoroughly grateful once more for Erik's plush carpets that would keep him safe and comfortable. The one thing she absolutely insisted upon was for a new screen to be fashioned for the fireplace. Even in the earliest days of summer when the heat became uncomfortable above, a fire was still necessary to ward off the chill of the underground. Erik created a very imposing structure that allowed for warmth to permeate the room and was quite attractive with its ironwork, but would ultimately keep their boy far away from danger.

But what thrilled Christine most was that Keane's eyes had steadily changed over the past months, and instead of the pale infant blue they had once been, they now appeared more like his father's. It was rather startling at first to see her husband's eyes peering back at her from her baby's round face, but that soon gave way to a comforting feeling that something of Erik's could be so readily seen in his features.

Unfortunately, they soon discovered that particular feature had an unexpected consequence.

Erik watched Christine ruefully as she strode about their home, dusting for the third time that morning, huffing all the while as she did so. He had grown used to these fits of restlessness, and he patiently waited for her to finally speak to him about what she required for distraction. It was not yet midday and it was rare that he ventured above at this time, but not entirely unheard of. Since Keane was born they had only emerged in the earliest morning hours and after dusk, though they all agreed it was far easier for Erik to simply procure supplies on his own. So their outings were confined to walks through empty parks and strolls through the sparsely populated streets.

But he waited for her to speak of her desire aloud, already mentally preparing himself for the tedious process of applying his full mask to his face. Whether a positive or not, he had grown used to not wearing a covering of any kind while in his home, and although his skin would never truly improve in appearance, it did at least in quality.

Finally she did so. She scooped up Keane after he had wriggled and rolled his way over to her, and she looked at Erik imploringly. "Might we go for a walk?"

He rose and kissed her cheek. "Of course. You need only ask."

She waited impatiently for him to prepare, and he felt a moment's resentment that this façade was necessary for him to be able to go above during the daylight hours. But that too past when he reminded himself firmly that he had to be grateful for the genius necessary to create such an apparatus, and that he had a family with which to spend the day.

Christine practically bounced along the tunnels, and on more than one occasion he had to take hold of her arm to keep her from abandoning him altogether. Even without a lantern she had become quite fluent in the twists and turns necessary to reach the entrance of the Rue Scribe, but that did not mean he wished for her to plod ahead of him.

Aside from his bout with colic, Keane was not prone to crying. He would whimper or perhaps even produce a whine of displeasure, but neither sound lasted overly long. So when Erik pushed open the door and the noonday sun blared bright and hot, they were unprepared for his full and despairing sobs.

Christine had been holding him at her hip and whatever excitement she had felt at being outdoors was quickly overshadowed with concern. Keane was trying to bury his face into her chest as he clutched at her bodice. Erik was used to the moment's adjustment that was necessary when going from blackness to daylight, and while it could be uncomfortable, it was not excessively painful.

Surely this would pass.

But Keane continued to wail and Christine turned to him pleadingly.

"Please, help him!"

Despite the warm weather Erik never felt comfortable leaving his home without a cloak. It housed his lasso and was therefore a necessary part of his attire, regardless of the weather. And now as he tucked his son into the garment and hid him as best he could from the offensive light, he was grateful for his fastidious and protective ways.

Erik's first impulse was to retreat back into the tunnel, but he did not know if this was simply a part of maturation, and if Keane was merely surprised by the change in brightness. But Christine was clutching at him and pulling him back to the doorway from whence they came, and he decided that they could discuss this matter further when their boy was not still whimpering his distress.

They did not speak on the way back through the tunnels, and Christine kept herself close to her husband while also keeping a comforting hand on Keane's back through the cloak.

He was still sniffling when they went through the front door, and he remained cuddled against Erik's chest as he sank down upon the settee.

Erik swallowed and allowed his fingers to stroke the soft hairs that had suddenly begun to become more plentiful. "He could simply have been startled. It does not mean that something is wrong." Even as he said it he could tell that he did not truly believe it. Keane was not one for dramatics, and he was more curious by new and exciting things than frightened.

Christine settled down beside him and he could practically feel her anxiety. "No. I think we did this."

Erik flinched and closed his eyes, clutching more fully to his boy that was grasping at his father's collar. Keane was perfect. Even if something proved to be wrong, he was their *boy* and he could not bear if Christine blamed him for some malady.

His wife took his hand and gave it a gentle squeeze, but he could find no comfort in it. Not now.

"We have been selfish, Erik. You and I tried to tell ourselves that we were thinking of him by remaining down here—that it was for his safety. But I think we were afraid to *try* living above. And now he is suffering for it."

Erik allowed his lips to skim over his son's forehead, the guilt eating at him painfully. "It is safe down here," he replied weakly.

Christine pressed against his side and gave his hand yet another squeeze in reassurance. "I know that. But we can be safe elsewhere because we will be together. And we have to decide how we want our boy to live. I am seventeen years of age and it still hurts my eyes to go above when it is sunny. I can only imagine how it is for him when he is still developing!"

She took a deep breath and reached to touch his cheek, looking dismayed that she could not actually come into contact with his flesh when this particular mask was in the way and she was unable to remove it. "We have to put him first, Erik. And I want for him to have choices in the world. If we remain down here he will not have them."

Erik wanted to growl that she was wrong. He should never have given her those books on childhood development or else she would not be insisting about such a thing. But she had wanted to know how Keane would grow and he being the foolishly indulgent husband that he was had offered her a variety of tomes of the subject.

But as he looked at his boy's huddled form and he remembered the cries of pain and discomfort that had issued from his tiny lungs, he knew that he would do absolutely anything for his son.

Anything.

But how could he agree to this when it would only put his family in danger? People could not have changed so very much in the decades since his childhood. A flimsy façade would not protect him from the stares and the questions—not when he had to live and work amongst them. Already his face felt irritated and uncomfortable from being so completely covered, and to have to *live* in this manner...

Anything.

How was he to keep them safe when his very *presence* could bring them to harm?

He tried to imagine leaving them. He would purchase a small cottage far away from the bustle and depravity of the city and allow Christine to raise their boy in the sunlight and the goodness of the country where he could flourish and grow unimpeded. He would continue to live in the underground, visiting them on occasion to bring supplies and see that they were safe and happy, while also keeping a careful distance so as to ensure he was capable of tearing himself away once more.

"Perhaps it would be better for you and Keane to live above. It would be a risk for me to be seen living with you as it would raise questions from any neighbours." His heart ached even as the words escaped him, but he had to do what was best for his family.

Erik did not expect to feel Christine tearing at his mask. Her hands were feverish as she scratched at it until it gave way and she could peel it away from his flesh, and she tried to soothe it as best she could with gentle fingertips even as she glared at him with such ferocity.

"You will *never* suggest such a thing *ever* again, Erik. Do you hear me? You think I could ever agree to rip out my own heart while you wither away down here alone?" She leaned back and looked at him with such anguish and disbelief that it sent another pang of guilt through him for even proposing it. "Do you doubt my love for you so completely?"

She was crying, and he had done that, and he felt ashamed that he had caused her such despair. "Christine..." He finally managed to tear one hand away from his boy so he could rest it upon her shoulder as he tried to offer comfort, but she lurched away violently.

"No, you do not get to say such things and then dismiss them as if they did not matter. Such thoughts should not even enter your mind! We are a *family,* Erik, and that means something to me even if it does not to you!"

He blinked at her incredulously, his own ire rising at her insinuation. "It is only *because* my family means so much to me that I would be willing to do so! I must keep you *safe,* Christine. You do not know what it was like for me to live above!"

Erik took a shuddering breath as he pushed down the memories of the taunts and the looks and even the stones that were thrown at him.

Devil. Demon. Abomination.

They were silent then aside from their mutual breathing. What were once harsh pants turned to calm breaths, and Erik could not help but shiver when he felt Christine's hand once more in his. "Let us start this conversation again, my husband. Our baby needs for his parent's to live aboveground. How can we accomplish this to all of our satisfactions?"

He glanced at her and while her indignation had apparently cooled, there was still a hardness about her shoulders and the tightness of her lips that told him quite clearly that she would not be moved.

And then he started to cry.

He did not mean to and he tried to stop the sobs from bubbling up from the depths of his soul but they would not be quelled. He clutched at her hand and at the small body still pressed upon his chest as he murmured his apologies. "I am sorry, my rose. So very sorry! Of course we should remain together, even if your poor Erik is to blame for our son's discomfort."

He brought her hand to his lips and peppered it in kisses, willing his contrition to seep into her skin and she would believe him.

"Oh, Erik," she sighed.

Christine moved closer and embraced him as best she could with an exhausted Keane slept upon him. "I do not *blame* you. We did not know that living here for so long would be problematic, and now that we do we shall remedy it. That is all we can ever hope to do. You told me once that we would make mistakes as parents and this was one of them."

She was looking at him so intently, and while her compassion was still evident, there was now a tinge of pain that flittered about her features. "But you must promise me that you will never speak of living apart ever again. I could not bear it, Erik. And Keane needs his father. I could not care for him all alone! And *you* keep us safe. Always. Not some cottage in the country."

The faith she placed in him was truly overwhelming, but her sincerity was so blatantly obvious that he could do nothing but trust her. He swallowed thickly and felt her brush away the remnants of his tears. "I promise, Christine."

She stared at him intently for a moment longer, evidently trying to judge his sincerity. Eventually she smiled faintly and kissed his cheek in comfort. "We are getting better, you and I. I know we are. We are allowed our little bumps in the road now and again."

Erik scoffed. "You do far better than I ever shall." Her bouts of memories and darkened thoughts were few and far between. And even when vivid reminders were set before her, she only needed to turn to him for comfort on the rarest of occasions. Her nightmares had all but desisted, and when they were at their most vulnerable during intimate relations, she hardly ever had to ask him to pause because some remembrance had shaken loose.

She shook her head. "It is not a competition." Her eyes darkened. "And you know very well the life I would still be living if you had not grown to love me."

He certainly did know of it, though it sent an ache through him to even think of it for a moment. "How could anyone not grow to love you? You are everything that is good and lovely."

Christine kissed him, softly and briefly, a mere brush of contact because she said he was sweet, and she settled down beside him once more.

"Let us think of this another way. Eventually there will be more babies," Erik's pulse quickened at the thought, "and if it is a girl, they cannot share a nursery." She turned to look at him. "At least... I do not think so. Do siblings share a nursery?"

Erik shrugged, grateful for the pleasant diversion, regardless of the fact that he felt a bit unprepared to be contemplating another addition so soon. "No daughter of mine is going to share a bedchamber with her brother."

Christine smiled and this time it was genuine and relaxed him. All he wanted was for her to be happy.

For both of his loves to be happy.

"Well, there we have it. I doubt I should like to move when I am pregnant, so we are merely making early preparations for our future." She rested her head against his shoulder, and he allowed his to rest upon hers. "So no feeling guilty. Either of us."

How easily she made such a pronouncement.

But she was his wife and even he could admit that the idea of finding a home that could suit all of their needs was a tantalising prospect. There would have to be many rooms. A parlour for his Christine, and a room entirely devoted to music—one with a door for those occasions when privacy was needed. There would have to be multiple bedchambers, for he most certainly was not about to forego relations with his wife unless she specifically requested it, and he would always welcome whatever babes she gifted him.

Even if he still had a lingering feeling of worry that they would not be quite as perfect as his wife deserved.

But he pushed away such thoughts for they were not justified, and discredited the loving nature of Christine and her ability to care for even him.

Deciding to play her game, he wrapped his arm around her and pulled her close. "We shall need a bedchamber that allows morning light through the windows. I quite think I should like to make love to you when your hair glistens in the sunshine."

He waited to see if she would be angry for his impudence, or perhaps disgusted that he would mention such a thing when he had been so foolish only moments before. But she merely sighed and nestled closer.

"That sounds lovely."

Indeed.

XLVI

Moving was a tedious process and Erik hated it.

Well, perhaps that was a bit harsh. But he hated how flustered and unhappy it seemed to make Christine, and that would always cause him equal distress. He tried to assure her that they could furnish their new home with whatever she desired to purchase, but she insisted that she was not about to leave Keane's baby things behind. Not when they were so very special.

Expediency was paramount, as while they could pretend they were moving for the sake of their future little ones that would require more space and beds of their own, it was never far from Erik's mind that the longer they waited, the more difficult it would be for Keane to adjust .

Never had he been more grateful for the Daroga's friendship as when he called upon the man to help him find a house. To his credit, he had not gloated when Erik painfully recounted the episode of taking their boy into the noonday sun, and instead he had shown nothing but sympathy.

"Of course I shall make enquiries for you. You three deserve somewhere special."

Erik had informed him that money was of little object and that the main focus should be on privacy and safety. The Persian had waved a dismissive hand. "Yes, yes. But do not remind me of your years of extortion. I know far too much about your less than savoury practices."

Perhaps he would have been more offended by the man's impudence except for the fact that he had come down to the lake the very next day with the details of a residence that seemed perfect for them.

It was just beyond the borders of Paris. Not so far that if he wished to continue his duties as Opera Ghost he could not do so—though the Daroga had glared at him when he had commented on that particular point.

They travelled by coach in the late evening, a sleepy Keane nestled in his mother's arms as they traversed the Paris streets. It was a château—one of the forgotten relics of the Revolution that had laid victim when its previous master had attempted to flee and had made a grisly end. At least, that is what the Persian had relayed from the solicitor.

The grounds were extensive and parts of the building would require widespread repairs, yet overall it was pleasing to behold. It was far smaller than many of the other grandiose structures that Erik had seen. The architecture itself was magnificent, but the relative size was not so large as to feel overpowering.

The last thing he wished was to purchase a home where he could not easily find Christine.

"What do you think, my rose? Would you prefer a small apartment in the city?"

He cringed even as he said it, but when Christine ran forward into his chest and waited none too patiently for his arms to enfold her and their son, his half-hearted worrying ceased. "I shall be a queen!"

Erik looked at her indignantly. "You have been a queen for quite some time, my lady. The entire Opera House has and forever shall be yours. Did you require a château to realise it?"

She nibbled her lip absently and then grinned at him impishly. "It certainly does not hurt."

He had rolled his eyes at her and kissed her soundly on the mouth for her impertinence, and then focused his attentions on precisely what would be necessary in order to ensure his lady would receive her manor.

As they were leaving however, something caught his eye. It was just a small catch in the middle of a dark wooden panel, and as he saw Christine cooing down at Keane about how many stars they could see when away from the Paris lights, he allowed himself a short investigation.

One press of the latch and a panel opened, showing a darkened tunnel beyond.

Perhaps this would prove an admirable home for him as well.

In less than a week it was theirs, and they would move as soon as they could pack up all of their essential belongings and the cottage was prepared. Christine appeared equally excited and devastated at the news. While he wanted her to enjoy her new abode, it still warmed his heart that she was truly so very fond of his underground achievement. "Some of my sweetest memories are here," she told him. "I know we must leave, but I will miss it."

It was satisfying that he was not alone. Knowing where they were to move was a blessing, and the fact that it was so secluded was a tremendous comfort. If he did not want visitors he had to but bar the gate and none could enter. The fence surrounding the property was high and had faced the test of time quite admirably—even if the interior of the home itself had not.

They had made arrangements to stay in one of the small cottages on the property that had not suffered quite so badly. It could do with a cleaning, and Erik had already employed a washerwoman to tend to it so that his wife could be spared the drudgery. They would remain there while the construction on the actual house was completed. Christine did not have to try to live in the midst of all the workmen and dust, and Keane would undoubtedly be annoyed at the constant disturbances.

Christine was currently repacking her trunk for the third time, fussing about every wrinkle and mussed skirt that would apparently be impossible to press later on.

Erik took her hand and considered dropping it once he received her glare, but pulled her gently to the sofa and sat down. "What has you so anxious, my Christine? You were so very excited earlier."

It was true. She had awoken full of life and energy and excitement for the move later that night. But as the day progressed her mood had darkened and Erik was nearly waiting for her to demand they cease the entire prospect of moving altogether.

Except they *had* to. That much was clear.

How it pained him when she cried! But she could not seem to stop as she flung herself into his arms and sobbed, her hands clutching at his lapel and mussing it.

Not that he would complain.

"Erik, I am *frightened.* You think I am healing well but I know that I am not! Every time I think about having all those workmen about and what could happen if you are called away and I am left alone with them..." She chewed at her lower lip to keep it from trembling, and he grew concerned that she would bite it off completely.

With a gentle hand he cupped her chin and tugged the abused lip from between her teeth and stroked it soothingly. He would like to have kissed it better but she was still crying and his heart felt heavy that she still should fear for her safety, even on their own property. "We have to leave, my rose, you know we must. They are building you a home worthy of your beauty, Christine. But I will not leave your side the entire time they are there if you should wish it."

She sniffled and shook her head. "I know you would not employ anyone... like... *that.*"

He would like to be able to promise he would not, and while he had chosen a reputable man to oversee the work, that made for no guarantees. Evil could dwell in the heart of any man, even when they had all the appearance of goodness.

But to speak such things to his wife would only upset her further, so he simply stroked her curls and filled her head with all of the wonderful things they had to look forward to. "Remember, my Christine. We are doing this for that future daughter you promised me. It would not do for her to share with her brother. And you shall have a cottage all of your own that is far away from any prying eyes." He kissed her temple, willing her to believe him. "You will be safe, *mon ange.*"

If she was not so obviously upset he might be insulted that not a week ago she had been the one to assure *him* of his capabilities as a protector. At one time his sensibilities might have been insulted that her opinion and confidence could be shattered so quickly, but some husbandly part of him understood. It was not truly about the workers. She was leaving all that was safe and familiar for the unknown. And if that prospect frightened him, surely it was distressing for her as well.

The Daroga knocked upon their bedchamber door, a fussy Keane in his arms. "I am sorry to interrupt but I believe this little one would like some supper before we depart."

Christine nodded and held out her arms for their boy, and Erik strode determinedly from the room with a slight push at the Persian to ensure she was afforded privacy. "She is nervous."

They had moved some of the furniture already to the cottage. Most of their possessions would be remaining down below—reassurance for both Erik and Christine that should the need arise to return to their sanctuary, it could easily be accomplished. But the heavily cushioned rocking chair that Erik had designed had been transported at Christine's insistence, and he was glad of it.

He could easily tell that she was pleased by his little gifts that he bestowed, but it still sent a thrill through him when she coveted them so jealously. He had reminded her that he could easily commission a new one, but she had glared at him fiercely. "I nurse our son in that chair, Erik. I will not leave everything behind."

He had not argued further.

While Keane nursed, Erik and the Persian took another trunk up to the waiting carriage. It had been *borrowed* from the stables of the Opera House as it would arouse fewer suspicions than to allow an unknown cab driver to watch them transport their luggage from the bowels of the theatre.

Dusk was already giving way to night, and the time to depart was quickly approaching. Their hope was that Keane would adjust more gently if he was allowed to awaken with the sun instead of thrusting him into more brightness than he had ever known, and it was passing his usual bedtime. A sleepy Keane was an unhappy Keane, and they certainly did not need the added strain of an exhausted little boy.

By the time they made it back down below his final evening meal was complete and he was already dosing in his mother's arms—who struggled between allowing her son to rest and needing to finish her third repacking.

"Will you finish? You are neater than I in any case."

Erik sniffed imperiously. "Quite true."

It pleased him that she finally made this allowance, not simply because he appreciated her acknowledgement that he took excellent care of his possessions, but because he was in fact far more capable of the meticulous folding necessary to ensure the least amount of creases in her more elaborate garments. She looked on in fascination, mumbling to herself about her wretch of a husband who surpassed her in skill at every turn.

He steadfastly ignored her, although he felt quite satisfied with himself when he managed to contain almost her entire wardrobe within the confines of the trunk, and he tried not to smirk *too* openly.

The Persian entered quickly and took up the final trunk, Erik's own wardrobe having been packed and readied that morning.

"Are you ready, my rose?"

Christine was still seated on the sofa and her eyes roamed over their bedchamber for what felt like the final time. They could always return—*would* return if life proved too dangerous for them above—but there was a finality that felt nearly overwhelming.

She was crying softly and adjusted Keane in her arms and kissed his forehead, reminding herself of why exactly they were leaving the home they both loved so much.

Erik thought he would feel worse about leaving. He had built this structure with his own two hands, and while he was leaving behind his most treasured instrument as the pipe organ could most certainly not be moved, he found that with the knowledge that the wellbeing of his wife and boy would only improve upon their relocation, he did not mind so very much.

He took her hand gently and helped her rise, pulling her into his embrace quickly. "We may return at any time, Christine. This need not be forever."

She sniffled and rested her head against his chest. "I want a bathtub just as large as this one. And a sitting room fire that is just as cheerful."

They made their way to the front door slowly, and when they were about to exit Christine gasped loudly and hurried backward. Erik grew concerned, but before he could enquire or even exclaim she was rushing back, her biscuit tin in one hand while Keane remained supported by the other.

"We will not change when we live aboveground, will we? You will still bake me sweet biscuits and help with our boy, and we will sing the afternoons away, will we not?"

He took the tin from her hand and returned her to his side, guiding her through their front door. "No matter where we are, we shall always be Erik and Christine." He leaned down to whisper in her ear. "Remember, we are doing this for our little ones, present and future."

She took a shuddering breath and held Keane a little more firmly.

"And a garden. Where perhaps you can grow roses." She looked up at him almost shyly, and he could not help but kiss her in the darkness of the tunnel.

"A rose for my rose."

The knowledge that the Daroga was waiting to drive them to their new home made him pull away, though it was barely enough incentive. Kissing her soothed the ache of her temporary unhappiness, and reminded him of the joy that only she could bring.

As long as they were together, all would be well.

"I will not miss the darkness."

She was huddled against him and he almost agreed, aside from the fact that he quite enjoyed the way she would cling to him—he had from the very first time he had taken her through these same passages. And while at the time he had warred with himself over such desires, he now found it tantalising and wonderful.

Christine must have had similar thoughts for she burrowed further still—quite a feat given her already close proximity. "Soon we will get to walk like this on our land. There will be noonday picnics and lounging in the sunshine." She giggled, and it warmed his heart to hear something besides her tears. "Perhaps we will not be so pale any longer!"

He grimaced, knowing that his sallow complexion would not give way simply because of exposure to the sun, but he remained quiet. Erik suspected that Christine could only grow more beautiful as her rosy skin would only be enhanced by the occasional stroll in the garden. "Perhaps, my

Christine. Perhaps."

The Persian was waiting for them when they finally emerged from the tunnels. "I suppose I should not complain that Erik will be forcing me to drive the carriage all alone in the night air."

Erik helped Christine into the carriage, ensuring she was settled properly before turning to glare at his friend. "You suppose rightly." And just because he was a foolish and impudent man, as soon as Erik was seated next to his wife he gave a rap upon the roof to signal his readiness for departure.

The Daroga's chuckle wafted freely from above.

The ride to their new home was pleasant enough. Erik never preferred carriages as the bumps and rumbling over the cobblestone streets could be jarring. Walking was far superior. He was in control of his movements, and any potential dangers could easily be circumvented.

But when Christine rested her head upon his shoulder and sighed deeply, he decided that this mode of transportation was not so very dreadful.

One of the benefits of travelling at this time of night was that few others were lingering about. The narrow streets were clear and so before long they were on the very outskirts, the large gate that guarded the entry to their new home standing proudly and ominously ahead of them. Christine had fallen asleep against him but stirred when the Persian hopped down to the gravel below so as to open the imposing obstacle.

The road to the cottage was even further than the château itself, and as Christine looked out at the moonlit grounds she eventually turned to her husband. "Who will care for all of the grass? It must be dreadful to maintain by oneself." It was true. What once must have been manicured lawns that would put any aristocratic manor to shame was now overgrown and shabby.

Erik shrugged. "I suppose we shall need to hire a flock of sheep to come and live with us. Should you like to be a shepherdess?"

She narrowed her eyes at him. "No eating any of the lambs from my flock. They will purely be for tending to the grass."

He placed a hand quickly over his heart. "You have my word, my lady."

Erik had never much cared for lamb in any case, so it was an easy promise to make. And he had absolutely no intention of slaughtering anything.

Perhaps it seemed hypocritical as he rarely had much issue dispensing with human life, but animals were far different. They were not capable of *evil.* Stupidity surely, but not evil. That was reserved for fallen man alone.

As they turned the final corner and their cottage came into view, Erik felt the first twinges of excitement. It was amazing what a few weeks and relatively unlimited funds could produce. These small structures had withstood the years of relative neglect quite well, but he was not about to move into a home that did not have running water. The Daroga had searched out the very same workers who were beginning on the château and informed them of precisely what the consequences would be if they could not finish the endeavour in the allotted time.

He might have hoped that Erik would never have gone through with that particular threat, but the workmen apparently had no desire to find out. The money was good and times were difficult and they were happy for the work.

Erik helped Christine down from the carriage and ushered her through their temporary front door.

It looked *homey.* There was a fire already going from the earlier trip to deliver some of the furniture and trunks. This time the sitting room had a sofa, not a settee, and it looked quite welcoming for long evenings when the cool summer breezes filtered through their new home. Christine's rocking chair was situated next to it, and Erik could easily picture her tending to their boy there. There was a kitchen with an attached dining area with far less formal a table than they were used to, but it would serve its function admirably.

There was no separate nursery for Keane and Erik tried to reassure himself that this would not in fact impede his sensibilities. For more *intimate* activities they could make do with the very inviting sofa, or simply use one of his other bassinets so he might sleep peacefully in the sitting room.

Christine was smiling as she took in every detail that made this feel more a home. Erik had made sure that a plush rug had been placed upon the floor, and as she made her way to their bedchamber she saw a similar one waiting there for her as well. It was lovely to see *windows* again, with drapery hanging on either side for those days when she wished to sleep in and forget that the sun existed for a little while longer.

"Will this do, my Christine? Until I finish your château?"

She settled Keane into his bassinet in their room and hurried to throw her arms about her husband. "It will do perfectly."

And after they had shooed the Daroga away—Christine thanking him profusely while Erik glared—they were able to put on their nightclothes and climb into their new bed with its same bounty of pillows and fall asleep beside one another.

Perhaps moving was not so very bad. Not when his wife and boy were still near.

XLVII

Erik awoke quite disoriented the next morning. Christine had reminded him the night before that it would defeat the entire purpose of moving if they sequestered themselves from the ensuing sunlight, so it was a bright and cheerful day that greeted him.

He wanted to go back underground.

It was dark there and comfortable, and the brightness this early seemed far too troublesome to be worth it.

But then he turned and saw the way the sunbeams looked as they settled in his wife's hair and the way her skin glowed, and he found that his mouth grew dry and his breath short.

She was *so* beautiful.

The previous night must have exhausted her as she continued to sleep even with the infernal daylight blaring down upon her. And as Erik glanced at their boy in his bassinet, he saw that he was not the only one awake.

Keane was looking about the room, obviously unsure of his surroundings. He was not yet demanding the attention of his parents but seemed content to peer about, his little brow furrowed as he took in the strange new room that would be his home for the next few months.

Erik rose quietly, pausing only briefly to ensure that Christine was not disturbed before he went over to his boy and murmured, "And what do you think, little one? Is daylight to your liking?" He had been out in this before but not very often. The test of course would be about midday and afternoon when the sun was highest, but for now Keane merely waved his arms, evidently tiring of being by himself and wanting his father's embrace.

He was only too happy to oblige.

By the time Keane's diaper had been changed and Erik's own needs tended to, Christine was blinking at them from the bed as they re-entered the room. "Good morning," she said sleepily.

She held out her arms expectantly for their boy, and Erik was briefly struck by the similarity to what Keane had done not so long ago. Both thoroughly expected him to comply whenever they utilised the action, and it truly did not occur to him to deny either of their wishes.

He wondered if he should be offended.

Keane happily went to his mother and impatiently tugged at her nightgown while Christine clumsily undid the bow and exposed a breast.

Erik sniffed. He was far more proficient at the action.

He kissed her forehead briefly. "I was going to take a short walk and see if the workers have arrived. Is there anything you require before I leave?"

Rather anxious to oversee the work at the château he hoped she would refuse, and thankfully she settled back into her mound of pillows and sighed. "No, thank you. We will have breakfast when you return."

He nodded because he knew it would please her, and after dressing quickly and donning one of his most simple masks, he departed.

Though she insisted that he eat more consistently, he never found that he relished the frequent necessity of *meal time.* He enjoyed being with her of course and he readily acknowledged that she needed meals throughout the day, but he had tried to explain that his body did not require nourishment as hers did. She was after all providing food for more than one person, but she had merely scoffed when he mentioned that particular aspect. "You are a man, Erik, like any other. And you have to eat. You do not want me to be lonely do you?"

As if he could ever argue when she looked at him that way.

Spring was once more giving way to summer but the morning was still cool and he found the open spaces of actual *land* to be delightful and refreshing. It would offer little cover should there be enemies about, but the lasso was still tucked into his cloak. And while he would always be vigilant, he could sense no impending danger.

The foreman was a competent enough man. Erik had followed him home one night and seen that he had a wife and five children of his own, so he was fairly confident that he would do all that was necessary to keep the craftsmanship consistent and on schedule.

They had agreed upon six months. Erik wanted the house ready for when winter came, as although he was certain the cottage would suit them well enough, there was something enticing about spending the holidays and winter months holed away in their new home. The sooner they began making their memories here, the sooner it would feel like theirs.

And Erik knew Christine needed that security, just as he did.

Marc was there, bright and early, ordering about his host of lads as they began the ground work for plumbing the house. They were beginning in the kitchen as it would to be the easiest to retrofit. Since the house was so old, there did not appear to be many bath-rooms actually established, and that would hurriedly be rectified.

His Christine wanted a tub as large and luxurious as their previous one, and he would most certainly oblige.

A few of the men stopped to look at their strange employer, obviously intrigued by the mask. If any had looked too long they would have been dismissed on the spot, but Marc had barked at them to continue working and all had promptly gone back to their tasks.

He appeared rather embarrassed and scratched at his neck awkwardly before addressing Erik. "Sorry, Monsieur. They're only curious. Please don't take offense."

Erik had half a mind to throttle the lot of them, but nodded his head stiffly. They would most likely not be so accommodating if the money had not been so good and the work so desperately needed.

However, he was satisfied that the work was being seen to properly, so he decided to do a bit more exploring of their new grounds. As he looked across the lawns he remembered Christine's enquiry. He had been partly jesting about the flock of sheep, but that seemed the most practical form of maintenance.

Erik ambled along one of the many overgrown paths, not at all appreciating that some of the weeds and grasses tugged at his trouser legs.

He would most assuredly be investing in sheep.

There was a walled structure that piqued his interest and he hastened to reach it, knowing that Christine would be waiting for him should he linger much more. Beyond the stone wall was a garden—wild and untamed, but a garden nonetheless. What caught his eye the most were the roses. He was no expert at flora, but he knew enough to know that these had been left to their own devices as they were lanky and far taller than the pruned and orderly bushes he was used to seeing.

But they blossomed all the same and he took out the small knife that tucked into one of his cloak pockets so nicely and cut a few for his wife. Though he knew he should hurry as it was cruel to deny his Christine breakfast for much longer, he took the time to strip the stems of their thorns, while also inspecting the petals for any insects. On the few occasions he had offered Christine a rose he had visions of her going to appreciate their scent and an arachnid or any other sort of frightening creature emerging from within, so it seemed a prudent measure.

Today he was glad of his precaution for a spider emerged from the depths of the rosebud, and he flicked it carefully back onto the plants where it belonged.

He did not wish the ugly beast ill, but he would not subject his lovely wife to it either.

Satisfied with his small bouquet he hurried back to their cottage, finding the morning air to be remarkably exhilarating. He had nearly forgotten how it felt to be outdoors in the country, and while he had always thought himself partial to the bustling and lively nature of a city—at least for short lengths of time—the open air had its own charms.

Christine was waiting for him in her rocking chair, Keane bouncing happily on her lap as she sang and giggled at him.

He stopped and looked at them for awhile from the doorway, marvelling that *this* awaited him in his home. But Christine soon caught sight of him and turned her attention away from their grinning little boy. "Oh Erik, those are beautiful!"

She rose quickly and held out their son to him, her greedy hands taking her flowers as soon as she was able. "Perhaps you will not have to plant my roses after all!"

He caught her about the middle and pulled her in for a kiss, finding that it had been far too long since he had felt her lips upon his own.

She blinked up at him dazedly when he finally released her, and it took her a moment to realise she still held the roses tightly in her grasp before she pouted at him for distracting her before scurrying off to the kitchen.

He followed at his own sedate pace, placing a squirming Keane on a blanket on the floor before watching in amusement as she rifled through the trunks and boxes looking for the lone vase that had accompanied them from their previous home. The new pipes groaned as they tried to do her bidding and fill the vase sufficiently, and she beamed at her husband triumphantly when it finally produced the water necessary. "You take such good care of me."

Erik was certain that Christine would have adjusted perfectly well to any home he provided and these modern conveniences were more his insistence than hers. After all, she would have grown up with the more traditional methods of outhouses and basins as her father was not a wealthy man.

But he came up behind her and wrapped her in his arms and kissed her temple, simply because he could, and whispered in her ear. "You are easy to spoil, my rose. And you are very beautiful in the daylight."

She blushed and nibbled at her lip and did her best to arrange her roses while still within her husband's embrace. "Are they working on our new house?"

Erik looked at her carefully, trying to judge if she enquired out of excitement or of fear that there were unknown men upon the property. She had not stiffened and the crimson of her cheeks remained, so he supposed she was merely trying to make conversation.

If she did not require breakfast he would have preferred to occupy her in *other* ways, but he sighed and pulled away.

His wife must be fed.

"It is. Marc seems a capable man and his workers respect him." That much was clear. A project only ran as smoothly as the foreman maintained, and Marc seemed a good sort that knew his men well.

Christine walked over to the kitchen table and placed the vase upon it, fiddling with an errant rose until it stood pleasingly with its brethren. "High praise indeed coming from you." She said this teasingly, but there was an undercurrent of relief that did not escape his notice.

She came forward purposefully and reached up to skim the corners of his mask. He rolled his eyes but removed it, knowing it was far easier to comply than to argue. Each of the workers had separately been warned by the Daroga that while the master would be on the premises at all times, but by no means were they to look for him. Marc was given the direction that if any problems arose, he was to come to the top of the small hill and wave, but he should most assuredly not approach any of the cottages littering the grounds.

Erik raised a challenging eyebrow. "Are you saying that your husband is difficult to please?"

His impudent wife hummed and stepped a bit closer, brushing her hands over his lapels. She glanced up at him coyly and her fingers delved and found little slivers of skin that made him shiver as she touched them. "No, not when you know how. And I like to think that I know how."

He tried to remind himself that he should make her tea and a bit of breakfast, but when she tilted her head just *so* he found his hands burying in her hair before he could stop them, and his lips descended upon her own welcoming pink mouth.

It was only Keane's impatient cries from the sitting room that tore them apart. It was just as well as Erik was already envisioning making use of their new larger table for purposes that most certainly did not include eating. They both were short of breath when Christine returned to the sitting room to see to their boy.

Erik took deep breaths as he tried to cool his body's reaction to his wife, and he set about locating their supplies for tea. That was yet another thing Christine had insisted was necessary. "I will not have our lovely tea things entombed," she had retorted when he had the audacity to suggest they buy something new.

How he loved her for her sentimentality.

In anticipation of Christine feeling a bit out of sorts about their relocation, Erik had ensured that some small treats were prepared and purchased for her breakfast. He had taken special care to keep them hidden away but now he located the parcel of muffins he had made the day before and heated them in their new range. There was no butter to be had and they would need to find the closest market in order to see to such supplies, and he hoped Christine would not be too disappointed. There were fresh fruits, and as he considered the rapidly warming morning, he felt rather discontented at the idea of tea.

His wife entered the kitchen looking rather disgruntled. "Your boy rolled under the sofa. Please tell him he must be more careful."

Erik raised his eyebrows before narrowing his eyes seriously at his unashamed boy. "That is very naughty, Keane. You must not worry your mamma."

He merely waved his arms about in response and giggled when Christine tickled and kissed. Apparently a mother's ire was easily assuaged.

Erik watched them both with amusement, and when their little fit ended he took his wife's hand gently. "Take a walk with me."

She looked up at him in surprise, eyeing the range thoughtfully. "But... breakfast!"

He rolled his eyes and returned to his preparations. "There are such things as picnics you know." He tried to keep his tone from sounding petulant and found that it was much easier to do so when Christine rubbed at his arm and stood on tiptoe, placing a kiss upon his cheek.

"Silly me. Of course I shall walk with you."

She worked at unearthing a basket while Erik carefully wrapped the now warmed muffins in napkins and selected the ripest fruits. He considered taking a knife so as to make the succulent peaches a bit more dignified for eating, but ultimately decided against it. There was something rather comfortable about sacrificing decorum on occasion, especially when one was about to eat out of doors.

"Success!"

Only his wife could seem so triumphant at locating a simple basket, but he applauded indulgently to which she offered a curtsey. And soon they had their little feast assembled, Christine stopping to collect the blanket Keane had been using upon the floor while Erik donned his mask yet again, and then they headed out the front door.

"Would you like to pick our direction, my lady?"

Christine was staring at Keane warily, as the sun steadily climbing higher even caused her to blink at the change in brightness. His brow was furrowed and he shut his eyes tightly before shoving his head into her arm, but made no other cries of protest so both his parents considered their first outing a relative success—and hopefully he would even grow to appreciate the outdoors once his eyes adjusted.

She sighed and gave him a reassuring pat before pointing, seemingly at random. "That way."

He was relieved that she had not selected the path toward their château, for while he would be happy to show her the progress that was already underway, he had no great desire to see if the workmen valued their jobs enough to keep their eyes away from his wife. It was one thing to ignore the master and his mysterious mask—it was something else entirely to disregard the mistress and her comely appearance.

Erik had never walked this part of the property, and there were a great many trees and what appeared to be a once cared for orchard. Early summer fruits were already beginning to ripen, and he was fairly certain that with pruning and some attention they could have regular provisions whenever they wished— at least while the weather held.

He allowed Christine to set the pace, and he found the stroll to be very pleasant. Keane eventually peeped out from his mother's arm once the shade of the trees proved sufficient, and he peered around curiously at the world about him.

In time they reached a clearing. Instead of the field he expected, there was a lake—a large willow hanging low, its branches nearly skimming the glistening water beneath it.

"Oh!"

He stopped, turning to his wife with concern. There were tears in her eyes as she looked at the water in astonishment. "We get to keep our lake after all."

His peculiar little wife picked such odd things that seemed to be of such great importance to her. But as she quickly handed him their boy and set about unfolding the blanket and promptly began unlacing her shoes, he quickly saw her intent. She cherished the things that held the sweetest memories. And apparently for her, she was going to miss those few occasions when he had sat with her upon the shore of their own private waterfront.

"Sit with me, Erik. Please."

Unlike the previous time, however, she had been wearing stockings, and Erik was treated to the alluring view of his wife's hands delving beneath her skirt as the gossamer silk rolled down her pale legs.

Minx.

He obeyed with only the slightest of sighs, and Christine held Keane on her lap as her toes dipped into the water.

"I do hope the temperature is more welcoming this time," he said dryly, amazed that once again a single word from his wife had him divesting his shoes outside the privacy of his home.

She sighed contentedly and wiggled her toes about. "It is glorious." To Erik's bemusement she held Keane so that his own tiny toes were also dangling within the water, and he squealed, kicking furiously in delight at this new experience.

Erik's own feet joined hers in the shallows, and unlike the rocky shore of his previous abode, this one was soft and squished pleasantly beneath his toes. "Must you insist on every male of your acquaintance indulging your need for dipping your appendages into lakes?"

Christine tossed her hair imperiously. "I will have you know that it is only the males whom I *love* that get to share in this particular act. You do not see me asking M. Daroga to participate."

Erik sniffed. "Certainly not."

And as they indulged in crumbly muffins and peaches so ripe the juices dribbled down their chins and hands until Erik could do nothing but taste his wife's mouth once more, simply to know if she would make the flavour all the sweeter, they decided that they liked their new home.

Even if Erik felt slightly abashed for displaying so much affection for his wife while his boy was present.

XLVIII

Life was good.

While they would have liked to have had a separate nursery for their boy, the cottage was a cosy retreat from the busyness at the château. Summer had come and gone, it was truly starting to resemble a liveable home. Christine had been thrilled when Erik had taken her to commission furnishings for her parlour, though she had insisted that their bedchamber was far more important. The day the bathtub was installed was an exciting one, and Erik had taken great pains to ensure that this one was even larger than the one previously enjoyed by them both.

Christine had marvelled at the size and grinned at him coyly when she had first seen it. "I believe this has certain implications, Monsieur. Whom do you expect will be bathing with you in such a large tub?"

He had pulled her close and nibbled at her ear, grateful that he had waited to show her until after the workmen had departed for the day. "My little minx of a wife, of course. Who else?"

But even more enthralling than the state of their new home was the milestones that Keane had reached. The many books they had read on the subject insisted that babies liked to crawl before even considering walking. Erik had wrinkled his nose at the prospect and very firmly informed his boy that such would not be necessary—not when it was such an undignified position.

And miraculously, Keane seemed to listen.

Ever since he had turned six months of age he had begun rolling about the floor. Some months later, he reached the wall and had hit it with a mild thump that sent his parents rushing toward him to check for injuries.

Instead he had looked at it thoughtfully and with the wobbliest of appendages, climbed up onto his two legs—which promptly collapsed beneath him.

Keane seemed quite startled that his attempt had landed him once more on the floor, and this time he was a bit steadier and more prepared for balancing against the wall as he took a wobbling step forward, his little hands still pushing against the wall for support.

Unable to contain herself any longer Christine had lurched forward and scooped him up into her arms, whispering her praises as she showered his face with kisses. He squirmed, obviously not understanding why his mother was impeding his new discovery, and Erik chuckled as he bid Christine release him. "I believe our boy was in the middle of something, my wife."

Wriggling determinedly, Keane looked directly at his mother and with an insistent voice declared, "Mum!"

Christine burst into tears.

Erik and Keane both looked at her with matching stares of bewilderment, and she eventually gave her boy one last squeeze before returning him to the floor. He still gazed at her oddly for a moment but returned his attention to his latest venture, toddling against the wall in a very determined fashion.

Christine turned to Erik and looked so heartbroken that he could not help but move closer to wrap her in his arms. "Why does this upset you so?"

She sniffled and did not wait for him to retrieve his handkerchief, but allowed her fingers to drift into his coat and find the hidden pocket that housed the square, and she dabbed at her eyes quite thoroughly.

Presumptuous wife.

"My baby is growing up."

He wanted to remind her that this was supposed to happen. Keane would learn to walk and talk and soon resemble more of a little person than a babe. But Christine was obviously upset at the prospect and so he soothed her as best he could with tender touches—while still keeping his eyes resolutely on his boy.

"He will still need you, Christine. At least until the next few months when he uncovers the hidden secret that walking does not in fact require a wall."

Evidently the last bit of attempted levity was unhelpful for Christine glared at him, though he saw a small glimmer of humour that gave him hope he had not completely failed in his attempt to comfort. "You will not like it either when he grows up and wants to move away."

Erik's eyes narrowed. "Why should he wish to do that?"

Christine resettled her head against his chest and they continued to watch their boy take tiny steps around the perimeter of the sitting room, falling occasionally but seemingly determined to reach some unknown destination.

"Life is passing so quickly." She finally turned to Erik and placed her hand upon his uncovered cheek until he tore his gaze away long enough to look at her. "You must promise that we will not take it for granted. We will appreciate every moment with our boy, even when it is hard."

He wanted to remind her of the difficulties they had faced when he was first born—the sleepless nights where she was near tears because she simply wanted to rest but he required so much nursing and care. There were also some *very* unpleasant episodes when he required changing. And then of course there was the dreadful stage of colic in which crying seemed to be the only thing that interested him.

And there were also those occasions when in the middle of his attempts to love his wife in more intimate ways, Keane would awaken and whimper and babble and not quite cry until one of his parents felt sorry enough for him and brought him to their bed for cuddles and attentions.

He treasured them all, even the most disagreeable because it meant he was alive and he needed them.

His boy.

"I promise, my rose."

She eventually nodded and gave him a gentle kiss on the cheek in thanks before going to the kitchen to tend to their evening meal. "Do not let him walk into the fire!"

Erik sighed and tried valiantly to keep his eyes from rolling. If they had sufficiently barricaded the hearth for when he was only capable of rolling, surely it would withstand his short little bouts of walking.

But he checked the screen all the same.

Another two months passed and Keane celebrated his first birthday. Erik had tried to explain to Christine that he would most likely not remember the event so gifts were unnecessary, but as usual she did not heed him.

"Then why do you refuse to allow him in our room when we are *occupied?*" From her tone and the significant glance there was little missing precisely what she referred to, and he sat a little straighter in indignation.

"I am merely taking precautions."

She huffed and shook her head, apparently annoyed by her husband's seemingly impossible standards. "At the very least we are making him something special to eat."

Erik looked at his wife suspiciously. "Are you certain you are not using this as an excuse for *you* to eat something delectable and *special*?"

Her hands went to her hips and she glared at him, and he knew that he was in fact correct. "I am not going to dignify that with a response."

Very correct.

On Keane's birthday there were muffins and biscuits and even a small Swedish cake that Christine had spent a copious amount of time perfecting. Erik had not had anything like it, and it contained the same marzipan that made her *frangipanes* so enticing.

If their boy received nothing else from his mother in terms of his features, he made up for it with their shared love of sweet things.

Erik was dismayed by the amount of crumbs Keane acquired through each of his birthday meals—although he supposed it was not so very different from his normal eating behaviour. When Keane began stealing items from his parent's plates and stuffing them into his mouth it became rather evident that he was ready to begin eating solid foods.

Christine had been a little upset when he had stopped nursing as frequently, but thankfully there were no tears to be had. She merely treasured their evening time all the more when they could still rest in their special chair.

Erik acquired some new toys for Keane as his contribution to the festivities. The wooden blocks in all different sizes would allow him to begin understanding geometric shapes and structural integrity as Erik showed him how to build all manner of objects. Keane watched with great interest, helping his papa with rapt attention, although Erik could not help but roll his eyes when his concentration finally waned and he found that knocking over the blocks proved equally amusing.

But in addition to his new building materials—and perhaps the most extravagant gift he received that day—was the intricately carved rocking horse that now adorned the corner of their sitting room.

Their boy looked in complete fascination for a long while before walking towards it slowly. Erik rather thought he would continue to be wary of the new object but instead, as soon as the little hands touched the smooth wood, Keane launched himself quite admirably onto the seat and wiggled and squirmed until his father, in an attempt to save his son's dignity, helped place him on it properly.

Keane was *delighted* by his gift. As Erik showed him how the wooden horse rocked and how to correctly hold the thin leather reins— to which Christine rolled her eyes as it seemed impossible that their small boy could remember such a thing—Keane laughed and showed more enthusiasm than either of his parents could have anticipated.

A week after their little celebration, Marc had appeared upon the hill, waving dutifully as he had been ordered if there were any troubles that required Erik's attention. He had hurried to don a mask and fasten his cloak before entering into the crisp November air, feeling anxious and excited all at once. Unless there were any unforeseen setbacks within the last few days, it was possible the foreman was coming to inform him of the completion of the château.

"Yes?"

Marc was not dressed nearly warmly enough for the upcoming winter, and Erik thought briefly of the scarf carefully packed away in his trunk that his wife had knitted for him last Christmas. Did not all wives see to their husbands as efficiently as his Christine?

The foreman gave a broad smile, barely concealing his pride. "I believe we have finished. Would you and the Madame like to see?"

Christine had rarely come into contact with the workmen. There truly was little need for it as Erik oversaw much of the renovations, and her input was mostly conducted with different shopkeepers as she ordered whatever furnishings she wished. But on occasion she had expressed a desire to see their home during the interim stages, and although she had been shy and visibly nervous, she had braved the strangers commendably.

Marc had been especially kind, and while at first Erik had been suspicious of his motivations, it seemed that he was merely a gentlemanly sort who saw her discomfort and tried to alleviate it as best he could.

So with that in mind, Erik returned to their cottage. "Is something wrong?"

Keane was standing at her side holding onto her skirts and he toddled forward determinedly when his father entered once more. "Papa!"

It always amazed him at the sheer enthusiasm of his son whenever Erik came home. His jaunts were always short, the longest being to the Opera House to collect his income and to deposit notes to the managers. On occasion he would also conduct some sort of mischief just to ensure they continued to remember him even though he no longer haunted their halls as frequently as he had in years past.

He scooped up his boy and gave him a welcoming tap on the nose and turned to his wife. "Marc believes that they have completed our home and wanted to know if you would like to come and see."

Christine's large smile and bouncing toes very clearly communicated her desire. "I shall fetch my cloak!"

He chuckled as she flew to their bedchamber and he watched her rifle through her trunk as she remembered that she would have to actually put on shoes and stockings in order to be able to walk outside. Erik was more than happy to stand and watch her as she raised her skirts and petticoats and fastened her garters, but she gave him a petulant glare that gave him pause. "Do not simply ogle, husband. Dress our boy!"

He gave her a mock salute that Keane tried to copy before he set about ensuring that their son was properly bundled. It was not *too* cold so he would not require more layers, but now that he insisted upon walking whenever possible, shoes were now becoming a necessary accoutrement. Like his mother he had no great fondness for the additional coverings, and he had a tendency to kick his legs about quite unhelpfully whenever his father attempted to place them on his feet.

"Keane," Erik said in his sternest voice. "You must be still or else I shall have to carry you the entire way. I will not have your toes freezing off because you want to run in the grass without shoes."

Perhaps he obeyed more because of the tone than the actual spoken words, but Keane's legs stilled and he was pliant enough when Erik fastened his small coat about him. The cap was another matter, but with a stern look that too also managed to stay on his head long enough for his father to be temporarily satisfied, though Erik was not foolish enough to think it would remain in place for long.

Everyone properly clothed and situated they vacated the cottage, walking swiftly toward Marc who was patiently waiting for his employer. "Madame, good morning! I hope I didn't disturb you, but I know my wife would not like to be kept waiting if she had a house waiting for her as nice as yours."

Christine blushed and huddled into Erik's side, glancing at him briefly. "My husband is very good to me."

Erik cleared his throat awkwardly, grateful and a bit embarrassed at her praise in front of another man. Perhaps it was rude but he was starting to feel anxious now that their home was potentially completed and he strode purposefully onward, allowing Marc to follow at his own pace. He was mindful of course of his wife beside him, and he had to pause on numerous occasions because Keane decided to squirm and fidget once the sheep came into view.

Their boy was fascinated by the fluffy creatures ever since the flock had first arrived. The Persian had proved useful once again when he made arrangements with a nearby farmer to allow some of his sheep to graze on the property, and in exchange Christine would be given skeins of wool when it came time for sheering.

The exterior of the house looked as imposing as it always had. They could not begin the landscaping until spring so it still resembled something out of a gothic novel rather than the cheerful home in which their children would be raised.

Marc held open the door and smiled at Christine encouragingly as she passed him. Her hand was firmly within Erik's and as she took in the new foyer she could not help but gasp. It was so *beautiful!* Far grander than she ever could have imagined, and each bit of wood and marble that comprised the décor seemed to sparkle with new life.

"My wife and a few of my workers wanted it nice and tidy for when you moved in proper. Your husband said you wouldn't be taking on any servants and it didn't seem right for a new mother to try to clean it all by herself."

Christine's first impulse was to hug the man, but she held herself back thinking it too bold and that her husband would not appreciate the gesture. So instead she offered her hand which he took with a welcome smile. "Thank your wife for me, please. It means a very great deal."

He nodded, bowing his head shyly before waving for them to explore the house. "I think you will be pleased."

Erik watched the interaction with his wife with narrowed eyes, but curiously, he did not feel threatened. This seemed more a step for her recovery than any indication that he might lose her, and so for a brief moment while he watched her extend her hand with barely a tremble, he felt *proud.* Proud that she was growing in confidence and that she truly did believe that not all men were intent upon doing her harm.

And so when he put Keane down so that he could toddle about his new home and tucked that same delicate hand into the bend of his arm, he felt quite contented.

Erik was not certain who was more excited about each room, their boy or Christine. She seemed delighted by the way the furnishings she had so carefully selected looked now that they were properly situated, while Keane would run as fast as his little legs would carry him, collapsing a few times on the Persian rugs that adorned every room.

Erik simply watched his little displays wryly. He was his mother's son, no matter how Christine tried to insist that he was the spitting replica of his father.

Erik was quite certain that he never behaved thusly, even at only twelve months of age.

But even with such thoughts, Erik loved the way his little family reacted to the house he had provided. He especially approved when Christine would see some small detail that while seemingly insignificant to anyone else, would cause her to *beam* at him and run back to his side to bestow a kiss. This was mostly done when little mementos from home were artfully arranged on side tables and mantle pieces.

"I am glad you left those horrid Scorpion and Grasshopper figurines behind. I never liked those quite as well as some of your other pieces."

Erik blinked at her, never thinking how disturbing it might seem for such gruesome creatures to adorn his previous mantle where his sensitive wife might be offended—especially given their hidden capabilities. "Our new home did not need such trifles."

Christine smiled and nodded and continued her explorations.

The parlour was all light colours and feminine features, and his Christine looked especially radiant as the morning sunshine poured generously through the front windows. For the first time Erik was to have a study, and as he saw the meticulous way the books had been dusted and returned to their proper order, he knew that he would be leaving Marc a significant amount of coins for that work alone. He had not asked any of them to do the cleaning—had truthfully intended to simply hire a washerwoman to come in before they moved—but it somehow touched him that his little wife, and possibly himself, could mean something to these workers for them to volunteer for such drudgery.

The small ballroom's floors shone with all the scrubbing and apparent wax that had been subjected to it, and Erik had visions of Christine and Keane in stockinged feet sliding about merrily, most likely wishing for him to join in their silliness before long.

He sniffed at the thought, but promised himself that he would indeed dance with his wife in that room before long.

While a château in terms of grandeur, it truly was not that large of a home. There were plenty of bedrooms for them to fill with little ones should the time come, and the few servant's quarters in the attics were perhaps wholly unnecessary, but as they wandered the gilded hallways it did not feel overly large and imposing.

It felt like home.

Especially when Erik opened the final room of the first floor and saw his new *pianoforte* standing proudly, waiting for him to finally coax forth its potential.

"Oh Erik, it is lovely!"

He had strung the piece himself. While he had gone to the most reputable musical store in the city, there was something wholly personal about communing so thoroughly with the instrument before playing. He knew its every eccentricity, and that would be critical if he should bring forth a masterpiece.

Which he most certainly would be.

Christine's fingers were gliding over the wood reverently, and her eyes glistened as she regarded him from his position in the doorway. "We will be happy here, Erik. Of that I have no doubt."

His ridiculous wife.

He would be happy anywhere as long as he was with her.

But before he could tell her precisely that, Keane came barrelling into his legs. "Papa!"

And his boy. Perhaps their little imp of a son was necessary as well.

XLIX

It soon became apparent from living in their much larger abode that they did not actually require the additional space. They were used to always being in one another's company, so the concept of closing doors and being a floor away was an odd one—to which they still had not become accustomed.

Christmas came and went along with Christine's eighteenth birthday, and both were thought to be highly satisfactory by all. The Persian had joined them once again for a Christmas morning breakfast, but this time it had been by invitation and he had waited patiently at the front door until Erik deemed he was ready to answer the beckoning knock.

Christine had rolled her eyes at him but let him be obstinate if he so chose.

Their anniversary was a special affair.

The Daroga had graciously offered his services as childminder, and while by no means was Erik prepared for him to take their boy all the way to his apartment in the heart of Paris, they did go to the cottage that still housed enough furniture to be comfortable for an evening.

"You are certain you are capable of tending to him?"

The Persian rolled his eyes dramatically. "Perfectly capable, though you offend me deeply by questioning my skills."

Erik sniffed in response.

Christine was surprised when he appeared the afternoon of their anniversary and had told her of Erik's plan. She looked rather alarmed, and although she blushed thoroughly while mentioning it, she felt it necessary to say all the same. "He still nurses in the evening. Will you... bring him back for it?"

The Daroga's eyes softened and he took her hand gently in reassurance. "We shall both be here when Keane informs me it is time. Do no fret, little Christine, he shall be perfectly well."

She felt rather unconvinced but when he promised they would stray no further than the cottage that had once been their temporary home, she relaxed slightly. She kissed her boy's forehead and though it tugged at her painfully when she watched the Persian take Keane's hand and allow him to set the very slow pace towards the cottage, she allowed it.

Because if her husband made these arrangements, he must have felt it important.

Erik drifted to her side and held her close. "Are you angry with me for wanting this evening for ourselves?"

His hands were on her hips and he was pressing soothing circles into her hipbones, which could have driven her to distraction if she was not still watching her boy walk across the grassy knoll. Away from her.

She took a deep breath and turned to her husband, trying her best to give him a smile. He frowned at her attempt and touched her cheek gently. "If you would like him to return then you had merely to say the word. I do not wish for you to be unhappy."

Christine shook her head determinedly. Their boy would be well cared for and she would see him in a few short hours.

And it was her anniversary with her husband, and he wished for her full attention. She would not begrudge him such a thing.

She put her arms around his neck and pulled, placing a kiss upon his lips. "I am not angry and I am not unhappy. I just was not prepared for that."

He eyed her warily, evidently trying to judge her sincerity before he eventually smirked and tugged at one of her errant curls playfully. "One is not generally prepared for a surprise."

Erik took her hand and brought her to the formal dining room. It was rarely used as they had become rather accustomed to the homey comfort of a kitchen table, but they still tried to occasionally partake of their evening meals in the formal setting. Erik insisted that Keane would grow up with proper table manners and he could only do so through example.

Christine thought it was sweet that he was so determined their boy become a gentleman, so she would dress in her nicest gowns and enter as regally as she could before sitting down to eat the food that she and her husband had prepared.

They were perhaps a little odd living in such a fine house without any servants, and while her husband had offered her a cook and a maid, she always declined.

This was her home and she liked making use of it to the fullest.

He had not given her time to dress, but as she took in the table before her, laden with candles and all of her favourites, she realised that this was not about solemnity. It was about appreciating one another through the mutual consumption of delightful goodies, and she was not about to argue.

It felt so wonderful to hold conversation together once more. While she would always treasure the way Keane could so wholly monopolise their attention with his childlike wonderment, it seemed quite adult and refreshing to hold conversation with her husband without interruption.

After they had eaten their fill, he stopped her when she began to clear the dishes, tucking her hand into his arm with a pat of encouragement. "The dishes can wait, my rose. There is something more important that I should like for us to do."

She tried to hide her look of disbelief as it was a rarity that Erik put off the common household chores for much of anything. On those days when he was utterly consumed with his new *piano* he would wave away thought of food or the like, and it would take a great deal of her more feminine enticements to distract him from his work.

With that in mind, she half assumed he would be leading her to their bedchamber. But instead, he opened the door to the unused ballroom.

It was beautiful.

The entire room was aglow with candlelight, and while before it seemed rather a wasteful space as the manor itself seemed too small for any large gathering, it now felt intimate and lovely. "Why did you..."

He twirled her around and brought her into his arms.

He looked a little bashful even when he did so, although she could easily see he tried to hide it. "I have never danced before, my Christine, but I rather thought I should like to try with you."

She nibbled her lip to keep the tears at bay. How did he expect for her to remain unaffected when he was just so *perfect*?

Her papa had taught her some of the more basic movements, telling her that someday she would marry a fine man and would go to all kinds of soirees in her fancy gowns that would shimmer when she glided across the dance floor.

She had laughed at him at the time and kissed his cheek as she promised that she only wished to dance with him, not some fine gentleman.

But now, as her Erik held her in his arms and began to sway ever so gently, she realised that she was precisely where she was always meant to be.

He hummed softly in her ear and she assumed it was one of his new compositions, and it touched her deeply that he might have written it for this moment alone.

Erik's natural grace soon overtook them both as he moved her along the ballroom. "I believe you may have deceived me, husband, for you are far too accomplished for a beginner."

He appeared almost relieved at her encouragement, and he gave an imperious sniff and bowed low, this particular set seemingly over. "I may have studied some in preparation. I would not wish to disappoint my bride."

She took his hand and squeezed it softly, willing him to fully appreciate her earnestness. "*Never* disappointed, Erik. You are more than I could have ever hoped for."

He looked down at her for a long moment and she was entirely unprepared for when he grasped her around her waist and pulled her in for a kiss. It was voracious and passionate, and just enough to leave her completely breathless. She worried that his arms would grow tired so she adjusted only enough to put her arms around his neck, rubbing at his soft hair as she did so. She attempted to be additionally helpful and wrap her legs about his waist, but was impeded by her skirt.

The effort however made him groan and eventually he released her, his eyes heated as he considered her. "I should like to take you upstairs now."

If he were any other man she would have suggested he take her here in the ballroom—beds or cushions forgotten. But her husband liked his comforts and he above all else liked *her* to be comfortable, so she reached up to press a final kiss upon his lips. "That sounds lovely."

She giggled as he scooped her into his arms, and the pace he set indicated that it was not for the romantic gesture but for the sole purpose that there was no possibility she could have mimicked his gait—not with her shorter legs and heavy skirt and petticoats.

Their bedroom was a mutual comingling of their tastes and styles. Erik had offered to allow her to design everything in their home save his music room, but Christine had been insistent that this would be a *shared* chamber and she desired his input. It was lighter and brighter than any room he had possessed previously, and the one stipulation his wife put upon him was that there was to be no black. "There is more to life than black, husband." When the shopkeeper briefly departed to select another book for them to peruse, Christine gently stroked his lapel. "And besides, I think your bride looks far better in white, do you not?"

How was he to argue when she looked at him with eyes full of intention?

So their bedchamber was both masculine and feminine. The bedstead was of dark mahogany, yet the draperies surrounding it were light and wispy—just like his minx of a wife.

But most of all, just as he had desired, the morning sunlight came through the large windows on the eastern side, and he liked to watch his beauty's hair shimmer as she blinked sleepily awake.

And on more than one occasion he had woken her with kisses as he pet her hair, simply because he could not help himself from touching her golden strands.

Carrying his bride up to their bed would always be a delight that he would treasure. Even now, as he hurried along the corridors impatiently, he relished her laughs and the way her soft body moulded to his. When she first came to him he thought she had looked like a more feminine version of him—all papery skin that seemed to be stretched too tightly across the unforgiving bones beneath. But now—now after he had plied her with proper foods and her own appetite had increased from the birth of their boy, she was all softness and curve and feminine beauty that appeared especially crafted just for his enjoyment.

And the pleasure he could provide *her* in turn for being so very lovely.

He growled at the latch, not for the first time missing his previous doors that opened at his whim. Christine laughed and reached up to place a kiss upon his cheek, her other hand opening the obstruction neatly as she did so. "Patience is a virtue, husband."

He glared and kissed her impudent mouth, striding over to the bedstead purposefully. Erik was always careful when he placed her upon the bed, but this time he released her with slightly more force, though he grew immediately wary as he did so. He hoped she would giggle at his enthusiasm and not grow fearful that he would become too impassioned and forget to see to her needs.

He did not receive a womanly titter, but instead a groan and he felt very worried indeed that he had been overly rash.

But then her hands were at his throat as she tugged at his cravat, undoing the tidy knot with determined fingers even as her mouth sought his and she brought him to cover her with his long, lean frame.

His little minx had become quite adept at undoing masculine clothing. A part of him might miss the shy fumbling of her timid and inexperienced fingers, but when her mouth departed from his so that she could kiss the slivers of flesh she uncovered, he could only moan and know unequivocally that he would not trade the intimacy they had forged for anything in the world.

Despite his hurried movements to get them to reach this precise position, he still took his time to savour the way she felt against his palms. Christine seemed more voracious than usual in her explorations of him, eventually pushing him onto his back so she could kiss and caress every inch of his chest that she could.

Before too long however they both grew too needful, and the knowledge that Keane could demand to return home loomed ever closer, but that made their joining no less pleasurable. There was something exciting about the possibility of interruption—one that would not mean leaving one another because their boy was crying or lonesome, because the Daroga would keep him sufficiently distracted until either Erik or Christine was decent enough to open the door.

After, when they lay in each other's arms, affectionate and languid yet both unwilling to move to put on their proper nightclothes for when their son and his minder returned, Christine rolled slightly so she could rest her head upon his chest and still look at him, her expression soft and satisfied. "Happy anniversary, my love. I want you to know that these have been the happiest two years of my life."

He brushed away some of the errant curls that always seemed to grow all the wilder after their lovemaking, and did his best to tuck them behind the shell of her ear. "I love you, my rose. Every day with you is the happiest I have ever known."

She placed a kiss over his heart and nestled all the more against him, and if he had not been so thoroughly sated he would have felt the stirrings of desire once more by her mere closeness.

But true to his word, the Persian could be heard knocking at the door. They both waited for a moment to see if he would simply enter, but he made good on his long ago promise to respect their privacy and waited.

"You may remain here if you wish. I shall simply collect our boy."

Christine shook her head firmly, rising quickly to don a shift and dressing gown. It would be obvious what their activities had contained as both were in their nightclothes, but while once she might have been mortified—and truthfully now still felt the twinges of embarrassment—she reminded herself firmly that the Daroga had once had a wife of his own and knew the importance of celebrating anniversaries.

"No, I would like to welcome him home properly. He should not feel as though we wish to be rid of him."

Erik gave her a curious glance and saw to his own attire, pulling a mask on his face last of all. It always bothered her slightly that he felt it necessary to wear one in the presence of his friend, but he gently explained that while he appreciated the Persian's friendship, they were not bound by the love that he shared with his family. Christine had sought to argue that surely he would not begrudge Erik being comfortable in his own home, but her husband would not be moved.

And so long as he removed it when they were once more alone, she did not find it imperative to argue too vehemently.

While she was very grateful for the private time she had been afforded with her Erik, now as she rushed down the stairs she felt a poignant pang of *need* to see her boy. In her haste to dress she had apparently grabbed one of Erik's dressing gowns, and on one of the final steps down to the foyer she tripped. She felt a moment's panic as her limbs got tangled and she clutched at the banister to keep from tumbling down to the unforgiving floor below.

But then a firm hand was at her elbow, keeping her steady as she found her footing, and Erik was glaring at either her or the garments she wore quite reproachfully. "I would appreciate if my wife did not tumble to her death on our anniversary." The words were biting and she nearly retorted that she did not trip purposefully, but his chest was heaving as evidently he had needed to rush forward in order to save her.

She had frightened him.

So instead she hugged him to her and she whispered her apologies into his sleeping shirt. "I will be more mindful of the stairs, Erik. I am sorry I worried you."

Another knock reminded them that there were people waiting for them at the door, and Christine suddenly felt horribly guilty that she made her boy wait out in the cold.

And she supposed M. Daroga.

Erik flung open the door and Christine crouched upon the floor and opened her arms in welcome to their little one. "My boy! Mummy missed you terribly! Did you enjoy your evening?"

Keane flung himself into his mother's arms and mumbled a quiet, "Yes," into her collarbone.

The Persian watched on wistfully. "He was very good. Your little fellow is quite a cook, but was getting anxious to return home." He smiled at the boy fondly.

Erik sniffed. "Of course he was." Christine gave him a glare, silently communicating that he should be kinder when the man had done them a favour, sacrificing his evening when he did not have to.

He sighed before nodding. "Thank you for your assistance, Daroga."

The man looked at their manner of dress pointedly, to which Erik rolled his eyes. "I hope we did not interrupt anything, but Keane was very clear about seeing the both of you." He appeared genuinely concerned that he had not managed to keep their boy occupied long enough for them to fully appreciate their evening, and though she blushed, Christine felt it necessary to set his mind at ease. "Your timing was perfect. Thank you so much for all you have done for us."

He shifted awkwardly at such praise, and he rubbed at his neck absently. "I will leave you to the rest of your night then." He nodded to Erik and gave Christine a smile. "Happy anniversary, little Christine. I am glad your husband understands the importance of remembering."

Erik had apparently had quite enough of the interruption and shut the door firmly—the Daroga's parting chuckles barely audible through the heavy wooden door.

Keane was still snuggled into her neck and Erik was hanging back, looking at them both with that same odd expression on his face. "Please remove your mask now. It should not be worn in our home."

He sighed but obliged her, tucking it into the pocket of his dressing gown.

She moved to take Keane up to the nursery, more cautious this time of the overly long garment she wore, but as she turned to ensure that her husband was following, he still held back slightly appearing rather petulant and empty.

Her silly husband.

"If you wanted to hold him all you had to do was say so."

Keane obligingly went to his father, his arms wrapping around Erik's neck tightly even as he buried his head into the crook.

"We would never get rid of you, Keane. I hope you know that."

Christine stopped on the upper stair and looked to her husband in astonishment, not truly thinking he would say something of that nature to their boy. He was barely conscious and she briefly wondered if he would even be awake enough to nurse, evidently the trek to and from the cottage a bit much for his little body.

"Papa," he sighed contentedly, and Erik closed his eyes as he held his boy to him.

"I love you, Keane. So much. Maybe even more than your mamma."

That earned him a glare and a huff as Christine walked to the nursery, her devious husband following behind her.

L

The kitchen of the château was obviously intended for a cook and a small gathering of servants to be able to eat within it comfortably. There was a large table with benches on either side, and Erik had found his wife there many times with their ever growing boy, knitting as bread baked or as their supper simmered in the heavy pots that she often asked him to lift for her.

His delicate little rose.

On this particular occasion it was a rainy day in April, and after he had taken Keane to the nursery for a long overdue nap, he began his search for his wife. When he had not found her in any of her usual haunts he made his way down the many stairs to the kitchen.

Christine was there, staring down at a seemingly untouched cup of tea. She swirled the contents about absently and did not even look up when he cleared his throat in the doorway. "Christine? Is something troubling you?"

She flinched sharply and his brow furrowed in concern. He approached her cautiously, each move carefully considered before he made it so that she would not startle any further. "You can tell your husband." He tried to keep his voice from quivering—to make his tone coaxing and soothing all at once so she could not help but unburden her mind to him—but even to his own ears he could hear the strain of worry.

Christine took in a deep breath and gave him a watery smile. "It is nothing. I am just being silly."

Erik sat down beside her on the bench, nearly afraid to touch her when she was so visibly upset.

"It is most certainly not *nothing* if it makes you cry." He reached over and felt her teacup, noting that it had gone cold long ago. Erik removed it from her grasp with a grimace. No wife of his was going to be subjected to tepid tea.

He refilled the kettle and allowed Christine to continue to brood while he waited for it to boil—which seemed to take entirely too long. Eventually however it finally bubbled and roiled and he was able to set a pot to steeping, carefully enfolding it in the black tea cosy his wife had so lovingly made for him.

Erik poured her a fresh cup and placed it before her, and tried to not grow more worried when all he received was a mumbled, "Thank you," her eyes not even lifting from her tea.

He sighed and sat down again, this time leaning in close. He would not touch her if she found it troublesome—Erik had long ago come to realise that such moments were not a direct slight towards him, but were a remnant of her painful past that required his sensitivity. But he could use his voice to coax many to do his bidding, and his wife was certainly no exception.

"Tell your Erik what is wrong. I cannot help you if you do not tell me." His words were soft and cajoling, and when she shivered he assumed they had their desired effect.

What he did not expect was the sob that followed. He blinked at her, entirely unprepared for her reaction. Despite her tears, she managed to finally stop looking at her now steaming tea and rested her head against his shoulder, and he tried to assure himself that this was at least a step toward communication.

He debated whether or not to put his arms around her when she was in such a strange mood, but as she continued to cry the familiar ache he felt in his very soul whenever she was distressed came back with a vengeance.

He pulled her into his arms and hummed softly, his hands pulling soothingly through her hair. "Please, Christine, what is wrong?"

She sniffled and once again her hands reached into his coat pocket in search of the handkerchief residing there. Perhaps it might seem presumptive of her—to take it before he could offer it freely—but he knew that she was merely being thoughtful. He did so like to keep his clothes tidy.

She wiped at her eyes and smoothed his shirt and coat, patting it gently. "I am sorry that I am being so dramatic about it. I just..." Christine took a deep breath and finally took a sip of tea. Erik took that as an excellent sign that she was returning to herself and would cease dwelling on whatever unpleasantness was causing her such trouble.

Erik stared at her purposefully, willing her to begin speaking plainly.

"You know that my courses have been... less than regular since Keane was born."

He braced himself, not at all prepared for *this* particular conversation.

Erik swallowed and nodded. "Yes." It was impossible to miss when his wife did experience her menses. She was weepy and despondent and then of course there were the awkward conversations when she had to explain that they could not indulge in any lovemaking until she was finished.

As if those words actually had to be spoken aloud.

"How am I to know if I am pregnant if they do not come consistently? And can I even *become* pregnant until then? What if I must stop nursing Keane completely in order to have another babe? Is that unfair to him? I am being selfish again."

All of this was said so rapidly that Erik could barely make out the words. Her hands trembled and the sheer agitation so clearly evident was nearly disturbing. She had not been like this when she awoke that morning. Everything had been perfectly pleasant. They had sat in the music room with Keane and she had sung a bit and listened to him play. Keane had been especially helpful when he decided it was time to sit upon his papa's lap and commence his first lesson.

He was far worse at listening to his teacher than Christine, and preferred instead to plunk his little uncoordinated fingers down on the keys in no particular order. Afterwards he had looked to his parents as though he had created the finest of masterpieces, and from the way Christine had gushed and cooed at him, it only cemented his notion.

Erik had sighed and kissed the top of his head, making future note of this first attempt and what subtle or blatant instructions were required when he was older. If his lessons with Christine had taught him anything, it was that patience and kindness were absolutely essential. Things did not necessarily come as easily to others as they did to him, and he could not begrudge them for it—at least, he could *attempt* to contain any frustration. He was not always successful.

However, when his boy had smiled up at him, obviously looking for his father's approval for his little performance, Erik could find no cause to withhold it. "You will make a very fine pianist someday, Keane."

But now his wife was in tears, this morning's happiness apparently forgotten.

He swallowed thickly, not at all sure of her desire. "Are you upset that you might be pregnant or that you might not be?"

She groaned and buried her head in her arms upon the table. "I do not know," came the muffled reply.

Erik hummed, understanding the conflicted feelings all too well. Ever since they had resumed their marital relations after Keane was born, now over a year ago, he had wondered when she would come to him with news of being with child. It had surprised him how long it had taken for any semblance of her courses to resume, but he did not particularly mind their absence—not when they made his wife so miserable.

"Would you like to go see Aida?"

Christine peeked up at him, her shoulders relaxing at his offer. "Yes, please."

Erik made no move to see to the preparations for travel. "How long have you felt this way? You cannot have worked yourself up so completely in the course of an hour."

She shook her head ashamedly, though to his relief she returned to her normal sitting position. She crept a little closer to him and leaned her head against his shoulder once more, even going so far as to pour him a cup of tea into the empty cup residing on the table.

He smiled at the care she showed him and pressed a kiss upon her temple in gratitude.

"I was so sure when I was pregnant with Keane. I have been wondering for a few months now, but half the time I still do not even feel like *me*—not really."

Erik glanced down at her in surprise. "What do you mean?"

She laughed incredulously and gestured over her body—the very body that he desired so absolutely and treasured so lovingly.

"When you took me in I was a skinny little slip of a girl. Then just when I was starting to look like *me* again, I was pregnant and my body changed, *so* much." She made another vague wave over the most prominent changes—her breasts and hips. While Erik thought them to be the womanly changes that he found so wholly enticing and desirable, he supposed he could understand that any significant transformation could be rather daunting.

But she was still being ridiculous.

"Christine, you were so young when we married. Most likely you were not even finished growing." He did not like to think about their ages—he, decades older while she was pure and sweet and perfect. And while he had avoided his reflection at all costs, especially during adolescence, he knew with certainty that many changes took place between the interim of childhood and full maturity.

He felt awful speaking of it as he had long since viewed her as far more than a simple child, but it seemed important to reiterate. "You are a woman now."

She laughed, and it made some of the pain he felt at her distress fade just a little by the mirthful resonance. "Yes, I am quite aware of that, but I thank you for the reminder all the same."

He felt embarrassed since apparently she did not in fact require him to speak such words, and this time he rose to see about preparing the carriage.

One of the most obvious necessities since their relocation was for Erik to acquire a horse and carriage. It was small, nothing overly large or ostentatious, but for those occasions when their business required going beyond the small shops and markets that made up the small town nearest them, another mode of transport beyond walking was mandatory.

Christine reached out and grabbed his arm. "Wait, Erik, please. I am sorry that I cannot express myself well. It is terribly unfair to you." She huffed and her hand crept to his wrist where she began rubbing at the hidden scars, seemingly as an aid to ordering her thoughts. It comforted Erik tremendously, and he wondered if that was perhaps her greater intention.

"I love our little family, Erik. But what if everything changes when we have another?"

So many thoughts flew through his mind. He wanted to snap at her that she should have voiced such concerns *before* they had consistently committed the act necessary for *begetting* babes if she was so unsure about it. He wanted to teasingly remind her that they had purchased this home with the idea of filling it with more small babes since he had refused to allow for his son to share his nursery.

But instead he found that he stiffened and it took a very great deal of effort to keep from moving his arm from her grasp. "Certainly it will change. It will always change. I had to grow used to being distracted from my music when we first married. We had to grow used to not being alone whenever we wished when Keane was born. But *I* was under the impression that we both agreed these sacrifices were worth it."

Christine took a step back, evidently stung by his words. "Of course it is worth it."

He did not know exactly why he felt so protective of the mere concept of another child.

But he did.

He loved Keane with his entire being, and to hear Christine even question that there would be anything but joy that could come from another of their little ones toddling about the house—

It hurt.

Because what the past two years had shown him was that he would do anything to protect his wife and children, and she seemed to question it.

"Erik, do not misunderstand me."

He shook his head, turning from her to vacate the room, but she held fast to his wrist. He could have easily dislodged her, but her touch was insistent and her grasp firm and it would have taken too fierce a motion to accomplish it—and even if his feelings had been bruised, he would not cause her that particular alarm.

She tugged once more and while he did not wish to sit, when she sighed and he saw the obvious worry and fear on her face he could do nothing but oblige her.

"What are you trying to say?"

Christine had yet to release her hold on his wrist, and for the first time in a long while her touch did nothing to soothe. His irritation was still too near and poignant now that he had heard her question whether another of their little ones could possibly disrupt their happiness.

"Please do not be angry with me for having reservations. You *know* I will love any of our babies, whenever they come. But I am allowed to have worries and you should assuage them, not censure me for the mere having of them."

He opened his mouth to retort that the ones she had yet stated were not truly worth fretting over, but as he took in her quivering lip and her pleading expression that so contrasted the firm resolve of her words, he realised that she was correct.

Whether or not her fears were justified, he was her husband. Being angry at her for the thoughts he had coaxed her into voicing would only keep her from speaking them in the future.

And he would know his Christine, even when he found her to be a ridiculous little wife.

Because she was his.

And he was hers.

With all the preposterous thoughts and demons that accompanied them.

And so he took a deep breath and embraced his wife. "Can you please... *try*... to not be so wary of another of our little ones? It hurts your Erik so."

She took his face in her hands and must have seen the wounds that she had not meant to inflict, and she pulled him forward until she could place a kiss on each of his cheeks, and one more on his lips just because she wished to.

"I told you, I am just being silly. We will go to Aida and she will set me to rights."

But their excursion had to be postponed since the rain did not relent and

Christine absolutely forbade Erik to drive the carriage when he would instantly be soaked through. He had protested of course as he truly did not mind a little wetness—not when it would set his wife's mind at ease, but his Christine would not give in.

The next morning proved bright and cheerful, much to Keane's chagrin. Though he no longer cried when faced with morning and midday sun, he never showed any particular fondness for it. He much preferred to be indoors, exploring anything and everything. At least, that was until Erik first showed him their new horse.

It was a gelding, tall and strong but mild in manner—of that Erik had been very clear. While Erik had experience with horses he was by no means an expert, and if this large beast was to be about his family he required that it be well behaved.

And Keane thought it was fascinating.

They did not allow him to stand near the feet as it seemed probable that such a large beast would not realise a small boy was trying to examine each of its appendages and might cause him harm. But Erik held him and allowed his son's tiny fingers to explore the velvety texture of the gelding's nose, and he relished the delighted squeal of surprise when the horse sniffled at Keane's palm.

And although he showed Keane the more appealing aspects of horsemanship, he had hired Marc's eldest son as a stable boy as he did not care for mucking out stalls himself.

Henri was a good lad, and was always cheerful about his work—which Erik could not even begin to understand given the drudgery, but he supposed he was grateful for it. He was there in the mornings as was usual, and was more than happy to help prepare the carriage. "You and the Madame going for a drive? Will you be gone long?"

It felt tremendously peculiar to hold conversations with someone so young, but Erik begrudgingly made an effort as practice for when Keane was able to do more than simply proclaim his parent's titles and the name of an occasional artefact. "We will return this afternoon, so I still expect you to be here in the morning."

Henri nodded and tipped his cap before trudging off to find his wheelbarrow and pitchfork to begin his work on the stall.

A part of Erik would have preferred that Christine and Keane remain in the interior of the carriage so they both could be more comfortable, but his wife insisted that she would much prefer to sit with her husband. "And besides, Keane would most likely hang out of the window for the entire journey as he tried to see everything that passes by."

That was true enough, and he was always glad to have his lady love beside him.

Christine had never asked to accompany him back into the heart of Paris, and he had never suggested it. She seemed to be quite content to remain in their new home and he was glad for it—even if he did feel a pang of longing for his companion while he wandered the Opera's tunnels.

"What if she is away for a birth?" His wife had been silent for a long while, as the job of wrangling Keane from tipping over the edge in his excitement to see some new and fascinating bit of nature proved more consuming than she had originally expected.

Erik rolled his eyes. "Then we shall return another day."

But Aida was indeed in, though she seemed quite surprised to see them. "Why, my most mysterious couple! What brings you to me on this fine morning?"

Her eyes drifted down to where Keane was clutching at Erik's trouser leg, noticing how he alternated between burying his head in the fabric and peeping up at the stranger. The midwife, far from insulted, laughed at his shyness and ushered them into her front room. "It is always good to see one of my successes looking so well. You made a very fine boy."

She gestured for them to sit and Erik placed their *fine* boy on his lap. "That we did."

Christine was seated next to him and they declined their hostess' offer of tea. "Aida, I was wondering about a second pregnancy."

The woman smiled knowingly and turned her gaze back to Keane. "He is about the right age for another. You have been the one to nurse him? And have your courses returned?"

Christine blushed. "That is why I came to you. Everything seems different and the few times when I thought they had come back there was little regularity."

Aida's eyes shifted to Erik. "You are a good man for listening to all of this. Most husbands would be waiting outside with the horse as it offends their sensibilities."

Christine took Erik's hand. "My husband is not like most men."

The midwife rose. "I am certain he isn't. But for this particular part I shall insist you wait here with your son. I would like to examine your wife and I doubt you would like your boy to be exposed to such a thing."

Erik was grateful for the mask that covered what he felt certain was evidence of his own embarrassment. "Indeed."

He had an idea of course of why privacy was requested. Midwifery required perusal and evaluation of the feminine organs and while it made him distinctly uncomfortable that someone other than himself would be examining *those* particular details of his wife, it was ultimately up to Christine to decide what would make her most comfortable. Apparently knowing for certain if she carried a new babe overcame her sense of modesty for she followed the woman to the back room where Keane had entered the world.

They returned a short while later, a teary looking Christine and a smiling Aida emerging through the doorway.

Erik rose to meet his wife with concern, and she curled into his side. "Congratulations, Monsieur. You are to be a father again, in about six month's time."

He looked down at Christine who still looked rather distressed. "But I have not been sick. I was terribly ill the first few months with Keane." Her hand strayed over her womb as it so often had when she was first with child. "Does that mean something is wrong?"

Aida smiled at her gently. "Every pregnancy is different, *mon amie.* From all I can tell your little one is growing quite nicely."

Christine started to sob, and as Erik held her he realised very clearly that perhaps that was her fear all along. If she was indeed pregnant she had not felt it—not like with Keane. Her upset in the kitchen must have stemmed from her worries that even if she had been with child, she thought she might not have been able to keep it.

His poor little wife.

And so with this new understanding he thanked Aida and gave her a few coins for her time, and then took his pregnant wife and boy home.

LI

This pregnancy was indeed different from her first. She had very little nausea—for which Erik was grateful. Any ache and pain seemed to cause him equal distress in sympathy, and she wondered if someday it would grow tiresome when he doted and made constant enquiry as to her condition, cringing at every declaration of discomfort. *She* was the one growing a new life inside of her after all, yet he sometimes acted as though every mention of a sore back made him feel it as well.

But for now she found it sweet when he fretted so.

Telling Keane of his impending new sibling was a challenge. He had little exposure to other children except for those occasional walks they took to the village for foodstuffs when other younglings milled about, clutching at their mother's skirts or fashioning all kinds of interesting toys out of sticks and other objects collected from the nearby woods.

Erik had wanted to explain it immediately upon hearing of her pregnancy, but Christine had reasoned with him that it would be far easier and more meaningful once she was actually showing. He was remarkably perceptive and only a month after her expectancy was confirmed, he had placed his little ear against his mother's womb and listened intently. She had begun feeling movements only the week before which had relieved much of her anxiety. If her little one could kick and stretch then surely they were alive and well—even if it already proved kinder than Keane had by allowing her to keep down her meals.

Keane frowned when he had felt a push against his cheek, grimacing and pulling away quickly.

Christine had laughed quietly and ruffled his soft brown hair. "Your mummy is going to have another baby. Should you like to have a brother or sister?"

They were sitting in the nursery, the first of what would eventually be two. Keane had long since forgone his bassinets, and Erik had commissioned a small bed to be made. It would be too short for when he became an older child as his limbs already seemed long for his age, but it made her feel better that he could not risk falling out of a larger bedstead.

Warily, he placed his ear upon the swell of her abdomen again, waiting for another bump that as of yet did not come. Unlike Keane who had seemed to enjoy nothing more than roiling about his mother's belly, this babe was far more docile. While she was only in her fourth month of pregnancy and it stood to reason that the stronger her baby grew the more pronounced the gestures would become within, yet so far she felt this child was not quite as sturdy as her son.

And because of that, she had secretly begun calling her newest little one Lotte.

She did not want to hear Erik's lecture that it would somehow insult their baby to be called by the improper name, so she kept it to herself. Even so, on those occasions when her husband had caught her whispering and humming to herself as she rubbed absently at their growing baby, she could sometimes tell from the narrowed eyes and the suspicious glances that he knew she had already named her.

But for now, her boy was still eyeing her womb suspiciously, obviously unsure about what having a sibling would entail.

Erik entered then, and from the way he scooped up his boy he had evidently been standing in the doorway for some time. He tucked him into his small bed, kissing his forehead before speaking. "Soon there is going to be another little person to love you, Keane. You will get to show them how to play the piano, and how to use your spoon properly," Erik leaned in close and his son watched in rapt attention. "And most importantly, how to pick up all of your toys."

Keane pouted, and Christine could not help but smile at how similar it appeared to some of the looks she had received from her husband. He did not like to speak overly much, and she had a sneaking suspicion that he would be one of the children she had read about who waited until their vocabulary had grown before contributing much in terms of conversation.

But Erik always managed to coax at least a word or two from him and when he hummed Keane's lullaby and ensured that the blankets were properly situated, Keane managed a mumbled, "Night, Papa," before falling asleep.

"Come along, Christine. Let us leave our boy to rest."

Even after knowing Erik for so long, it still startled her when he managed to whisper in her ear from across the room. It was a curious skill that she had asked him about on multiple occasions, but he had only sniffed and waved his hand dismissively. "Your husband has many talents, my Christine. Some of them should perhaps remain mysterious."

Infuriating man.

He took her hand and led her down the stairs to the study. That had become a favourite of theirs for sitting in the evenings as the dark woods and the surrounding books gave it a cosy feel that reminded both of them of their underground home. There were fewer windows and even though spring was burgeoning on summer, a small fire still managed to be pleasant in the hearth.

There was a large leather sofa that was also a tempting reason to select this particular room as a favourite, especially when Christine added her customary blanketry. Erik had sighed of course when she threw a few over each arm, but when she had then proceeded to cuddle with him underneath the copious amount of fabric, her hands straying to decidedly inappropriate places, he relented that perhaps there was something quite nice about their arrangement.

But for now he was content to simply lounge with her, and she sank upon the sofa with a tired sigh. "Charlotte," he said.

Christine blinked, her eyes perfectly happy to droop as she used her husband for both a *chaise* and a pillow, but at the name she forced herself to alertness. "Pardon?"

Erik moved his arm so that she could more fully rest against him, wrapping it about her shoulders. "Our little Lotte. While I have no objection to the name, I do think it important that she have a bit of her own. Do you agree?"

She shifted to look up at him, hopeful that he would allow her to name the baby so early—even when they could not be completely certain of the sex for another five months. "Truly? You do not mind?"

Erik sighed mockingly, tugging at her curls playfully. "Would I allow a child of mine to be given a stupid name? Please, be reasonable, wife."

Her answering smile was bright and while he was slightly horrified by the delighted squeal she emitted, he was quickly distracted when she pulled him close and kissed him. Erik sincerely wondered if his beauty had a penchant for blankets of all sorts, because she did so insist on using him like one. He worried that she would become despondent when her pregnancy disallowed him to cover her so fully, as it seemed whenever possible she liked to tug at him until his frame covered her own.

He had questioned her on it before and she had always blushed and glanced away from him, fiddling with whatever was most convenient. "It makes me feel safe when you are above me. No one could find me or do me harm because you are there." And then she had looked at him coyly and pouted with her delectable lower lip that taunted him so when she did that and whispered, "Do you not like it?"

Just as he was doing now he had kissed her fiercely, her eager hands and mouth communicating what words could only attempt to relay.

Despite Christine's seemingly easier pregnancy, Erik was not so certain she was any less miserable. Before she had been able to wait out the hot summers underground, cocooned in her blankets whenever she desired and free to shun any notion of going outside unless it was night and a cool breeze promised relief from the heat.

Their château offered no such respite.

By mid July she was near tears.

"I am moving into the wine cellar," she declared that afternoon. She had begun refusing to wear any of her maternity gowns that were not made of the thinnest of linens, and on most days it seemed even a chemise was unbearable.

Erik of course did not mind this so very much, though he did try to insist she stay away from the windows lest Henri catch too intimate a view of her lovely body. This perhaps was a bit unnecessary as she had taken to closing all of the draperies in their home so as to block as much of the sun as possible.

"Christine, you are not moving to the cellar."

He had meant the words to convey that no wife of his was going to be subjected to an unfurnished cellar. His original thought had been to forbid her from any cellar at all, but he appreciated just how hypocritical that would be. They had lived quite comfortably in their previous home, and as she fanned herself with the fine lace fan he had procured for her, he realised how much she must miss it.

She glared at him, apparently dissatisfied with his proclamation. "I believe you think I am jesting, Erik. I can assure you I am not."

He grimaced at her tone, but decided that it was far better to offer distraction than to reason with her.

He rose from his chair in the study and held out his hand to her. She eyed it suspiciously, her gaze flitting between his proffered hand and his face. "I am far too uncomfortable for lovemaking if that is what you intend to do with me."

Perhaps his masculine pride should have been offended by her very blatant rebuff, but he merely rolled his eyes and made a sweeping bow. "I can assure you, I merely wish to offer relief."

She stared at him a moment longer but eventually sighed and took his hand, and he led her miserable form from the room.

His first thought was to the walk to the nursery to locate Keane, only to find him curiously occupying himself in the hallway outside the study. He brought all of his blocks from the nursery and was attempting to construct some sort of bridge. "Come along, Keane, we are going to make your mother cool."

At first he looked ready to protest as his project was apparently unfinished, but Erik picked him up and tickled him until his blocks were promptly forgotten and he was amiable to follow his parents.

It was late enough in the day that Henri would have already returned home, so Erik did not feel it necessary to ask Christine to put on more clothing than she already wore. She glared at him fiercely when he led her to the front door and gestured for her to exit.

He sighed, though he tamped down his own irritation. Not wishing to upset her by coming too close when she was already feeling cramped and uncomfortable, he allowed his voice to carry to her ear and whisper softly, "Trust your Erik, my rose. I shall make it better."

She shivered and this time relented as he led her outside. The sheep that so dutifully kept the grounds properly razed also appeared to dislike the heat. They clustered under the shade of the many trees, languid and uncaring when the family passed by.

Once they reached the path to the orchard Christine's spirits rose, both because the sun overhead was now occluded, and also because she knew their ultimate destination. Her pace quickened and Erik chuckled as Keane's legs kicked excitedly against him as he was carried, sensing his mother's enthusiasm.

The lake was peaceful and serene, only the slimmest rays of light managing to find their way through the large canopy of shade the trees provided.

Christine positively *beamed* at him, kissing his cheek before abandoning him for the sake of the beckoning water.

He smiled as he watched her wade into the depths, and he was comforted knowing that there were no traps at the bottom that would swallow her hole should she dare to swim too close to the snares. While she would have had little need to find relief in the water of their previous home, it still made him feel glad to know he could provide something she obviously enjoyed.

Erik supposed that this particular body of water more resembled a large pond than a lake, but as he appreciated Christine's satisfied sighs and the way she floated upon the surface after having drenched herself thoroughly, he supposed it did not matter.

"I am glad to know you can swim. I should have hated to need to dive in after you."

Christine huffed at him and playfully sent a small wave of water towards him.

He glared in mock outrage.

Keane was wriggling and anxious to join his mother, but Erik hesitated. It was one thing to allow Christine to float and wade in the water, but it was something else completely to allow his entire family into the shallows.

His wife ceased her floating and stood, and he noticed just how enticing she looked with her now transparent shift clinging to her body.

"Down!"

Christine smiled at him and drifted a little closer. "I will hold him, Erik. Nothing will happen."

But as he stripped Keane of his clothing and handed him to his wife and listened to his boy's delighted shrieks as the cool water lapped at his heated flesh, he realised that he felt strangely excluded.

Not by his wife's intention, but because he was too prideful to shed his many layers of clothing and join his little family in a glorified pond.

And that was ridiculous.

When Christine saw him shedding each garment and placing it carefully on the cleanest bits of grass, she smiled at him encouragingly. Down to his shirtsleeves he contemplated just how nude was reasonable and would not be too poor an example for his son, and decided that his underclothes would be acceptable bathing attire.

His were black of course and were far more modest than what his wife was currently wearing, and he felt almost gratified that she was casting him covert glances and blushing prettily as she did so.

Perhaps lovemaking did not seem so wholly intolerable anymore.

He hissed a breath at the change in temperature, but as Christine drifted a bit further away—not *too* far as she thankfully understood the importance of keeping a firm footing when holding their boy—he renewed his determination and crept closer. He held out his hands for Keane who kicked and laughed at the new experience, allowing his wife to continue her swim unimpeded.

Before she went any further however she came very close to him, and he bent slightly so she could bestow her kiss without having to balance on tiptoe in the marshy bottom of the lake. "Thank you, Erik. Both for bringing me here and for joining me. That is where you always belong."

With one last beaming smile she swam a bit farther off, enjoying the occasional ray of sun that broke through the trees but mostly relishing in the feeling of comfort that could only come from feeling a *normal* temperature.

Erik did not feel it necessary to wade much deeper, except that Keane evidently desired to be further submerged. At the moment only his toes were able to skim the surface and as he squirmed and looked up to his father in dissatisfaction, Erik chuckled and obliged.

Christine remained in the water far longer than her husband and son, though eventually she too began to chill and joined them upon the shore. She collapsed upon the green grasses that apparently the sheep had managed to find if evidenced by its short length, and she smiled up at the few patches of sky that could be seen above. "This is perfect."

Erik hummed in agreement, and adjusted the now sleeping Keane across his chest. Whether or not his mother wanted an afternoon excursion did not apparently mean his naptime differed in the slightest.

"Does this mean you shall be content to live with your poor husband and stay *out* of my wine cellar?"

She giggled and tore off a few blades of grass and threw them at him teasingly. "Perhaps. But only if you promise to bring me here whenever I wish."

He sniffed, stroking his son's hair softly. "I suppose that could be arranged. But if you wish to go in the mornings you *will* be wearing more of a covering. Henri may be young but he is old enough to know a beautiful woman when he sees one."

His little minx had the audacity to giggle and took his lone free hand in hers. "Are you jealous, husband? Of a thirteen year old boy?"

Erik scoffed. "Hardly. Merely acutely aware of what it is like to *be* an adolescent male. And besides, it is not beyond my awareness that he is far closer to your age than you are to mine."

He had not meant to speak of it. Truly, he did not like to consider their ages much at all. He had accepted that he was far older than his Christine and that should have been the end of it. But when he considered younger men—her sweetheart of old perhaps—he could not help the feeling of wistfulness that she deserved someone more akin to her own age.

She rolled onto her side, the better to look at him. "You cannot be serious."

Erik shrugged gently, careful not to jostle his boy overly much with the movement.

He felt a sudden thud on his shoulder and glanced at her in surprise. She had *cuffed* him. "How could you be troubled by such a thing? I can assure you that your age has never bothered me. Your reticence in even giving me a hint as to what it might be, I admit has been troubling, but only because you are keeping secrets!"

Despite her exuberant discord, she had thankfully kept her voice relatively low so as not to disturb Keane and he did not have to try to shush her—which undoubtedly would have upset her more.

"I told you, I was not privy to my date of birth," he hedged. "That is hardly keeping a secret."

Christine huffed. "You must have *some* idea. I would accept even a guess."

Erik resumed stroking his son's back as he considered her request. He did not doubt her love—did not doubt that even if he estimated on the higher end of his supposed age that she would continue to do so. This was his own issue, one that as he listened to his boy breathe and felt the flutter of his heartbeat so close to his own, he realised was only one because he made it so.

"A guess then." It had never seemed overly important and he kept no running tally in his mind of the years that passed. Until two years ago it had been too lonesome and painful to contemplate for long—each year a vivid reminder of just how alone he truly was.

He supposed he was about forty years of age when they met, and if two years had passed...

"Forty-two. Will that suffice?"

She nibbled at her lip thoughtfully for a moment before creeping closer and kissing his cheek. "Yes, it shall. Though I do almost wish you would pick a birthday so we might celebrate."

Erik shook his head. "Between Christmas, your birthday, and our anniversary, I believe you tire your husband quite thoroughly as it is."

Christine pouted, rolling onto her back once more. "But with this baby due in October, that means we have all of spring and summer with no celebrations."

Erik grunted. "Time for vital recuperation, my rose."

She sighed and was quiet for a long moment. "I do not like that you would doubt me. I am carrying *your* child after all."

He raised his arm in welcome and to his relief she cuddled close, her hand curling around his as they looked at their boy. "I do not doubt you,

Christine. If you had wished to leave me I could far sooner believe it would be for someone handsome, not necessarily someone young."

She squeezed his hand insistently, and her words were infused with the utmost sincerity. "But I would *never.*"

He kissed the top of her head and held her close, grateful that she was apparently cool enough to allow such contact once again. "I know that, my darling girl. But that does not mean I would like to parade you in front of impressionable young men simply to prove that I trust you."

She giggled and kissed his still bare chest and they lay there well into the afternoon.

And Erik felt wholly triumphant at his abilities to distract his wife from any and all discomfort.

LII

Christine required her husband to fulfil his promise many times over, although she also made sure that on those occasions that a morning swim sounded too delightful to deny, she did indeed don one of her dresses so as to maintain a modicum of modesty.

His revelation of his age did not surprise her—she had in fact supposed that he was much older than his estimation, but she would never reveal that to him. Regardless of his physical age, he was an old soul. His genius had meant his intelligence had accelerated his skills and abilities, and the pains he had suffered had taught him from a young age to be self-reliant.

But to hear him say that he did not doubt her—that he knew her love was true—that was what warmed her heart.

Eventually however summer had faded into the crisp clear days of autumn, much to the relief of all. No matter how much she wished to, she could not in fact live at the lake, especially when her pregnancy progressed and it became more necessary to ensure proper facilities were easily accessible. Too many times she had awoken Erik as she tried to creep to the bath-room unnoticed, but it was difficult to do anything stealthily when she felt as though her once light gait now more accurately resembled a waddle.

As her time drew nearer to delivery, the important arrangements for the midwife became ever more pressing.

"Are you certain you require Aida? I am quite sure we could find someone nearer who will be willing to perform the duty."

They were sitting in the garden, enjoying the autumn leaves and the last of the roses, Keane running about inspecting all manner of foliage and insects that happened to be near.

Christine and Erik were seated on a cushioned bench, specifically placed so that she could lounge and appreciate her roses to the fullest, even when pregnancy made it nearly impossible for walks of any significant duration.

She turned to her husband, giving him a very cross look at his suggestion. "But I did so well with Aida. I should hardly like to risk it with someone else."

Erik scoffed beside her. "I believe for the majority of the birth you had *me.* And I would still be at your side, regardless of who caught the babe."

Christine pursed her lips at his description. "There is far more to it than that."

He hummed and adjusted his arm to pull her closer to him, his hand straying into her hair to run through the curls soothingly. "If you say so, my dear."

They were quiet for a moment, content to enjoy the afternoon and watch their boy as he scurried about, occasionally calling out gentle reminders to not wander from view. He was a very obedient boy, and while both would have liked to take credit for instilling that particular attribute, it truly appeared to simply be a part of their son. Despite his curious nature he seemed to have an intrinsic need to please his parents and that they be proud of his attempts at accomplishment.

Christine sincerely hoped it lasted into the future.

"Should we return below then? It would be far closer for when the time comes."

Her hand strayed to her swollen womb as she contemplated his offer. While she felt comforted knowing that she had come through her first experience of childbirth unscathed—and with a beautiful boy to show for it—she still felt nervous at the prospect of doing it again. The pain she had suffered during the process seemed somehow detached. She knew that it had hurt almost beyond what she could bear, but she *had* borne it. She only need remind herself of that.

Often.

"It must be so dirty by now. I do not like to imagine it so..."

Erik's hold about her shoulders tightened. "You like remembering it as it was." He leaned in close and kissed her temple, his lips drifting to her ear tantalisingly. "Perhaps you like to remember our evenings before the fire. You did so have a fondness for nests."

She shivered, vividly remembering just how wonderful it had been.

And it was true. It would make her heart hurt to see it so abandoned after they had so many happy memories there. She had become a wife and a mother in that home, and while a good scrubbing and some refurnishing would return it to its former glory, she worried that she would feel the temptation to remain there.

"I do not think I could clean it in this state, Erik. It would hardly be liveable now."

He appeared deeply offended. "You think your husband so unkind that he would make you tend to housework while waiting for childbirth to commence?"

She smoothed her hand over his lapel calmingly. "No, I do not. You take excellent care of me."

He sniffed and she took the sound to mean that although his sensibilities had been trodden upon, if only for a moment, she was still forgiven.

In the beginning of living in the manor, Christine had tried to keep up with most of the housework herself. For the most part she was successful, and between her and Erik the cooking and the cleaning of the bedchambers were easily managed. However, when Henri had shyly told them that his older sister was in look of some honest work, she had been eager for the help. After her pregnancy had become more pronounced and Christine less capable, Lucie had eagerly accepted more responsibility.

She had been wary of Erik at first, though not to the point of rudeness. For the most part she did not see him, as the mornings when she came to work he would shut himself away in his music room—which Lucie was banned from cleaning—or take Keane for some adventure on the property. This was mostly done because Christine had tried to forbid him from wearing the mask, and he would not subject a young girl of fourteen to witness his face. His wife might have been overly kind and understanding, but he knew that more impressionable children could still easily be frightened.

And he rather relished the excuse to make use of the tunnels and passages he had restored throughout the house.

"We could stay with M. Daroga."

She had not meant to be humorous, but at her husband's loud chortle she must have unwittingly been successful. "That will not be happening, my Christine. Not while your dear Erik draws breath."

Christine huffed, but relented. It was already October and there was truly no telling when the babe would come. It would be terribly rude to impose in any case, even if they did make some financial restitution for the inconvenience. She had never been to his home to know if it would even be suitable—it had just been an errant thought.

"Then tell me, oh wise husband, how will we arrange it?"

He narrowed his eyes at her, evidently trying to decide if he was going to be offended by his designated title. "I believe it would be far more preferable that you remain in our home. I will send the Daroga to retrieve the midwife when it is time, assuming she is amiable to travel the distance."

Christine's brow furrowed. "And how will you communicate with him?"

Erik sighed, her question apparently tedious. "He will come to stay in the cottage. Then he shall not be underfoot."

She hummed, not truly caring how he arranged it with his friend. Theirs was a special relationship—one that seemed from the outside like there was no fondness at all. But the longer she knew both men, the more she had come to realise that the curt, perfunctory way they dealt with one another was merely the way they communicated.

Perhaps all men were as odd as the ones in her life.

They had corresponded with Aida and told her of their home. She had been surprised to hear of their request as during the previous pregnancy they had also alluded to the fact that they were not nearby, yet had made arrangements for the delivery to take place at her apartment instead of transporting her there. But she had ultimately relented, telling them that if they provided transportation, she would be more than happy to aid them however she could.

The Persian had also been accommodating. "A bachelor does not much care where he rests, as long as there is a bed and a warm meal."

He made light of his situation but even Christine who did not know the full story of his life could see the lingering pain at being so. He would look at her swollen womb at times with a wistfulness that made her sad. Perhaps if it was anyone else she might be disturbed by the covert glances, but she knew this man's intentions, and the reminder of growing life and family must be very hard when one was all alone.

It was a very odd thing to have another at their dining room table. It was odder still to *use* the dining room. While in the beginning they had made sincere efforts to make use of the space, as Christine's pregnancy progressed and her feet protested climbing so many stairs, the kitchen table was far more favoured. The Persian had offered to eat in the kitchen as well, and even assured her that he could eat in the cottage so as to not be in the way or troublesome, but she had merely smiled and handed him a few dishes. "You can help carry. That is all I ask."

Erik hummed from the doorway, having already taken up his own burdens—including a waiting Keane. He stalked over to his wife and scooped her up into his arms, breathless giggles escaping her as he did so. "Yes, Daroga, you carry dishes. I have something far more important to see to."

Later, after their supper was consumed, the dishes washed, and a sleepy Keane tucked into bed, Erik had taken his wife to her own nest of pillows and blankets.

"I have been thinking, my rose."

She smiled at him welcomingly, patting his rightful side of the bed. "You are too far away for discussions."

He chuckled softly. "I am a fortunate man indeed that my wife still appreciates my company even after it was I that inflicted such discomfort upon you."

His tone was light and teasing, but she caught a faint undercurrent of very real remorse. She took his hand and brought it to cover her belly, and she sighed in contentment when he rubbed at it soothingly. "Perhaps other wives resent the husbands who do not try so very hard to pamper them. You do not hesitate to rub my feet or take me swimming when the days were unbearably warm. You carry me up the stairs instead of making me waddle up and down."

He scowled. "You do not *waddle.* You are merely *slow.*"

"Regardless," she said, tugging at his sleeping shirt until his face was close enough that she could kiss his cheek, "You are perfectly wonderful, and I shall always want you."

Erik smiled wryly. "I shall be sure to remind you of that when your labour begins."

Their hands were still entwined over her stomach, and their little Lotte sent her greetings with a gentle nudge. "I think that was an elbow," Erik commented, rubbing at the spot quietly.

"Let us all hope that she has inherited some of my features this time, Erik. I should hate to look foreign in my own family."

He rolled his eyes dramatically. For a moment she had frozen, suddenly afraid she had crossed the unspoken line that compared their physical features with their boy. It was so evident to her that Keane resembled Erik—who he would have been if whatever had gone wrong when he was just a little thing had not happened. But it had and she loved him anyway.

And though he had stiffened slightly, he quickly recovered—his response evidence that she had not unthinkingly angered him. "I think our children would be very grateful if they were not petite like their mother. You can barely reach the upper shelves in the kitchen!"

She nibbled at her lip, refusing to confess precisely how she reached those shelves. There was nothing *barely* about the situation. The upper shelves held quite a bit of the taller cookery, and when her stomach had not protruded in such a cumbersome manner, she would usually climb upon the counter so as to better reach her needed item. If Erik was near she would simply ask, but thankfully he had not yet caught her doing something she was certain he would find dangerous.

His eyes narrowed but he did not press her, for which she was grateful. She would not lie to him of course, but she did not relish the outrage she was certain would follow if she told him of her method to handling the kitchen.

In an effort to distract him further however, she returned to talk of the baby. "I think she was conceived on our anniversary."

Erik chuckled lowly, his thumb tracing delicate patterns through her nightgown. "Is that so? And what makes you so sure of such a thing?" He leaned in closer and placed a kiss to the sensitive skin behind her ear. "I believe we were quite *engaged* many times before and after that date."

She whimpered, his voice always sending that pleasant chill through her body, and she wondered how she could make her voice do similarly so as to affect *him* so completely. Christine noted wryly that *that* particular talent was not covered in her vocal lessons.

She tried her best to appear coy and appealing, and from the way he looked at her she must have at least somewhat succeeded. "I just know. And when your wife is with child you are to agree with her in all things."

Erik smirked at her. "Indeed."

And then his hands were massaging and coaxing and she wondered that any wife could wish to deny their husband when he made her body feel so languid and wanted, even when she looked down at herself and she felt more akin to how one of the ewes outside appeared when pregnant with twins and had yet to be sheered.

Erik was always sure that she was comfortable and oh so very willing before he ever considered instigating *more.* There were plenty of nights when his soothing hands only managed to induce a deep slumber, and not the kindled passions he was most likely intending.

But they both remembered the exhaustion and the forced abstinence that was to come once the baby was born, and they treasured these moments for as long as they could, knowing full well they could come to an end at any moment.

If only for a time.

It was two weeks after the Persian had taken up residence on their property that Christine awoke feeling strange. Erik might take her ways of *knowing* with an indulgent air of barely contained disbelief, but when a few hours later she felt the beginning tugs at her lower back, she was quite sure that her labour had begun. Whether or not it was possible that she could be so certain that she would have their baby that day was now deemed irrelevant, as when Erik heard her first intake of breath and watched her try to soothe the spasm with massaging hands, he had no choice but to believe her.

She was far calmer this time, and knowing that she did not have to rush to the midwife's home brought her some comfort. She still made Keane his breakfast, and though Erik hovered about her, she felt much less frightened than she had anticipated.

At midday, Erik demanded that the Daroga immediately depart for the midwife. Christine was confident that the actual delivery was a few hours off, so in theory they had a few hours before her presence would be strictly necessary.

She was currently in the study, finding the books and the smooth leather comforting. Erik had tried to keep Keane occupied in his room, but it was difficult when he frequently left his boy in order to check on his wife. "Mummy?"

Keane was holding Erik's hand in the doorway, and they both wore matching expressions of concern. She would have found it adorable had she not been trying to breathe steadily through one of her pains. Eventually it too passed, and she patted the sofa beside her.

Her boy ran to her quickly, hugging her as best he could when her belly was so large and swollen.

"He was worried about you. I believe he has received your remarkable pouting abilities, my wife."

She smiled ruefully; placing tender touches on her son's hair and leaning close so as to kiss his cheek. "Your little sibling is going to be born today, Keane. You need to be good for your papa and do as he says." Shifting her gaze to Erik briefly, she returned her attention to her son. "But perhaps you can convince him that a few extra biscuits would make you feel better today," she whispered conspiratorially.

That at least earned her a smile, and when he rushed passed his papa to scurry off to the kitchen, Erik had the audacity to glare. "I would have words for you, wife, if you were not so indisposed."

Christine grimaced and his expression turned once more to distress, and she waved him off. "Go tend to our boy, Erik. I will rest easier knowing he is being cared for."

The hours passed and by the time the Persian arrived with Aida, Christine was propped up in the spare bedchamber.

Before her labour had begun, Erik and Christine had many conversations about precisely where the delivery would take place. He had offered their marriage bed, citing that perhaps she would be most comfortable in the familiar space. It was sweet for him to suggest it and she had told him so, but it was evident that he cringed even at the suggestion. Their bed was for *them,* and while something wonderful would come from her pain and temporary misery, she did not particularly wish to soil it with the mess that followed.

He had been relieved and they decided on one of the other furnished rooms.

When they had renovated their home they had decided on making a few of the additional rooms actual bedchambers, simply for lack of any other need. Now, as she lay amongst the cushions and felt each contraction bring her steadily closer to the actual delivery, she was grateful for their unintended forethought.

Aida bustled in assuredly, smiling at Christine calmly. "Hello, my dear! How are you feeling?"

If they had not already gone through this process Christine might have felt it necessary to snap that she most certainly did not feel *well,* so the question was inane and unnecessary.

But Aida was experienced and she knew that the query was aimed at more specific criteria. "I do not feel like pushing quite yet. But I think it is close."

She nodded and seemed surprised to see that the Persian lingered in the doorway. "Out, Monsieur. I thank you for bringing me, but I believe you should be tending to another of their little ones at this moment."

He gave Christine an encouraging smile before nodding and soon Erik took his place in the room.

As he should have.

Every part of this seemed more accelerated than her last pregnancy. Aida patted her leg comfortingly when she gasped and cried as she spluttered out that it almost seemed better to have each step come along more slowly. "I told you, *mon amie,* each one is different."

Erik held her hand through it all, and to his very great credit did not even flinch when she squeezed his hand too tightly when she began to push. He hummed and encouraged and through her haze of tears and frustration when she just wished for it to be *over,* she could see how much it affected him to see her so pained.

He promised it would be worth it.

And though in the beginning of their relationship he had not always kept his word, she now believed him with her whole heart.

While still in the midst of the discomfort and burning and strain

Christine had a moment's sincere belief that her babe did not *want* to meet her, but then Aida proclaimed that her little one was almost out and if she could hold on just a little longer...

And with one last push a mewling cry was heard, and Christine was crying and then a wet, wiggling little girl was placed on her chest.

She was so *small.*

And she was perfect and she was here, and Christine thought her heart might burst from the love she felt for her.

"Little Lotte."

This time Erik did not linger by the walls as if afraid to meet his child, but knelt beside the bed and touched her tiny head, his long finger dwarfing her delicate features. "*Bonjour,* sweetling. We are going to take such good care of you."

He placed a kiss upon his daughter's head and then his attention turned to his wife. "My Christine. Look what you have accomplished."

And then he kissed her too and she saw that he was crying as well, and their tears mingled as they drank in every detail of their newest addition.

And Christine knew in that moment that she had never felt so complete.

LIII

Having two little ones was very different from one.

Perhaps that should have been obvious before Lotte had even appeared, but it still took a great amount of adjustment on all their parts.

Keane's especially.

He found his sister to be a curious new object, one to be studied and then when realising that she could not do much beyond whimper for milk or blink at the new world around her, he abandoned her for far more interesting things. Yet that was not to say that he did not like her.

He would bring her his toys and hold them up so she could see, and under Christine's guidance he would stroke her head or study her tiny fingernails, comparing them to his own modest hands. "She's small."

Erik chuckled and ruffled his soft brown hair. "Indeed she is. And you are going to have to help me protect our little Lotte, for that is what brothers do when they are bigger than their sisters."

Keane nodded, and after inspecting his new charge for another minute, he scrambled off and brought a book and held it out to his father. "Read, Papa."

Christine smiled and continued to hold her Lotte, enjoying the sound of Erik's voice as he read aloud.

Despite his intermittent fascination with the new member of their family, what Keane did not seem to appreciate was that his sister got to spend the night in his parent's bedchamber.

Rarely did he wish to sleep with them. He was content with his nursery that held his toys and specially made picture books that his father had illustrated for him. Even in the first few days after Lotte had been born they were careful to maintain their routine. Christine and Erik would bring Keane into their bed to read, and then Erik would take their sleepy little boy back to his own room.

But now he was discontented about leaving.

Lotte had her own nursery, but she was most assuredly not yet settled to any sort of sleeping pattern. As such, her bassinet had migrated, much to Keane's displeasure.

A week had passed since that delightful day in October when their daughter had graced them with her presence, and Keane was pouting and refusing to go to his bed. Christine was nursing in a nest of pillows, tired and worn herself from the sleepless nights. Their daughter did not require nearly as frequent meals as their boy had, but still found it absolutely essential that she eat in the middle of the night.

"No!"

Erik stood with his arms folded, looking down firmly at their nearly two year old son, who glared up at his papa with the same ferocity. "No."

"It is time for sleep, Keane. Of which you are quite aware."

With a bit more fumbling, their boy was able to mimic Erik's crossed arms as best he could, his little brow furrowed as well. "No."

Christine sighed, torn between amusement at her two men and the need for her son to understand the importance of obedience. Erik cast a quick glance at his wife, apparently gauging her reaction. His eyes narrowed at their daughter, and then he smirked. "Very well, Keane, you may try sleeping here for the night."

She was mildly surprised that he relented, but he had a bit of a devious look about him that made it clear that he had some plan that superseded the need for discipline.

Christine trusted him so she made no comment, only kissing Lotte's pale pink forehead before Erik took her into his arms and to her bassinet. "Goodnight, my little sweetling. Your papa sends you all the sweetest dreams you can bear."

She had thought him gentle with their boy when he was so young, but now watching him with their littlest—he was tenderness itself. He hummed and stroked her delicate feet until Lotte fell asleep, and then returned to the bed.

He reached over their triumphant boy and kissed her briefly, her eyes already drooping and her mind fuzzy, but grateful all the same that he had not forgotten her.

They were awoken some hours later by Lotte's mewling cries. Erik had been very insistent that the bassinet be placed on his side of the bed so that he could be the one to soothe if she merely needed comfort, as on some occasions that was all she required. "It is understandable," he had told her on the second night. "She has gotten to be with you for all of her life so far. I would find that terribly lonesome to suddenly wake up all alone."

Her tender-hearted husband.

Tonight however, Lotte had suckled slightly less before sleeping and she continued to bemoan her plight until her papa kissed her and passed her to Christine, who blearily set about undoing the neckline of her nightgown and placed her baby to her breast.

Keane was also awakened, his brow furrowed and eyes wide and blinking. Even in her own befuddled mind Christine was quick to notice that her boy shared his father's luminescent eyes, clearly visible in the moonlight. "Sleep, baby. We sleep."

Even with Christine's pink nipple firmly in her mouth, Lotte was still releasing little whimpers that clearly communicated she was unhappy to be awake. And Keane covered his ears.

He looked up at Erik pleadingly. "Sleep, Papa."

Erik clicked his tongue and shook his head, his arms once more folded over his chest. "You wanted to sleep with us, Keane. I believe your papa *told* you about being in your own bed."

Christine held out a weary hand and ruffled her boy's hair. "We are not having fun without you, Keane. Your sister just needs some extra looking after for a while and then she shall be in her own nursery. But you need your sleep if you are going to grow up to be as tall as your father and make some very lucky lady have to stand on tiptoe just to kiss you."

This earned a fierce glare from her husband, but she returned the look with an unrepentant smirk. "I love you for your height." Keane was beginning to appear frustrated by his prolonged wakefulness, and Christine smiled at him encouragingly. "Give your mummy a kiss goodnight, then be off with you."

He scrambled over to do as he was bid, placing a kiss upon her cheek and one to the top of Lotte's head unprompted. "*Sleep,* Lotte."

Erik watched the little moment with pride, but as he took their boy into his arms and placed him on his hip—Keane's overly tired head already drooping against his shoulder—Erik sniffed, evidently his mind returning to her earlier declaration. "I love you for your wit, my lady." He then left the room mumbling under his breath about impudent wives who filled his innocent boy's head with nonsense, and Christine leaned back into her pillows with a sigh of content.

Lotte had finally quieted and seemed to be intent on suckling herself to sleep. Christine allowed a finger to stroke gently over the plump cheek of her daughter, marvelling at how different she was from her brother.

Keane had always favoured Erik in appearance—at least in resemblance if not actual feature. His skin held a yellowish hue, and the long limbs and nearly colourless eyes that only burned a fierce amber in the darkness easily bespoke of his father.

Her little *chérie* was pink and small and delicate. She had a little rosebud mouth that would someday put even her mother's to shame, and Christine wondered what the fine wisps of hair would someday be. At the moment they appeared to be the same blonde tresses that her Erik adored so very much, but she supposed they could easily turn to her husband's darker shade.

Both her children were beautiful in their own unique way, yet if she looked at them objectively—or as objectively as she could manage—they did not bear much likeness to one another.

Erik entered a moment later, rubbing at his temple absently, obviously intent on returning to his place in their bed. When they had first begun to share a bed there had been a question of sides. Christine thought it mattered little since they always seemed to end up connected in some way—either the simple touching of hands or her curled up against his chest.

But Erik insisted that it was his husbandly duty to sleep nearest the door in case of any unpleasantness, and while she had rolled her eyes at the time and teased him for it when he still insisted upon it during their subsequent relocations, she could easily admit that she found the gesture to be sweetness itself.

"You are still awake? And you look as though you have been thinking." He climbed beneath the bedclothes with a tired sigh, and although she was careful not to jostle her now dosing baby overly much, she did her best to inch her way closer to his side.

He smiled at her movements and took pity, closing the distance between then and wrapping his arm about her shoulders. "Has my Christine been plotting in her sleepy state?"

She laughed softly, certain that it was her sleep deprived mind that made his teasing tone and words so very humorous. "I was just marvelling at how very different our children look."

Erik's eyes narrowed and he allowed the hand not occupied with his wife to stretch out a long finger and feel the fine texture of his daughter's hair. "They are the product of their parents."

She glanced up at him and noted the slightly shuttered expression, and realised how carefully she should speak of this particular matter. "I like to think they are the best parts of us." Christine smiled down at her daughter. "I think she shall grow up to be far prettier than me."

Erik scoffed openly at that. "Impossible."

Christine hummed, her mind already beginning to slow as sleep began to take her. "I love you, Erik. I do not think I say it enough."

She felt a soft kiss upon her lips and he held her a bit more firmly. He would stay awake awhile longer, she knew, so that he could place their baby back into her bassinet when she had finally taken the last of the milk she required for the night. And though she might have imagined it, she thought she heard him murmur in her ear, "You say it plenty through your actions, my rose. But your Erik does so love to hear it."

Life settled into a routine after that. Lotte eventually decided that she quite liked sleeping, and often they had to wake her in the morning for her breakfast as it appeared she rather favoured the idea of sleeping until all hours of the day.

When this new pattern became evident, Erik would shake his head and hand of their little *chérie,* who looked bleary and unhappy about being awoken. "You have passed on your dreadful sleeping habits, Christine."

She rolled her eyes at him, cuddling her little one close. "Do not listen to your papa, Lotte. He is jealous of our youth and vitality."

Erik sniffed indignantly and set off to find their boy.

A little less than three weeks after Lotte was born, they celebrated Keane's birthday. It was a quiet affair but he all but insisted that the Daroga be invited, as apparently he told very great stories of the *hot land.*

Erik had blanched at that and interrogated his friend the next time he had seen him, but the Persian had merely held up his hands defensively. "I can assure you, Erik, I have spoken of nothing untoward. Most are simply fables that *all* children find fascinating."

The unspoken mention of the Daroga's son lay thick in the air, much to Erik's chagrin. He did still managed to glare and threaten the man that any of Erik's personal dealings within Persia should remain undisclosed, but he ultimately allowed the showy stories from faraway lands to continue.

"It is all right to speak of it, you know," Christine later told him. "I have not asked questions because you do not seem comfortable about it. But you can tell our son stories if you like. I shall not pry."

Erik shifted uneasily, and she was once more amazed that such a simple action could look so graceful when performed by her husband. "He will grow up and remember them. And then ask questions. You would forgive me for that time since you are capable of understanding what pain and loneliness will do to a person. Our children will *never* know of such things through experience, so I doubt they..." His voice trailed off and he shrugged, his eyes not meeting hers.

It was so simple to forget their pasts when their lives were filled with little ones and one another. They occasionally had dinner with the Daroga, and although the weather now denied them the ability to picnic in the gardens, the sweet memories of doing so beckoned with the knowledge that this winter would soon pass.

"We are not going to hide who we are. If something prompts them to ask a question then we shall answer it. *Appropriately* of course." She took his hand and grasped it firmly with hers, the other seeking and finding the ring of scars about his wrist that she liked to soothe with her thumb. "They love us, Erik. They will understand."

His eyes narrowed and while she could see he wished to believe her, his voice was still disbelieving. "You are going to inform them someday that you were raped?"

She flinched, and his eyes immediately softened, and then he was the one catching her hand before she could pull away. The word was dark and painful, and she did not like to hear it. That part of her life seemed a distant memory, one that had no place in her true home—and not coming from her husband's lips.

Christine waited for his apologies—his eyes to widen in horror at having said the word they so resolutely avoided—but he offered none. He waited patiently for her reaction, though he seemed rather guarded as well. "Why would you say that to me?"

His smile was sad and he traced her features softly with a lone finger. "Because even though you are blameless, you still feel ashamed. I am fully responsible for my actions in Persia, for the choices I made, so imagine the shame I now feel for what sins I have committed."

Put so blatantly she understood. Their children loved them, but to hear such things from their parents—the wrongs that were performed to them and by them—it would be devastating.

"I do not wish to lie to them. We must be honest, even when we are embarrassed."

Erik sighed and nodded reluctantly. "But that does not mean we must volunteer the information."

She hoped they made the right decision. If she were to in some backward way find out such details about her beloved papa, she would feel devastated and frightened.

Someday they could revisit the issue, when they knew their children better as the individuals they would become, and when they had matured as parents themselves.

But for now, she was happy to embrace her husband and remind herself that he did not mean to hurt her by bringing up the pains of her past.

And when his hands found her hair and he kissed her oh so gently, she realised that the mention of her wounds did not pain her as much as they used to.

Perhaps they had healed each other after all. At least, enough for now.

Christmas was a grand affair. She decorated the house as best she could with ribbons and bows. On one December morning Erik had bundled up their boy and kissed her goodbye, informing her that they would return shortly. She eyed them both curiously but did not press the matter.

An hour later Erik returned, this time with Henri following behind him as they both dragged a large tree into the foyer of the house.

"What are you doing?"

Erik had done his best to brush off the bits of snow and loose needles that clung to the large fir, but he still glared at the bits that still held firmly to the greenery. "I foolishly thought you might enjoy a Christmas tree. I see now that they are troublesome decorations that should be immediately disposed of."

He eyed her shrewdly, and though she felt nearly overwhelmed by his unexpected participation in her attempt to make the holiday festive, she could see that he was waiting none too patiently for her to exclaim over his efforts.

Ignoring the fact that Henri was present as well as Keane, she flung herself into his arms and pressed her lips soundly against his. "It is perfect, and troublesome, and messy, and I love you for it."

He pulled away in mock offense, smoothing his rumpled cloak all the while, but she could see the way his mouth twitched and knew that her reaction had pleased him.

In addition to the décor throughout the house, Christine had also purchased new clothes for her children—a small black suit for Keane so that he could be as handsome as his papa and a frilly silk frock for Lotte that was entirely frivolous and would most likely be soiled within an hour of her donning it. But it did not matter for it was Christmas, and she wanted them to look their best as they made their way to the church for the service.

It was a small nearby parish, with a congregation that was not so very fine. Most wore their bests but even that appeared rather shabby—at least compared to the brand new clothes that Erik was able to afford for his family. Marc and his brood were in attendance, and they smiled at Erik and Christine fondly, waving cheerily from their seats near the front.

Before they had arrived, they both had discussed whether or not Erik should don the mask that made him appear like any other man. Marc had certainly seen his plainer masks, and while they tried to avoid the blatant stares that were given, they ultimately decided that he should forego such pretence. They had built a life here, and as Christine rightfully pointed out, the more accustomed they grew to seeing him about the village and markets—especially when there were *francs* to be had—the more widely accepted he would become.

When the service was over Christine was able to finally meet the rest of Marc's family. He introduced his wife Aimée, who smiled at them warmly and complimented Lotte's ruffles. Henri and Lucie she obviously knew, but there was now a new babe and three other children who bowed and curtseyed shyly, some clinging to their mother's skirt. "I was so happy to hear of your daughter, Madame. Girls are such blessings."

Keane tugged at Erik's trouser leg, evidently feeling uneasy by these strangers that were much closer to his size than he was used to. His father obliged and picked him up, slightly uncomfortable himself but hiding it reasonably well. His hand was firmly in Christine's and while he was not smiling, he was not the imposing and menacing figure she knew him capable of being.

It was progress.

Soon however they excused themselves to return home, and Christine felt him relax as soon as they were once more in the open air and all bundled in the blankets she had piled within the carriage to keep them warm. "You did very well, Erik. I am proud of you."

He scoffed. "Your husband is the epitome of gentlemanly behaviour. It is good of you to notice."

She laughed merrily as she laid her head against his shoulder, her arms too full of little ones to embrace him more completely.

"Perhaps someday a few matches will be made between our families. Marc and Aimée have a beautiful family."

Erik glanced down at his children, not at all able to imagine a time when he would be willing to allow either of them to marry and leave him. But if they were in love...

He could not imagine a life without his Christine.

So he sniffed and returned his eyes to the road. "Then perhaps I shall have to see to their education. For no daughter of mine is going to marry a stable boy."

Christine rolled her eyes but turned her head, fully expecting him to place a kiss upon her waiting lips.

Erik did not disappoint.

And then he tucked the reins into a lone and fully capable hand and wrapped his free arm about her shoulders, pulling her into his side and making her feel safe and secure. *"Joyeux Noël, my rose."*

Christine sighed in contentment and enjoyed the feel of her husband's strong arm around her, and their sleepy children nestled against her.

This was happiness.

"Joyeux Noël, Erik."

LIV

Time was an odd thing.

Some days, when her children were fussy and the idea of napping rejected by all until she simply wished to cry and beg for them to allow her a moment's respite, it went so incredibly slowly.

Then other times, when they were little angels and her husband was so very attentive, she felt as though it flew by too quickly. Her little *chérie* was the perfect addition to their family—one they did not even know they required. As soon as she was able to sit up on her own and seemed more alert and did not sleep *quite* so much, Keane found her to be a very interesting playmate. She could not actually do much beyond sit and stare and coo any encouragements, but evidently their son liked an audience.

Now that he had the ability to form more sentences, he was quite the chatterer, often telling her in minute detail the plans and schemes behind his elaborate block towers and cities that transformed Christine's parlour into the new epicentre of the modern world.

Lotte would smile at him and although he would scold—and occasionally scowl in a very Erik-like way—he was generally very gentle with her even when she would disrupt one of the foundation pieces with her little fingers.

Erik and Christine watched it all with pride. Both of them having no siblings of their own, it had not truly entered their minds that there could be any difficulties introducing another baby into their home—not when they were mindful that both children had to be loved equally and individually. They spent time with each on their own, reading and cuddling and ensuring that neither felt neglected because of the other. It was easier to make time for Lotte as she insisted every few hours on a meal, so Christine could retreat with her to the nursery for some quiet time together.

On those occasions Erik would read to Keane. Weaning him had been an absolute necessity as when Christine's pregnancy progressed, the act of nursing had become a torment to her sore and sensitive breasts. To his credit, Keane had been relatively amiable; no doubt seduced by his father's excellent baking skills that distracted from the lure of his mother's milk.

Their routine was so established that now when Lotte would start whimpering Keane would run to the study, pulling out all manner of books and waiting impatiently for his chuckling father to amble in as well. If Erik was enthralled in his music, he would run to his papa and tug at his trouser leg until he received his full attention. "Time to *read,* Papa."

Erik still had moments where he slipped into his bachelorhood, desiring nothing but to be confined to his music room and coax all manner of concertos and melodies from his *pianoforte* until he felt spent. At those times he nearly felt resentful when there would be a knock at the door, and on more than one occasion he would steadily ignore it until the intruder either departed or violated the sanctuary.

And when he saw the faces of his family, either his son or his lovely wife as they entreated him for company, his compositions flitted away as if they had never been, and he remembered what truly mattered.

With that in mind, whenever he began to hear Keane's pattering feet in the hallway as he came rushing toward the music room, Erik would begin the sometimes painful process of disengaging from his work. The last thing in the world that he wished was for his boy to feel unwanted, and while he treasured his music, his care for it was a mere pittance when compared to his love for his boy.

At times he tried to convince Keane that an impromptu music lesson was far more desirable than a book, as Erik was ever ready to begin indoctrinating his son as to proper theory and method when approaching a piano.

Not *pounding* as he had done when he was smaller.

But Keane would wriggle free and pull on Erik's hand, a larger replica of his own long fingered appendage. "*No,* Papa. *Read.*"

So Erik would sigh resignedly and scoop up his insistent boy and he would read all manner of subjects to his son while he knew his Lotte was being tended to in the nursery.

That was not to say that his children did not have a fondness for music. In the afternoons when Christine was not too tired or some household chore did not impose itself as being of utmost importance, they would all cluster in the music room and Erik and Christine would resume their lessons.

They were not immediately instigated after Lotte was born, and it had taken some of Christine's more *practiced* wiles to persuade her husband to tell her what was wrong. Music was important to both of them, though she knew her own passion for it paled in comparison to Erik's. A few years of having a proper family might have done wonders to promote his healing, but he would always be grateful for his lifelong friend. That had been his only companion for the majority of his life, and evidently he began to feel despondent and alone when he felt as though his music was no longer a priority to her.

She did not begrudge him for it, although it still made her sad to think of it.

For herself, it was something that made her feel connected to her papa. It was a true joy to see just how greatly their children loved Erik, but on occasion it sent little pangs of longing for her own father. He would have loved her little ones and enjoyed spoiling them with affection and robust violin playing that would send their feet dancing until they could do nothing but collapse into giggles.

Keane at least. Lotte would bounce on her plump rump and clap her hands, smiling and laughing all the while.

Her little fantasy made her sad and Erik must have noticed for he immediately asked her what was wrong. She smiled at him as best she could and wiped away the few tears that had escaped without her notice. "I just miss my papa today, that is all. Nothing to worry about."

Erik's eyes narrowed and he seemed unconvinced. "Would you like a distraction?"

She rolled her eyes, vividly imagining just what kind of *distraction* he could be referring to. But as she remembered thinking of the joy that could be found by an uninhibited violinist, she decided that she had a very fine player offering his services and it would a shame to waste it. "Yes, I think I would."

Her son was far more reserved than his sister, and Christine could easily see the reflection of Erik's insistence on *dignity* within him. But unlike his father, Keane could be persuaded that certain times called for a bit of childishness.

And when she placed a pair of socks on his feet and a pair on her own and asked a bewildered Erik to play them a tune on his violin, she showed him that the ballroom was very great fun for sliding and twirling and collapsing until the world stopped spinning and all was right again.

Erik played dutifully but she could see that he thought his wife and son had caught some sort of sickness whose primary symptom was temporary derangement.

But he could plainly see that Christine's mood had dramatically cheered, so if prancing and slipping on a polished wooden floor made her happy, then so be it.

Although *he* much preferred those occasions when he would carry her into the ballroom and whisper a quiet tune in her ear as they glided over the dance floor.

But perhaps that was simply because more often than not, that particular form of dancing led to *other* pleasurable activities—activities he would never object to.

And if he was being imaginative, he could almost suggest that marital relations were yet another form of dance, ones where seasoned partners that knew each other so very well could reach new heights of beauty and fulfilment through bodily expression.

Yes, perhaps dancing was a very fine thing indeed.

Even when not heavily pregnant, when summer reached the château Christine insisted on many of their midday meals to be eaten by the lake.

On one particularly sunny day Christine found Erik in the kitchen, preparing a basket for an early luncheon. She watched him amusedly as he organised everything just *so,* seemingly uncaring that everything would become jostled once they began walking outside. "Are we going somewhere?"

She had yet to make her declaration regarding her desire for another lakeside afternoon, and Erik rarely initiated them.

"You and I are, yes."

She smiled at him incredulously. "Oh really? And where pray tell will our children be while we are having this adventure?"

He rolled his eyes at her dramatically, tucking a loaf of freshly baked bread into the basket and nodding his head in satisfaction as he closed the lid. "The Daroga has graciously offered his services. I believe he is teaching Keane the intricacies of the scimitar."

Christine gaped at him. "You cannot be serious."

Erik sniffed. "Perhaps not, but he will be minding him for the next hour or so. I believe I am in need of your company." His eyes shifted to meet hers, and she saw a bit of raw vulnerability that he did not quite manage to conceal. They loved their children with all of their hearts, but there was something to be said for stolen moments alone.

As Lotte grew older she adjusted relatively easily to sleeping in her own nursery, but there was still the ever present possibility that one or both of their little ones could need them at any moment.

They had to take time for one another.

So Christine relented and kissed her babies and thanked the Persian before taking Erik's hand and following wherever he led.

She gasped as they made the final turn to the lake. Packing the basket of food was evidently the last part of his little scheme, as there was a waiting blanket and even pillows laid out in welcome.

Erik was looking at her shyly from the corner of his eye, and disregarding that one of his hands was still occupied with the basket, she flung herself into his arms. She did not know how much she had truly missed him until moments like these, when they were alone and could simply *be.*

Her husband was able to catch her and hold her to him with his lone arm, and she rewarded his strength with a long and unhurried kiss. She eventually released him for she felt young and free and wanted to enjoy her husband in every way she possibly could.

His eyes widened in surprise when she first began undoing the light linen dress she wore, but they quickly darkened as every bit of bare flesh became open to his view. She still did not feel it necessary to fully dress in the mornings, so petticoats were forgotten. The dressmakers always tried to convince her that corsets were an essential, but her husband had forbidden them, and she did not feel it necessary to argue.

And at moments like these when she could easily slip out of her dress, underclothes, and chemise, she was grateful for her husband's peculiarities.

He moved to grab hold of her naked form but she smiled impishly and waded into the water. It was slightly too cold and made her skin prickle, but against the heat of the summer's day it felt delicious and refreshing.

If only her husband would join her.

He stared at her incredulously from the shore. "You cannot ravish me if you are over there," she called out encouragingly.

His mouth pursed and his eyes narrowed, and as he began tugging nearly angrily at his clothing she could not help but laugh as she enjoyed the feel of the water against her skin. It felt so *good* to be unencumbered by clothing, and to be able to glide through the crisp clean lake felt entirely indulgent.

Erik stalked toward her purposefully, and though she tried to swim away coyly, he caught her easily and drew her to him. "You are a minx, wife, and it is horribly unfair to use your feminine wiles on your husband." His eyes flickered to the shore. "Now my clothes will be rumpled."

She followed his gaze and saw that his usually impeccably folded clothes were now in a messy pile, obviously discarded in haste.

Christine nibbled her lip and tried to look penitent, but she must have been a truly terrible actress indeed for he still pouted. So she did the only thing she could and tugged at his neck until she could kiss him properly, and she could not help but groan at the delicious way his naked flesh felt against hers.

He pulled her fully into his arms and her legs went about his waist for balance as he stalked back to the shore, laying her down upon the blankets and pillows, evidently having had enough of her games.

And ravish her he did.

By the time he had finished with her, her hair was nearly dry and quite wild from his frequent ministrations therein. She felt completely languid and sated, happy to cuddle with her husband as they enjoyed the afternoon, though she knew they would soon have to return to the house and relieve their poor friend from his profession as childminder. He might be able to entertain them with his stories of faraway lands, but he most assuredly could not provide Lotte her meal when it was time.

"I must go to the Opera House tomorrow."

His fingers were trying to undo the many tangles in her hair, and she hummed as he rubbed and caressed her scalp and tickled her back as he trailed his digits through her long tresses. "Already? It feels as though you just went."

He kissed her temple. "The beginning of each month, every month. And you know I must do my best to keep apprised of their workings." He gave a curl a playful tug. "We would not want to be responsible for the demise of the theatre, would we?"

She smiled and placed a kiss upon his chest. "I suppose not."

They lay there for a while longer, Erik occasionally feeding her bits of fresh bread and cheeses from the basket, neither caring that they were completely nude in the middle of the afternoon. It amazed her somewhat that she could be so comfortable being intimate in the outdoors given her previous dealings, but as she listened to her husband's soft breaths and gentle heartbeat, she felt no shame.

She had grown, both in body and in mind since she was a lost child on the streets of Paris. And perhaps that meant she should be a bit bolder in her manner.

"I think we should go with you sometime."

Erik looked down at her in surprise. "*Why?*"

She rolled her eyes. "Not to haunt, though I would not mind one of those adventures again. Perhaps we could do *that* when the children are older." His expression remained unchanged, although an eyebrow rose as he waited for her to explain. "I mean that we should go with you into Paris. We could visit the park while you work." She took a deep breath and glanced up at him. "I do not want to be afraid of a city, Erik."

He was silent for a long while, and she waited for him to dismiss it altogether. But instead he kissed her temple once more and gave her shoulder a gentle squeeze. "Allow me time to get used to the idea, my dear."

She nodded, content to enjoy the rest of their stolen moment without dwelling on any unpleasantness.

What Christine did not expect was for Erik to take an additional three months to grow *used* to her idea. But come the first of October, when she resigned herself to watching her husband ride away for the entirety of the day, she instead saw the carriage prepared and waiting.

"Really?" She asked him excitedly.

He took a deep breath and placed his hands upon her shoulders, his expression serious. "You will stay at the park. You will not wander off with anyone while I am not there to..." He shuddered and his eyes closed tightly, until finally he rested his forehead against hers. "Please be waiting for me there."

Christine reached up and stroked his masked cheek gently, grimacing at the feel. Her husband may not be the handsomest of men, but there was something special about the feel of his skin—slightly raspy yet silky all at once, and she would choose it over the feel of the cold and impersonal façade with no hesitation.

"Do you say that because you are worried for my safety or because you do not trust me?" Her heart felt heavy that she even felt the need to voice such a question. Erik loved her with his entire being; she knew that to be true. But jealousy was a terrible thing and they lived such a secluded life that it stood to reason he might feel insecure in her loyalties when faced with other men.

It made her feel ill to even contemplate it.

"Oh, my rose." He kissed her then, softly and sweetly. "I worry for your safety, not your fidelity. Forgive me if I sound more like a childminder than a husband." His breathing hitched and his hands clutched at her waist firmly, but without pain. "If anything were to happen it would be *my* fault."

She bit her lip, willing the tears that threatened to come to quiet so that she would not add to her husband's pain.

He did so hate to see her cry.

"Erik," she began, proud that her voice quivered only the slightest amount.

"It would not be your fault. We both decided that our pasts were painful and harrowing, but ultimately they led us to each other. Perhaps you will think it selfish of me, but I would never change our histories—not if it meant I did not get to be with you."

His thumb brushed against her cheek and she realised that despite her best efforts, a few tears had escaped. "You should never have been in pain. Someone should have protected you."

She went on tiptoe and pressed a kiss upon his thin lips. "Someone did. And I thank God for him every day."

He smiled at her wryly and placed one more all too brief kiss upon her cheek before pulling away. "I suppose we should depart then."

She grabbed hold of his wrist. "Not if you are too uncomfortable or think it too dangerous. I *do* respect your opinion, Erik, as you know more of the world than I do."

She would be disappointed, but if something *should* happen, the last thing in the world she desired was for Erik to somehow fault her for the event.

But in her experience, monsters came out at night. There was a beauty to Paris in the daylight, with the ladies in their fancy skirts that swished as they walked with their gentlemen, and the sounds of the horses clomping along the cobblestones was one that always brought comfort.

Erik straightened to his full height and seemed to overcome the last of his fears. "No. We will go and you and the children will have a lovely day at the park while I tend to the Opera House. Then we shall all return home in the *same* condition we left it."

She regarded him for a long moment trying to gauge if he was truly satisfied with the arrangement. Eventually he rolled his eyes at her. "Must you always make your poor husband fetch your cloak? And I believe we have children to collect."

Christine could not help but smile as she hurried off to ensure that her little ones were dressed properly for the autumn afternoon. The sun was warm but there was a cool breeze that foretold of a chilling winter, so cloaks and blankets were a necessity.

The ride into the heart of Paris was always an interesting one. Some streets were so narrow it appeared impossible for a carriage even as small as theirs to be able to fit. But her husband was a capable driver, and she remembered how fine he looked atop the horse when he would travel here alone.

Keane had already expressed great interest in horsemanship, and though Erik seemed almost chagrined at the notion, Christine knew that in a few years he would ultimately relent. But first their boy's legs had to grow long enough to sit astride the large gelding, and she comforted herself with the knowledge that such would be far into the future—at least, she hoped it was.

The park was busy at this time of day. The perfectly polite couples walked hand in arm, murmuring quietly as a chaperone kept careful watch to ensure nothing untoward took place. Children squealed and laughed as they scurried about after one another, some slightly older boys using fallen sticks as weaponry for a swordfight most likely begun for the hand of some fair maiden.

Erik's brow crinkled in distaste. "You are certain you would like to remain here? Perhaps the children are not too young to begin haunting after all."

Christine leaned over and kissed his cheek. "Come along, Keane, say goodbye to your papa. We are going to enjoy the afternoon." Keane did as he was bid, both wary and excited by the unexplored sights before him. Erik gave Lotte a kiss and she threw her little arms about his neck in return before allowing herself to be placed upon her mother's hip.

As she watched Erik drive the carriage away she almost called out for him to return and spend the day with them. She did not feel frightened exactly, but she was not used to being around all these people—especially not alone.

But she had wanted to feel capable again, to test her courage and know that while she would always *want* her husband, that she did not in fact *need* him in order to feel comfortable.

As he had told her long ago, she was a woman now, not a frightened girl forced into the world far before she was ready.

So she took her boy's hand and relished the way he seemed to absorb all of his surroundings, already trying to pull free so he might investigate at his own pace. "Do not wander far, Keane. I must be able to see you."

The park had many trees and benches, with grassy areas for children to run and Christine supposed the occasional picnic to take place. She and Lotte settled on a bench a little farther away from the other occupants, content to enjoy the sunshine.

They had been there about three quarters of an hour before Christine saw Keane disappear into some shrubbery. She was not overly concerned, but then when he finally did emerge he was holding something lumpy and furry, and she rushed to cover the distance between them. "Stay there, Lotte!"

"It's a kitty, Mummy! We will keep him."

It was indeed a kitten. It was filthy and looked frightened, and cowered into her son's arms at her approach. "I believe your father and I will decide such a thing, Keane." He glanced up at her in disbelief, his lower lip already beginning to quiver. "But she's scared all by herself!"

Christine sighed and ruffled his hair. "Come sit with your sister and me and we will discuss it with your father when he returns." Knowing her husband and his penchant for caring for sad and broken things, there was little chance they would leave the kitten to fend for itself.

But any thoughts flew from her mind when she turned to return to the bench that had once held her daughter, only to find it empty.

Her little Lotte was gone.

LV

Driving away in the carriage was perhaps one of the most difficult things Erik had ever done. It seemed ridiculous and risky and if anything should happen...

But he had faith in his wife. Whether or not he agreed with the importance that she prove herself capable of being alone with a bunch of strangers was not for him to say.

He could simply conduct his business at the theatre as quickly as possible so that he could return to her all the sooner.

The Opera was much the same as it always was. There were some new ballet rats that he had not seen before, and he watched them titter and flit about backstage with detached amusement. They were not much older than his wife, but there was a maturity they lacked that was startling. If his Christine had ever been accepted at the theatre, would she have gossiped and whispered as enthusiastically as these young girls? Or would she have been detached, wondering at the simpering nature of feminine girlhood, just as he was?

His little Lotte was every bit the delicate rose that her mother was, yet he could not imagine her *simpering.* She was far too intelligent for such nonsense.

He went quickly to his box and true to their word, twenty-thousand *francs* resided within. Only once since he had vacated the premises had they tried to cheat him of his salary, and he had been forced to act accordingly. No one was hurt in the endeavour—at least, not seriously. He had considered proving his ire by collapsing the grand chandelier that hung proudly over the audience, but ultimately decided against it. Instead he had caused one of the scenes to fall upon the stage, and one of the flirting buffoons below had not stopped ogling one of the chorus girl's breasts long enough to get out of the way.

And that could hardly be considered Erik's fault.

He caused a bit of mischief backstage simply to keep the spirit of his ghostly company ever present on the performer's minds. Erik rolled his eyes at the peel of girlish screams that sounded when he chuckled through the walls and sliced one of the ropes, sending one of the sandbags crashing to the ground. He was careful, ensuring that no one would actually be injured this time as this was merely for show and not for any sort of retribution.

The little Jammes and Giry girls immediately began regaling the newcomers with tales of Erik's horrifying face and his dastardly deeds throughout the Opera.

Their eyes were wide and excited, their hands gesturing wildly as tales of his relatively simple exploits grew to impressive new heights.

Ever since he had married Christine, his conscience had grown. Not to the point where he had any great love for his fellow man, but he no longer felt it was his right to do as he wished merely because of the past misdeeds against him. God did not shun him because of his face—otherwise he would never have provided his Christine, and later the two perfect children that came from their union.

But it was obvious from watching these girls that they *enjoyed* the excitement of the haunted building—the way they would creep about the theatre at night, certain that if they even breathed wrongly they would be snatched away by the mysterious Phantom that roamed the halls looking for victims.

And his signs kept the management under control and the music alive.

On any other occasion he might have tarried longer, listened to rehearsals and overseen the different departments so he would know precisely what suggestions to make in order to improve the productions.

But not today.

For today his wife was not safely tucked away at home with their little ones, and instead was facing her public with all the fierce determination that he both loved and resented. While it was that quality that saw her through the most difficult times, and indeed what saw her through a good portion of their marriage, that was also what kept her striving for them both to be *better.*

And though he might be tempted to feel sullen and sulky when she reminded him that they were imperfect—which was of course absurd—it was that part of her character that brought them so close in the beginning when he was too cowardly to do so himself.

He snorted softly. If it was not for that quality, they would not even be married. Most likely he would have kept her living down below, a maestro and his pupil who shared music and little else—most certainly not a bed.

If it had been up to him, they most likely would not have consummated their marriage. It was her willingness to *try*—to prove herself a worthy spouse and a capable lover that inspired him to attempt to do the same.

And his boy and his sweetling would not have been born.

His wife was perfect for him, and he would be a fool not to love every part of her—even the parts that asked him to take his shoes off and enjoy a too-cold lake. Even the parts that made him ruin a perfectly acceptable coffin. And most especially the part that convinced him to try his hand at baking and all manner of cookery.

He was ready to go home.

Even with the relative infrequency of his visits to the theatre, he still knew how to manoeuvre the routes and tunnels that led to the outside with ease.

What he did not expect was to see the Daroga lurking about. He could have just continued on his way. His wife was waiting for him, and the longer he was away from her, the more urgent he felt the need to return. He did not belong as some spectre any longer. He was a husband and a father and he should be with his family—even if his role as Opera Ghost was in fact how he provided for said family.

Perhaps it was time to begin investigating a new profession.

The man was walking up the front steps purposefully, and it took little effort for Erik to creep up behind him. "Ah, Daroga. What brings you here on this fine afternoon?"

The Persian jumped, whirling around and his expression one of profound guilt. He looked even more surprised to see Erik's mask. Despite the fact that it was far better for him to wear his Death's head when prowling about the theatre, he was not about to draw unnecessary attention to his family with his more fanciful masks. So for this occasion he had donned the mask that made him appear as anybody else—one that the Daroga did not seem accustomed to.

"Erik! What are you doing here?"

He looked at him incredulously. "I believe I am employed here and was merely collecting my wages. But I believe *you* confessed to prowling only in search of my whereabouts. Why then pray tell would you look for me here?"

The Persian appeared sheepish, his hands fidgeting absently. "I have found that I rather enjoy watching the rehearsals. I thought perhaps I could be useful to you by giving any suggestions for improvement—ones that would not require people to be hurt for their incompetence." He tried to make his voice sound accusing, but instead he merely sounded sad.

Erik's eyes narrowed. "Surely that cannot be the reason. Are you certain that some little ballet girl has not caught your eye?"

The man blanched and walked down the steps hurriedly. If not for the fact that such was also the direction of the stables Erik might have allowed him to continue on his way unimpeded. But as he was *going* that way in any case, he could not help but prod. "Oh, come now. You are not *so* old as to be considered lecherous for simply admiring."

The Daroga turned sharply. "I am *not* infatuated with a ballet girl!"

Erik firmly believed that his ability to spot the slightly guilty expression in the man's face was wholly due to living with his wife. Every small detail could have a larger significance, and he had learned to pay attention to every nuance that could give him a clue as to her thoughts and feelings.

"But there is someone." He tried to gentle his voice and keep the amusement from permeating. Perhaps at some other time he would have reminded his friend of his commitment to his first wife—the woman who had borne him a son and that he still grieved over to this day. But to hear that he had nothing more pressing in his life than to idle away his days listening to operas that he could not understand seemed depressing.

And he realised how their lots had changed.

"Who is she?"

He mumbled something so softly that if Erik had not possessed such fine hearing he would surely have missed it. "Mme Bertrand."

Erik could not help it.

He laughed.

The Daroga groaned and stalked away again, throwing the occasional furious glance over his shoulder. "It is not amusing!"

Erik's legs were longer and it took little effort to close the distance between them. "My apologies."

The Persian sighed and stopped walking, turning to his friend, all traces of humour or outrage suddenly gone. "When I was searching for you, I had a purpose. I thought I was doing something good keeping an eye on you to ensure that your madness did no one harm."

Erik sniffed indignantly.

"Do not give me that look, Erik. You know it is true. That wife of yours saved you from yourself, and you cannot deny it."

"I would never try. My Christine saved me, just as I saved her."

The Daroga smiled sadly. "That much is obvious. But every time I see your family, it makes me miss my own. And then I begin to wonder if it would be so wrong to..." He shrugged, and as Erik stared at him, he felt the oddest pang of...

Sympathy.

During his time in Persia, he *never* would have thought that someday he would be in this moment. He had hardly considered this man an acquaintance, let alone someone worthy of his compassion. But as he watched the man struggle to reconcile his desire for a family with the memory of those he had lost, he saw a reflection of himself.

And the need to be with his wife became all the more urgent.

He cleared his throat awkwardly. "I must collect my Christine. She and the children decided to spend the day at the park. Would you... care to accompany me?"

His wife was easy to soothe. Soft touches and reassuring words were all that were necessary to calm her when something was particularly distressing, but he had not the slightest idea of how to offer the same reassurances to the man before him.

The Daroga smiled faintly. "No, thank you. I think I shall just return home."

Erik shook his head. "Return to the Opera House. Their prima donna should be performing her aria soon and I should like an untrained opinion." And with that he continued on his way to the stables, but turned back before he lost his courage. "I think... I think your family would wish for you to be happy. Even if that meant having to be with someone else. They loved you after all."

He hurried on after that, not wishing to see if his attempt at conciliation was ill received.

The journey to the park seemed to take twice as long as before, though if he tried to remain objective the roads were in fact clearer and fewer people milled about impeding the carriages that needed to pass by.

He gave the horse a gentle pat and pulled out an apple from his cloak pocket. While the deep pockets therein were originally intended for weaponry, they now more readily housed apples and knitted goods for his children to wear should they catch a sudden chill.

Though the lasso remained firmly in place.

The gelding munched happily on his treat, and Erik stroked his nose affectionately before facing the dreadfulness of the public park.

He did not immediately see his family, but he tried to remind himself of Christine's promise to actually *be* here before panicking. It was a large space with many trees and shrubs that could easily hide them from view—and as he stalked forward and saw some young lovers engaging in some rather passionate repose, he realised that the laurels provided excellent covering for *other* things as well.

What he did not expect to find when he walked further was to see his little sweetling sitting alone on a bench, a strange woman beginning to encroach while her gentleman friend looked on distastefully.

"Lotte."

It would have been inappropriate and drawn far too much attention to actually call her name aloud, so instead he threw his voice to her ear, and when she whipped her head to follow the sound of her father's voice, he knew he had been successful.

She smiled widely and began her clumsy descent from the bench, much to his dismay.

His daughter was so different from her brother. While he had begun using the walls to maintain his posture as he walked about the perimeter of the room, his Lotte was nearly a year and had yet to take her first steps on her own. If Erik held up her hands in support she happily trudged along, looking very proud of herself for her accomplishment as her father and mother showered her with praise.

However, when it came to moving on her own, she much preferred to crawl.

Erik chose to believe it was because she was a delicate little flower and the prospect of falling when her legs were still uncertain was distasteful to her. Christine had begun to worry, but they refused to actually speak of it as though something was *wrong.*

She merely refused to do things at Keane's pace—as was her right as his sweetling.

But now he watched her place slightly unsure little feet upon the grass, and after she was certain she was not going to collapse, she all but ran into his arms.

Or at least, she tried to.

He stalked forward hurriedly so as to save her from the fall he was sure would come from her inexperience, but as he met her and she fell against his legs, hugging them close to her slight body, he could not help the feeling of immense pride that followed.

His little Lotte.

"Well, look at you, little sweetling. Had to run before you walked, did you? You had your mummy worried."

She smiled up at him, all things trusting and loving with her golden wisps of curls and blue eyes that looks so much like her mother's. And he could not help but chuckle as he leaned forward to scoop her up into his arms.

The couple that had been so close to her drifted forward. "Are you her father? I was concerned seeing her sitting there all by herself. It is not right to let a child her age be unaccompanied."

He would have scowled, or at the very least rolled his eyes, except for the fact that his Christine should have been with her.

And a feeling of dread washed over him.

He ignored them both, his eyes flickering about as he tried to locate his wife, only to catch sight of her crouching by their boy some distance away—what appeared to be a furry lump held within his son's hands.

Relieved that nothing serious had befallen them besides Keane's own inquisitive nature—something that caused plenty of chagrin and pride in turn—he turned back to the interfering couple.

"I thank you for your concern," his eyes flickered to her ring finger, "Mademoiselle, but I can assure you, my wife was nearby tending to our son."

"You see, my dear? We did not have to interfere. And I am certain you offended the man by assuming his daughter was unprotected."

Erik's gaze finally drifted from over the woman's shoulder where he watched Christine cajole and speak with their boy.

Only to then see the Vicomte de Chagny was the man speaking to him.

How he hated this man.

Not because he saw him as a rival for Christine's affections—no, not that. It was difficult to be jealous about a few stolen kisses in Christine's girlhood when *Erik* was the one who knew how to please her so thoroughly. She had welcomed him into her body and into her heart, and Erik had no intention of ever betraying that trust with hurled accusations stemming from his bruised pride.

He hated him because for so long Christine had thought him her only hope. If she could find *this man,* then she would be saved.

And when she finally did see him, he spurned her and called her a thief.

But there was a small part of him that was grateful. When this man refused to truly *see* Christine, it allowed him the opportunity to right his wrongs to her. And from that opportunity came their marriage.

He glanced over the lady's shoulder once more, only to see Christine's wide and horrified eyes as she looked at the empty bench, and his heart reached for her. Erik could remain where he was and tell this impudent young man of the girl he had shattered, or he could comfort his wife.

And when he thought of it in that way, there truly was no dilemma.

He bowed slightly and gave no further reply, striding forward with his sweetling in his arms so he could reassure his wife that there was no great peril.

She nearly started sobbing when he came into her view, and she rushed forward hurriedly in order to seek out his embrace while also caressing their daughter, evidently looking for injury. "I am sorry, Erik! I only turned for a moment because Keane had drifted into the shrubbery and now he wants to keep a kitten and she was *gone.*" All of this was said in a rush of words punctuated by little kisses upon Lotte's pink cheeks.

Erik glanced down at Keane who had drifted near them, his arms indeed full of a tiny animal. His boy looked up at him with those eyes so like his own, his expression forlorn. "Can't I keep her, Papa?"

How was he ever to say no to such a query?

"What say you?" he murmured into Christine's ear.

Her sobs had begun to quiet and as she glanced down at her son, he felt his own heart lighten to hear her laughter. "Keane, how is your father supposed to say no when you look at him like that?" She glanced back to her husband and gave him a soft smile. "I do not mind if he would like a pet. Though I have never had one myself."

Little did she seem to realise that their boy was merely copying the look so often utilised by his mother—which also happened to result in his acquiescence on many occasions.

Lotte began to wriggle insistently, her eyes focused on her brother and his new familiar, and Erik placed one last kiss upon her temple before putting her down. Christine watched in amazement as her daughter no longer plopped immediately onto her bottom, but stood without assistance, her gaze fixed upon the tiny animal.

"She is walking?"

Erik smiled down at his daughter fondly. "Our daughter is apparently now *running.* She was quite enthusiastic about my approach and did not wish to wait."

He considered whether or not he should mention seeing her previous *friend,* but ultimately decided against it. He was not keeping a secret from her, but instead was truly trying to consider her feelings. She was happy and contented, and he did not wish to distress her unnecessarily.

Mentioning the fop would surely do so.

Christine moved closer to his side, burring her head in his chest as they both watched their little ones below. "They grow so quickly. I feel as if I do not watch them constantly I shall miss something important." Her voice grew rather wistful. "I *did* miss something important."

Erik stroked her curls, a mature representation of what his daughter's would someday become, and he understood her sentiments. "We can only do what we can, Christine." And just because he had decided that he had experienced quite enough of this separation business, added, "But perhaps we can be all the more efficient at ensuring we witness these events when we are *together.*"

Christine hummed and he felt her hand sneak between his shirtsleeve and glove and found the sliver of flesh that she so favoured. "Perhaps you are right."

Their attention was drawn once more to their children when one of Lotte's small hands reached out to touch the fuzzy creature, its blue eyes looking at her warily from its huddled position in Keane's arms. "You must be gentle, Lotte. She is very small and you would not want to hurt her."

Keane nodded sagely. "*Gentle,* Lotte."

She made contact with the kitten timidly, a bright smile crossing her face as she felt the soft fur for the first time. "Kitty!"

Erik had drawn many pictures for her of the different animals, rightfully realising that while she enjoyed the voices and stories he could construct from one of his many books, pictures would be far more useful in establishing her vocabulary.

"Kitty comes home with us," Keane explained patiently, glancing quickly up at his papa who had yet to give the final approval.

"Of course she shall. It has been far too long since we have had an addition to the family."

Christine gave him an incredulous look, their daughter not yet even a single year of age, but he sniffed unapologetically.

Perhaps in the future there would be more children. A few more little boys and girls that would look such a perfect combination of their parents that many an evening could be spent arguing over whose features were more pronounced.

And perhaps the many bedrooms in their home would be filled, either by babies or by stray kittens that his children found wandering about the grounds. And he would love them all, for they were an extension of his ever-growing family.

They began walking back to the carriage at a sedate pace, Keane with his nuzzling and mewling burden, and Lotte still trying to reconcile her legs into a more natural gait instead of an enthusiastic run.

Christine remained tucked into his side, his arm about her waist and her head against his shoulder—precisely where she belonged. "It is good of you to accept every stray that comes your way, Erik. Not every man would be so accommodating."

He hummed, his arm tightening slightly around her. "Fortunately for you, as you were the first." She gasped and stared up at him indignantly, but he placed a kiss upon her impudent mouth and then he leaned forward to whisper, "But I think I like you most of all. You have given me *everything,* my rose. And I shall be forever grateful for it."

She sighed, her ire melting away at his gentle words, and he gave her one last kiss before they resumed their walk. Their children were only a little ways ahead, evidently arguing over true ownership of their new kitten, Keane seemingly remaining steadfast in his position as original finder. "You are the same for me too, Erik. I hope you know that."

And he did.

Her every action and word made it abundantly clear that he was her saviour, just as she was his. They loved each other truly, with a depth born of trial and pain, and both had become the stronger for it.

"I love you for your perseverance, my Christine."

She placed her hand in his and gave it a gentle squeeze. "I love you for your tender soul, my Erik. I would have been lost without it."

And as he lifted all of his beloved charges into the carriage and began the journey home, he felt a peace he had only recently come to fully recognise. Christine had granted him the gift of her love—and with it came what he truly needed.

A family.

And as his rose began to whisper of precisely how she would like to spend the rest of their evening after the children had been put to bed, he could not help but think he was the most fortunate man that had ever lived.

For no matter how wretched his beginning, he was now truly blessed.

All because of his rose.

His living wife.

His Christine.

EPILOGUE

"Papa?"

Erik looked down at the glimmering keys of his piano with a sigh. Even with most of his children grown—or at least seemingly grown—he never seemed to have enough time to devote to his music. Something had sparked anew in him of late, and his desire for solitude and more time for his compositions appeared to be steadily growing.

Perhaps he was growing old and the amount of youth in his house merely depressed him.

But as he saw his eldest and only son peering in from the doorway—an apologetic yet serious look upon his face—he as quite aware that he was simply withdrawing so he could avoid this particular conversation for as long as humanely possible.

But apparently even a man with certain *inhuman* qualities could eventually be found by his offspring.

"Come in, Keane, you might as well interrupt me completely."

Keane grimaced but obeyed, coming to stand near the piano. His son was proficient in the instrument, though he reserved most of his playing for bouts of dreary weather. True to their suppositions from childhood, Keane much preferred to spend his mornings riding his horse about the property, though now that he was older his afternoons were spent on business instead of education. Christine had been terribly nervous when he had first begun his lessons, absolutely certain that he would be thrown from the large beast at the first possible moment. But Keane had a way with horses, or so they had been told by the horse master that had agreed to tutor their boy on the intricacies of true horsemanship. And other than a few scrapes and bruises over the years, Keane had suffered no great injury.

Erik watched his son fidget with some amusement, although he was rather confident that a deepening sadness would soon replace any humorous reaction. "Did you intend to speak or were you merely going to stare at me as I work?"

Keane rolled his eyes, quite used to his father's drollness. "Forgive me, I was trying to find the words."

Erik sighed and his eyes fell once more to the keys. Whether or not he liked where this conversation was inevitably leading, he should make more of an effort to be understanding. *He* had not been forced to confer with anyone before marrying his sweet rose, and as he continued to watch his son—his fully grown son of two and twenty, with eyes that so matched his own, he knew that he should put away his own feelings of loss in order to encourage his boy.

Or at least *attempt* to do so.

While Erik had not attended many weddings, his fingers still knew precisely how to coax the traditional wedding processional from the piano and from the corner of his eye he saw Keane's shoulders visibly hunch.

"Who told you?"

Erik hummed quietly, a pang of sadness at the confirmation that was so terribly obvious now that he stopped to consider the signs. "Your mamma might have mentioned something."

Keane sighed and stared at the sleek wood of the piano, pulling out his handkerchief to rub away an errant mark. Erik might once have been proud of his son's attention to the care of the instrument—another testament to their similarity as Keane seemed to also have inherited his fastidiousness—but now he knew his son was only trying to avoid looking at him.

And while previously that might have been the cause of horror, now it signalled how frightened his son truly was. All of his children did so desire his approval.

"Ellie is a fine young woman."

Keane glanced up at him sharply. "She is."

"And you have asked Marc's permission? She is his youngest. Perhaps he does not yet wish to part with her." He knew how closely he held on to each moment with his littlest girl, and he loathed the idea of ever being forced to give her hand to any man, regardless of how worthy.

"Papa, she is twenty years of age."

A lone, sparse eyebrow raised in question. "I was not aware that once your child had grown you would love them any less, nor cease to desire their company."

Keane huffed, but conceded. "He laughed at me."

"He denied you?" That would have shocked Erik indeed. Keane and Ellie had been friends for quite some time—ever since Lucie began bringing her along to clean when she was still a little thing. She would follow her elder sister with a dust cloth and always marvel at the small coin that Christine would place in her hand afterward as payment, but more often than not Keane would convince her to abandon her employment in favour of exploring with him and Lotte.

And while Erik questioned whether her wages should be docked, he had merely been softly cuffed by his wife for his enquiry.

And when Keane had begun to work with Erik more diligently as an architect and designer during adolescence, he had clearly stated his intentions to someday make Ellie his bride. Erik had scowled and sighed—or *pouted,* as Christine liked to call it—but there was no denying that what their boy said was true. He worked hard to make money of his own so that he could someday bring home his wife.

But perhaps Marc had other objections that had yet to be voiced.

Marc was far better off now than when Erik had met him years before. While he had once sacrificed and scrimped in order to feed and care for his brood, when Erik had approached him with an arrangement, things had changed considerably. When Erik finally retired as Opera Ghost and he began working exclusively as an architect—purely through correspondence of course—his services were highly sought out as Paris and the surrounding cities continued to grow and flourish. And with Marc as his personal foreman who oversaw each of his projects, there was little they could want for.

And although Erik might not like the idea of another of his children marrying, he could not deny the insult he would feel should the man have denied his son.

Keane smiled softly and fiddled with his handkerchief a little longer—and for the first time, Erik noted the delicate embroidery in one corner that could only have come from Ellie's skilful fingers. "No, he only asked if I had spoken to you. He said that there was no point in him giving me an answer unless I had your blessing." He finally glanced up at his father, a look of worry plainly evident. "He said that you might not be willing to be without another male presence in the house and refuse your consent."

Erik should be insulted.

He loved all of his children and the idea that he would somehow deny any one of their happiness just so he could keep his only son near was preposterous.

At least, he hoped it was.

But as he stared at his son, he knew that there was little he could say—or *want* to say to keep him from marrying his lady love.

"You know you are providing me yet *another* daughter. Lotte at least had the good sense to give me a son."

Keane quirked an eyebrow of his own. "Somehow I do not think you would have appreciated that as much as you think you would."

Erik sniffed. "Perhaps not. But you are doing nothing to relieve me of the Daroga's incessant insults."

Keane laughed, his father's reaction apparently easing some of the tension he felt. "They are hardly meant as insults. There *are* quite a few girls in the family."

Erik glared at his impertinent boy. "Having three daughters and a wife is hardly a harem."

His son shrugged. "So far I am only interested in bringing one more into the family. We shall see if she provides us any other additions to your hoard."

Erik gestured toward the door. "Be gone with you. I have obviously failed to raise a proper gentleman, and I pity what Ellie shall have to live with for the rest of her days."

Kean's answering smile was wide and from that expression alone Erik knew he had said rightly. "Thank you, Papa!"

After all, their lives would not change so *very* much. Keane would continue to help him in their business, and he had worked hard to fashion the old cottage into a space for his new bride.

So really, it would only be the manor that would feel the most loss, as the estate itself would continue to house those he loved most.

Keane practically ran from the room, obviously intent on finding his future wife and giving her the happy news. And as Erik was left once more alone with his piano, he felt a sudden melancholy that made the idea of remaining in his room—sanctuary that it might be—nearly intolerable.

And so as he often did when his music ceased to hold his interest, he went in search of his family.

As usual, they could be found in the kitchen, baking and drinking far too much tea than was good for them, and laughing as if they were truly as amusing as they thought they were.

It made his heart hurt just a little to look at them.

He waited a moment until they quieted, and then came through the door with a longsuffering sigh. "Your boy is abandoning me, Christine. I shall be lost in a sea of long hair and curls with no respite in sight."

Christine shot him an exasperated look while she continued to knead what appeared to be a fresh batch of scones. Over the years she had taken most of the responsibility of cooking for the family, but never once did she make sweet biscuits. Those were Erik's jurisdiction, and every day of their marriage he ensured that her little tin from so long ago continued to house some morsels should she wish them—though more than once he had found the small greedy hands of his children inside instead of his wife's.

And with his children's ingenuity, placing the tin on a higher shelf did little to cease their thievery.

So instead one day a mysterious *new* tin had appeared, and inside was a note that told them quite explicitly that while they could help themselves to the provisions within *this* coffer, they were to keep out of their mother's.

For that was his Christine's, and she deserved to have something special of her own.

And miraculously, his children had obeyed.

But now his second daughter was up on tiptoe as she placed a kiss upon his unmasked cheek. "Poor, Papa. Keane should have been more thoughtful. Not to worry, I will not abandon you quite yet."

Erik sniffed. "You have at least granted me *one* sensible child, my rose."

Mari beamed at him, always happy to receive a compliment, especially from him.

She had been christened as Marguerite but the name never did quite seem to suit her—at least according to his then five year old boy. He had barely glanced at her before pronouncing that Marguerite was a ridiculous name for a girl so small and that he would only ever call her Mari.

And while Erik had thought Christine would be affronted since she had been the one to select the name, she instead had laughed and from that moment, Mari she had always been.

Unlike his two eldest children, Mari did not have a prospective spouse from childhood—at least, not one that could readily be detected. When she was young she had plenty of friends between her siblings and the village children, but now that they had grown none yet seemed to interest her beyond the friendships they had always been.

Erik hoped it would remain that way.

Christine warned him that it could mean Mari would be a part of some torrid romance, as some handsome stranger whisked her away to a far away land where she would be deliriously contented raising their children on foreign soil.

Erik had nearly forsaken their bed that night in favour if his study for the mere suggestion of such a thing, but Christine had professed her apologies and coaxed him into remaining with all-too skilful hands and kisses that he was powerless to ignore.

"I believe these are *your* children as well, husband, and you would do well to remember it." She tilted her chin just so, and though a moment before she had apparently been annoyed with him, he still dutifully approached and placed a kiss upon her waiting cheek.

"My demanding little wife," he whispered lowly into her ear.

She shivered and he watched with fascination at how even after so many years of marriage, her skin still prickled from where his words caressed her.

And just as she opened her mouth to reply, with some scintillating retort about *later* he was certain, he felt a hand tug at his trouser leg, and he did not even have to turn to know who sought his attention.

Nora was their surprise, and the completion of their family. Their first three had appeared so quickly and with such relative ease they were rather confident their family would soon rival Marc and Aimée's in sheer number. But after Mari was born, no matter how they seemed to try Christine did not become pregnant.

Many years had passed and both had learned to become contented with the children they had been given. Both Keane and Lotte had been adolescents, and Mari was soon to follow. But then one day Christine had come to him, eyes shimmering with tears and she had sobbed into his lapel that she was pregnant.

And neither had to question or worry if their baby was wanted by the other—not when long ago promises were still so vivid for the both of them.

So their little Nora was born, and now at five years of age she clearly favoured her mother in appearance, much to Erik's pleasure. And while Lotte had been all smiles and bouncing exuberance, and Mari nearly equally so, Nora was quiet and shy and liked nothing better than to be perched in her father's lap—which was a desire he was all too happy to oblige.

Erik did not even bother to ask what she wanted from him; instead placing one last kiss upon his wife's lips he scooped Nora into his arms and sat down with her at the large table.

Lotte smiled at him tiredly from her seat beside him, and he leaned over slightly so she could place a kiss upon his cheek. As she did so, he could not help but notice how her hand rubbed absently over the small swell of her abdomen. "And how are you, Little Lotte? Could you not convince your brother that marriage is a dreadful business?"

She groaned and rested her head against his shoulder. "You know I would not even try, Papa, Henri is so good to me. But I do not know how you and Mummy did it all by yourselves. I have you two to help me with Peter and yet I am still exhausted!"

Christine laughed and finished placing her scones on a pan before wiping off the excess flour that covered her hands and most of dress—apparently the fine white dust finding it a personal challenge to find each nook and cranny not completely covered by her apron. "Oh, Lotte. You are *pregnant*. Whether or not you have a three year old you were going to be exhausted!"

Erik shifted slightly so he could place his arm around his eldest daughter in comfort. "Where is my grandson?"

Lotte sighed and rested more fully against him, her tiredness plainly evident. "Henri agreed to watch him for the day."

Erik nodded, a little disappointed not to see his little grandson. It was a rarity that Lotte and he did not make the trek from one of the farthest cottages on the property to the welcoming kitchen of the manor. When Erik had originally bought the château he had fully intended it to be a gift to his Christine—a way to provide her a house aboveground where they could safely raise their children. But somehow as each of his children had been born he had begun allocating a cottage for each of their future use if they should have need of it.

And while when Lotte was born he had intended on a very different cottage to be set aside for her—one that resembled something from one of the storybooks he had illustrated for her—he had swiftly changed his mind when it became apparent that an attachment was growing between her and their previous stable boy.

True to his word, Erik had seen to Henri's education, not seriously considering he would someday become his daughter's husband. The lad had always been a diligent worker, and it seemed a pity to have him waste such an attitude on drudgery when there was the possibility of more potential. But Henri was not one for figures, and though he appreciated the occasional novel on particularly thrilling bouts of heroism, it was not until Erik began to teach him the intricacies of woodcarving and masonry that Henri showed particular interest.

His height could be attributed to the stature of his father, but it was the long days implementing Erik's grandiose designs that made him strong.

He was not proficient immediately of course and Erik had arranged for him to tutor with some of the best masters in Paris, but eventually Henri was able to handle the craft on his own—even under Erik's stringent scrutiny.

What Erik had not foreseen was one Christmas Eve service when both families had joined to celebrate the season at their local parish. Lotte had been a mere fifteen years of age and Henri a man fully grown, yet when Erik saw the way his ears grew pink as he stared at the beauty that was his daughter, he knew that the man was lost.

And Erik could not fault him.

It seemed that what had appeared to him to be a few short years had instead been enough time for his little girl who adored running about his grounds as fast her as her chubby legs could carry her to turn into a woman.

And it took every bit of effort to keep from scooping her up into his arms and storming away from the Mass immediately.

It was not until Christine took hold of his arm, her eyes flitting between the two of them even as she did so, that he began to calm. "Do not fight it, Erik. He is a wonderful man, and she has been besotted with him since she was little."

That he could not deny. While Keane would beg to visit the stables for the sake of the large gelding that he deemed to be fascinating, Lotte thought that Henri was the more amusing creature of the two that inhabited the structure. He did not scold her when she threw pieces of hay in his direction, and it was a exceptional thing to see dirt upon one's clothing. Ever used to little girls from his own family, Henri had cheerfully obliged her, and many times Erik would hold his tongue from rebuking him from carrying her upon his shoulders.

Even then Christine would take his hand and remind him that interactions with others were *good* things.

But apparently the years had changed their opinion of one another.

And he supposed he had a begrudging affection for their stable hand.

So that fateful Christmas Eve he had gazed down at his wife, clinging to her hand and dreading the change that was to come while also firmly reminding himself that he would not deny his daughter's happiness.

As long as Henri proved himself capable as a husband and provider.

"At least he is not a stable boy any longer."

Christine had rolled her eyes at him—ever his impudent little wife—but she smiled all the same and gave his arm a gentle squeeze. "No, you have seen to that."

Erik hummed, reproaching his misplaced generosity, while also deciding a test was in order should their intuition prove correct regarding the budding fondness between his Lotte and Henri.

Indeed, Henri began to walk his sisters to the manor when it was their time to clean, claiming he thought it dangerous for them to walk unaccompanied in the snow. Erik always ensured he was there to open the door, and he tried valiantly to keep his glares to a minimum.

Lotte was at first surprised by his visits, but eventually began to offer to walk with him to the gates. Erik had opened his mouth to object quite vehemently, but with ears steadily turning pink—was it some sort of medical condition Erik had failed to notice before?—Henri had done it for him. "That is very kind, Mlle Daaé, but I should hate to see you catch cold."

His cap was clutched between his hands, and he fiddled with it nervously, a strangely boyish posture for a man so large and sturdy.

And from the way Lotte had blushed a matching shade of pink to Henri's ears, and smiled at him softly—Erik grimaced to note it was a way Christine had often smiled at him in the beginning—she had nodded and he had taken his leave.

The door had not been closed for more than a moment before his daughter turned to face him. "I am going to marry him, Papa."

Erik tried to remind his heart that she should profess such intentions *someday,* but it still beat wildly at her declaration. Outwardly however, he was rather proud of how composed he remained. "Is that so? I do not suppose I am allowed to have any say."

She had the audacity to giggle at him and tugged at his sleeve until she could deposit a kiss upon his bared cheek. "Not particularly. For although you like to grouch about him now, I know you are very fond of him."

Erik sniffed.

She was far too like her mother.

He watched her return to whatever activity had previously held her fancy before their *visitor* had appeared, and he found himself longing for the wild blonde ringlets of old to once more don her lovely head. Instead as she matured her hair had darkened to a shade that nearly rivalled Keane and Mari's, and she had forsaken her girlish poise for the quiet assurance of womanhood.

And as he often did when his children made him feel old and despondent, he sought out the company of his wife—who was always all too glad to comfort him.

Despite his own feelings, he did allow Henri to begin courting his Lotte, and he did inform him that there was lodging available on his property should he be able to furnish it properly. Prolonging their romance would only cause bitterness between all parties, and Erik knew the happiness that *he* had discovered with a girl he barely knew—surely theirs could be an even happier marriage when theirs was built on mutual love and affection. But for his own sanity, and perhaps just a bit selfishly, he had instead changed the cottage he would allow them—this time to one in need of the most repairs.

Lotte remained oblivious to Erik's scheme, but Henri took to the challenge with relish. He worked on it daily, even enlisting the help of some of his brothers to ensure the cottage—which at the end was possibly too large to strictly be considered thusly—was worthy of the bride he someday wished to call his own.

At the end of the year when the families were assembled at the parish in December, it was to celebrate the union of Henri and Lotte. She looked radiant, dressed all in ivory, her groom staring at her shyly from his position near the priest.

The Daroga and Aida had of course been in attendance. They had been married for a good many years, though Aida had laughed at him at first when he proposed and suggested they move closer to Erik and the children.

"I have women to see to! I have no issue taking you as a husband, but I am no young bride happy to go where her husband pleases. I have families who need me and I shan't abandon them."

The Persian had blinked at her, realising that the woman he had come to admire was far from the demure wife he had once been blessed with, but found that he enjoyed her ferocity. Her chuckles had finally quieted however when she saw that he was perhaps a little hurt by her response, and she took his hand firmly in hers. "But any time that young Christine needs my help, you can be certain I will be there, even if it is just for a bit of childminding. And you can also be sure, I will never begrudge you going to get your fill of the children, either."

And true to her word, she had not. The Daroga rarely announced his visits, but as the years passed and Mari joined their little family, Christine would grow all the more pleased to see him, though Erik continued to huff and demand at least two week's *written* notice before he stepped foot upon the property. However, despite Erik's dry greetings, on more than one occasion he was left to mind and feed the three young ones that thought him one of the grandest men they had ever met, while Erik and Christine would slink away for a few hours—or the occasional night—away for themselves.

Erik held his then-pregnant Christine as they watched their daughter stroll away with her husband down the lane to their new cottage. Erik was rather sad he would not be able to see Lotte's reaction to her new home, but he was certain Henri would do an adequate job of relaying each detail that had been placed there by the men she loved to ensure her comfort.

The Daroga approached them cautiously, grateful for his own wife beside him. "They are a fine pair, Erik. And remember, you have another on the way, that should bring you comfort."

"None could replace my sweetling, Daroga. Do not be stupid."

Erik cursed the way his voice failed to have its usual vehemence, and the way Christine nuzzled into his side had made him feel all the more emotional.

And now, a mere five years later, his son wished to also marry.

He kissed the blonde curls of his little Nora, thanking God yet again for the blessing of another. While he would always treasure the joy that his grandson brought and he looked forward to the months ahead with the emergence of whatever child Lotte currently carried, he was not yet ready to part with his role as parent.

He loved being *needed.*

He loved that she would come pattering down the hallways at full speed, hesitating only slightly before creeping into his music room and begging him to remove the spider that was tormenting her dolls.

He loved that he was still the man she loved best in all the world.

Later that night, as he held his wife in his arms and pulled his fingers through her tresses she must have sensed his despondent mood for after placing a kiss upon his chest she tilted her head up and touched his cheek, bidding him to look at her.

"Are you truly so unhappy about him marrying? We shall still see him every day."

Regardless of her fingers, he turned his head away and glared at the ceiling. "But it will not be the *same.*"

Christine sighed and played with one of the buttons on his black sleep shirt. She was quiet for a long moment and he nearly thought she would let the subject drop, and he oddly felt rather disappointed at the prospect.

"Do you remember when you took me back to the Opera House?"

He glanced down at her in confusion. "I have suffered no great injury that has robbed me of that memory."

She rolled her eyes and huffed in vexation. "I should think not. I was *referring* to what we discussed."

In actuality they had returned to the Opera House on numerous occasions. For a while he enjoyed taking Keane and lurking about the halls, and their boy thought it was great fun to use his eyes to mimic his father's as the unsuspecting performers saw not one but *two* pairs of eyes skulking through the darkness.

But eventually Erik had found that he much preferred a profession that could foster qualities in his son that might help him engage with the world, and not merely hide from it.

So though he no longer performed his duties as the Opera Ghost, he still felt certain ties to the structure that would never be severed.

And apparently some of these were shared by his wife.

It was six years after Mari had been born that he had surprised her with an evening at the Opera. They had attended as any normal patrons, sitting in a private box that was *not* reserved for a Ghost. And Erik had actually paid for their admittance.

Christine had nearly cried at the splendour of the performance, and Erik begrudgingly admitted to enjoying the experience as well. He had worn the mask that made him blend in with any other man, and though it saddened his Christine briefly to see it, there was little other option.

But seeing his wife so happy and the way her eyes shone in the twinkling lights of the stage made him feel nearly giddy. So after the performance he had taken her to one of his tunnels, and they waited there until theatre grew quiet before they emerged once more.

He had pulled her onto the stage , directing her to stand tall and proud as his Prima Donna, visions of her beauty, grace, and talent stunning all of Paris once more flitting through his mind.

The once vibrant melodies from his long abandoned *Don Juan Triumphant* returned with a vengeance, and he kissed her thoroughly as the passion of forgotten wants returned to him.

Christine was breathless when he eventually pulled away, and even in the dim remaining lights of the empty auditorium he could clearly see her surprised, yet pleased smile. "What has you so excited, husband?"

He took her hand and gestured widely at the neat rows of seats that filled the large space. "Think of it Christine. Our children are older now, and you have grown *so* much. Perhaps the time is right for us to think of you taking your rightful place upon the stage."

Christine stared at him quietly, apparently too surprised by his sudden idea to voice any opinion of her own.

"Do you..." She swallowed thickly, and he waited as patiently as he could for her reaction. "Do you think that is why I have not been able to have another? I am meant to sing?"

She glanced about the theatre, and to his disappointment she appeared to nearly shrink upon the stage. Over the years he had continued to tend to her voice, and her age had only brought maturity and range that was previously impossible.

And then to his horror, she began to cry.

"I love our children, Erik, *so* much. But I would gladly exchange all of this for another of our babies."

Erik stood quietly, the realisation coming upon him like a torrent. Years had passed and wounds had healed, but they were still the same couple that yearned for simple things.

A home and family was their reward, and he had once again become consumed with the idea of fame and beauty.

He kissed her softly, wiping the tears from her eyes. "As would I, my rose. For blessedly, our babies tend to look like you."

She giggled lightly, and as they usually did her fingers sought his handkerchief of their own accord before he had a chance to offer it freely.

His presumptive little wife.

"But Christine..." He waited until she had dried her eyes and her attention had mostly returned to him. "Change need not be so very bad. We changed when each of our little ones came and we will change when they are grown. But as long as you are by my side, I know that we shall be happiness itself."

It seemed so *simple* when he was using such words to comfort her, but now as she lay within his arms and reminded him of their long ago interlude, it seemed a difficult thing indeed.

"You have me, Erik. Me who loves you for your devotion to our children, and who loves you for your worry, and *especially* for the way you huff and puff about our kitchen after our boy tells us that he is marrying the woman who completes him."

She placed one more kiss upon his chest before surprising him as she quickly sat up and situated herself across his chest, her long tresses brushing against him teasingly. "And I quite thought you were *fond* of a sea of curls with no respite in sight."

His mouth felt dry as she sat up and slowly undid the ribbon of her nightdress, and that lovely, *lovely* hair was soon the only thing covering her delicate pink nipples from his view. "Treasure our children, Erik, but remember, our family is as strong as you and I make it."

In a moment he would ravish her. In a moment he would divest her of her chemise completely and thank her in every way he knew how.

But for now, he clutched her to him and he relished the way his face was buried in her hair—her beautiful, *luscious* hair, and murmured his words that his body would soon equally express. "I love you for your wisdom. I love you for being my rose. And most of all, I love you for your sea of curls." His voice grew dark as he breathed the last of his words, "*Both* of them."

And had her eyes not also darkened and she kissed him with such fervour, he was quite certain she would have cuffed him.

He was only mimicking her own impudence after all, so it was hardly his fault.

But as the night grew longer and he enjoyed the every curve of his loving rose, he decided that whether or not his children loved him best—whether or not they found spouses and children of their own to fill their days—he had the love of this woman.

For she was his.

And he was hers.

And that was all he could ever truly need.

Forever and always.

CPSIA information can be obtained
at www.ICGtesting.com
Printed in the USA
LVOW13s0619200917
549387LV00015B/441/P